WIN A 5 STAR G
THE CULLODEN

courte

HASTINGS
HOTELS

Hastings Hotels has teamed up with Poolbeg Press to offer a reader and three friends the opportunity to win 'One Night Only' at the luxurious Culloden Estate and Spa!

Nestled high in the Holywood hills and overlooking Belfast Lough, Culloden Estate and Spa in Cultra, Co Down is Northern Ireland's most prestigious 5 star hotel – celebrities such as Michael Douglas, Robbie Williams and Lionel Ritchie are previous visitors!

The lucky winner will enjoy overnight accommodation with breakfast in the luxurious Amethyst suite, which can accommodate up to four adults. This stunning split level suite is perfect for a girly weekend.

To avail of special offers contact Hastings Hotels on 028 9047 1066 or visit www.hastingshotels.com

To enter just answer the question below, fill in your contact details and send this page in an envelope to: *One Night Only* competition, Poolbeg Press, 123 Grange Hill, Baldoyle, Dublin 13.

Q. To which county do the girls in *One Night Only* escape for their big night out?

Answer: _____

Name: _____

Contact number: _____

Address: _____

E-mail: _____

one night only

Also by Emma Heatherington

All Over Again
Playing the Field
Since You've Been Gone

And writing as Emma Louise Jordan

Beyond Sin
The Truth Between

All published by Poolbeg Press

one night only

emma heatherington

POOLBEG

Published 2013
by Poolbeg Press Ltd.
123 Grange Hill, Baldoyle,
Dublin 13, Ireland
Email: poolbeg@poolbeg.com

A catalogue record for this book is available from the British Library.

ISBN 978-1-84223-462-4

Typeset by Patricia Hope in Sabon 10.75/15

Printed and bound by CPI Group (UK) Ltd, Croydon, CR0 4YY

www.poolbeg.com

About the Author

Emma Heatherington is from Donaghmore, County Tyrone. She has three children – Jordyn, Jade and Adam – and she works in PR and as a freelance writer.

She also writes under the pseudonym Emma Louise Jordan.

Keep up to date with Emma at:
emmaheatherington.com,
facebook.com/emmalou13
or follow on Twitter @emmalou13

Acknowledgements

For research purposes only, I must confess that I was handcuffed and shown to a cell when planning this book. It was interesting and fun but handcuffs are heavy in real life, believe me! And cold!

So, first of all, a big thank-you to the real-life Mr Copalicious from PSNI for helping me to get to grips with the nitty-gritty of all things 'arresting' and for showing me around a police station.

To my fantastic editor Gaye Shortland – it is always a privilege to work with you and we always manage to have a laugh. I don't think you will ever look at the names Seán or Pat in the same way again, so thanks for all your seánience – I mean 'patience'!

Thanks to the wonderful people at Poolbeg for bringing this one to life, especially Paula, Sarah, Ailbhe and David who do such a great job with all of my books.

Thanks to Ger Nicholl, my agent, who gets my jokes, tells me I'm great when I need it most and kicks my behind when I need that too.

Thanks so much to Julie at Hastings Hotel Group and to all at Duffy Rafferty Communications, Belfast.

The Irish media, north and south, have been a great support to me since I began this novel life, so thanks to you all. A particular mention goes to Paddy and Karen Scott from Alpha Group Newspapers, Annamay McNally at Tyrone Times, Ronan McSherry at Ulster Herald, Kerry McKittrick at Belfast Telegraph, Carolyn Stewart at U105, Laura Murphy at *The Newsletter*, Martin Breen at *Sunday Life*, Róisín Gorman at *Sunday World* plus all at UTV, RTÉ and TV3 who have had me on 'the telly' to talk books.

Everyone loves a good girly night out and I have been lucky to have experience of plenty of those down the years with great friends, so thanks to all of you for giving me plenty of material to work on.

To all of you who go out and buy my books and come back to me with such heart-lifting and motivational feedback, thank you so, so much. I had lots of fun writing this book and can empathise with many of the characters who I really grew to love – I hope you like them too!

And finally, huge, massive thanks with kisses and hugs to my brother David, my sisters Vanessa, Rachel, Lynne, Rebecca and Niamh, my dad Hugh and my children Jordyn, Jade and Adam. Love you all so much.

For my aunt and Fairy Godmother
Kathleen McCausland –
thank you for encouraging me to be a writer.

1

"Do I still turn you on?"

Polly stood at the end of the kitchen table and stared at James. She gripped the handle on her coffee mug and awaited her husband's answer. Okay, so it wasn't the usual question to ask a man as he chewed the last mouthful of his dinner on a Tuesday evening, but she needed to know. She put the mug down and the coffee slopped out onto the red-and-white gingham tablecloth. The spillage caught her eye but, instead of rushing to fetch a cloth like she normally would, she ignored it. She fiddled with the bottom of her old faithful apron and wished she had at least taken it off before she asked him the question. It said *Bisto Mum* and was far from sexy.

"Huh?"

James didn't take his eyes off the television. The noise of it was like a whirr in Polly's mind – reports of good weather kicking in at last was dominating the news but Polly could feel a storm brewing right there in her kitchen. Everything was just so damn noisy these days – the television, the radio, the people in shops, the children,

1

everything. It was like no one had time to listen to anyone else and having a conversation with her husband was almost impossible.

Her *Groundhog Day* existence was a far cry from the life she had planned when she married her childhood sweetheart on the eve of the millennium. Yes, she had anticipated babies and burps and bumps of all varieties, but not the engulfing loneliness that she'd felt lately. James was a hard worker and she knew the construction industry was a tough business these days and that he worried into the night about where the next project was coming from, but a little communication with his wife wouldn't go amiss!

She had always been so glamorous, so confident in her own skin, but right now she felt like an invisible doormat, a servant, a voiceless walkover whose own needs were frozen to meet the needs of her husband and three young boys, who she loved and adored more than anything in the world.

"James?" she asked again. She knew she was nagging. She hated nagging.

"What?"

"Just answer the question, James!" She needed to know if there was even the slightest spark there between them. She still found him sexy as hell but she knew his mind was anywhere but on sex these days. "Do I still turn you on?"

"Polly, honestly!" said James. "The kids will hear you! And I'm trying to watch the news. Where the hell did this all come from?"

"Where did it come from? I'm trying to save our marriage!" Polly retorted, feeling the familiar burn behind her eyes as tears threatened to burst through. She wouldn't let them. Not this time. He was always watching the news, or reading the paper, or checking sports results, or doing his books for his business, or pricing a job – he was always doing something that avoided discussing their floundering relationship.

"You need to stop this," said James, pushing his dinner plate to the side.

He wasn't eating much these days either which insulted her greatly. He'd always loved her cooking.

"I don't know what has got into you these days but these random bloody questions are really wearing thin."

Polly didn't expect the rise in his voice and it set her back immensely. He was pissed off. She was pissed off too.

"Wearing thin? Look at me, James! Oh, that's right. You don't. You never look at me any more. You'd rather stare at the TV or at your bloody dinner plate. You never even look at me!"

His eyes darted around the kitchen.

It was true! He could barely look at her. She remembered a time when they couldn't keep their eyes or their hands off each other. People envied them. Other couples admired them. They were love's young dream, childhood sweethearts who had grown up together and now, after twelve years of wedded bliss, they were growing apart day by day.

"Mummy, can I –"

Frankie walked into the kitchen at exactly the wrong time. He glanced at both of his parents, and Polly sensed he was aware once again that a row was in the air. It seemed to be the same thing at the same time every day now, only it was usually a one-way conversation where Polly talked but as far as she could tell, James didn't listen.

3

"Not now, Frankie," said Polly. "Your dad and I are talking about – about holidays and stuff. I'll – I'll just be a few minutes."

Polly watched her nine-year-old son walk out and tried to swallow the enormous lump in her throat. She hated having to turn Frankie away like that but for once she had raised a response in her husband and she wasn't letting this opportunity go.

"I've a lot on my mind," said James. He got up and took a fresh mug from the cupboard and flicked the kettle on to boil. "I don't mean to take it out on you."

"But that's the thing," said Polly. "You don't even *do* that. You don't even take it out on me. It's like I don't exist."

"Ah, come on!"

"It's like I'm in this different world, or at least on a different time zone. Me and the kids. And you are on your own little journey with blinkers on. You go to work, you come home, you have dinner and then you watch TV until you fall asleep. We don't do anything together any more. We don't even talk like we used to."

James leaned on the worktop with both hands and stared at the kettle. She noticed his breathing, strong and steady. James never had a temper but, to an outsider, he very much looked like a man who was about to lose it.

"Is this about sex?" he asked. "Are you going to make me feel worse by throwing that up in my face?"

It was a big part of it, thought Polly, but she didn't want to rub salt in the wounds. She could see it was a sore point.

"Not only that," she said. "It's like there's been a blackout in our relationship. We never do anything together any more. Remember the times when we used to go out for

4

dinner, or even catch a movie, or even have a laugh about something the kids had said or done? It's like it's all gone. It's like what we had is dead and gone."

"Don't nag me, Polly. You know I hate nagging. It's this constant *yak-yak-yakking* every time you go on one of your deep and meaningful rants. I'm honestly not in the mood. Oh for fuck sake, kettle, hurry up!"

He had shouted louder than he had ever done in her company and it frightened her.

"Would you keep your voice down?" she said. "What the hell has got into you?"

She looked at her husband, barely recognising the man in front of her any more. Yes, he was a little greyer round the temples as the strains of being thirty-something set in. His laughter lines ran a little deeper than before, his eyes creased up a bit more, but it was in his eyes she saw a change that age had nothing to do with. His beautiful brown eyes that always made her heart swoon were empty and lifeless and she just couldn't get him to say what could possibly be wrong.

On paper they had it all – a comfortable lifestyle in middle-class Ardglass Villas, a circle of friends that were a mixture of old school-friends and family, and most importantly three healthy adorable boys who idolised them.

Polly and James were the cardboard cut-out picture-perfect couple of Cranmore, the rural Irish village where they had both grown up. Everyone knew them and everyone loved them and they used to have such fun together. They used to be as tight as a drum.

But now, behind closed doors, it was a very different picture. Now, in their own homely kitchen with its Aga and American fridge with its funky magnets and children's drawings and all the trimmings of a white-picket-fence lifestyle surrounding them, they stood like strangers with a world of difference between them.

"I'm going to the pub," said James. "I need to get out of here before I say something I regret. I'll be back by ten."

"James!"

Polly closed her eyes and winced as the door slammed, its noise thumping her brain as she felt panic rise within her. Her worst nightmares were coming true. James had no interest in her any more. She was a harpy, a nagging wife, a 'ball and chain', a 'handbrake', the 'trouble and strife' . . . and she had no idea how she had become one of those women. It frightened her, it made her feel old and worn but, most of all, it made her wonder if this was really what life was all about. Is this what she had worked so hard for? Was this really . . . was this really it?

"Dad, please, can I . . .? Oh. Where's Dad?"

Polly opened her eyes and took a deep breath as the sight of Frankie brought her back to her senses. His face was still grubby with ketchup from dinner and his hair was sticking up in his own unique spiky style that made her want to squeeze him and nuzzle into his familiar, welcoming cuddles and never let him go.

"He's – he's just popped out. To the shop. What is it you want, love?"

Frankie blinked and screwed up his freckled nose and Polly felt her heart warm up at the sight of his innocence.

"Nothing. It doesn't matter . . . can I go and call for Johnny? He has the new FIFA game and he said at school I could come over and play. I've done all my homework and –"

"Yes, of course you can go. But half an hour, okay? I think we all need an early night."

"Thanks, Mum," said Frankie and he wrapped his arms around Polly's waist, gave her a tight squeeze and then ran outside.

"*Door!*" she called after him.

"Sorry!" He came back and closed the door gently, leaving Polly alone in the kitchen.

She had the freedom to let her tears flow at last. But only for a few seconds. She didn't have time to mope. She had too much to do. She had to bath the twins and get them to bed. And get Frankie's school uniform ready for the next morning. And do some laundry, and then the dinner dishes and then check over homework and make up packed lunches. She had a PTA meeting that she would now have to miss and she had to make a list of things to get the next morning, including remembering to make a dental appointment for the children and a medical appointment for herself. Then tomorrow she would have her part-time job at the post office to tend to and she'd promised to meet her sister Tess for a coffee after that. Her life was all go, go, go with very little time for herself.

Polly thought of her husband, sitting on his familiar stool at the local pub, sipping a cool pint as it washed his troubles away. She would love to run away to the pub when the going got tough. She would love to run away *anywhere* sometimes and never come back. But she couldn't. And even if she could, she wouldn't . . . would she?

This was her life. This was what she had become. She would just have to put up with it.

"Who the *hell* put that on the stairs?" Polly shouted later

7

in the direction of her children but got no reply. She was out of her mind. She didn't normally swear at under-fours. Well, never on a Tuesday anyhow, and not when she had the noise of the hoover to compete with. She cursed her own judgement every time she looked at the dark green carpet on the stairs. It needed more attention from the hoover than any other part of the house.

She thought she heard the repeat of the word 'hell' from one of her three-year-old boys in the living room – Max, she thought – but ignored it. She would beat herself up for it later. She was good at doing that.

"Mummy, I want more Coco Pops!" yelled Thomas but she was in too much agony to reply. She had knelt on a piece of Lego on the stairs and the pain was excruciating.

In the almost ten years since she had first encountered motherhood, standing on Lego was right up there on her 'Things That Get On My Tits' list, along with forgetting to put the overflowing bin out for collection, cleaning up mashed-in food and worse from the carpets and night-time feeds with new-born twins. She was halfway through her evening chores and had been getting on so well until she stood on the offensive bit of plastic and it was doing absolutely nothing for her mood. In the midst of her rant, she heard a knock on the door, so she hobbled downstairs still muttering to herself in expletives.

It was seven thirty in the evening. No one ever called on a midweek evening and those who did (like her sisters) didn't ever knock. For a split second she thought of James. Had something happened? Had he been in an accident? Her stress levels rose as she approached the door.

She gasped at the sight that awaited her on the other side.

"Oh, you poor thing!" she said.

It was Gina from next door and she was in a terrible state.

"How long have you been knocking for?"

Despite her own troubles, Polly was genuinely concerned. Gina was soaked right through so that her tiny breasts and their tiny nipples were very obvious and her hair looked like rats had been sucking at the ends of it.

"Ages," she said and Polly could tell from the look on her face and the rainwater dripping down her forehead that she really did mean *ages*. Plus, Gina never exaggerated and never, ever told lies.

She just wasn't the type . . . except when it came to explaining the bruises on her face or arms or legs. For that, she could lie for Ireland, North and South and every border in between, not even a problem.

Her tracksuit bottoms were on back to front, her hair looked more like a bird's nest on top than it normally did and her chapped lips looked extra, well, chapped. Poor Gina, as she was affectionately known, was living proof that money couldn't buy you happiness. Never in a million years. And the saddest thing was that beneath all of that was a very beautiful young woman screaming to get out.

"Come on in," said Polly in her best Women's Aid voice and for a second she thanked the Lego for having brought her away from Henry the Hoover so she had heard Gina's pathetic wee knock and come to her rescue. But this sympathy wasn't to last.

Thinking that Gina too had witnessed a life or death encounter that evening, Polly forgot for a split second about everything else (i.e. The Pain and the row with her husband) and concentrated fully on Project Gina.

9

"What's wrong, love?" she asked. "You look terrible. I'm sorry, but you do."

"I – I – I've run out of milk," she said. "Again."

Honestly, you would swear by the look on her face that she had been given hours to live. She had run out of fucking milk.

"What?" asked Polly, cursing her for not having hours to live because for a split second her knee had been okay again but now the pain was back with a vengeance.

"I've run out of milk," said Gina. "There isn't a drop in the house and my Trevor is due back home in a while and it's our anniversary tomorrow and I have no way of getting to the supermarket and back again on time but I just can't . . . I can't be out of milk."

Polly could have punched her right there and then, but she was not the violent type. She was a middle-class mother of three and had learned long ago in a previous life how to control her temper. Plus it was a well-known fact that Poor Gina had been punched enough.

Ever since she moved next door, Polly had picked up the pieces and covered up for when Gina had accidentally walked into the door or hit her leg on the kitchen table or bashed her eye when she stood on a rake. It was like a secret code between them. Polly would never question it, and Gina would never divulge the truth. Perhaps she would someday, Polly told herself. But, in the meantime, she would never push her.

"Oh . . . okay, here you go!" she said, taking a carton of semi-skimmed milk from the fridge and placing it into Gina's red, shaky hands whilst trying to breathe as her leg buckled beneath her in pain. "Tell Trevor to put that in his tea and, erm . . . drink it!"

10

"Thanks, you're a darlin', Polly," Gina said in her strong Dublin accent. "But the thing is, I need another few things too."

"Like what?" asked Polly with a desperate nip in her voice. Teabags? Bread? *Blood*?

"Something for the tea," she said. "I haven't a bite in the house. I swear on me child's life. Not a bite. I couldn't get groceries at the weekend cos I – I hurt my leg when climbing the stairs and the car is in the garage and he'll be starving if – I mean, when he comes home. You know what men are like . . ."

Hurt her leg when she was climbing the stairs? That was a new one though Polly had just done that very thing herself. But Gina had no need to swear on her child's life. There really was no need for that when both women knew the ugly truth.

"Could you take me over to the Spar?" she asked, as if she was asking for Polly's last tenner. "Please? I'll only be a minute or two. I promise."

Polly looked at Gina standing in her kitchen. She really was a hopeless sight in her wee flip-flops with the desperate wee quiver in her voice. But Polly loved Gina and would drive her to Cork and back if she asked her to. She was the gentlest, kindest soul who had been dealt a sorry deck where husbands were concerned. One day, thought Polly, one day she'll realise that he is not worth it and she will finally get up and go.

"Of course I will, love," she said, just as she always did. She would have to temporarily ignore the rest of her 'to do' list for the evening. So what if things ran half an hour behind? She could bath the twins when she got back. The stairs would wait. Gina needed her help.

11

So, with a quick bribe of a promise of a Milky Bar, Polly packed her twins and Gina's only child, six-year-old Danny, into her Jeep, rang Johnny's mum across the road to keep Frankie till she got back and set off to the Spar to help Gina in her hour of need, remembering en-route that she needed ham. And bread. And toilet roll . . . gosh, it really never ended and despite the whirling list that was circulating her brain, her troubles had only really begun.

Because when she ran into the Spar to grab a few bits and pieces, Polly bumped into Ruth Monaghan.

Not metaphorically. Oh no. In her speed to get back to the twins in the car she actually *bumped* into Ruth Monaghan beside the Toilet Duck and knocked a glass-covered air freshener out of her hands so that it smashed into smithereens all over the supermarket floor.

"I'm so sorry – toilet roll – twins in car," she mumbled like a lunatic, but it was only when picking up the pieces of the citrus-scented Air Wick that she caught sight of the other lady's equally flustered face and they recognised each other with great surprise.

Ruth Monaghan looked like she had won the Lottery. She really did.

Polly looked like she'd seen a ghost. She really had.

"Polly *Woodhead*!" screeched Ruth, totally over-emphasising Polly's maiden surname.

"Sweet Jesus, it's been years," said Polly, and Ruth nodded, much more flabbergasted than Polly was. And that was a lot.

"Polly, is it . . .? Is it really *you*? What on earth has happened to your hair?"

And just as Polly used to in high school, she wanted to thump her so hard her head would spin. But just as in

high school, she didn't. She smiled and said something
totally soft and stupid instead: "I knelt on a piece of Lego.
I'm not really feeling myself today. And I'm Polly *Knox* now.
I'm married." Polly wanted to add in the word 'happily' but
that would have been a stretch of the truth in the day that
was in it.

"Well, nothing is forever these days," said Ruth.
"Whoops! Did I say that out loud?"

Polly glanced at Ruth's wedding finger. It was bare. She
wished she had said 'happily' after all. Shit.

"What a surprise. It's been years!" said Polly. "But
anyhow, I'd best race on. I've left my twins in the car and
you know what it's like, I'm sure . . . family keeps us all
busy, doesn't it?"

Polly cursed herself at giving in to the game that
women played. The 'my life is better than yours because I
am married with children' versus the 'mine is much better
because you are living a big fat lie and you know it'.

"I've just moved back home from London," said Ruth,
her voice changing now, as if she recognised the game and
no longer wanted to play. "Look . . . I . . . I know I was a
bit of a cow to you in school, but we're all grown up now
and . . . well, do you fancy a catch-up over coffee? I'd love
to hear what you've been up to. I'd love to hear all about
your twins."

That was a lie. The twin bit. Polly guessed she would
rather stick pins in her eyes than hear about twins.

But coffee? With Ruth Monaghan? Get to France!

Polly looked at Ruth, a hint of concern on her face. Ruth
looked at Polly, taking in her every feature. Neither of them
had changed much at all, despite the years that had passed.
Polly still had big innocent doe eyes, a lightly freckled nose

13

and bee-stung lips that used to drive all the boys in school mad with desire. Ruth was still bigger, a little rougher round the edges, with dyed red hair and black clothes – like an oversized, can't-grow-out-of-it nineties Goth. She was scary-looking back then and she was scary-looking now.

"Er, yeah, okay," said Polly, afraid to say no and clinging for dear life onto a four-pack of toilet roll. She feared Ruth would hit her if she said no.

Ruth rummaged in her huge black handbag and found a business card with her contact details and Polly took it from her, flipping it over, impressed and surprised as she examined the little red, white and black card. The colours matched Ruth's appearance.

"Graphic designer, eh?" Polly said with a raised eyebrow. "You always were so artistic, Ruth. Good for you. Look, I'd really better race on but I will definitely be in touch. Hope you settle in well. Nice to see you."

She walked away, still feeling Ruth's dark eyes on her.

"Polly?" Ruth called to the back of her head.

"Yes?" she replied. She stopped and turned, still gripping the toilet roll.

"I'm sorry," she said. "I'm desperately sorry for being such a bitch to you at school. To you, and your sister. How is Tess?"

"It was a long time ago," said Polly, ignoring the question about her younger sister. Tess would murder her if she thought she had given one inch of information to Ruth Monaghan! She turned away from Ruth and walked towards the till.

The bloody cheek of her! Polly's heart thumped as she handed over her debit card, feeling Ruth's stare, and she was transported back to the days in school where the very mention of Ruth Monaghan's name was enough to bring her to tears.

On her way out of the Spar, she caught Ruth's eye again and Ruth smiled. It wasn't a threatening 'I'm gonna get you on the way home' smile like she used to throw at Polly when they were fourteen. It was a nervous, almost desperate 'please be my friend' smile and Polly, being the soft touch that she was, smiled back.

"Nice to see ya," said Ruth.

Polly nodded and left the supermarket as fast as her feet could carry her.

Despite her size and her dark clothes and her heavy make-up, there was a deep sadness in Ruth's eyes that stood out for miles and Polly felt her heartstrings tug despite her head telling her to wise up and walk on. She contemplated going back in and making proper arrangements to meet up, but then she forced her mind to recall the days at school when the very sound of Ruth Monaghan's voice was enough to give her diarrhoea. Forgive and forget she could do, yes. But best buddies? Nuh-uh!

She stopped outside the shop near a litter bin, Ruth's card and the shop receipt still in her hand. She stared at the business card, knowing that Ruth was still watching from inside. Polly was shaking like a leaf. Then she pretended to drop the business card in the bin while in fact only letting the receipt go.

Then she hurried to the Jeep and climbed in, turned on the ignition and began to reverse before remembering she had to wait for Gina.

"What about my mum?" asked Danny from the back.

"Oh, sorry, Dan!" said Polly, turning off the ignition again. "Silly Polly forgot. Don't worry. She won't be long."

15

She turned on the radio and tried to hum along to distract her heart and mind. So, Ruth Monaghan was back in town! Shit. And she had sort of, kind of, in a half-hearted way agreed to meet her for coffee. Double shit. Her sister Tess would hit the roof when she found out. Shit, shit, shit!

2

"Ruth *Monaghan*! Ruth bloody Monaghan! The biggest bully our town has ever known! Are you off your head?"

Polly had called in to Tess as agreed the following afternoon for a quick coffee before her shift at the post office, and just as expected, Tess *was* hitting the roof. She was going Chicken Oriental Mental! She was on a roll.

"Did she *honestly* think that the moment she swanned back into our wee rural life from the bright lights of London people round here should actually like her? Should actually forgive her? *Did she*?"

"She just seemed so desperate," said Polly. "She looked really sad."

"And what?" Tess replied, fixing her make-up in her compact mirror in her sparkly clean kitchen, which Polly's gruesome twosome were doing their best to demolish with grubby toddler hands.

"I just think we should give her a chance, that's all."

"Lies," said Tess, with a sweep of blusher to her cheek. She was on a very quick lunch break from her teaching job at the local school and her make-up needed attention. "You are just dying for a nosey into her life since she left St John's with a three-month bump and a hickey on her neck."

"Well, maybe I am being a little bit nosey, but I do think we should just call around and –"

"Hold on!" said Tess, holding up her blusher brush in mid-air for effect. "What's all this *we* business? *You* are the one who bumped into her, not *me*. I don't feel the need to do anything. I don't even want to say her name, never mind call on her."

"But she said she was sorry! For how she treated both of us, not just me. Oh, come *on*. Don't make me do this alone."

"No. I am not meeting her," said Tess. "And anyhow, I thought you threw her business card in the bin?"

"I wanted her to think I did," said Polly, pulling out the very slick, very cleanly designed black, white and red business card from her purse. "It was the toilet-roll receipt I binned but I wanted her to think I was playing hard to get. I'm not the soft little Polly Woodhead I once was. I am Polly Knox now and I will never let Ruth Monaghan bully me again."

And oh how the gods laughed as Polly uttered those words! Polly was always a softie and Ruth Monaghan knew it. In all walks of life, Tess was the tougher, stronger one who said exactly what was on her mind. No one would ever walk over Tess. She was an independent newly-wed who knew exactly what she wanted and how to get it.

Tess and her husband Rob were in that wonderful, fuzzy honeymoon period of wedded bliss where they were still adding little bits of 'us' to their new home and couldn't keep their hands off each other when they came home from work in the evenings.

Rob, a six-foot-three fireman, sent Tess's pulse racing and her hormones into orbit and she would just have to have him, there and then. Life was as good as it could get. She had a sensible job teaching French at St John's, she had a strict daily routine that involved a morning jog, a read of the newspapers over breakfast with Rob, a hop, skip and jump to work for nine o'clock, a healthy packed lunch in tow with the option of popping home if she so chose, a visit to the gym (together of course) twice a week and, after dinner each evening, one glass of wine before relaxing in front of the telly and then heading to bed by ten for mind-blowing sex. Perfectly fine.

The only uncontrolled thing in her life was what she and her hubby got up to in the bedroom (or living room, or garden, *ahem*) and the only thing they ever argued about was when it was time to start a family – not so perfectly fine.

Rob wanted one now. Tess wanted one never. Well, not any time in the foreseeable future anyway.

At twenty-nine years old, the very thought of nappies and buggies and snotty noses and shitty asses just didn't appeal to her as much as say, a weekend at a Health Spa, or a night out at a wine bar or a long lazy lie-in on a Sunday morning. She just was not ready to give all that up. Rob *was* though. He was so maternal he would make Mary Poppins look like Attila the Hun.

"We have been married almost two years now, honey," he would say.

"Nineteen months and twenty-seven days to be exact,"

Tess would reply, quoting the exact timescale almost to the hour from when they'd both said 'I do'. "Don't exaggerate, babe."

Her sisters, of course, were on his side.

"It's much better when you have them when you're young," Polly would chirp.

But, looking at her strained face and sick-covered hair and dodgy clothing, Tess could always argue her case and feel like she had won hands down.

"You'll regret it when you're at the school gates and get called Granny," her eldest sister Mary would say. She had married at nineteen and was the perfect advertisement of why never, ever to marry young. She was thoroughly miserable and had no life of her own from what Tess could see.

"Wouldn't you want to have them before Mum or Dad kicks the bucket?" her sister Helen would say after a few glasses of wine.

Her minor, but growing, drink problem told Tess that she too was living a lie.

Tess could wait for all that. Rob would have to wait too. Right now, her career and her marriage were quite enough and she was very thankful for what she had in her life, no matter what anyone else would say.

No one would tell Tess Matthews what to do with her life. No one.

Tess returned to school that afternoon and greeted her first-year French class with a firm "*Bonjour, la classe*".

They filed into the room like mini-soldiers, clad from head to toe in navy and not as much as a hair out of place. St John's Grammar was an elite school for girls, nestled behind fir trees in the village of Cranmore, and pupils travelled from near and far to be educated within its walls.

Tess was a former head girl at the school and she took her job seriously and with great pride. She had excelled there as a student and was a real all-rounder with awards for music, drama, academia and sport coming out of her ears. With long legs and blonde hair and a complexion to die for, there was no doubt about it: of all the Woodhead girls, Tess was the golden child who had never put a step out of place. Well, not as far as her parents were concerned anyhow.

Tess was a model student in her day and she wanted to produce more model students by applying firm, fixed rules in her classroom. Her 'no shit' attitude had earned her great respect amongst her peers and she had her eye on a Head of Department job which would be in the pipeline as soon as old Droopy Knickers Wilson decided to call it a day and slump off into a long overdue retirement.

Tess's job was the main focus of her life. She ate, slept and breathed St John's and lapped up the admiration she received from parents and pupils alike.

"I like your dress, Mrs Matthews," said one of her young students.

Tess smiled and fixed her smart royal-blue wrap-over dress that brought out the deep blue of her eyes.

"*Merci beaucoup*, Alannah," said Tess. "That's very kind of you to say. Now, can you tell me the word for dress *en Français*?"

The little girl's eyes rolled back in thought. "Em . . . is it *une robe*?"

21

"*Oui,*" said Tess with a smile. She loved how she could always turn the simplest question or conversation with her girls into learning. "Everyone repeat after me: *une robe.*"

"*Une robe!*" said the class in unison and Tess's heart filled with warmth.

These girls were her babies for now. Her *job* was her baby. She couldn't possibly find anything in the world to top the high she felt when bettering her students and, for the moment, she had no great desire to. Motherhood would have to wait. She could meet any maternal instincts head on here in her teaching job at St John's and she would be the only one who would decide when it was time for her to do otherwise.

3

"So," explained Polly, "Tess chucked a wobbly with me, but what on earth else was I supposed to say? I mean, I couldn't be rude, could I? I couldn't just start a full-blown argument with Ruth Monaghan in the Spar over stuff that happened so many years ago! Frankie, eat up!"

"I don't like spaghetti."

It was dinner time in the Knox household, which meant a constant battle with Polly's eldest to eat, a war with the twins to stay at the table and a one-way fight to get her husband's attention. It was never easy to compete with the telly remote control and a plate of spaghetti bolognese.

"And then the atomic bomb exploded from my handbag and I ended up in hospital and they say I have weeks to live! Weeks!"

"Uh-huh," said James, entering the digits for Sky Sports News on the remote without having to take his eyes off the screen. "Very good."

Fooking *Groundhog Day* again!

"*Days* to live actually. I have days! It's serious.

Terminal. It was a terminal type of bomb-type thingy. That means it could kill me. And it's contagious too. So you might have it too. And the children."

Polly wouldn't normally joke about such things, but she was testing how bad the communication levels had become within her marriage. She was on transmit – he had switched off the ability to receive.

"Are there any more batteries for this thing?" he asked, shaking the remote with one hand and shoving a hefty forkful of spaghetti into his mouth at the same time.

Polly was hoping he would choke. "*James!*" she said, knowing exactly what his response would be.

"What? Sorry. What, love? I'm just checking on tomorrow's fixtures. United are –"

"I don't give a flying fudge what United are doing! I have been telling you about my day and you haven't listened to one thing I said!"

"Mum?" asked Frankie, playing with his food. "Should I swap Johnny a Rooney card for Scholes or not? Dad says not. What do you think?"

Polly looked at her son in his red football jersey, his little hands now full of Soccer Trump Cards and his dinner sitting on the table beside him untouched and her eyes widened in horror.

What did she think? What did she *think*? At that point, she couldn't think at all! She could only focus on breathing and not crying and screaming for some attention to come *her* way for a change! She caught a quick glimpse of her future at that moment and it truly gave her the willies. In her mind, there she was in ten years' time, surrounded at their family dining table by not one, not two, but four one-track-minded soccer fanatics who wouldn't care if she had days or weeks to live as long as Manchester Bloody United were winning the League or the Cup or whatever other life-changing competition they were competing in these days!

"Did you put Worcester Sauce in this again?" asked James in distaste, and that was it.

She had to get away before she threw something at him.

She pushed back her chair, took off her *Bisto Mum* apron, flung it on the table and stomped towards the back door, glancing back to see if her great departure had the desired effect on her nearest and dearest, but the look on her husband's face – or lack of it – spoke volumes.

He was still shaking the remote control at the television. He hadn't even noticed she had moved.

Bastard!

So she stomped into the living room instead and turned on the TV. If you can't beat them, join them, she thought, flicking through the channels until she found a trashy reality TV programme which followed a celebrity couple and their children around on their luxurious lifestyle. Just what she needed! Chewing gum for the brain! The dishes could wait, the homework could wait. Everything could wait because Polly Knox couldn't be arsed any more. And besides, she had no idea where else she could go.

Rob had the table set to perfection and a stomach-rumbling, mouth-watering aroma of garlic and ginger met Tess, along with a hefty glass of red wine, when she walked into her kitchen that evening. The lights were lowered in the candlelit room and it looked wonderfully inviting.

25

"So, how was your day, my favourite, most beautiful girl in the world?" he asked.

He was so handsome and the way he rested his hands on her hips and looked into her eyes as he spoke got her going every time.

"Mmm, let me think . . . six classes of teenagers who excelled in learning the beautiful language that is *La Français* and a meeting with a principal who I am desperate to impress but who would rather look down my top than talk business, so all in all, a normal day at the office. How about you?"

Rob pulled her closer towards him.

"Two games of poker at the station, one false alarm at the bank and a minor house fire where a little old man almost toasted himself in his electric blanket. He's all tucked up on a ventilator now, poor thing. All in all, not a bad wee shift."

He gave Tess a deep, lengthy look of absolute appreciation and pulled her face close for a smouldering kiss that went on for longer than she could remember. Rob had always been an amazing kisser and the longer they were together, the more she savoured his talent. He smelled of soap and his kiss tasted warm and salty and she said a silent prayer of thanks for the glow of happiness that filled her right there and then.

"Babe, were you smoking again?" he asked when he pulled back eventually. "Please don't smoke, Tess."

He wasn't angry. Rob was never angry at her but the way he said it spelt disappointment and she hated disappointing him. For all her amazing, top-of-the-class qualities, Tess had one little vice that she couldn't quite kick. She was a sneaky smoker.

"I just had one earlier on my lunch break," she said. "Oh, don't look at me like that, babe! I know I need to give up but it's seriously only when I'm stressed. I've been feeling a little bit more under pressure than normal this past few weeks and it's the only thing that settles me. You should be a smoke detective."

"Well, being a fireman, I sort of am," he responded immediately. "I'm trained to spot smoke, even of the tobacco variety. I can smell it and taste it a mile away."

"Well, from where I was standing, that kiss was yummy and this all looks and smells amazing. What's the occasion?"

He really had made quite the effort for a midweek dinner. Candles were flickering on the table, on the worktops, on the windowsill and on any other surface that was free to hold them and a tasteful shuffle of mellow music played in the background from the iPod dock.

Tess was truly impressed, but truly puzzled.

Very puzzled, until she caught a glimpse of the calendar that hung on the side of the dresser and that's when it all became clear. Rob had marked off each day with an 'X' as he always did (he blamed his mild case of OCD), but today's date had a circle around it. It glared at her then and she couldn't take her eyes off it. So she glared back.

"Why is today's date circled on the calendar?" she asked, secretly hoping that the reason swirling around her head wasn't matching the one on his mind. "Is it someone's birthday? Your mum's?"

Of course, Tess knew it wasn't his mum's birthday. She knew the dates of his parents' birthdays better than she did anyone else's. Being an only child, he always made a fuss of his parents so she knew it was nothing to do with them. Was it the anniversary of the day they had met? No. The day they first spent a full night together? No. The day they first said 'I love you'? No. They knew all those dates. They were soppy like that.

"Em, no, it's not her birthday . . . I . . . are you trying to change the subject?" he asked.

"What subject? Me smoking?"

"Well, yes, you smoking. You know I hate you smoking and it's not good if we're going to . . ."

He trailed off and at that moment Tess knew that her suspicions were true. Suddenly the delicious aroma of garlic and ginger turned sour, the wine she had just sipped tasted bitter and even the lingering warmth of his kiss made her shudder.

"Rob, I think we need to talk . . . again," she said and waited for his face to fall as it always did when they broached the whole baby subject.

"Look, I'm sorry! Just forget it. Let's not ruin what was supposed to be a lovely, romantic evening," he said.

She felt so bad for him. He had put so much effort into the food, the wine, even the background music was tasteful but the calendar had just thrown everything off the boil and now she wanted to shake him for not listening to what was now beginning to sound like a very worn-out, scraped record.

"I can't just forget about it," said Tess. "I can't just sit at the table and look lovingly in your eyes when I know you had an ulterior motive for tonight, Rob. I'm on the pill, Rob! My ovulation date is irrelevant! No matter how many times you try and trick me with your sperm disguised by a romantic dinner, it won't make one blind bit of difference!"

The bloody calendar was still catching her eye at every turnaround. She walked towards it and ripped it down.

"What are you doing, Tess? Sit down and relax. Please babe, forget about all that then. I shouldn't have . . . I just thought . . ."

"You just thought of yourself," she said, knowing that her words were cutting him in two but she couldn't help it. "You thought of yourself and your own desires but you didn't even discuss this with me. I feel as if you were sneaking behind my back. I feel like you've betrayed me, Rob."

His gorgeous face crumpled now and he couldn't even look her in the eye. She knew he wanted a baby. She knew that from day one but *he* knew that it would have to happen when they were *both* ready and that was something that they just couldn't agree on.

"Let's just forget about it and have dinner," he said, moving towards the cooker where everything was keeping warm at the perfect temperature. "Please."

Tess took a drink of her wine and then another and then another until the glass was drained. Then she rummaged in her handbag for the pack of Silk Cut that she kept for emergencies and moved to the patio doors where she lit up a cigarette, inhaled deeply and watched as the smoke filled the evening sky.

"Are you okay, Tess?" Rob called from the kitchen.

She tried to remind herself of how wonderful her life was in every way. She had a rewarding, if somewhat frustrating, job teaching a subject she adored even if the adorable little monsters she taught sometimes didn't; she had her health (despite the smoking – she knew she really should quit) and her wonderful if sometimes highly annoying family lived near enough to visit but far enough away to avoid; and most importantly she had a husband who loved her more than life itself and who totally rocked her world every time he said her name or looked into her eyes.

But despite hours of debate during the nineteen months that they'd been married, one thing just wouldn't go away. He wanted a baby. She wanted a baby too, she supposed . . . but just not yet.

And now he was monitoring her cycle, though how her being on the pill was factored into his scheme she didn't know. Was he trying to *trick* her into forgetting her pill or agreeing in the heat of the passion to stop taking it?

That hurt. That hurt a lot.

4

Gina Humphries looked out the window onto Ardglass Villas to check again for her husband's arrival. Lights were on in every house in the development where families gathered for supper or evenings in front of the telly, but Gina's house was silent and empty. Danny was in bed and there was still no sign of Trevor.

Gina loved anniversaries. She loved cards and trinkets and little novelties like hand-made photo frames or scrapbooks and memory boxes and quilts and home-knitted scarves and baking bread and meeting her son coming home from school with rosy cheeks and the smell of fresh air on his coat.

She was not a bad person. Her friends said she was kind and gentle and caring and that, with a little bit of care and attention, she might even be . . . pretty.

So why did he make her feel like she was worthless, every hour of every day, even that day – on their tenth wedding anniversary? Like she'd done something wrong, when all she had ever done was tried? Really, really tried.

"You wouldn't recognise me now if you looked at my wedding photos," she had once told Polly. "I was a Size 10 back then. I was beautiful, if I do say so myself. My hair was long and thick and glossy and I was radiant with health and happiness and hopes for the future."

But all that had changed. Her clothes were too big for her now and her hair was a ruffled, wiry mess. *Wretched*, as her mother would say.

"Did you ever dream you could just run away?" she once asked Polly. She asked Polly lots of things these days. "You know, like in that movie *Shirley Valentine* where she packs up and leaves and has this wonderful holiday fling by the sea and drinks nice cocktails on the sand and tops up her tan while leaving all her cares behind?"

"I'd love to do a Shirley Valentine." She remembered hearing her mother and her aunt say that with a giggle when they wanted to moan about their other halves, but of course they never would. They never could.

Gina never thought she would either. She had a young child to look after. And him. Yes, *him*. Trevor. Her husband of ten years and seven hours. If he knew that she had to go next door yesterday and ask for milk and a lift to the shop she'd never hear the end of it, but it was one of those quick decisions she had to make. Did she risk having no milk for his tea when he got home, and worse again having nothing prepared for dinner? Or did she swallow her pride by going next door and asking Polly for a neighbourly favour? Again.

Gina really liked Polly. She had one of those faces that everyone liked. *A lovely, lovely girl,* as her mother would have said. *A real lady.*

Polly's husband James was a decent sort too. Gina

32

would see him coming home from his work every day at the same time, like clockwork, and Polly always had a delicious smell coming from the kitchen or on sunny days she might be out hanging her washing on the line when he pulled into the drive in his nice Mercedes Benz.

It's not like she watched their every move at all. She wasn't a nosey person. Maybe just, well, a bit envious you could say.

She wished *her* husband would come home at the same time every day, with no liquor on his breath, nor snarl on his face, nor gravel in his voice when things weren't the way he liked them.

She had put make-up on that day for him coming home since it was their anniversary. She'd put the hot brush and straighteners through her hair too and even put on a skirt. She hadn't worn a skirt for ages. Her nice clothes didn't really fit her any more.

"You look pretty, Mammy," her son had told her. He had a look of sadness in his eyes when he said it, like he knew that she was trying her best and like he knew that it would all be for nothing.

She'd bought a few steaks down at the Spar and cooked them to Trevor's liking and, although she hated when he had a drink, she even put a few beers in the fridge for him just to mark the occasion. Their wedding day seemed like yesterday and she remembered that horrible feeling that she had made a terrible mistake moving north with Trevor Humphries. She was a Dublin girl at heart and it had taken her at least two years to settle into her new life up North where everything was different – different accents, different money, different cultures and a totally different way of life than what she was used to.

Everything was slower here out in the countryside. Yes, the village of Cranmore had everything a young family would need and there was a great sense of community but it was very strange to be plunged into the back end of nowhere when you were used to the bright lights of Dublin.

Gina remembered when they first went to the supermarket and she couldn't believe that everyone knew each other's name. Most families were related and Trevor Humphries was certainly a very well-known, highly regarded figure amongst the locals. He was a champion footballer and a shrewd businessman and although he was slight in stature – lean, one might say – he was a magnet for respect and Gina moulded into that sense of pride as a comfort to her loneliness in her earlier years of married life.

How that had changed as the years rolled by! Trevor was still the apple of everyone's eye in the local business and sporting circuit, but behind closed doors Gina had witnessed a very different side to the husband she once adored.

She remembered the first time she encountered his other side. It was a cool, crisp evening in September and she had just moved from Dublin to start a new life with her new husband in Northern Ireland. They had been to a barbecue down at the local sports club where Trevor was still, even in his mid-thirties, regarded as a bit of a hero. The *craic* was mighty and Gina had enjoyed a few glasses of wine with Polly and her sister Tess and they had giggled and laughed at some of the locals' attempt at karaoke.

Gina, in her little white summer dress and long black hair, was feeling confident under the influence and decided to give some of the locals a run for their money. It was all a bit of fun and when she sang 'Like a Virgin' the small crowd whooped in delight. Some even said she was a great singer and she returned to her table with a huge smile which would turn to tears when she got home.

To say Trevor Humphries wasn't impressed was the understatement of the year. He was humiliated, he said. He had never been so disgusted in all his life. The men in the club were leering at her, he said. The women were laughing at her, not with her, he said. You would never see Polly Knox get up and make a show of herself like that, he said. She never would sing again, he said.

And she didn't.

Danny had been impeccably behaved at bedtime earlier, just as if he knew that Gina was making a special effort for his daddy coming home and she had settled down to watch *EastEnders*, waiting for the key to turn in the door. When that would happen, she would quickly spray some perfume and bring him dinner as he watched the news or whatever it was he fancied. Maybe some *Top Gear*. He loved *Top Gear*.

But his key didn't turn in the door that evening.

And by ten that night it still hadn't. So there she was, all dressed up like a Christmas tree, her belly rumbling with hunger and nothing on the telly to distract her from the knowledge that her husband had let her down. He didn't care enough to come home because he was with *her* again. On their fucking anniversary. Yes, on their tenth wedding anniversary, Trevor Humphries was with his other woman.

Gina would never say their names together. She did know her name, but she would never say it out loud. To do so would be like she was acknowledging her existence, her place in his life – her place in *their* lives – and she could never do that.

She knew that people talked and that their opinion was divided. A couple of people admired her for being too proud to make a fuss, some pitied her for being such a weakling and a walkover, but the majority would love to give her a shake and tell her to get out while she was still young enough to make a new life for herself and her young son.

That was the one thing that baffled her about life in a small village where sport was religion and religion was a show. Trevor Humphries could get away with murder and they would forgive him for it. He could shag the entire village and he would get a pat on the back. It was the village's worst-kept secret that he had a mistress and Gina knew that she was more the fool for putting up with their big fat masquerade of happy families.

She knew she should eat her steak and go to bed and count her blessings that *she* (the other woman) was the one enduring his bad manners and dealing with his moods and grubby clothes when he came back from work. She knew she should be thankful that she wasn't on the end of his fist for once when she forgot to put the bin out or change the toilet roll on the dispenser or left the heating on too long.

But she was weak and powerless and she didn't have the energy to stand up for herself. She wished she had. She wished she had done it a long, long time ago.

5

"Do you fancy going to the cinema?" Ruth Monaghan asked her daughter whose fingers were in a flurry as she typed into her Blackberry with great gusto. "There's a new Liam Neeson movie out and I hear it's really good. You like Liam Neeson, don't you?"

Melanie's bedroom smelt like deodorant mixed with salt-and-vinegar crisps. Ruth couldn't say it was pleasant but it certainly didn't bother Melanie who looked very comfortable as she lay on her bed, lost in her world of teenage dreams.

"Melanie? Cinema?" she asked again, feeling defeated already.

"Nah," was her reply and she giggled at whatever message she just received on her phone. *Nah*. Not even a 'not in the mood' or a 'there's something good on telly'. Just *nah*. So much for quality time and making an effort to keep the lines of communication opened between mother and daughter. No matter what Ruth suggested, Melanie would answer with a nonchalant 'nah'. Her counsellor had advised on the importance of 'communication' and 'quality time' after her father left them two years ago, but Ruth's efforts were rarely rewarded.

"Do you fancy pizza for tea then?" she tried, hoping for a more fulfilling response. "We could go to that nice place in town? You know, the one with the waiter with the wonky eyes?"

Melanie shrugged. No words this time, just a lazy shrug. She wrapped a throw around her bare legs and continued to stare at her phone. It was the same thing every day since they had moved here. Melanie's phone was a permanent barrier between them, like a wall that Ruth had to jump over before she got her daughter's attention.

"Melanie!" said Ruth in a proper 'I'm your mother so have manners' voice.

"What?" she asked, as if Ruth had interrupted an intimate conversation with Chris Martin from Coldplay. Melanie was prime time in love with him. Not a crush. In proper, like, love, like. Melanie said 'like' a lot.

"I have just asked you two questions and you barely answered me!"

"I did!" she said, putting on the headphones of her iPod so she could listen to something, anything other than her mother's voice.

"Melanie! I am speaking to you!"

"And I answered you!" she snapped in her strong Cockney accent, then gave the kind of deep sigh that only a teenage girl can give. "I can't be arsed with the cinema and I had pizza at lunch time. You need your roots done, by the way."

Ruth breathed in and out of her nostrils, rather dragon-like as Melanie stared at her hair which to be fair, *had* seen better days. She had lost interest in her appearance and the stress of the move from England to the backwaters of Cranmore had really taken up all her time and energy, not to mention the worry of now being so close to her mother and feeling the urge to break down the barriers of the past by paying her a visit.

"I'll make an appointment tomorrow," said Ruth, running her fingers through her outgrown bob and feeling two feet high. "How about fish and chips for tea then? Melanie, please? Fish and chips?"

But Melanie wasn't listening at all now. She even had the cheek to sing along with Coldplay to drown Ruth out. That was it. Ruth had had enough of talking to a brick wall!

"*Melanie!*" she shouted and pulled the headphones from her daughter's ears. They caught in her hair which made her yelp like a wounded animal but Ruth wasn't one bit sorry. "Have some bloody manners!"

"*Ow!* I was listening to that!"

"Well, why don't you listen to *me* for a change? Do you want fish and flippin' chips or not?"

She made sure to say 'flippin'' rather than use another expletive because Melanie loved an excuse to swear and Ruth wasn't giving her one. No way.

Melanie recognised this and decided to take the piss.

"From the *flippin'* chippy or *flippin'* home-made?" she asked, as if it made all the difference in the world.

It probably did. Ruth's cooking sucked and they all knew it.

"From the chippy!"

"Then yes! Your chips are soggy."

Ruth resisted the urge to pull her hair again, on purpose this time.

"*Thank* you! Now, was that so difficult?" she asked but Melanie was away again, her nimble fingers working overtime on the Blackberry's tiny keys and her ears plugged with headphones.

All that just to find out what she wanted to eat! Ruth shuddered at the thought of getting an answer to a difficult question from her daughter!

She left Melanie to it, surrounded by her Coldplay paraphernalia and scatter cushions and dirty washing that she totally refused to lift from her bedroom floor and stormed down to the kitchen where she automatically reached for a bottle of gin from the cupboard. It was after six. Therefore she was not an alcoholic. It was 'evening'.

"Just one," she told herself, ignoring how her hands were shaking and her heart was thumping as she poured the cool, clear liquid into the glass.

She downed the drink in one go, feeling ignited as soon as the soothing effects of the alcohol hit her bloodstream. It was times like this when she wondered why on earth she had moved back to this dead-end town at all. If she was in London, she could have called on Cathy or Georgie to do something with, but round here all she had was a fourteen-year-old who gave her nothing but bad manners and a nineteen-year-old boy who was so obsessed with his new girlfriend that he couldn't possibly do anything that didn't involve her. Apart from sleep, when he probably . . . oh, Ruth didn't even want to think about what Ben thought of when he went to bed.

No wonder she spent far too much time in the Spar across the road talking to Sheila the shop assistant. Getting conversation out of her children was as challenging as a *Countdown* conundrum and she just felt so lost, so lonely and so good for nothing. She was thirty-four years old, living in a town where hardly anyone remembered her – and those who did, did so for all the wrong reasons.

She lifted her mobile phone, scrolled through the numbers and stopped at 'Mum'. Her thumb hovered over the dial button. She closed her eyes. Just press it, she told herself. Just press it.

She pressed the button and scrunched her eyes tighter and then hung up. She couldn't do it. She would one day, but not just yet.

"Oh God, how did I come to this?" she said, staring out the window onto unfamiliar streets and the clenched fist of loneliness squeezed her insides.

She stood in her new kitchen, poured herself a second gin and tonic and, knowing that Coldplay were upstairs kindly drowning out any sound effects she might make, she cried her eyes out, longing for someone to talk to that didn't involve a phone or a computer. She could feel herself slipping deeper and deeper into a horrible depressing cocoon-like state and she had no idea how to stop it. Loneliness was engulfing. It could swallow you up and break you down if you let it and Ruth Monaghan knew all about that.

She needed someone. She needed someone to talk to so, so badly. And no harm to Sheila the lovely Spar lady, but she just wasn't doing it for her any more.

Ruth Monaghan needed a friend. A real friend. And she needed one now.

6

Polly didn't speak to James for two whole days after 'Spaghetti-Gate' as she had since thought of it. Living with someone and not speaking to them was much more difficult than she thought it would be, but that's where a nine-year-old boy came in handy. It was difficult to begin with, but he soon got the hang of it.

"Frankie, tell your dad he has to call with Granny to change a light bulb in her bedroom. She can't reach and she can't see in the dark."

"She should eat more carrots," said Frankie. "They help you see in the dark, or so you grown-ups tell me. I have a feeling it's a bribe. And why can't you tell him? He's just on the sofa right there."

Frankie pointed in bewilderment at his father who lay with his feet up watching *The Simpsons*. The very sight of those yellow faces on television were enough to drive Polly batty.

"Be a good boy and pass on the message," she said in defiance. "Granny needs –"

"I heard you," said James, staring at the TV. "Doesn't your mother look a bit like Marge, Frankie? All she needs is the blue hair."

He smirked and she threw a cushion at him, regretting it at once because she shouldn't have acknowledged his presence at all.

"He says he heard you and that you look like Marge," said Frankie, still a bit put out by it all. Then he giggled as he realised it could be fun.

"Tell your dad that makes a change," Polly snapped, not thinking it was fun. She had to make her point. "And I do not look like Marge Simpson!"

"Mum says that makes a change."

"What makes a change?" asked James.

"What makes a change?" asked Frankie, his little head to-ing and fro-ing like a ball boy at a tennis match.

"Him hearing me!" said Polly, raising her chin in defiance.

"Touché!" said James.

"Touché," said Frankie. "What does touché mean, anyhow?"

And so it went on for two whole days.

Polly reluctantly gave in on Thursday morning when she couldn't find the ATM card and needed it to get her hair done. After the Marge comment, she needed to make herself feel better. She needn't have bothered speaking to him directly because, as always, she ended up finding it herself and when she did she also came across Ruth Monaghan's business card.

"Ruth bloody Monaghan," she said, fingering the card.

For a split second she contemplated calling her, just for a chat and to find out what had become of the school

43

bully of St John's who left with baby bump when everyone was studying for their exams. What on earth had made Ruth return here? What was making her so sad?

She wanted to call but, remembering Tess's reaction to the very idea of it, she put the card into her pocket and decided to sleep on it for a day or two. She would keep Ruth Monaghan at a healthy distance for a while.

She never, ever for one second expected Ruth Monaghan to land at her door the very next morning. That was a shock and a half and she had no time to decide how to react. So, she invited her in for coffee.

Ruth was empty inside and more down than usual when she visited the Spar that Friday morning. She'd had absolutely no intention of visiting Polly unannounced but, before she knew it, the words were out of her mouth to Sheila the shop assistant.

"Do you know Polly Woodhead, I mean, Polly Knox?" she asked as she paid for her pack of Kit Kats and Diet Coke. "We went to school together. I was thinking of looking her up."

She knew she sounded like a stalker but Sheila seemed to like her. She was one of her best customers after all. Every day she would call at the Spar on at least three occasions and every day she and Sheila would chat about everything from Cheryl Cole's hair to the price of a bag of crisps and how they were always half-empty these days anyhow. They just didn't make Monster Munch like they used to.

"Of course I know Polly. Her sister Tess teaches my daughter French at St John's. Lovely girls they are, the two of them. One of their sisters has a bit of a problem with the you-know-what."

Ruth loved how Sheila always threw in a wee titbit of gossip for good measure.

"Do you know where she lives? I don't have her number so I thought I'd pop round."

Sheila folded her chubby arms and looked up at the ceiling as if Ruth had asked her a phone-a-friend question for the biggest prize on *Who Wants to Be a Millionaire?*.

"Now, let me get this right," she said. "Tess lives out of town I'm almost sure, in the snobby end, and Helen, she's the one who's fond of the booze – she lives in Rushfield Park and then there's Mary the sensible one with all the children . . . yes, I'm nearly sure that Polly lives in Ardglass Villas. You know the posh houses at the end of the village? Her husband is very well to do and a real hunk into the bargain. Some girls have all the luck, eh?"

Ruth was already feeling like a down and out and, when Sheila told her about Polly's idyllic lifestyle, she felt even worse. She was fat and alone and no one wanted to know her any more, but Polly seemed kind. She was always much softer than her younger sister. Maybe if she gave Ruth a chance, she might see how much she had changed down the years. She wasn't a big bully any more. She was still big, but not a bully.

Yes, that was it decided. She would just drive around to Ardglass Villas for a nosey. The place hadn't even existed when she lived in the village as a teenager so it would be only right to check it out. She would drive through, have a look around and then go home and talk to . . . well, probably to the microwave or the television again. She wouldn't even get out of the car. She would just drive through and leave it at that.

So she got into her little Alpha Romeo and, before she could change her mind, she drove through the village and down to the entrance of the very beautiful and very posh indeed Ardglass Villas.

It was a well-to-do development, anyone could tell. It had redbrick pillars at its entrance which were framed with black cast-iron fencing and the name of the development was proudly displayed on a black marble plaque with gold lettering. Each of the detached houses was unique in design but similar in style and their very presence and stature reminded Ruth of the life she could have had with Jeffrey. Or Jeffrey the Bastard as he was more commonly known in her own muddled head.

Feeling flushed at the very thought of her ex-husband, she put down her window a little to let some fresh air in and turned the radio down so she could concentrate on taking in how the other half lived here in her home village, so many years on.

Who lived in these houses? Solicitors, contractors, teachers, accountants, she guessed. She thought even the birds chirped louder and more in tune in this place. Stepford Wives hung out their washing and retired gentlemen mowed their lawns in the morning sunshine. It was like a big cocoon of blissful living, straight out of an *Ideal Homes* magazine. It was just the type of sight that would make you boke.

By the time she had reached the middle of the development, the fact that she had none of this idyllic lifestyle any more began to creep in on her. Heaviness built in her chest and a choking sensation nestled in her throat.

She wanted to turn and get out of there fast. What if someone recognised her? She didn't belong around here. Everyone hated her. What if Polly saw her? She would think she was a maniac! She had to turn! She had to get out right away. At this point she realised she was in a cul de sac. She would pick a driveway, any driveway to turn into and pray there were no small children outside playing as she couldn't promise she would be able to avoid them. Or animals. She was sure to squash someone's pet Chihuahua with her flustered three-point turn. What was she thinking driving round, skulking about here anyhow? She wasn't that desperate for a friend, was she?

She randomly pulled the car into a cobbled driveway and checked her rear-view mirror in preparation for a quick spin back out again. The house had hanging baskets and window boxes and the garden was as neat as a pin. Ruth's eyes were a blur, she was so determined to get out of Ardglass Villas with its wisterias and cherry-blossom trees. But then she stopped. Because then she saw her.

Of all the houses and all the driveways to choose, she had to choose this one. Ruth's worst nightmare came to life when she saw the familiar figure of Polly Woodhead washing her windows from inside the house in front of her. Holy shit! It was too late. She was caught. She had chosen to turn her car, she had chosen to make her escape by driving straight into the lion's den!

"*Shit!*"

Polly looked puzzled and then waved at her in recognition through the window as Ruth wrestled with her steering wheel, pretending she had no idea where she was.

"Ruth!" she saw Polly mouth through the glass. "Hello!"

And before she knew it, Polly was on her doorstep and was making her way towards her.

"Oh! Polly! Is that you?" Ruth put on her best 'what a surprise' look. "What a coincidence! I was lost . . ."

"You stopping?" asked Polly. "Come on in."

Wishing she had an excuse to be driving around Ardglass Villas and scrambling to find one, Ruth tried to look casual as she parked up the car. She could feel her normally pale cheeks flush with humiliation as she scrambled out and walked up the pathway of Polly's very posh detached house with its picket fence and landscaped gardens.

"What a surprise!" said Polly as she opened the door.

Ruth knew she had made a terrible mistake in coming to Ardglass Villas. She felt like a bunny-boiling psychopath. She bet she *looked* like a bunny-boiling psychopath.

"Hi, Polly," said Ruth. "I – I didn't realise this was your house. I was just turning the car. Took a wrong turn. Have I got you at a bad time? You really don't have to invite me in. I was just passing."

I was just passing. That old chestnut!

"Em . . . no, not really," said Polly with her sweet smile that was just oh so Polly. "I'm just getting the kids ready to go to their gran's for the morning. I normally catch an hour of Pilates on a Friday but, to be honest, I'm not that fussed today. Come in."

Ruth couldn't believe it. She was just so nice. How could she have been so cruel to her all those years ago? She used to call her Fanta Pants because of her ginger hair. Or Ginger Minge. That used to drive Polly insane.

"I wasn't going to come in, but then you waved so I thought I might as well and anyhow, I was just wondering if you would like to go for that coffee anytime soon?"

Now she was *sounding* like a bunny-boiling psychopath with her shaky voice and fidgety hands. "I mean, no pressure. I know I've just sprung this on you but, you see, I was in the area, took a wrong turn and . . . well, I'm here now and I remember you saying that Friday mornings were good. Did you say Friday mornings were good? Maybe I just made that up. Anyhow, I'm here now, so maybe if you've time . . . look, I'm sorry . . ."

She was rambling and Polly's startled, wide eyes added to her acute embarrassment.

"You've already apologised, Ruth. You don't have to keep doing it. Come into the kitchen and meet my twins."

Ruth could have hugged her, but she didn't. That would have been the beginning of the end. Polly would definitely have called the cops and had a restriction order issued if she had hugged her. Besides, Polly was tiny and Ruth was huge so it would all have ended in tears. Instead she sheepishly followed Polly through the hallway underneath its huge chandelier and between cream walls and over wooden flooring and, even though she was so unbelievably grateful to Polly for inviting her into her home and not being a snotty cow like she had every right to be, Ruth was feeling more and more jealous with every step she took.

Polly 'Fanta Pants' Woodhead had become Polly 'Blonde Bombshell' Knox and was well and truly living the two-point-four lifestyle with her health and her wealth and her sanity. And where had Ruth got with *her* life? Divorced, working from home, isolated and lonely and well out of her depth in this backward village where everyone had moved on and done very well for themselves thank you very much.

She felt a wave of emotion engulf her and she began to feel really sorry for herself. More so than ever. More than the early-morning sweats she'd get when she'd panic about living so far away from the man she had loved but who now loved another, and with no real family to fall back on apart from her Aunt Ida who she believed hated her guts for coming back into her life and upsetting her bridge games and afternoon job in the bingo hall. And a brother called Brian who should have been named Judas. Oh, and her mother who hadn't spoken to her for more years than she could remember and who had probably decided to forget about her very existence.

She had nothing.

Yes, she had money and two wonderful children and a small but thriving business to call her own but inside she felt that she had no idea who she was any more. Who on earth *was* the real Ruth Monaghan?

She had absolutely no idea.

Polly, on the other hand, seemed to have everything and Ruth felt so inadequate as she stood in her perfect kitchen beneath her perfect black-and-white family portraits with her three sons and drop-dead-gorgeous husband with his light stubble and take-me-to-bed eyes. She could have cried right then.

She could have cried even more when there was a knock at the door and in walked Tess.

Super-talented, naturally blonde, long-legged, beautiful Tess who had the looks of an angel but the tongue of a viper.

Polly was a walk in the park. Tess was an obstacle course in the dark.

Now Ruth *really* wanted to cry.

Tess had sped through the hallway and then stopped dead, like someone had pulled a handbrake on her, and she couldn't help but glare. She gulped and then she glared more.

A deathly silence followed and Tess felt her smile turn upside down like a cartoon character. She could feel her skin crawl, like she was being turned inside out. No one – *no one* had any idea how much this girl – this useless lump that was Ruth Monaghan – had made her life such a misery back in the day when she should have been more worried about getting caught wearing lipstick to school than what shadow Ruth would leap out of to call her names!

"Em, Ruth was just passing by and popped in to say hello," said Polly, making faces at Tess behind Ruth's back which begged her not to slice the woman's head off with a breadknife. Tess *hated* Ruth Monaghan. And she had every right to.

Ruth used to tease and taunt Tess so badly. She would tease both of them about their clothes, about their hair, about the way they walked, the way they talked. Everything. To Tess, Ruth Monaghan was a big fat bullying bitch and the very sound of her name made her stomach churn.

"Hi, Tess," said Ruth.

Hi? *Hi?* What the hell did she want? A hug? A high five? You don't just make someone's life a misery for years and then say 'Hi!'

Tess could tell Ruth was shitting herself which gave her a satisfactory glow of power even though Tess too was shaking in her high-heel boots at the very sight of her. It was like stepping back in time. It was like she was standing there in her school uniform being taunted and teased at the school gates, plagued by name-calling and cruel jibes.

Ruth hadn't really changed that much. She still had the same shoulder-length hair. A bit more limp than it used to be and dyed a dodgy colour of red with dark roots. Not ginger or a pleasant auburn red, but an in-your-face pillar-box red which made her look paler than Tess ever remembered her. Underneath the shock of clown-like madness, she had eye make-up that was a little too dark on her slanted peepers and the same podgy face with a dimple on her chin. She looked like she always had. Like she didn't really fit in and that made Tess feel kind of . . . good. This was *their* little world and she had no place around here any more. If she tried to apologise, Tess decided right there and then, she would pull her spiky eyelashes out.

"I'm . . . It's good to see you again," mumbled Ruth.

"You haven't changed a bit," said Tess. "You look . . . you look exactly the same."

Tess was eyeballing her now for all she was worth.

"I have changed," said Ruth. "Believe me I have changed more than you know."

Silence followed and Tess could hear the other woman gulp with nerves.

"You look great," said Ruth.

"Oh, *do* I?" said Tess. "That's rich."

"Yes, you do." said Ruth. She looked like she was going to cry. "In fact you always did and that's why I probably treated you so badly. I was jealous. I've thought about it for years. I'm –"

"Don't you dare say you are sorry!" said Tess, thinking Polly looked like she was going to pee her pants with fear that she actually *would* pull Ruth's eyelashes out. Polly was such a softie. She hated confrontation. Tess thrived on it. She would take on anyone, anywhere. Was it any wonder she had that school principal eating out of her hands? Even the parish priest turned to mush when Tess was around and he was the most ignorant, snooty-nosed beast of a man you could ever meet!

"I just . . . I was confused back then," Ruth continued. "I didn't have many friends and my parents were going through a divorce when no-one else's were and then I found out I was pregnant and –"

"*Oh, boo fucking hoo!*" Tess snapped. "Do you expect me to listen to this shit? I don't care what you were going through! You didn't need to take it out on *us*! We didn't make your parents divorce! We didn't bloody impregnate you! Tell it to someone who cares!"

"Tess! Don't be so rude!" said Polly as she ushered the twins into their playroom. Polly was all pious when it came to swearing and still hadn't forgiven herself for saying 'hell' in the children's hearing when she'd knelt on the Lego.

"*Me? Rude?*" said Tess in her best high-pitched teacher voice. "I think I have every right to be rude! Don't you remember the horrible names she used to call you? Or the fact that she stole my medal when I won the Cross Country Schools Under Twelve Championship?"

"No, I will never forget that," said Polly. "You have never let it go, either. Are you sure it's not down the back of Mum's sofa?"

Tess was on a roll. "Or the way she terrified you into taking a different route home every day for two whole years? Huh? You have a very short memory and you are way too soft!"

"Did I?" asked Ruth. "Did I really terrify you that much, Polly? Oh God, I'm –"

"Don't say it!" snapped Tess. "Don't dare!" She glared at Polly who was scratching her head and fixing the string on that stupid apron she always wore to make her look like Mother-fucking-Earth.

Polly mumbled a response. "Em, well . . ."

"Oh, just tell her, Polly!" Tess squealed, enjoying the look on Ruth's face as she squirmed at the ugly truth. She was only starting . . . "Tell her how she used to make you piss the bed when you were old enough to be at discos and how you didn't keep on Biology which you loved because she was taking that class too and you were too afraid to be in the same room as her!"

"I honestly am so sorry," said Ruth, a quivering wreck now.

But Tess still had saved the best to last.

"Or how about the fact that you couldn't eat for five days and vomited up everything you did eat in fear of her horrible, evil bullying after she threatened you for picking up her schoolbag by accident? You have a cheek, Ruth Monaghan. You have a cheek coming back into our town and expecting us to forgive and forget! You're a callous, conniving, backstabbing bully and I would advise you to get out of here right now and never show your sorry face again!"

There, she had said it. She had said what she was longing to say for years. It was out. It was gone. Years of pent-up frustration and lack of closure had come to an end.

And then it all went terribly wrong . . . because Ruth Monaghan – all five feet six and fifteen stones of her – started to cry.

Tess hadn't meant to make her cry! Well, she had sort

of meant to, but not in the way Ruth was crying. Tess had never seen anyone cry like that before. Not even at funerals or wakes and without a doubt, her family went totally over the top when it came to wailing for their dead. But this – this was like a condition of some sort. Like a type of crying that there should be a medical name for. Big, heavy, straight-from-the-gut, breath-taking sobs that drained Ruth's energy so much that her knees actually did buckle beneath her and only for the island in the middle of Polly's kitchen, she would have been on the floor. It was a bit like watching the Wicked Witch from the West melting but instead of singing along with the Munchkins, Tess was actually feeling sorry for her! This was certainly not the outcome Tess had intended when she saw her standing there in Polly's kitchen on a Friday morning on her free period from school!

"Ruth? Ruth, it's okay!" said Polly. "It really is okay. I ate after that. Lots. I even got fat for a while. Please, it's okay."

But Ruth most certainly was *not* okay. She could hardly breathe so she was anything *but* okay. Tess felt so bad. She felt like she'd been caught holding a bloodied knife while her victim lay below her dying and she didn't know what to do or what to say. The damage was done.

"Do you think we should call a doctor?" she asked eventually, totally convinced that this was a lot more than a bully feeling guilty for her actions years ago. The woman was in pieces! She was bloody hyper-ventilating!

"No, she'll be fine," said Polly, nice and calm as Polly always was. "Get her some tea, Tess. Tea with sugar. Quick. The kettle's boiled."

Tea with sugar. Tea with flaming sugar! Only Polly would think of that, thought Tess.

55

She would be more inclined to have rung the doctor, run out the door and left him to it, but typical Polly had a nice, warm, homely solution which proved exactly why she did not feel up to becoming a parent. There was a time to cry, a time for tea and sugar, but all Tess could identify with was a time to run.

So, feeling extra guilty and forgetting she was late for school, Tess made the tea from Polly's kettle that was always on the boil (yes, 'Polly Put the Kettle On' – the old ones are the best) and brought it to Ruth who was now sitting at the kitchen table, her face stained with dollops of mascara and her eyes blood-red from her (as Tess was to later know) mental breakdown. It was a horrible, horrible thing to watch.

"Thank you," she said. "Thank you. Both of you. Thank you."

Ruth gripped the cup with both hands and raised it to her lips.

Without taking her eyes off her, Tess sat down on the chair opposite and watched in admiration as her sister took charge of what was now a very delicate situation.

"You know you can talk to me," she said to Ruth in a voice Tess only ever heard Polly use with her children. "No woman is alone when she has her friends, and everyone needs a friend. We all need our friends."

Friends? So all of a sudden they were *friends*? Yes, Tess could see the girl needed help. It was as plain as the fact that she needed her roots done badly, but friends? That was taking it a bit too far.

"I'm s-s-sorry," stuttered Ruth between shaky slurps of tea. "I shouldn't have called. I –"

"Yes, you should have called," said Polly. "You were right to call. You were *meant* to call. It's better that you let all this emotion out here than at home on your own. Tess was just venting off some long-withheld anger. She didn't mean to touch a nerve like that, did you, Tess?"

Tess looked at Polly with widened eyes and she reacted with a raised eyebrow – again, a look that Tess had only ever seen her use with her children.

"No, I . . . well . . . look, I need to get back to work," said Tess. "I was just passing through. Here –" She put the local paper on the table and wondered if she really should rush off but let's face it, she wasn't exactly Florence Nightingale, was she?

"What's that?" asked Polly, looking at Tess as if she was her mother. "Why did you bring me the newspaper?"

"Just . . . it's just, after Spaghetti-Gate I thought you may be interested in the ad on page twenty-five. It's a special offer. A weekend break. It's for this weekend, which is why it's so cheap and it might be impossibly short notice but I think it would do us the world of good, if you could get James to give you some time out."

"Time out?" said Polly, as if Tess had just suggested a cure for cancer.

"Time out?" said Ruth, letting out a dreamy sigh.

Tess looked at Ruth and realised that if anyone needed a break – any of the three of them – it was her with her snot-stained face and bloodshot eyes and look of utter despair. But despite what she had just witnessed, Tess couldn't bring herself to invite her. She just couldn't.

And anyhow, she knew – she just *knew* that she didn't have to. She knew that that little piece of the jigsaw would be left to her darling, caring sister. Yes, Polly would take care of it. In fact, Tess knew she would have asked Ruth along before Tess even reached the front door.

Gina didn't even notice Ruth's car in the driveway, such was her eagerness to tell her dear neighbour her most exciting news. She wouldn't have cared that Polly had a visitor, even if she had noticed. She was walking on air. She was giddy with excitement. She had to tell someone. She had to tell Polly.

"I've done it!" she said, shaking and giggling in shock when Polly led her into her kitchen, minutes after Tess had left.

Gina was clingy and giddy and she kept covering her mouth with her hand like a schoolgirl who couldn't quite believe her luck when she was announced best pupil in the class.

"You've done what, love?" asked Polly, glancing from Gina to the lady sitting at the table. Gina had never seen her before but she looked like she had been through the wars. "You've got a job?" Polly knew how much she wanted to get back to work.

"No, no," said Gina. "It's not about work. Though that might be my next move. I've left Trevor! I've done it, Polly!"

"What the –" Polly couldn't take any more drama. This was certainly a Friday to remember.

"Well, I didn't actually leave him as such," said Gina. Her eyes were wide and Polly had never seen someone before with pupils so large. "I told him to leave me. To leave us. He's gone. To her. He was gone within minutes. I'm free, Polly. I'm free!"

Polly led Gina to the kitchen table and pulled out a

chair opposite the other woman, who seemed glad to be out of the spotlight, but Gina was as stiff as a corpse. She wouldn't sit down.

"Gina, where is wee Danny?" asked Polly, totally sure that Gina was sleepwalking or on drugs or something.

"He's with his gran," said Gina, a stupid grin sitting on her face like a basket of chips.

"With Trevor's mum?"

"Yeah. Mrs Humphries has him. She's a lovely woman, is Mrs Humphries. Maybe Trevor was adopted!"

"How long for, love?" asked Polly. "Is he staying for the evening?"

"She said as long as I needed her to have him," replied Gina.

Polly beckoned her over and held her tightly. Polly felt so warm and motherly and – well, sane.

"That's really nice of her. You need time to think," said Polly when Gina finally let her go.

It was the first proper hug Gina'd had in months, maybe even years. Polly looked a bit out of breath when she finally loosened her arms from round her neck.

"I just . . . I just need a break," whispered Gina, looking into Polly's ever-so-sympathetic eyes. "Just a little break to get my head around it all, you know?"

Polly scratched her head.

"Oh, by the way, this is Ruth. An old, er – school friend of mine."

"I used to bully her. I'm so sorry," said Ruth and she began to sob again.

"*Shhh*," said Polly. "Now, sit down, Gina, and we'll get you some tea. This is turning out to be a very strange day indeed but I think we all know the solution."

59

"A solution?" asked Gina. "But I've already found my solution. I've kicked him out. He's gone. No more worrying about milk or dinner or fretting over anniversaries. I've done what everyone hoped I would do. What I hoped I would do. I've done it! Aren't you proud of me, Polly? I am so *so* proud of me!"

"Yes," said Polly. "But you also said you need a break."

"I do."

"And so does Ruth. And so does Tess."

Ruth slid the newspaper across the table and Gina sat down and read it.

The Cove Country Club, County Donegal. Last-minute special offer. Luxury Spa Weekend Break. Bed and Breakfast and Spa Treatment of your choice.

Gina looked up as the other two stared at her, nodding their heads.

"We could go in the morning," said Polly. "Just imagine . . . one night only. No children. No men. No worries. Just leave it all behind. What do you think, Gina? I'm no doctor, but I think it's just what the doctor would order if he was here."

"Oh, I agree! Am I there yet?" asked Gina, a dreamy, faraway look in her eyes.

"Let's do it," said Ruth. "That's if . . . well, I'm hoping I'm . . ."

"Of course you're invited," said Polly. "So you're in then, Gina?"

"I'm so in," Gina replied. "I can't believe I've finally done it. He's gone. Oh my God! Polly what have I done? I'm okay, I'm okay!"

Before the tears could burst from her eyes, Gina was

ushered upstairs, covered with a Thomas the Tank Engine duvet, ordered to have a wee snooze in Polly's twin sons' bedroom (with Ruth in the single bed across from her) and then when she woke up from a coma-like snooze, she was fed soup and sandwiches at Polly's kitchen table, instructed to go home and pack a weekend bag and the next morning, feeling refreshed and ready for action, they all – Ruth, Polly, Tess and Gina – would set off on a weekend break that would give them the time out they all so badly needed.

Like Polly had said, it was just what the doctor ordered.

7

On Saturday morning Polly woke up to the sound of dishes being done and the smell of bacon and eggs frying in the pan. She rubbed her eyes and pinched herself, just to be sure she wasn't dreaming that she was already in the four-star hotel Tess had found for their one night away from it all. She checked the clock. It was eight forty. She'd been allowed to lie in? What the – ?

"James? James? Is everything okay down there?" she called, but James couldn't hear her over the music that he was listening to as he cooked. James never cooked. He could barely boil an egg but now he was actually making a full-blown effort and frying bacon! There was a God!

She decided not to rock the boat and with contentment in her heart she put the shower on and stepped beneath its soothing spray and dreamed about the day ahead as she scrubbed.

A girly night out was within inches of her reach and she couldn't wait! One night away with her sister, her neighbour and a reformed school bully. The chance to get to know herself again. To relax, to switch off from mummy and wife duties. Just one night. It couldn't do any harm, could it?

She had applied a layer of tan the evening before, had shaved her legs so they were silky smooth, her hair had been freshly coloured and cut only a few days before so it would be easy to handle. And she felt a buzz of excitement she hadn't felt in a long, long time.

She never did anything spontaneous. Tess was always booking last-minute trips for herself and Rob, or having dinner with her friends, or doing 'date nights' at the cinema. Polly never went anywhere that didn't involve grocery-shopping or the post office or something to do with the primary school. She was always rushing around, working hard and taking very little time out for herself. She had lost her *va-va-voom*. No wonder James didn't find her attractive or exciting any more. She had become a boring, Plain Jane mum who cooked and cleaned and never did anything else. They were in a rut and this was one way of getting out of it. Time out. Time apart. A chance to appreciate each other more.

James had been much more understanding of her last-minute decision to get away from it all than she had expected. They had been arguing more than ever lately with the slightest thing sparking off a row and something as simple as a night apart might do them the world of good.

Of course, she wasn't just leaving him in the lurch. He wouldn't have the slightest idea where to start when it came to looking after the children on his own so, the night before, Polly had put a meticulous list of the children's routine for him on the fridge and by the sounds of things downstairs he was taking his new responsibility very seriously. He was already making breakfast and she hadn't even left yet! Things were looking up!

"Everything okay down there?" she called when she got out of the shower. Her clothes had been laid out from the night before – a pair of jeans and flat pumps with a T-shirt and light cardigan for the journey – and her overnight case was packed with a few options for her overnight stay. A few different outfits to choose from in case they went out for a nice meal, a swimsuit for the spa in the hotel, cosy pyjamas to chill out in and a fresh day dress for the drive home. Everything was planned to perfection and she felt very pleased with her decision to be a modern woman with independent needs, and not a needy woman who nagged all the time.

"You almost ready, babe?" called James from the bottom of the stairs.

Babe? *Babe?* He hadn't called her babe in a lifetime! Had something happened to her husband overnight? This was almost too good to be true!

"Nearly there. Is that bacon I smell?"

"Yes," he called. "But don't get too excited. I haven't turned into Jamie Oliver overnight. Tess is here and she has everything under control."

She rolled her eyes. Okay, so maybe she was expecting too much, but all in all things were looking pretty rosy in the garden. She should do this more often. She felt more appreciated already.

"Okay, *babe*," she said with a smile. "I'll be right there!"

By nine thirty, Ruth had arrived by taxi and Gina had hauled her suitcase over to Polly's house, both more than ready for the road. Ruth was obviously still in meltdown and she smelt a bit like gin but she looked a lot better than she had the day before. She was less pasty in the face and, although she was still clad head to toe in black, she didn't look as, well, as scary as she had been when they had first bumped into each other. Gina was second in the race to Loopy Land and, although still giddy and shaky, she looked just a tiny bit more under control – she had popped a sleeping tablet the night before to make sure she didn't walk the floors all night. Tess was as cool as always, but Polly knew she had just about kept her marbles after her grievance with Rob and the whole baby argument. So Polly felt that being ignored and feeling taken for granted (her reasons for going away) were probably the most minor problems. She was the driver, she was in charge, and therefore she felt it was up to her to make sure that everyone had their toothbrush, make-up, hair-straighteners and clean knickers packed. After that, it was each to their own devices. She was on a well-earned break from baby-sitting, but for the journey's duration she would make it her duty to play 'mummy'.

The girls packed up the car as Polly said her goodbyes to Frankie and the twins who, much to her disgruntlement, were almost oblivious to her departure. Through guilt, she had raced to Tesco the night before and bought them enough jigsaws and colouring-in books to keep them well occupied until she came back and she had prepared ham sandwiches for their lunch, and a stew for dinner and left it in the fridge so that James only had to heat it up and serve. The following day he was taking them to his mother's house for Sunday lunch so at least she knew her children would be fed while she was away.

"Mummy will be back tomorrow, okay?" she said, but they were all too engrossed in scribbling over Postman Pat's face to care.

"They'll be fine. Just go," said James, walking her to the door. "Don't be doing anything I wouldn't do." He gave her a light peck on the cheek.

Not exactly a mad passionate I'm-going-to-miss-you-so-much snog, but it was better than nothing.

"I won't be visiting strip clubs or getting arrested if that's what you're hinting at," she said as a joke with a jag. His stag night over ten years ago was still a sore point but she couldn't resist.

"Oh, when will you ever let that go?" he said, his jovial mood breaking ever so slightly.

"I'm joking!" said Polly. "Now you know where everything is, don't you? I hope I haven't forgotten anything. I will call, of course. Not a lot, but just to check in."

"I can look after my own children," said James, ever on the defensive. "You don't have to worry about a thing."

Polly longed to say 'that would be a first' but she buttoned her lip, trying to ignore the new-found heaviness in her heart at leaving her family to their own devices.

"Come on, sister!" said Tess, beeping the horn. "We want to get there today if possible!"

"Tell her to mind her own business," said James. It was no secret that he and Tess had a love/hate relationship.

"Tell her yourself!" said Polly and she made her way to the car.

"Mind your own business, Tess!" called James and they all laughed as Polly got into the driver's seat.

She started up the engine. "Alright in the back?" she asked Gina and Ruth who were staring out a window each as they pulled out of Polly's driveway. James waved them off with the little ones now in his arms and Frankie by his side and Polly gave him a good-luck sign (no, not the fingers although she would have loved to) and turned the Jeep out of the cul de sac.

"Into the great wide open!" Polly declared, determined to keep the mood light and jovial. "Here we go, girls. Let's make this a night to remember!"

"*Woo-hoo!*" said Tess, with her arm out the window, very *Thelma and Louise*.

They were turning out onto the main road when Gina spoke up in a tiny voice. "Do you have any George Michael, Polly? I do love George Michael. Can you play 'Careless Whisper'?"

Tess, who as the second in command was in the passenger seat, shot her sister a glance and rolled her eyes.

"How about something a little livelier?" suggested Polly, dreading that a row over the music selection would kick off before they even got out of the countryside.

"Adele?" asked Ruth.

"Oh, how about we just drive off a cliff now and put us all out of our misery?" said Tess, the sarcasm dripping off her tongue, but she had a point. As much as she admired the Grammy award-winning global songstress, listening to Adele at that moment would have been like cranking up the desperation levels which were already at an all-time high.

Polly ignored all of their requests and put on a cheesy eighties mix she had made up herself and smiled as the mood lifted with every mile. Soon, they were like four best friends without a care in the world as they sang along to Yazz and the Plastic Population, Bros, the Pet Shop Boys and a little bit of Wham thrown in for good measure which pleased George Michael fan Gina no end.

They made rules as they drove along – lots of rules. They were heading away to make each of them feel better. There were to be no personal bitchy jabs about the past, there was to be no moaning about men, no talk about kids, and under no circumstances no judging if anyone did have a moment of weakness when they cried into their champagne (but the rule was to avoid this scenario and politely leave the company if any one of them felt such a turn coming upon them).

"What about sex? Can we talk about sex?" asked Gina and Polly almost crashed the car in surprise and shock. The word 'sex' coming out of Gina's innocent wee mouth was a bit like a nun talking about her latest drug-fuelled orgy. It didn't sound right, but it was kind of funny.

"Depends on who you're thinking of having it with," said Ruth in a monotone that had them all in hysterics. "I wouldn't even take it from Johnny Depp at the minute."

"Liar," said Gina.

"Oh, okay then. But I'd make him beg for it first."

The thought of Ruth bouncing her big voluptuous breasts on top of Johnny Depp's beautiful face put images in Polly's head that she really didn't need at that moment, so she cranked up the tunes and concentrated on the windy road ahead.

Within the hour, they had crossed the border into Donegal and, with the sunny evening settling down to a comfortable haze outside, they turned off the main road onto a country lane that seemed to go on forever and took a sharp left through the magnificent gates that led to the Cove Country Club.

"Oh my God, it's flippin' gorgeous!" said Gina. "Where are we again?"

"Somewhere in Donegal, in the back end of nowhere, that's where," said Polly. "And doesn't it feel like heaven already!"

"It does," said Ruth. "In fact, I feel like taking my clothes off and streaking across the lawns. But I won't just now. I'll save you all that glorious sight for later."

Cue more unwelcome thoughts in Polly's head. Tess looked like she might vomit.

"Me too!" said Gina.

"Oh Sweet Mariah!" Tess exclaimed and they all burst out laughing.

Whatever was in the Donegal air, it was working a treat. They all felt better already.

As they gathered their bags and cases from the boot, Polly got a short sharp rush of guilt through her veins. What was she doing in this strange place, with strange company (apart from her sister who was only strange some of the time) and without her darling boys to keep her occupied? She wondered would James remember to have Frankie brush his teeth? Would he know how to soothe the twins with a verse of 'Twinkle Twinkle' if they wouldn't go to sleep? Would he even dream of telling Frankie a bedtime – ?

"Stop it!" said Tess, reading her mind. "Stop it immediately! It's one night only, for goodness' sake and you'll be back in your Weetabix-stained apron by tomorrow evening. You never do anything like this. Leave the guilt behind."

"Oh, I can't help it. It's normal, it's natural. Maybe I should just call and –"

"Look!" said Tess, looking her sister right in the eye. They were exactly the same height. "Out of all the husbands involved in this wee getaway, James was the most encouraging. He might not say much, but he knows how to keep things in control at home. And he said he'd call if he needed to know where the nearest hospital was!"

"Tess!"

"I'm joking. He said he'd be fine, didn't he?"

"Yes."

"And he will call if he needs to. Now come on. Let's not waste another second. It's almost eleven already and there is a whole new world awaiting us in this land of luxury."

"Okay, okay, let's get inside," Polly replied and gave herself a little shake. "I'll be okay once I have a nice cool glass of Pinot Grigio in my paw. Oooh, how my mouth is watering at the very thought!"

Ruth led the way into the hotel, her hunched-over, sad figure of only a few hours ago now a distant memory. She had been the giddiest of all on the journey but now that they had arrived, she seemed to switch into her confident business-like poise that she was obviously used to turning on when the time was right. Despite being overweight and complaining about it, Ruth did know how to carry herself well. She wore black as she always did and her heavy make-up made her look older than the rest of the gang but was obviously a mask she wore when Ruth the Businesswoman was in town.

Little Gina hurried along behind her, pulling her cerise-pink case by the handle and ignoring how it bumped and bounced along the gravel driveway. She was like a child going to Disneyland and Polly feared that her adrenaline-filled enthusiasm would explode into hysteria as the night wore on. But for now, she was happy to watch Gina's tiny figure scurry behind Ruth in her haste to see what this wonderful place had to offer.

"It looks gorgeous. Good find, sister," Polly said to Tess as they strolled alongside each other. "This is just the best medicine ever, isn't it?"

"It is indeed, but if you say it was just what the doctor ordered again I will stab you," said Tess, staring ahead at the unlikely twosome who were already approaching the revolving doors. Polly placed a bet to herself that mousey Gina and her pink case would get stuck. She did.

"You could murder me for bringing those two, couldn't you?" said Polly, wanting to get rid of the great big white elephant that stood between her and her sister.

Of course Tess had meant this little break to be for just the two of them, but Polly couldn't do anything about that now. She had been in Mother Teresa mode yesterday and it was too late to turn back the clock and change her mind.

"I'm sure it will be fine," said Tess in a tone that would have been better suited to a statement like: *I could murder you with a very sharp object but I shall refrain for the time being*.

"They're good girls, really," said Polly. "Harmless. Just a little bit troubled. They need a break as much as we do."

"That's enough of the excuses. Drop it," said Tess. She knew she really was bossy sometimes but she couldn't help it and, besides, Polly needed a firm hand every now and then. "Let's hit the bar. I need a drink. Last one in buys a double round!"

In her haste to obey Tess and in a twist of fate for having an inward giggle at poor Gina for getting stuck in the revolving door seconds before, Polly's own entrance to the hotel was not very graceful.

"Who invented revolving doors!" she said as her face met the carpet.

"Get up, Polly! Please get up!" hissed Tess in mortification.

Polly glanced around to see if any fellow guests of the Cove Country Club were watching her face down and star-fished on the swish cream flooring. They were. But she couldn't get up. She couldn't see very well and her nose was running . . . no, it wasn't running! It was bleeding! Her nose was bleeding! She'd never had a nosebleed in her life!

"You could try to help!" she spat back at her sister. Oh God, there was blood – *lots* of blood on the milky carpet.

Reluctantly, Tess put down her Prada luggage and scooped Polly under her arm then let go of her before she could even straighten her knees so that she flopped back down into injury position again.

"Oh dear," said a rather snooty voice with a German accent from Polly's right-hand side. "Is madam okay?"

"She's fine!" said Tess, almost shooing the owner of the voice away to avoid any fuss. "She does this all the time. It's her idea of a grand entrance. Everything's fine."

"Tess!" squeaked Polly, pinching her nose to stop the bleeding but managing to squirt more on the floor instead. "People will think I'm drunk! I'm not drunk."

"Can I be of assistance?"

Slowly Polly turned her head and, now in the attractive position of being on all fours, she looked up to see the face of the snootiest, most unlikeable, most condescending person she had ever laid eyes on in her whole life.

"My name is Pee-ta and I am your porter and I would like to help you up."

"I am not drunk in case that's what you are thinking," she hissed. "I tripped on my luggage coming through those bloody revolving doors."

"Mmm," he said, handing her a tissue. "I think the only thing bloody is your nose, madam. Welcome to the Cove Country Club and Spa. I'll put the cleaning bill onto your room charge, shall I?"

"Yes, you do that," said Polly. "Splendid. Absolutely splendid. Pee-ta!"

8

The rooms of the Cove Country Club and Spa were 'step back in time' Victorian velvet luxury and, despite the throbbing pain that went up into her eye sockets, Polly managed to really appreciate the fine surroundings of this cosy getaway. Everything was so romantic, so ornate and so bloody expensive-looking.

Crystal decanters sat on little mahogany tables. A four-poster bed formed a grand centre-piece and thick heavy swish green-and-gold patterned curtains framed huge windows that had window-sills so deep they were almost like an additional room themselves. The bed linen was thick and crisp and clean with a duck-down duvet so heavy that Tess and Polly joked at how it would be like having a hunky man lying on top of them all night – and the carpet – well, the carpet was so deep that they both took off their shoes and made orgasmic sounds as the pile nestled between their toes with every step. This was as close to heaven as either of them could ever have imagined, even if Polly did have an ice-pack held to her nose courtesy of Pee-ta.

A knock on the door (huge doors – huge!) brought Polly temporarily away from the carpet ecstasy and she tried not to laugh when she saw Ruth and Gina standing there. They looked hilarious together. Like two misfits that made up a comedy duo. Ruth was big and bulky and dark, while wee tiny Gina was so fragile and grey and weak beside her. They reminded her of an elephant and a mouse.

"What happened?" asked Gina, her voice more high-pitched and louder than normal. "We heard in the bar that you'd had a fall! It's the talk of the place!"

"Shh, come in," said Polly, realising that they had gone straight to explore the bar and had missed her spectacular arrival. "It was just a bump on the nose. No-one died."

The door was so big that they could both walk in side by side, still trailing their luggage behind them.

"Wow, this room is amazing!" said Ruth. "I hope ours is the same. But maybe we should have asked for twin beds. If I roll over on Gina I would squash her and we only met yesterday morning. That would be most unfortunate."

It was on the tip of Polly's tongue to suggest that they do swapsies on the room-sharing arrangements but luckily she caught the fear in Tess's eye in time.

"The rooms are exactly the same," said Tess, "and your bed is the same as ours, and nice and roomy, so I'm sure there will be no chance of Gina being squashed. But we didn't come here to stay cooped up in a room, did we?"

Sometimes Polly thought Tess might be a witch. She could tell what Polly was thinking far too often for her liking, but in this case it was a good thing. If Polly had suggested that Tess had shared with either Ruth or Gina, she might have been shoved into the open fire in the foyer at the next opportunity.

"Did we?" asked Tess again.

"No," said Gina and Ruth like two of Tess's grammar-school pupils.

"Good. Now, go and get changed and freshened up and we'll see what this place has to offer. I don't know about you lot, but I'm starving."

Like good little schoolgirls, Gina and Ruth turned on their heels to go and get ready, leaving the other two to do the same.

Polly had packed a little too much for one night away but they were all in the same boat judging by the bulging cases that had weighed down the Jeep on the way there. Her evening wear came down to one of three choices – a reliable Little Black Dress that was at least six years old but always did the trick, a slightly bolder cerise number that skimmed above the knees and went lower at the back than she would normally wear but which made her feel amazing, and a sexy red satin jumpsuit that she only ever had the courage to wear in front of the mirror at home before shaking her head, taking it off and hanging it back in the wardrobe. It still had the label on it.

"Wear the jumpsuit," said Bossy Boots Tess and before Polly could protest, she had taken the other two items and shoved them back into the wardrobe. "It's about time you dressed for your age and not like our mother. You have a figure to die for, now show it off!"

"You exaggerate terribly, Tess," Polly told her. "But I love it. Do you really think I can get away with it? It's sleeveless and shoulder-less and short and –"

"Did you put fake tan on before you left?"

"Yes."

"Did you shave the bits that need to be shaved?"

76

"Yes."

"Your hair looks fab, your skin is clear, your legs are long and you are a Size 10. Put it on. Now."

As always, Polly did what she was told but on this occasion she was quite glad to. Tess did have a point. She *was* a Size 10, she *was* petite and she *did* have good skin. The long-legs bit was a big fat lie but she appreciated her sister's efforts. And she did tend to dress like their mother with her apron covering up her thirty-five-year-young figure. She would wear the jumpsuit and she would wear it well. So there.

"What about you?" Polly asked her sister who funnily enough wasn't as decisive when it came to selecting her own attire.

Unlike Polly's daily uniform of leggings and tunic tops covered in breakfast, lunch and dinner, Tess's wardrobe was bursting with designer labels and she often talked about 'staple items' and 'necessary basics' when she had been on a shopping spree. Her staple items and necessary basics were flattering black trousers, well-cut jeans, classic crisp white shirts and a seasonal coat or jacket that went with almost everything from the very upmarket Bella's Boutique. Polly's staple items and necessary basics were spuds, milk, baby wipes and supermarket bread. With those items in stock, she could conquer the world.

"I'm trying to decide what approach to take to the evening," said Tess, holding item after item under her chin as she gazed into the massive mahogany mirror at the other side of the room.

Tess's day and night always had to have an 'approach'. She was a meticulous planner who was always prepared for last-minute action and no doubt had a suitcase on standby packed with all the necessities all year round. One for each season.

"I'm wondering . . . ah, feck it," she said. "Let's go the whole hog. I am going to get glammed up too and feel great. We are in the middle of nowhere and there is no one around to admire our beauty but it's how we feel inside that's important. I'll wear this."

Polly looked at her and gulped.

"Where's the rest of it?" she asked.

"The rest of what?"

"The – um, the outfit? The bottom half? That's not a dress, is it?"

Tess didn't answer her but instead began to strip off and put on the teeny-weeny, silky, sexy white, um, 'dress' that she had packed for the occasion, whatever that occasion was to be. Polly had no idea.

"What do you think? Too short? Too slutty? Do I look like a teacher?" she asked and Polly's eyes widened at the sight before her.

She didn't look slutty at all. She most definitely did not look like a teacher either. She looked outstanding and all of a sudden Polly's red satin jumpsuit felt a bit plain in comparison.

"Can I do your hair?" Tess asked, sensing that Polly was stuck for words, and within half an hour she had her fully coiffed, her blonde hair tied up into a loose bun, her cheekbones highlighted with some of her fancy make-up and her lips (which were by far her best feature, or so she was often told in days gone by) plumped up and painted in the most glorious shade of red that matched her outfit to perfection.

The sisters stood side by side and looked in the mirror,

both of them recognising those few seconds as an emotional moment – even for Tess who had normally as much sentiment as a goat.

"You look like a teenager," she told Polly and she put her arm around her bare shoulders. (Again, this was a one-off. Polly couldn't wait to tell the others at home. Tess never hugged anyone unless they were at least six feet tall, male and had the body of a sex god.)

"Well then, you look younger than a teenager. Not bad for two old married women!" said Polly. "Let's take a photo!"

And so they stood, giggling like teenagers and brimming with confidence as they snapped and posed for the camera in glorious surroundings and, for once in many years, it seemed like they hadn't a care in the world.

And it felt absolutely incredible.

9

Tess was right. Their room, which was just a few doors down, was exactly the same and therefore equally spectacular. Result! They also had the added advantage of a magnificent lakeside view and Ruth sat on the window seat (yes, it was big enough to hold even her to her great surprise!) and savoured the silence that filled the room, now that Gina was in the bathroom doing up her face.

Gina was a terrible chatterbox and not at all how she had appeared when they'd first met the day before in Polly's kitchen. They had very little in common apart from a hatred for their husbands and a deep love for their children. Oh, and that they both were at the end of their tethers. Ruth almost forgot that minor detail.

"I feel like such a rebel," Gina had said to Ruth in the bar when they'd first arrived. They didn't tell the others but they'd managed a swift double vodka each in the time it took Polly to fall, get checked in and make it to the room. "I've never spent a night away from my son, ever. Have you?"

"Well, mine are a lot older than your lad," Ruth had told her. Gina really was a pixie-like little thing and Ruth couldn't help but feel like a dinosaur beside her. Even though they were more or less the same age, Ruth felt ancient and huge.

"I'd imagine your business takes you places too," Gina said, her eyes widening as she said the word 'business'. "I always wanted my own business. Never had the guts or the know-how to go about it."

"Really?" Ruth asked her. "Why didn't you go for it?"

Gina's eyes dropped and she took a long gulp of her drink. So long in fact that Ruth felt at one stage she should stop her in case she drowned.

"Well, I always had lots of ideas when I used to work for the local Council," she said. "I was so bored with administration and longed to do something a bit more creative. Something that exercised the brain a bit more. But then I met Trevor and he encouraged me to give up my work when our son was born. He's a very successful contractor and felt we didn't need the extra money. He was right in that way, but now the little one is at school I would like to try something, you know, for myself. Trevor will go mad if I suggest it, of course."

Trevor *will* go mad? Mmm, wondered Ruth. Hadn't she just left him the very day before?

"Perhaps it's time to worry about what you want instead of always what Trevor wants?" Ruth suggested and decided to leave it at that. She had enough worries with her own domestic situation and was in no position whatsoever to shell out advice on relationships to anyone. Besides, she barely knew the woman.

Thankfully, Gina didn't mention Trevor's name again

for the rest of their time at the bar, instead proceeding to marvel about how great Polly and Tess had it.

"Polly's husband seems so attentive," she had said. "And Tess's man – well, he's a fireman. Say no more. Oh, what I would give to be able to look across a table at *him* every evening!"

She was back in the bedroom now, her face made up and her wispy hair styled up to one side. She looked much better already. Less vulnerable, less fragile. Ruth was a great believer in the power of make-up, even if she did wear too much on a daily basis.

"Beauty's only skin deep," Ruth told her, not wanting to acknowledge how good other people had it. "And besides, no-one knows what goes on behind closed doors. I'm sure no-one's relationship is a bed of roses. The grass always looks greener on the other side."

She wondered how many other clichés she could pack in to make her point. She was the biggest cynic in the world when it came to marriage and family life but, with her experience, she had every right to feel that way.

"Aren't you going to get ready?" Gina asked, watching as Ruth stared again out onto the glistening lake.

Ruth was tired now and not sure if she wanted to play the whole 'let's have a wonderful time together and pretend we're on top of the world' game. She was miserable and she wanted to show it and that big whopper of a four-poster bed had her name written all over it.

The huge sigh she let out gave her away.

"Come on, Ruth! When will you ever do this again?" asked Gina. "I don't know about you, but I haven't had a day out in yonks and yonks."

"I haven't had adult conversation in yonks and yonks,"

said Ruth, realising once more that her confidence levels were more unpredictable than a bloody rollercoaster in the dark.

"Well, I'm not claiming to be the most exciting person in the world, but if you don't make an effort to join in this weekend, you'll probably regret it in the morning. Come on. The others will be waiting."

The others. The Woodhead girls. Polly and Tess. Polly and Tess Woodhead. Never in her wildest dreams had Ruth Monaghan thought that those two girls would ever, ever give her the time of day again and there she was, dragging her heels at accepting any more of their goodwill. She had totally crumbled in front of them yesterday. She had let down her guard and cried and bawled her eyes out for what her life had become and now she was feeling like she had more to lose. She couldn't have more to lose. She had hit rock bottom and it was time to start swimming her way back up to the surface of life as she knew it. It might be a shitty place to swim to, but it was better than sitting at someone's kitchen table, mascara-stained and snotty-faced and feeling that the world was against her.

"Okay, okay," she said, "I'll get ready – but there is no way I will ever look as glamorous as they do. Or you. I mean, you too. Oh, you know what I mean!"

"Ruth?" said Gina, staring at her reflection in the mirror.

As big as the mirror was, Ruth didn't think it would have held her reflection if she'd stood so close. Never in a million years.

"Yes?"

"Do you think I look . . . do you think I'm . . .?" She tipped her head from side to side, biting her lip in uncertainty.

"I think you look wonderful, Gina."

"Really?"

"Yes, really," said Ruth and she meant it. "Your hair is pretty and your make-up is perfect and once you put on your dress and heels, you will turn many heads."

"Good," said Gina. "Thanks, Ruth. I really needed to hear that. I think we are going to have great fun."

"I hope so," Ruth told her new roomie. "I really, really do."

10

Polly and Tess were already in the bar when Ruth and Gina finally made it downstairs about thirty minutes later. Ruth had taken a bit of a wobble when she was about to leave the room but Gina had managed to talk her round. In fact, she'd actually steered her towards the door and pushed her out through it, which was no mean feat when you consider the difference in size between the two.

Ruth's confidence took a further dip when she saw the Woodhead sisters sitting on two high stools at the bar. Their blonde hair, long tanned legs and trendy outfits that would barely cover her big toe. That's both of their outfits sewn together.

"You both look stunning," said Polly. "What would you like to drink?"

"I'll have a double vodka and lemonade," said Gina without the blink of an eye. "Ruth will have the same."

Gina spoke before Ruth even had the chance to think about what she should have but she was in no position to argue. There was only one way she was going to get through this escapade and that was with the help of her dear friend, Mr Alcohol. Tried and tested measures were always best stuck to.

"We'll need to have some food soon," said Tess the Teacher.

Mind you, she didn't look like a teacher now. Hell no! Ruth noticed the barman drooling as he served them up their drinks.

"We could get bar snacks now or wait and see what the nearest town has to offer?" said Ruth. She was feeling claustrophobic already. Posh hotels reminded her of life with Jeffrey and it was a trip down memory lane that she didn't want to take right now.

"Let's hit the town!" said Tess, seductively sucking her cocktail from a straw. The barman looked like he was going to jump her bones right then and there. She looked amazing. It may have been only lunchtime, but they were all dressed for the evening ahead and had started as they meant to go on.

Polly didn't look so sure though.

"I'm not so keen on the whole town idea, Tess. I thought we had come here to relax," she said. "You know, just to get away from it all. I wouldn't know what to do in a big town. I'm a country girl at heart."

"You need to let your hair down," said Tess. "That's what you are here for. You can be boring all you want at home. This is the time to let yourself go. It's a time to find your 'fabulousness' again. We all need to find our *fabulousness*."

"To *fabulousness*!" said Gina, raising her glass of vodka and knocking it back way too quickly.

"To fabulousness!" said the rest of them and before they

knew it, they were piled into a taxi and on their road to 'town' . . . wherever that was.

"Isn't this exciting!" said Gina as the taxi rumbled along country lane after country lane until they eventually met a main road.

"It's like being on one of those mystery tours," said Tess. "I did one of those in Ibiza and it was amazing! It's the not knowing what's going to happen next that makes it all so exciting."

"Ha ha," chuckled the taxi driver who was their new best friend. His name was Larry and he drove a taxi on weekends for 'beer tokens'. During the week he was a fishmonger in Killybegs. "Ibiza this ain't, ladies, but when the men in this town see you lot, they'll think all their summer holidays have come at once!"

Ruth waited on him to say 'Except you in the back, Fatty' but he didn't, even if he was thinking it. She liked Larry. He was a nice taxi driver.

"So, where do you recommend?" asked Tess who had taken over from Polly as the captain of the ship. It made sense. What did the other lot know about nights out on the town? It seemed that Ruth had spent the past two years in hibernation since her separation and the other two still had traces of baby milk on their boobies.

"Well, to be honest, ladies, it's not the most happenin' of places," said Larry the Leprechaun as he later became known. "But if you try the Top O'The Road, there might be a bit of live music in there this evening. It's a cosy wee spot and they serve grub in there too."

"Top O'The Road it is then," said Tess. "Let's get this party started!"

87

Polly fidgeted with her handbag as the taxi stopped outside a small pub on the edge of a little street that was dotted with multi-coloured buildings – a little hotel, a couple of shops and the pub seemed to be all this place had to offer. The pub itself had a huge white sign with green-and-red lettering under its thatched roof and smoke billowed from the chimney, even though it wasn't exactly a day for snuggling up indoors. Apart from a light breeze, the weather was glorious.

"How about we look at the shops first?" she asked, but her suggestion was met with a glare.

"I don't remember anyone putting shopping on the agenda?" said Tess. "And unless you want to buy the local paper or a stick of rock, I don't think this is exactly a shopper's paradise."

"Oxford Street it certainly isn't," said Ruth. "Anyhow, I'd rather slam my tits in the door than go shopping. I'm sick of shopping."

"Well, *I* can see where you are coming from, Polly," said Gina. "I feel a bit tipsy already so a nice walk and some fresh air might do us all good."

"Oh, shush, you lightweights! You'll be okay once you have some food," said Tess and she pushed the door of the Top O'The Road pub open, where all eyes turned towards her and her three trusty companions.

"Mmm, that was simply delicious," said Polly, delicately dabbing the sides of her mouth with her napkin. She had chosen a fish chowder and home-made bread and it was more than satisfactory. The Top O'The Road was as cosy inside as it looked from the outside and its food certainly didn't disappoint. Larry the Leprechaun knew his stuff.

"I think I need a snooze," said Gina.

Again she was met with a glare.

"You snooze, you lose," said Tess. "We didn't come here to snooze. Just relax and enjoy the freedom."

They sat back in the little snug of the pub and savoured the atmosphere around them. It was as traditional as an Irish pub could be, with postcards from all sorts of exotic locations surrounding the bar area and flags and emblems of all nationalities lining the mirrors that stood behind the optics. There was horse-racing on the nearby television and a group of older men let out the odd holler and name of a horse now and then but, apart from that, the place was relatively quiet.

"Do any of you fancy a flutter?" asked Ruth. "I used to be quite a gambler in my day. Won buckets at Cheltenham every year."

"No way!" said Gina. "You really are a dark horse!"

The other three girls burst out laughing, much to Gina's bewilderment. Then eventually the penny dropped. "Oh, I get it. Cheltenham. Dark horse. *Doh!*"

"So, did you like, have a gambling problem?" asked Tess, hoping for some juicy gossip. "Please say you did. I can just imagine you down at the bookies!"

"No, not at all," said Ruth, sitting tall and feeling very much in her comfort zone now that a subject close to her heart had come up in the conversation. "My husband, I mean, my *ex*-husband, was a jockey."

Tess and Polly's eyes widened. Ruth on top of a jockey! A jockey on top of Ruth! No, no, no!

"I'm joking! I thought that would get a reaction!" laughed Ruth. "Imagine me and a jockey in the sack! I'd swallow him up in one gulp! No, my ex-husband Jeffrey was a trainer. A professional trainer. One of the best, if I do say so, and he owned his own racehorse, *Melanie's Way*. We named it after our daughter." Her eyes glistened as she spoke. "Horse-racing was our life, really, but he was away a lot. I stayed at home and looked after the children in the early years, but then I did a course in graphic design and started my own business from home. With his huge connections, it grew and grew and then before I knew it I was set up in the centre of London and it was all going really well until . . ." She trailed off and took a sip of her drink.

"You don't have to talk about this if you don't want to," said Polly, placing a hand over Ruth's. "We can just go and stick a fiver on the nose of the horse with the coolest name if you want? That's how I work the Grand National. I close my eyes and stick a pin on the page and I even won a tenner once."

"No, no, I think it's important I do talk about it," said Ruth. "My God, I've been dying to talk about it for ages but my friends in London . . . well, who was I without the great Jeffrey Landsbury?"

"Jeffrey Landsbury! What a posh name," said Gina. "He sounds like a character in a crime novel. Jeffrey Landsbury!"

"So, what happened?" asked Tess and Polly gave her a sharp dig.

"Tess! I think Ruth knows what she wants to tell and what she doesn't. Don't force her!"

"It's fine," said Ruth. "I've been talking to counsellors for years about what happened so it's nice to have some real people to communicate with for a change."

"Go on," said Tess, enjoying the gossip.

"Well, basically, Jeffrey was going on one of his

business trips to Dubai," said Ruth. "The Dubai Grand National was growing to be the richest horse race in the world and it's a huge event every year. Normally I travelled with him to that event if it suited me but this particular year I was too busy in work to leave."

"I'd love to go to Dubai," said Gina.

"Shh!" said Tess. "Go on, Ruth."

"Anyhow, Ben, my eldest – well, obviously he wasn't Jeffrey's son as I had him when I lived here – but he had developed a real flair for horses. He looked like he had really caught the bug from his stepfather and he wanted to go with Jeff but Jeff wouldn't have it. He said he would be too busy to have a teenager tag along so he went on his own. I should have smelled something fishy there and then. Jeffrey would have taken Ben anywhere normally."

Ruth paused for effect.

"The rat!" said Tess. "Who was she?"

"What do you mean?"

"Oh sorry," said Tess, rather sheepishly. "I thought you were insinuating that Jeffrey had another woman in Dubai. Which is why he wouldn't take Ben? Sorry, Ruth. Do continue. Me and my cynical old mind!"

Again, Ruth paused and then she took a deep breath as if she was deliberately holding back on the punch line. And a damn good punch line it was going to be too. She couldn't wait to see their faces when she told them.

"Oh, there *was* someone else, Tess," she said. "You got that bit right."

"Who?" asked Polly. "A young show jumper? His secretary? A wealthy widow in Dubai? Who was she?"

"Who was *he*, you mean?" said Ruth, awaiting their obvious reaction.

91

"No way!" said Gina.

"Way," Ruth continued.

Polly and Tess were too stunned to speak.

"He?" muttered Tess eventually.

"It was, ironically, a jockey," said Ruth. "Spencer Baker is his name. I've known him since he was a teenager. He was always at our house and his father was Jeffrey's biggest fan. How humiliated was I when I found out that, all the time, young Spencer and my husband were riding a whole lot more than horses around our paddock while I was tucked away in London? No wonder my business was flying. It suited him to have me out of the way. He probably paid my clients to keep me busy, and I am *not* joking."

"The dirty lying cheating bastard!" said Tess. "I hope you cut his balls off! I mean it. I would have done time for that motherfucker –"

"No," said Ruth. "I didn't do anything."

"Ruth!" said Tess. "Why not?"

"You don't understand the power of money, ladies," said Ruth. "I'm not talking thousands here. I'm talking *millions*. Spencer Baker's family are worth their weight in gold."

"*Wow!*" said Gina. "*Wow!*"

"Wow indeed," said Ruth. "Jeffrey was minted too. I had all the trappings of a wonderful lifestyle. I had a home in Surrey surrounded by stables and the car of my dreams on the doorstep. I had a circle of friends – well, that's what they called themselves – they were never my friends. They were *associates* as I know now. They were friends of our money, not friends of mine."

Ruth twisted her napkin and stared at the table. It was a shocker, but it was no laughing matter. Ruth was obviously still very stung by Jeffrey and his little boy racer.

"So what happened, Ruth? I can't believe this. You have been through the mill!" said Polly. She couldn't believe her ears. It was like a whole big different world. Like something out of a Jilly Cooper novel.

"It was a huge shock to me that Jeffrey was gay, let alone that he was having an affair," said Ruth when she got her breath back. "Of course, *I* was the last to know. The whole Landsbury 'set', as they called themselves, knew it was going on for ages. Then eventually I was asked by William Baker, Spencer's father, to quietly leave and he would make sure, if I didn't make any noise, that my children and I never wanted for anything."

"Oh Ruth, you poor thing!" said Polly. "So did you leave there and then?"

"I had to," said Ruth. "I didn't have a choice. These are very powerful people and without Jeffrey I was nothing to them. Besides, what could I do? I had very little dignity left. I was humiliated so I decided to hang on to whatever little dignity I could scrape off the floor and get out of there."

"And what about the children? Do they know?" asked Polly.

Ruth shook her head. "No, they don't know the full story. I couldn't tell them, not yet anyhow. All they know is that Jeffrey had found someone else and that I was in too much pain to stay in London. They have been so strong, even though Melanie does irritate the life out of me sometimes."

"Bastard! Some men . . . *eurgh*!" Tess was finding it hard to hold back what she really wanted to say about this Jeffrey Landsbury character! If Rob ever did that to her she would murder him! Cold-blooded murder!

"I didn't ever see Jeffrey again after that," said Ruth quietly. "He and Spencer didn't return from Dubai until recently when I was finally safely packed up on a plane and guaranteed never to come back. Mr Baker had asked me where I wanted to go. I could have chosen anywhere, but I chose here. I just wanted to go home."

Gina was thinking of where she would go with a one-way ticket to anywhere in the world. Yes, Ruth was right. She would probably go to Dublin. Home is where the heart is and all that.

"I wouldn't blame you," she said. "Everyone wants to go home in a crisis. Home to their family."

"Well, that's another story," said Ruth. "But I'm home now. Almost."

She took a long deep breath through her nose and out of her mouth, closed her eyes for a few seconds and then she smiled.

"I bet you all think it's hilarious, don't you?" she said with a wry expression.

"Hilarious? Not a bit hilarious. I'm in shock," said Tess.

"Why would we think it was hilarious?" asked Polly.

"Because of all the misery I put you through at school. I got my comeuppance and I got it hard. I don't blame you if you feel smug."

"I don't feel a bit smug," said Tess. "I still can't believe you left without a fight. Did you at least burn the place down before you left? Tell me you did something to get revenge on the wormy wee bastard?"

"I need another drink," said Gina. "I thought my Trevor was bad with She Who Must Not Be Named, but your fella left you for a jockey! Are you sure this Spencer one was definitely a man?"

94

Ruth looked at Tess and Polly and they all exploded with laughter.

"Yes, Gina. Spencer was a man. A very small man, albeit. But a man with a willie he was."

"I definitely need a drink."

"So, anyhow, on that note," said Ruth, "who fancies a flutter? I may not be able to live that life any more, but I sure know enough about it to make sure the drinks are on the bookies tonight!"

"I'm up for that!" said Tess.

Gina was already at the bar.

"Hear, hear!" said Polly and they all raised a glass to whipping some ass at the horse-racing.

11

After their fourth win, the girls had well and truly captured the attention of every single punter in the Top O'The Road, with Ruth holding court as she predicted win after win with only the odd loss of a few quid in between.

She scanned the newspaper like an expert, circling her top three choices and then carefully placing her bets. They made a 'kitty' for their gambling money and Polly, chosen as the most sensible after a very fair vote, was in charge of making sure everything was accounted for.

A tenner each way started them off and, after each win, their confidence grew until Ruth decided it was time to up the ante.

"So what d'ye predict this time, love?" asked Duncan the barman. He was Scottish and round and was in awe of Ruth's talent, not knowing of course the fine stock she came from and the background knowledge on horse-racing that just couldn't be bought.

Ruth bit the inside of her cheek and her heart thumped

as she scanned the listings for the 4 p.m. at Cheltenham and their last bet of the day. She had known this day would come. She knew that if she got over this hurdle, she would get over anything and now, in a back end pub of Donegal surrounded by people she didn't know and girls who used to hate her guts but who had now given her a chance, her deepest fears were right in front of her in black and white.

"*Melanie's Way*," she said, matter of factly and she circled the name of the horse so deeply with her pen that the newspaper tore.

"What? As in *the* Melanie's Way?" asked Tess. For some reason she now felt like she was in the presence of a celebrity.

"Do you think it will win?" asked Polly. She felt a little bit scared. Ruth's eyes were wild and out of control.

"I know it will win," she said. "I know it will as well as I know that Jeffrey Landsbury is a queer."

"So, what are you thinking? It's 6/1. Fifty quid each way?" asked Gina, feeling all knowledgeable. She hadn't bet on a horse since her father used to put a pound on for her and her sisters in the Irish Grand National and feared she might get used to it.

"Put it all in," said Ruth, tilting back her chin.

"All of it?" asked Polly. "But we have won nearly five hundred quid! We can't put it all –"

"Put it all on!" said Ruth.

Polly lifted up her hands in surrender. "Okay, okay, it's your game. I mean, it's your call. Really?"

"Really!"

Tess linked Polly's arm as the bet was placed online by Duncan the barman and they waited for the race to start.

"My nerves are shattered. I think I need a smoke," said Gina.

"You don't smoke," said Polly.

"I do now," said Gina and she followed a sign which directed her out the back to a tiny smoking area that you could barely swing a cat in.

"Did you see who the jockey is?" asked Ruth. "Wee Waspy Ass himself, Spencer Baker."

"No way!" said Polly. She was beginning to sound like a teenager but she really couldn't believe this wonderful, if traumatic, chequered past Ruth Monaghan had up her sleeve.

"And only that I'm dealing in cold hard cash, I'd be praying the wee bastard came off at the first jump. God forgive me but I'd love to see him do a head-over-heels tumble on live television."

"I think that alone would be worth gambling five hundred quid," said Tess. "I don't know how you can even stomach to watch this, Ruth. If that were me, I'd be throwing my stilettos at the telly, never mind placing bets on him to win."

"Ah, but it's some sort of satisfaction," said Ruth. "I don't need money. I have plenty of that, but if anything can come out of that whole sorry mess, it's that we all have a good time tonight and not one of you goes home with a penny less than you came here with. I owe you big-time, girls. You have no idea how much this all means to me." Ruth felt her lip tremble and her eyes fill up so she fanned her face with her hands and took several deep breaths.

"You know, if it doesn't win there'll be no hard feelings, Ruth," said Tess. "It's only a bit of fun. There's no pressure whatsoever."

"It *will* win," said Ruth. "I know this horse like I know my own children. I know the ground he likes and the weather he thrives in. He will win. Come on, Melanie's Way, you wee beauty!"

"It's on! Oh my God, they're lining up to start!" said Polly. "I think I'm going to be sick!"

"Drinks are on me, ladies!" said Duncan, who had sneaked a wee nifty fifty on the horse's nose himself, and they grabbed their glasses from the bar and stood amongst at least ten Donegal men, waiting for the off.

He was a beauty, that horse, and every time Ruth saw him in the newspaper or on the box, she stared at him and wondered if the horse knew any of the scandal before she did. She wondered if Spud, as he was known on a daily basis, had witnessed any of Jeffrey and Spencer's dirty shenanigans when she was working in London or when the children were at school.

"Go on, yeh wiry wee hoor yeh, Baker!" shouted one of the men at the telly.

"He's a queer wee git!" said Tess and the punters roared in support.

And they were off!

Melanie's Way trailed behind to begin with, hard to spot amongst the flurry of hooves and colour and the girls squinted and strained their eyes to find him.

"There he is!" said Ruth. "I could spot him a mile away. Go on, Spud! Do it for your mammy!"

The race was frantic and somewhat disturbing with two horses falling at the first hurdle and another one at the second, but Melanie's Way under the slick guidance of Waspy Waist Spencer was making steady progress, making his way into fourth place, then swiftly onto third and with

99

only seconds to go, Spencer spurred him on with all his might into a mighty first. He had won! Melanie's Way had won!

"Holy shit, Ruth! You're a bloody genius!" screamed Tess.

"Buy that woman a drink! Who is she?" asked one of the punters who then made his way over to Ruth. He was a red-faced, red-haired, friendly chap who introduced himself as Michael.

"I don't need you to buy me a drink," said Ruth. "But thanks all the same. I've just won three thousand fucking euro! *Woo hoo*! Drinks are on me!"

The men scrambled to the bar, most of them trying to edge their way towards Tess and Polly, but Michael only had eyes for Ruth.

Ruth could feel her face flush. She wasn't used to attention from men, apart from when it came to racing tips, and this man had barely looked at Tess or Polly. Men *always* looked at Tess and Polly. They were like two men-magnets and Ruth, despite her size, had always been invisible in comparison. He was obviously after a tip but she still felt flattered.

"I can't believe you predicted all those winners," he said. "Are you some sort of psychic?"

"That she is," said Tess. "And a very wealthy one at that. We only take her to certain places. She's in big demand."

"I'm serious," said Michael and he produced a business card, but didn't hand it over. "I'm the editor of an online sports magazine called *Goldrush*. Have you ever used your talent in the media?"

"I worked in graphic design for many years," said Ruth, a little disappointed to have it confirmed that he

100

was after her racing knowledge, not her. "And I've written the odd bit of brochure copy but nothing like what you are talking about. But I do know my stuff as you can see."

Tess took the hint and butted out of the conversation.

"Well, I'd really like to talk to you about the possibility of doing a horse-racing column, paid of course. If you're interested?"

She looked up at him in disbelief. A column? For real? She loved writing! It was her favourite part of her design work and the copy she wrote for past clients had always been regarded even more highly than the actual designs she came up with.

Michael was taller than Ruth. He wasn't as red in the face as he had been during the race but, as Ruth later found out, that was because he had one hundred pounds on the horse that came second and his blood pressure had risen to the max with worry. She liked him. He was friendly. Ruth didn't suffer fools gladly after what she had been through but there was something about Michael that made her feel at ease.

"I would really have to think about it," she said. "Me – writing a column – it would be quite a commitment. It would be a great challenge, but it would be a big step and might take up a lot of time."

She was doing her best to play hard to get. She would *love* to write a column on horse-racing. She knew all there was to know.

"Of course, no pressure whatsoever," said Michael. "I just know talent when I see it and I don't like to waste an opportunity. What brings you here anyhow? A hen party? Business?"

Ruth laughed and took a sip of her drink. She felt all

funny inside. A bit flirty perhaps? Michael certainly was holding her attention and it appeared that she was holding his too. Was something happening here after all?

"Well," she said, "it's a long story. But let's just say we are out to have a really good time and it's just got better."

"Yeah," said Michael. "Three thousand pounds up would make any good time seem better."

"Oh, it's not only the money," said Ruth and she giggled. She *was* flirting! She waited on the bombshell. He was probably married or gay or, as in her experience, both.

"The wine, is it?" he asked, cocking an eyebrow at her.

"Yes, the wine," said Ruth coyly. "That's exactly what I meant. The wine."

He slipped his business card into her hand at last and held it there for a little while longer than he needed to. "Well, here are my details. Think about my proposition. One column a month. Name your price – though go easy on me! I'd love to have you on board. I think we'd make a winning team."

He winked and she felt her legs turn to jelly. She saw him look at her bare wedding finger. His was the same. Ringless. *Result!*

"Ooh, you have all the lingo, don't you?" said Ruth, batting her eyelids. She really was feeling rather funny inside.

"That's only the tip of the iceberg. I'll let you get back to your friends, but you know where I am once you have, you know, thought about it. It was lovely to meet you – ?"

"Ruth," she said with confidence. "Ruth Monaghan."

She reached into her purse and gave him one of her own business cards which had all her current details including her website which she was extra proud of.

"I like your style," said Michael. "I like it a lot, Ruth Monaghan."

The way he said her name and looked into her eyes with a smile made her stomach do a leap. It was butterflies! She hadn't experienced butterflies since she was a teenager! Not even with Jeffrey! And with that Michael was gone, back into the snug where his mates were awaiting his return with a pint of Guinness.

"*Ahem*," said Tess.

"What?"

"What on earth was that all about, Ruth 'Mystic Meg' Monaghan?" asked Polly.

"I'm not quite sure," said Ruth. "But I think I may have just pulled!"

"What? Already?" asked Tess.

"Don't look so surprised! Some men do like the more voluptuous look!"

"I'm not surprised! I'm just saying fair play to you! I'm pleased for you, I really am. Do you like him?"

"You know what, I kind of do," said Ruth, glancing over at Michael who was looking right in her direction. "Watch this space, ladies. Watch this space . . ."

"Where's Gina?" asked Polly a few minutes later, after they had dragged Ruth over and over her conversation with Michael the journalist.

"Shit, I thought of that earlier. She left for a smoke before the race began. That must be at least half an hour ago. I'll go outside and see," said Ruth and she was gone in a flurry of black clothes and red hair.

Polly and Tess looked at each other, each feeling a little bit tipsy as the manic drinking that came with the win hit home.

"I can't believe her husband was gay. What a shocker!" said Polly. "I feel so sorry for her."

"I can't believe she just won us three grand!" said Tess. "She sure knows her stuff. Who knows, maybe this Michael guy will give her something to look forward to. She definitely deserves a lift after all that trauma!"

They didn't have any time to discuss Ruth's proposition as she was back within seconds.

"Gina's gone!" she said, slightly out of breath.

"What do you mean she's gone?" asked Polly. "She can't be gone. There's nowhere round here to be 'gone' to!"

"She's not out there and she's not in here and I've looked in the loos – the ladies and the men's. She is gone! I'm serious, girls! Gina has disappeared!"

12

Gina leaned back in the Jacuzzi and closed her eyes. The bubbles were warming her from the inside out and she had a woozy, drunk feeling that made her feel like she was floating over the water.

"You know, I don't think I have ever felt this good in my whole, entire life. Can I stay here forever?" she asked.

"Won't your friends be wondering where you are?" asked Marco – the gorgeous young man she had met exactly sixty-seven minutes and forty-two seconds ago outside the pub next door. She had bummed a cigarette off him and the rest was history.

"I'm sure they haven't even noticed I'm gone yet," said Gina, opening her eyes for just a few seconds and then letting her eyelids drop again. She hadn't decided yet if Marco was her type at all. He was young. Very young. And far too good-looking. She hadn't even snogged him yet but she would. Damn right she would. So far, so good, Marco, and what a brilliant idea it was to come and see his Jacuzzi! Whether or not he meant for her to get *into* it was another story, but it was too late for that now. She was in it and she had absolutely no intention of getting out. Not in the next twenty minutes anyhow.

They had been discussing the tourism industry in Donegal when the subject of seeing his Jacuzzi had come up. That was over an hour ago and yet she was so comfortable with him that she felt like she might have known him in a previous life or something.

"Excuse me," she had said, flopping down beside him on the picnic bench outside the Top O'The Road bar, a little more clumsily than she would have liked to. She was a single woman now and had to remember to be graceful, even when under the influence of alcohol. "Could I be awful cheeky and ask you for a cigarette? It's just my friend is a compulsive gambler and I can't bear to watch her any more. My nerves are frazzled."

"Never let your nerves be frazzled, that's my motto. Or one of them anyhow," was his reply and he handed her a cigarette and then lit it for her.

She decided then and there that this was a very nice man indeed. She liked the idea of never letting your nerves be frazzled. That was an excellent motto.

He was definitely younger than her. A lot younger. About twenty-eight, she guessed, but she was too busy smiling at him and he was too busy smiling at her to ask a lot of questions.

Then she realised that she really should strike up a conversation in case he got bored looking at her cheesy grin and left her to smoke all alone. He might go inside and see Pretty Polly or Hot Teacher Tess and he would never smile at her again. And, aside from that, Gina did like a good chinwag when she was having a cigarette. You had to be a real smoker to enjoy one on your own.

"I take it you're not a Donegal man with that accent?" she said, trying to look seductive. She couldn't really remember how to do that, but she was giving it her best shot and she thanked the Lord above for the invention of fake eyelashes.

"No, I am not even an Irishman. I am from England," he said.

"England? Ah . . . I see."

"You look disappointed?" he said with a laugh, as if he got the same reaction all the time.

"No, no, why would I be disappointed?" said Gina. "Surprised, yes, but never disappointed. You look – you look more exotic than an Englishman, no offence to all those Englishmen out there. Lots of Englishmen are hot. I mean, you'd hardly kick David Beckham out of bed for spilling crumbs, would you?"

"No offence taken."

Damn but his smile was electrifying!

"My parents are Italian but I was brought up in humble old Berkshire. My name is Marco. What's yours?"

"I'm Gina," she replied and she saw a very inviting twinkle in his eye.

"Gina," he repeated softly. "That's a very pretty name. Gina is an Italian name too, you know."

"I like the way you say it," said Gina and then she hiccupped and covered her mouth. "I'm sorry – I'm a little bit tipsy! I've had quite a bit to drink already and it's only . . . what time is it anyhow?"

"I have no idea," said Marco. "I don't check the time when I'm here. You're very pretty, Gina."

The way he said her name was really making her heart leap inside. He said it so long and slowly as if he was holding on to it on his tongue for as long as he could. She liked her name on his tongue. She wanted him to hold on to *her*. Oh God, she hadn't felt so much like a teenager since . . . since she was a teenager! Not since that summer's day that Trevor asked her out for the first time round the back of Micky Martin's chip van all those years ago! She might just go for it and have an orgasm there and then, in broad daylight in a little village in Donegal.

"Do you know something?" she said to Marco who had lit up another cigarette. Great. He wasn't going anywhere too soon. *Do you know something?* was a great conversation-keeper.

"I'd like to think I know lots of things," he said.

"I'm sure you do – but what I was going to say was that I have absolutely no idea where we are. Don't know what time it is, don't know where we are. No idea whatsoever."

"What, you mean you and me?" asked Marco. "We've only just met. We're strangers. We aren't really anywhere yet."

He laughed again and once more she resisted the urge to jump his sexy bones.

"No, no, I mean I have no idea where in Donegal we are. All I know is that I am staying in a very, very posh place a few miles away and that the sun is shining and that I feel so free I could kick off my shoes and dance around this table."

Marco's eyes crinkled when he smiled. She liked that.

"What a wonderful way to feel," he said. "Donegal is such a beautiful county. I have been coming here for many, many years just to switch off and reflect on life. We all need to take time to reflect. That's why I never check the time. I eat when I'm hungry and I sleep when I'm tired. It's the best way to be, when life allows it."

"Reflecting is good," said Gina, nodding. "I can see my reflection in your eyes. Yes. There I am. Hello, me!"

She waved and Marco laughed again. Gosh, he even thought she was funny! Probably in a semi-drunk kind of mental way, but she was making him laugh and smile and it felt good.

"I used to work in the – *hic* – tourism section of my local Council," she said. "That sounds terribly boring but – *hic* – it was fun at times. We used to go on what we called 'familiarisation trips' to other counties and Donegal was always my favourite. It's like a different, slower way of life. The whole wide world should move to Donegal."

She held her breath to try and get rid of her hiccups.

"But then, if the whole wide world moved here to Donegal," said Marco. "There would be no room for you and me, and we would never have met and shared such a pensive –"

"And reflective. Don't forget reflective!" said Gina.

"Exactly. We would never have shared such a pensive and reflective moment over a cigarette."

Gina swung her feet back and forth like a schoolgirl. "Moments like these don't happen very often." She leaned back and her arm brushed against Marco's. So she did it again. And again. And again. And Marco laughed. Again.

"You seem very, very happy," he said.

"I am," said Gina. "I'm free at last. You don't how good it feels to be free!" She stretched out her arms when she said it, with a little more gusto than she realised and hit Marco's handsome face full whack with her left hand.

"*Ouch!*" he said. "That's some left hook you have for such a little person! I wouldn't like to see you angry, if that's what you do when you're happy!"

He held his hand to his face and Gina leaned closer to him.

"Oh sweet Jesus in heaven, I am so sorry," she said. "Does it hurt?"

"*Ouch!*" he said again when she pressed his cheek with her finger. "It does when you poke it. It's okay. I will survive. Nothing a long soak in the bath won't cure, which is what I am planning on very, very soon."

"Mmm, a bubble bath! I haven't had a bubble bath in ages and ages. I never seem to have the time any more, but I will from now on. I'm sick of a quick shower here, and a quick shower there. Yes, I want a – *hic* – bubble bath. Shit, these hiccups! I do apologise!"

"Now, a bubble bath," said Marco, leaning his elbows on his knees, "a bubble bath, next to Donegal, might just be the best place in the world to reflect."

"Ah, I see what you mean," said Gina. "If a bubble bath is the best place to reflect, next to Donegal, then a bubble bath *in* Donegal would have to be the bestest, bestest place to reflect in the whole wide world!"

"That is exactly right," said Marco. "And if a bubble bath *in* Donegal is so, so good, then imagine what a Jacuzzi bubble bath in Donegal might be like!"

Gina let out a gasp. "Well, I'm afraid I might find that a little bit too much to take! I mean, the excitement would be a little bit too much. I might have a heart attack."

"You have a beautiful accent," said Marco. "The way you said 'heart attack' there really got me. You've a great way with words."

Gina gave him a friendly slap on the leg. She really should stop with the violence very soon.

"It's a very strong Dublin accent I have," she said. "And I have absolutely no problem with words. I never have had. I just wasn't listened to for a long, long time. Now where in the world is this Jacuzzi? I simply have to see it."

"Really?"

"Yes, really. I want to see where the best place in the world is to reflect."

"It is right up there," said Marco, pointing to the top-floor window of the building next to the Top O'The Road pub.

"You're having me on! It's really that close?" said Gina, staring up at the little open wooden window with its white curtains flapping in the light breeze. She looked at the sign above the door – *The Wayward Inn*. She would never have noticed it in a million years. And she would never have dreamed that it was home to a Jacuzzi bath in another million years!

"That's where I stay. That's my room," said Marco. "It's a little gem of a hotel. My room is the only one with a Jacuzzi and I stay in that room every time I visit. You should have a look around. I just know you would love that place. You look like the creative sort."

Gina was feeling very daring indeed. She would climb every stair in that place if it meant she could get a look at Marco's Jacuzzi.

"I am very creative," she said. "I paint a lot."

"Really? I'm impressed," said Marco. "Portraits? Landscapes?"

"A little more abstract," said Gina. "I've framed a few and hung them up around my house but I've never really appreciated them. Other people have commented loads and gave me the whole 'you're wasting your time just doing housework' speech, but I've been too busy to do anything about it."

They sat thinking together in comfortable silence.

"So, can I see it then, or what?" she asked, giving her eyelashes an extra flutter.

"But we have only just met," said Marco. "I don't show my Jacuzzi to just anyone, you know! I am very selective as to who I reflect with."

Gina knew he was teasing. In her mind they were already examining the place and she really did want to see what the hotel had to offer. She loved finding places that weren't what they seemed from the outside. Like the Top O'The Road pub – they had been expecting baskets of sausage and chips or soup and a roll, but instead it was the very best of homemade deliciousness on the menu!

"Well, we have been reflecting and putting the world to right for about twenty minutes now," she said. "So I thought I was already in the Reflecting Gang, but if I have more work to do to prove to you that I am worth reflecting with, then that's what I'm prepared to do. It's not every day you come across a – *hic* – handsome stranger called Marco with a Jacuzzi bath in the back-end of Donegal. This I have to see."

Marco stood up and put his hands in his pockets. Then he took them out again. Then he put them back in.

"Well, at least let me buy you a drink first?" he asked. "I would feel terribly bad if I showed you my Jacuzzi and hadn't even at least bought you a drink."

"Okay," said Gina. "Let's go inside this little gem of a hotel of yours and have a quickie."

one night only

He looked startled.

"A quick *drink*, I mean!" she said and she linked his arm as they walked towards the little hotel. Sure, this single life was great *craic* altogether!

"Maybe you should just text or give one of them a quick call," said Marco twenty minutes later. He was very responsible, thought Gina. She wasn't feeling responsible at all. She had filled the Jacuzzi straight away, told Marco to look away and, when she was sure his eyes were averted, she'd stripped off and stepped into the hot bubbles.

"I would text them," she giggled, taking a sip of pink champagne from the flute that Marco had poured for her moments earlier. "But I don't have their numbers!"

She laughed out loud and then noticed that Marco really did look concerned.

"Shall I pop next door and let them know you're here?" he asked. "I don't want them thinking I have kidnapped you or anything . . ."

"You, my dear," said Gina, "can kidnap me any day of the week and twice on a Sunday. Now, come here!"

Gina reached out her arm and pulled Marco towards her. She was a tiny little thing but she had him under her spell and he did what he was told.

He smelled of cigarettes and alcohol and a musky man smell that got Gina very excited indeed. She hadn't had the love of a man in well over a year and, boy, was she ready! Not proper lovemaking, anyhow. She'd had plenty of rough, horrible fumbles with Trevor when he'd come home drunk and the last time they did it he called her by the wrong name. That was at least six months ago and he hadn't even tried to touch her since. No, she would make real love with

113

Marco. Hot, passionate, 'I don't care if I never see you again' sex! She wondered what time it might be. The sun was glaring through the hotel window so it was still early, but she was drunk and for the moment she was in love.

Sex with a stranger! How exciting! The girls would never believe it when she told them. They would be delighted, that was for sure, she thought, because in her drunken mind it was just what the doctor ordered. And that was their motto for the day, wasn't it? Just what the doctor ordered!

"Talk about sobering up quickly!" said Polly. "I can't believe we've lost her. Out of all of us, not Gina! She's the most fragile of all of us!"

"Speak for yourself! I'm not a bit fragile," said Tess. "Don't be putting me in the tragedy group! I'm fine!"

"Oh, I know *you* are," said Polly. "But poor Gina!"

They were marching along the little village street, stopping each person they met (which wasn't a lot of people – maybe two so far) and asking if they had seen Gina but to no avail. The people who worked in the corner shop were treating it very seriously and wanted to put up a Missing Person poster even though it was only over an hour since she had last been seen. It was obviously the most dramatic question they had ever been asked in their combined 150 years of life in this tiny village.

"Was she wearing a pretty dress?" asked the lady. "You girls all look very pretty in your dresses."

"Yes!" said Polly. "She was! Did you see her?"

"No. She definitely didn't come in here," she said. "You three are the first to wear pretty dresses round here in a long time. Was she a tall girl or a small girl?"

"Small." Tess wanted to tell the old lady to stop talking about Gina in the past tense. She wasn't dead. She hoped she wasn't dead. God, what if she was dead?

"It's safe as houses around here," said the old man. "But you never know, do you? It's the quiet ones you need to watch. You just never know who is lurking about waiting to pounce. Look at that wee town in Galway on the news last week. You'd never have thought the Credit Union there would be robbed, but it was! Tragic altogether!"

"She's in a bit of a fragile state," said Ruth, wanting to get her tuppence worth in. "She's not thinking straight at the moment, so it's very important we find her. Here is my card if she does come in. Please ask her to call me straight away."

"Ah, a card!" said the old lady. "How clever! Is she bad with her nerves? You know old Kitty O'Connor? From Tullygreen Road? She was bad with her nerves. They found her by the river. She was nearly a goner, I tell you, a goner. Only for Seán Sullivan and his wee terrier, she'd be six feet under now. What's this you called that wee dog of Seán's? Lovely wee thing it was too."

"No idea," said Tess. "And we have no idea who Kitty O'Connor is but we're all glad she is alive and well and not at the bottom of the river. Come on, girls. Let's look elsewhere."

The old couple in the shop looked very disappointed that their detective work was over already.

"If you need to phone the Gardaí just come back here and you can use our phone," said the old guy as the girls scurried out through the door.

"Thanks!" said Polly who was last out. "Thanks for all your help."

"Ah bless him," said Tess when they got out onto the street. "Offering for us to use his wee phone. They mustn't have mobiles round here yet."

Ruth let out a guffaw.

"Who are we to slag him off, though?" she said. "We hadn't even the brains to swap numbers to prevent this happening. Now we're running around like headless chickens. Oh where on this earth will we look next? And don't say the river or I'll vomit my wine up!"

"Well, it was good enough for Kitty O'Connor to escape to, so who's to say it's not where our Gina is now?"

"I think I'm going to cry," said Polly.

"You don't have time to cry," said Tess. "Now, come on."

13

Gina reached over and touched Marco's earlobe. He had very nice earlobes. In fact, everything about Marco was simply delicious and being with him made Gina feel very delicious too.

She could hear light noise from the street below – cars passing and people chatting – but it was all at a level that was at ease and full of peace. No one rushed around here. There were no busy streets or beeping horns or people almost trampling over each other to get from A to B. Even the cars sounded like they had Hush Puppies on their tyres – as if they apologised for disturbing the village as they passed through. Marco was right. This was the best place to reflect in the world, ever.

It was beginning to get dark now and Gina knew she really should get up. But it was cosy and lovely and Marco had just given her the ride of her life. Yes, it was that good! He had been such an easy lover – gentle at the right times and a little bit rough when needed. Not rough like Trevor was. Oh no. Trevor was just *wham bam thank you, ma'am* and he would have his way and then roll over on the bed and fall asleep with his mouth wide open and snore so loudly that she would sometimes want to put a pillow over his head. She'd end up moving into the spare room feeling used and frustrated and would cry herself to sleep, full of self-pity and a deep hatred for the life she had made for herself and her son.

But this – this was like an almighty, earthmoving awakening! Marco had released the girl inside her and she truly felt like she had been reborn. When he touched her, she was so aware of his fingers, so aware of his tongue and his lips – and even the way his legs moved when he lay on top of her had heightened every sensation in her body and made her feel dizzy with desire.

"You are so beautiful," he had said repeatedly as he moved inside her. "You are such a beautiful woman, Gina, and don't let anyone ever make you feel any different to that."

She sighed as she drank in his every word. She thought she might drown in his dark-brown eyes as he held her gaze and pushed and pushed inside her.

Then, just when the rhythm was becoming too much to bear and Gina was moaning towards a climax, he would change positions and build and build the glorious rush within her again – until finally she couldn't hold back any longer and exploded into a mind-blowing, toe-curling, head-spinning orgasm! It was so wonderful that she had to remind herself to breathe. But the best bit – the best bit was that instead of falling straight to sleep and snoring for Ireland or England or Italy or wherever he was from, he lay facing her, staring into her eyes with his arms around her until they both drifted off into a most satisfactory post-coital slumber.

Gina woke up about fifteen minutes later. She knew her time was up. She hated leaving him but his job was done and she really had to go.

"Thank you," she whispered to him and his eyelids fluttered as he slept.

She should wake him and say her goodbyes but that would be like taking away all the mystery from what had just happened. Marco had known what she had wanted all along. He didn't need her life story. He didn't need to know her plans for her future or what had really taken her to this backward village that she still didn't know the name of. All he needed to know was that she wanted a man to make her feel alive again, to reassure her that there was a vibrant, lively young woman who had a lot to give to this life and, in just two hours, he had done just that.

Now, it was her time to go.

She tiptoed into the little bathroom where the champagne flutes still sat by the Jacuzzi. Two towels lay on the floor so she picked them up and folded them over a radiator, unable to stop smiling as she revisited the scene of where their lovemaking had begun. She stepped into the shower cubicle and lightly washed him off her, moving her soapy hands across her body with a new-found confidence. She was totally invigorated from the inside out.

When she was back in her glamorous dress and heels, she sprayed perfume and fixed her make-up which had done quite well on the survival stakes despite the steam of the Jacuzzi, shower and not to mention the heat of the lovemaking session. Then she took one last look at Marco.

119

He was a stunning young man. Well out of her league and she knew it, but he had enjoyed it too. He said so. He was meeting friends for dinner later that evening. He had a life of his own to get on with. He had done his job.

"Goodbye, my lover," she whispered, feeling like an exotic prostitute, and blew a kiss towards him.

She carefully opened the door, stepped outside and closed the door behind her, leaving Marco in a very contented sleep. He had given her a real-life memory that was only ever in her dreams before now and she would never forget him for it.

When Gina went back inside the Top O'The Road pub next door, it dawned on her that the girls might, just might, be worried about her at this time of the evening and her elation was threatened with the fact that she might be in trouble.

Then a tall, burly man approached her with a look of great concern.

"You must be Gina?" he asked. "Jesus, you've given those girls a terrible fright! Do they know you're okay?"

Gina shook her head like a disobedient schoolgirl and a wave of panic rose inside her. "Oh, I didn't mean to cause any trouble! Do you know where they are? I need to find them quickly!"

"Why didn't you at least call them? They've probably called the Guards!"

Oh, he really was cross.

"Well, I would have, but, you see, I don't know any of their numbers. That sounds strange but before this trip we didn't really need them because Polly lives next door and –"

The man fished a business card from his pocket and

began to dial a number on his mobile phone as Gina stood looking up at him.

"Ruth? It's Michael. Hi . . . No, not Michael from The Butcher's Apron – Michael from the pub. The Top O'The Road? Yeah. Your friend is here and she is safe and sound. I'll stay with her till you get back here. Okay . . . okay, love. No, it's no problem whatsoever. See you in a few minutes."

He hung up and pulled out a stool for Gina by the bar.

"You had them worried sick," he said. "Can I get you a drink? They're not too far away."

"No, no," said Gina. "I mean, thank you for the offer and thank you for getting in touch with Ruth but I think I've had quite enough to drink for this time of the day. I feel terrible for causing such worry. I was totally carried away. More than you could imagine."

She giggled and stared at a beermat, listening to Michael slurping his pint. He was a very big man compared to Marco. He had the look of a man who should wear a Stetson, she thought. Yeah, he was like an American. Like a red-haired Texan if there was such a thing. He seemed friendly and she felt safe with him but he had told her off big-time and now she was ever so slightly afraid that she, in her tipsy loved-up world of great sex and pink champagne, was in deep, deep trouble.

At that the girls burst in through the door like a scene from an old Western. Gina knew from the look on Tess's face that they didn't know if they wanted to hug her or hit her.

"Gina! Where on earth have you been?" cried Tess.

Tess was definitely the scary one. If she had been Gina's teacher at school, she would have been petrified.

"Thank you so much for getting in touch, Michael," said Polly. "Thank God you had Ruth's business card from earlier. We had just begun to search along the beach and we'd already done the river. Jesus, Gina where the hell were you? We didn't even have your number to call and see if you were okay."

Michael stood up from his bar stool. "Well, since my good deed has been done for the day, I think I'll head home and put my feet up for a while. Ladies, it's been a pleasure. Ruth, I do hope to hear from you very soon."

"Oh, you will," said Ruth, feeling her cheeks blush. "Thanks again, Michael. It's been a pleasure for me too."

"Believe me, the pleasure was *all* mine," said Michael and he left the ladies to it.

As soon as he walked through the doors of the pub, the interrogation of Gina began.

"Holy crap, you scared the absolute shite out of us, Gina!" said Tess. "We were seconds and I mean *seconds* from calling the Guards to start a search for you! We thought you had done a Kitty O'Connor and gone to the river!" She was manic with anger, now that the relief of finding Gina alive and well had set in.

"I swear, I was starting to think of funeral arrangements," said Ruth. "I was even thinking we would have to play George Michael songs or use the money we won to get a tribute act to come and sing over your corpse."

"You didn't really think that, did you?" asked Gina, and she burst out laughing. "Look, I am so, so sorry. I really can't emphasise how sorry I am."

"So where the fuck were you?" asked Tess.

Polly was been unusually quiet. In truth, she was imagining the George Michael tribute and inwardly commending Ruth on her thinking. She would never have thought of such a cool idea. That's what living in London could do for you. Teach you to think outside of the box.

"Well," said Gina, her brown eyes widening under her false eyelashes. She fixed her pixie-like dark hair and took a deep breath. "In the words of the song from my favourite movie, *Dirty Dancing*, I have had the time of my life. I really have! *Nobody puts Gina in the corner!*"

"Have you been hit on the head?" asked Ruth.

"The time of your life? Where? With who?" asked Polly, snapping out of her George Michael funeral fantasy.

"With Marco! In his Jacuzzi! Drinking pink champagne!"

The three girls stared at her. Tess was the first to break the silence. Maybe she *had* been hit on the head.

"And who in their right mind is Marco? What do you mean the time of your life? You're not thinking straight! Are you sure he didn't harm you? Did he force you to do anything you didn't want to do?"

Tess was leaning with both hands on the table as if she was preparing to go and find Marco and give him what for. If she had been wearing sleeves, she would have rolled them up.

"No, no!" said Gina. "I swear it wasn't like that! It was wonderful! It was gentle and romantic and he has a really big willie and he knows what to do with it! I just left him. I snuck out – he's fast asleep. I think I've worn him out!" She put her hand over her mouth and began to giggle at the thought of what she had just done. It hadn't been planned at all and that's what made it even more out of character. It was spontaneous, it was a case of being in the right place at the right time and, most of all, she enjoyed every second of it!

"You dirty rotten harlot!" said Ruth with a surprised grin. "I'd never, ever have thought it, not for one minute. Not for a millisecond! Good on ya, Gina! Fair play!"

Ruth lifted her hand for a high five. Polly grabbed Gina's hand before she could reciprocate the gesture. She just didn't agree.

"I'm in shock," said Polly. "Gina, I didn't think you had it in you. So you just had sex with a hot stranger and left his room without saying goodbye?"

"That's exactly what I did!" said Gina. She was feeling more hyper than ever now. "I'm sorry if you were worried but I was somewhere between ecstasy and heaven and to be honest you three were the furthest thing from my dirty mind!"

"And did he really have a big willie?" asked Ruth. She was enjoying this story to the full. All the searching around the village, all the worry and panic they had for the past two hours was worth it to see Gina on such a high. Ruth would give anything for a big willie.

"Massive!" said Gina. "I never saw the like of it! He makes my Trevor's look like an AA battery!"

Even Polly had to give in at that. In truth she was a little bit jealous. She would love to have sex with a stranger. Maybe that's what they all needed! The girls roared with laughter until they were told by the barman (Duncan from earlier had finished his shift) to keep it down as people were in for evening meals and the rowdy crowd of punters had moved on.

Perhaps it was time for them to move on too.

"Well, so far this has been a very eventful outing!" said Polly. "Three grand on the horses, Gina gets the shag of her life and Ruth is offered a job. Cheers to Top O'The

Road but I think it's time we saw what else this little backwater has to offer!"

"I'll drink to that!" said Gina.

"You're on the water for a while!" said Tess. "Now, let's get the flock out of here."

The girls didn't have a clue where to go next but they knew one thing was for sure – they had money and they wanted to spend it. With the evening wearing in and the Top O'The Road exhausted, they decided it was time to be sensible and soak up some of the alcohol from early in the day with a slap-up meal.

"I fancy Chinese," said Tess. "Mmm, I'd love a big dirty chicken dish and rice and noodles and prawn crackers!"

"Oh, my mouth is watering! But what's the chances of getting a Chinese restaurant in this place? I think that wee pub, the shop and Gina's den-of-iniquity hotel are the only establishments around," said Polly. "Maybe we should have bought a map?"

"A map?" said Ruth. "A *map*? Who on earth uses a map these days? We have smartphones to help us get around and we also have Larry the taxi driver to call on. Let's get him to pick us up and take us to the nearest Chinese restaurant. It can't be *that* far away."

Larry the Leprechaun taxi-man arrived within minutes and seemed very glad to see a bit of glamour again.

"I hear one of you went missing," he said, before they even had their seat belts on. "Gosh, did I laugh my socks off when I heard that! I mean, how on earth would you get lost around here? It's hardly Dublin City!"

Gina chewed on her lip. She had to see the funny side.

"And how on earth did you hear that?" asked Tess.

125

"Do you know how many times we went to the loo, too?"

"I couldn't tell you exactly," said Larry, "but word gets around here very quickly. I told you the men round here rarely see a good-looking woman and when three or four turn up at the one time, it doesn't take long for the word to spread. I hear the Top O'The Road was packed earlier. It's not normally like that of a Saturday, you know."

He drove along, chuckling to himself and singing along to Daniel O'Donnell on the radio.

"So, where did you find your missing one?" he asked eventually. The events of the day were beginning to take their toll on his passengers and they were being unusually quiet.

"She was down by the river," said Ruth. "Just like –"

"Like Kitty O'Connor?" said Larry. "Jeepers, she was nearly a goner. Only for –"

"Only for Seán Sullivan and his wee dog," said Tess. "What's this you called that wee dog?" Polly couldn't restrain herself from laughing.

Gina, of course, was oblivious as to what they were talking about.

"What's this you called it?" asked Larry. "That'll bug me for the rest of the evening, you know. I'd nearly call in to Seán himself and ask him. What was that wee dog's name? And what the hell did you have to mention him for? That'll wreck my head all night."

Larry pulled up in the centre of the next town where the mood was much livelier than the village they had spent the day in.

"If we find out, we'll let you know," said Polly. "Now, how much do we owe you?"

126

"Thirty-five euro," said Larry with a glint in his eye.

"Thirty-five euro! Our asses have hardly warmed the seats in this car! Ahh, go on, ye wee beggar," said Ruth, handing him the money. "I've no doubt you heard a whole lot more about what we got up to today when you come out with a price like that!"

"Sure, ye can well afford it," said Larry. "Loaded ye all are, loaded! Gimme a shout later and I'll get you back to your hotel safe and sound. Have fun, ladies!"

14

The sun was well and truly down when the foursome walked along the cobbled pathway of the town with no name. It did have a name of course, but they didn't need to know it, nor did they particularly want to. It was a town and it had a Chinese restaurant and they were ready to stuff their faces to the max.

"Oh, that smell is just delicious!" said Tess when they entered the restaurant. It seemed clean and pleasant, if a little old-fashioned with its paper Chinese dragons hanging from the ceiling and red and green décor. They were shown to their seats by a huge window that gave a bird's eye view of what was going on outside and around them in the restaurant.

"Now, remember, ladies," said Ruth. "Eat as much as you want. Let's treat this like a proper feast. I am so ready for this. Good call, Tess."

"I'm starving too," said Gina and the others lifted their heads from the menu and then they all let out a giggle.

"Somehow, that doesn't surprise us!" said Tess. "You've

probably burned off more calories than you have consumed in a fortnight!"

Gina was still the star of the show in the wake of her rampant ride with Marco, the Italian Stallion from Berkshire.

"Did you not feel a wee bit guilty leaving Marco without even saying goodbye or getting his number to stay in touch?" asked Polly. She seemed very concerned about poor Marco's feelings but then that was typical of her, always thinking of how people felt inside.

"Honestly, Polly," said Gina, over the top of her menu, "I don't think Marco will be too concerned. He comes here every year to reflect. I'm sure I am only one of many women to have shared his bed down the years. He is a virile, hot, gorgeous man and I'm sure he has forgotten me already. It's a bit like that song – you know, the one about the rainy night and the woman picks up the man at the side of the road . . . what's it called?"

"Oh, yeah I know the one!" said Tess and she began to sing the chorus of Heart's 'All I Want to Do is Make Love to You'.

"I love that song," said Ruth and she began to sing too.

"Didn't she get pregnant in that song?" asked Tess. She loved her music trivia.

"I have no idea but there's no hope of that happening to me," Gina said. "We took all precautions necessary and I'm pilled up ever since our Danny came along. Trevor never wanted any more. I would have loved another child."

"You know, all this talk of rampant loving is kind of stirring my loins," said Ruth, shifting in her seat and rubbing her thighs. "See, Gina! See what you started! And here was me saying that I wouldn't even take it from

Johnny Depp when we left home this morning. Right now, I'd take it off that Chinese waiter if he offered. Not that he would."

The girls eyed up the waiter who was approaching the table. He looked a bit cautious, as if he knew he was the subject of a very illicit conversation and the girls singing had caused a more riotous atmosphere than what he was obviously used to.

"Everything okay?" he asked. "You ready to order?"

"Oh, everything is wonderful," said Gina. "Just wonderful and floaty and *ahhhhh* . . . very satisfactory."

The poor waiter looked scared. He glanced around him for help.

"Satisfactory for some," said Ruth. "For others, everything is a little bit frustrating and green-eyed and envious of others in the company."

"I think the gentleman would like us to order some *food*," said Polly, giving her best mammy stare.

"Okay, okay, sorry, Mammy," said Ruth. "I know exactly what *I* want."

"*Food*!" said Polly.

"Chicken Fried Rice to be precise," said Ruth and she stuck her tongue out at Polly who was being very pious as bloody usual. "And can I have some chips and prawn crackers and some Kung Po sauce. Oh, and can I have spring rolls to start. We are having starters, aren't we?"

"Of course," said Tess. "Let's go the whole hog! I'll have barbecue ribs –"

"I'd love a big barbecue rib," said Ruth, and Polly pinched her under the table.

Tess was seeing the funny side and was slowly taking a fit of the giggles but Gina was still locked in a dreamy world of Marco and early-evening shenanigans back in the village.

"Then I'll have a really hot, steamy, yummy curry and rice please," said Tess, licking her lips suggestively. "I'm in the mood for something really hot, hot, hot!"

"Honestly, you two are behaving like schoolgirls on heat," said Polly under her breath. "I'll have duck and pancakes to start with and then King Prawn Chow Mein. Gina, what about you? Gina?"

Gina had a glazed, almost silly, look in her eyes and she wore a huge grin.

"Just anything," she said with a light shake of her head.

"Excuse me?" said the waiter. "I'm not sure what you mean?"

Gina took a long deep breath through her nose and then her eyes brightened, back to normal.

"Sorry, I was miles away, *ahem*," she said. "I do apologise. I will have . . . I will have the same as Polly. What are you having, Polly? Oh, it doesn't matter. Just give me the same."

The waiter looked very relieved to be leaving the table and Polly was not impressed at all.

"Honestly, girls, that was just rude!" she said in a firm whisper. "There is no need to be acting all giggly and girly every time you see a man. You'd swear that you had sex on the brain!"

"I have at the minute," said Ruth, eyeing up the waiter's backside. "I'm telling you. I so would."

"Stop it!" said Polly. "If you keep acting like that, you'll get us into trouble."

"Oh lighten up, sis," said Tess. "Have another glass of

wine and chill out. You're not at home giving out to James and the boys now. We are big girls. We know how to behave. We're only having a laugh!"

Polly's face fell. Was that how she was seen at home? As someone who 'gives out'? James had already called her a nag. She didn't want to be a nag, but Tess had hit a nerve and it stung very badly.

"I'm not nagging you and I don't nag James either," she said.

Tess sniffed and played with her cutlery.

"Tess! I mean it. I'm not being a nag! That poor guy was humiliated by you two drooling over him and Gina acting like she was still mid-orgasm – so just admit that you were out of line instead of taking it out on me and making me feel bad!"

The atmosphere at the table was dropping in temperature at a rapid rate and Ruth and Gina exchanged awkward glances.

"I'm just saying that you shouldn't feel like you need to treat us like you do your husband and children," said Tess. "We don't need you to tell us when we are right and when we are wrong. Save it for when you get home."

Ruth noticed that Polly's hand was trembling as she lifted her glass to have a drink of wine. Sisters could be so cruel to each other and she hated to see such tension between Tess and Polly. There really was no need and it certainly wasn't the right time or place for a domestic. Perhaps she should step in.

"Maybe we did go a bit far," she admitted. "But that was probably my fault. I started it with the whole barbecue-rib thing."

"Yes, you are good at starting things and letting others

take the blame, aren't you, Ruth Monaghan?" said the normally bashful Polly. She had a wild look in her eyes and she looked like she might cry. "This was my idea to have you all come away for the night and this is how I am treated, just because I think your behaviour was childish and over the mark!"

"I really think you should keep your voice down," whispered Gina.

Other customers were beginning to sense the high tensions at the table by the window and the waiting staff were giving glances in their direction.

"I think you'll find it was my idea to come away for the night!" said Tess. "I was the one who found the article in the paper with the special offer. I was the one who spotted that you were at the end of your tether trying to be a Stepford bloody Housewife when you were really living in misery! So don't give me all this 'only for me you wouldn't be here' nonsense. It was my idea, not yours."

"I don't really think it matters whose idea it was," said Ruth. She was well used to settling rows between her son and daughter who were like chalk and cheese. "We are here now and we have been having such a good time. Let's not ruin everything just because I got jealous that Gina got a shag and I didn't. It's okay for you two. You can go back to your husbands and get a full service from head to toe. My opportunities are rarer than hens' teeth and the waiter just caught my eye. Sorry."

Ruth's words cut the conversation between Polly and Tess in two. There was a brief moment of silence as the waiter returned with their starters. They all muttered a sheepish 'thank you' and tucked in.

"This is lovely," said Gina, trying her timid best to change the mood. "Who'd have thought yesterday that we'd be living it up in Donegal eating gorgeous food with such wonderful company? It's so lovely."

"It is," said Polly. "Look, I'm sorry for losing it. I really am. I just think you hit a nerve there, Tess. I don't want to be a nagging wife. Sometimes . . . you see . . . sometimes I don't want to be a wife at all."

The other three stopped eating as Polly continued to make up her duck-filled pancake with cucumber and hoisin sauce. Huge tears began to drip down her face.

"Oh Polly, don't say that!" said Gina. "You have a wonderful lifestyle. I've always envied you so, so much. What's the matter?"

Polly sniffled and wiped her tears with the back of her hand, then took a bite of her pancake.

"It's okay," she said, talking with her mouth full which was so unlike her. "I'm probably just an ungrateful cow. You're right, Gina, I do have a wonderful lifestyle. Just ignore me. I'm fine."

"Polly feels that James doesn't listen to her," said Tess.

Polly stared at her in shock.

"What?" said Tess. "I'm just being honest. You're among friends!"

Polly sat up straight on her chair, preparing herself to maintain her pride and protect her privacy. She would murder her sister for this!

"It's not that he doesn't *listen*," she said, a little bit of reluctance and denial in her voice and then she gave in. "Okay, actually that is *exactly* it. He doesn't listen to me at *all* and when I repeat what I said and he *still* doesn't listen then I get angry and he says I'm a nag and lately when it happens he just storms out and goes to the pub. Oh girls, just tell me, what on earth am I doing wrong?"

Gina chewed her food. She wouldn't be giving out any advice on this one. How could she do so with her sham of a marriage that had just ended unofficially the day before?

Ruth kindly picked up the ball and ran with it.

"It sounds like a very common problem," she said, chomping into one of her spring rolls. Ruth liked to talk a lot when eating. She missed the social part of her old life where they would talk around a table over a meal and the finest of wines for hours and hours on end. She missed having *anyone* to talk to these days.

"How do you mean, common?" asked Tess. As the baby of the group, she wasn't exactly qualified to shell out relationship advice either. She was still very much in the honeymoon period of her relationship and, apart from the baby issue, she and Rob were mighty fine thank you very much.

"Well, it's all down to good old communication and not taking each other for granted," Ruth said, waving her fork as she spoke. "It's the oldest story in the book. The good news is, if it's dealt with in time then it's very easily remedied."

"And the bad news?" asked Polly. She couldn't believe she was asking Ruth Monaghan for relationship advice but, then again, Ruth had a lot more experience than she did. She had been in long-term relationships since she was sixteen and was a mum by her seventeenth birthday. Yes, Ruth knew her stuff in a 'been there, done that' kind of way.

"Well, the bad news I suppose is that if it isn't dealt with, it can simmer and then eventually it starts to boil over and very soon it's out of control and there is nothing left to work with any more. Nothing left in the pot, so to speak. It's all gone. It's boiled dry," said Ruth. "Gosh, I should be a psychiatrist or a counsellor or something. That was a pretty cool description even if I do say so myself."

"Very visual," said Polly. "So, what do I do now to resolve it? How do I get him to talk about not talking or listen about how he doesn't listen without sounding like a nag? It's sort of like a vicious circle, isn't it?"

Ruth thought for a moment. "Well, it depends what end of the scale you feel you are at. I mean, are you at simmering stage where it's starting to be very noticeable and get on your nerves, or is it beginning to boil over and get out of control until it causes arguments?"

Polly felt a wave of panic overcome her and she pushed her plate to the side. Her appetite for food was waning. Her appetite for alcohol was like a hunger that couldn't be satisfied. Her marriage was boiling over. Soon there would be nothing in the pot left. She needed to fix it quickly.

"We are boiling over," she said and she felt the tears sting her eyes again. "Oh God, somebody tell me what to do! I don't want to be a statistic!"

Ruth raised an eyebrow while Gina sheepishly nibbled her food and said nothing. She was a statistic now. So was Ruth. No one wanted to be a statistic.

"Sorry, guys! You know what I mean!" said Polly. "It's not what any of us would have planned if we could have prevented it!"

Tess knew when to come to the rescue. "I think what my sister means is that in an ideal world we would all live happily ever after just like it's meant to be. Realising that your relationship is falling apart must be a very scary experience. I'd die if anything were to happen between Rob and me. In fact, the very idea of it is enough to give me the willies."

"I know," said Ruth, taking her last piece of spring roll. She could have eaten at least five more. "I know exactly what you mean. We all set out with the best intentions, don't we? I know I did when I married Jeffrey. Even he did, deep in his heart. He may have been in denial beneath it all, but his intentions were to be a good husband and father. And then along came Spencer fucking Baker, the wee –"

"Waspy-waisted bastard!" said Gina and Tess and Polly in chorus, which lightened the mood just a notch.

"So, to answer your question," said Ruth, enjoying her role as chief adviser, "I think it's time you and James sought some outside help. Sometimes just having a third party to hear you out can kick-start things and send you back in the right direction. But don't think about that tonight, pet. Try and enjoy your time away from it all."

They finished their starters and when the waiter came to clear the table, each woman was on her best behaviour, afraid to step out of line on what had become a very fragile subject. *Men*. Waiters included.

Their main course was served and by then Polly had come round a bit. She wasn't going to let her personal problems dampen everyone's spirits. Well, she would at least make a very conscious effort not to. And besides, it was against the rules of the trip. No men talk, no kids talk and no bitching about the past. The plan was to look ahead and enjoy their freedom.

"Mmm, this all smells delicious!" she said, and she

meant it. The curry looked flavoursome and her King Prawn Chow Mein was steaming hot and she could almost taste the garlic before it even reached her mouth. She would force herself to relax and enjoy her meal, plus the wine was going down a treat. Mind you, it might as well have been Liquid Nitrogen for all she cared at this stage of the evening.

"I'd like to propose a toast before we begin our main dish of the day," said Ruth as the waiter, who was becoming braver now and was doing his job with a lot more confidence, topped up their glasses. Ruth was sure he was giving her the eye but she wouldn't even dare to joke about it.

"Oh, go for it! I love a good toast!" said Gina. "I might even make one myself. Go, Ruth!"

Ruth cleared her throat dramatically and flicked back her red bob as if she had a longer mane than Melanie's Way. Truth was, the hair was more chopped and chunky these days.

"Here's to letting bygones be bygones, the future taking care of us and the present being what we focus on. Here's to tonight, and to the here and now. Onwards and upwards!"

She raised her glass and the others followed suit.

"Oh Ruth, that's just lovely!" said Polly. "I think that's exactly what we have to do. Concentrate on now. Tomorrow will bring its own new challenges and we will deal with them then!"

Tess rolled her eyes and took a gulp of her wine. "Honestly, you lot are just so deep and meaningful. Right, Gina – your turn. Ruth's was lovely but I'm counting on you to make us laugh!"

Gina wiped her mouth with her napkin and tried to control the smirk on her face but she couldn't. It broke into a huge smile and then a titter and then a full-blown, throw-your-head-back belly-laugh.

"What?" asked Tess. "Was it something I said?"

"No, no," said Gina. "Gimme a minute. Right . . . *ahem*! Here's to –"

And she was off again, huge laughter coming from her tiny body. Again, the other diners began to look their way and their waiter was looking a little unsure of himself again. He probably really hoped they didn't start singing!

"Okay, okay, I've got it now," said Gina, dabbing her mouth for the second time. She took a deep breath and fanned her face with her napkin. "Woh! Here's to . . . here's to . . . reflection! You just can't beat a good old reflection every now and then. To taking time out. To catching your breath. To pressing pause. Here's to that fantastic shag I had earlier and how I just can't stop buzzing since! And here's to happiness from now on for each and every one of us!"

"Hear, hear!" said Tess. "Love that you got your wee shag in there. I have a feeling it might be the highlight of our trip so far, even if you did give us the fright of our lives."

"Oh, I've one, I've one!" said Polly. She was getting tipsy again and felt much better even if the whole sentimental side of her brain was still in overdrive.

"Jeez, what have you started, Ruth? No, no – I'm joking, I'm joking! Go for it, sister!" said Tess, supposing that she should come up with something too before the food got cold. But it was Polly's turn. Please no tears, she thought. No more tears.

But Polly had no intention of shedding tears. She took a deep breath and raised her glass.

"Here's to good friends and to second chances," she said, looking at Ruth and Gina. "Girls, we have come a long way since yesterday and I'd like to raise a toast to both of you in particular. Gina, you're a very witty, very beautiful woman who has so much ahead of you now that you have made possibly the bravest, biggest decision you will ever have to make in your life, but you did it, girl! You did it! And look at that smile on your face! Long may it last!"

"Thanks, Poll. A lot of it's down to you, you know," said Gina.

"Oh, no, it's nothing to do with me at all. You're an independent, strong woman, which leads me nicely on to Ruth. You have really surprised me for the better, Ruth Monaghan."

"Do you always call me by my full title?" asked Ruth.

"Yes," said Polly. "And always will. But stop interrupting. I just want to say that I hope we can be friends for a long time. You're a changed person and I think it's enlightening to see that people can change for the better. You have become an amazing person, Ruth. I'm glad you came back from London. Good luck in your new life here at home and let that rich bastard whore around London all he wants! You are way too good for him anyhow!"

Ruth fanned her face this time and looked genuinely touched. "I swear, Polly Woodhead, if you make me cry I'll never forgive you," she said. "Polly Knox, Polly Knox, I mean! Sorry! The last thing I want to do at this stage of the evening is ruin my make-up!"

140

"Fair enough!" said Polly. "I'll shut up then."

"So what about me?" asked Tess. "Can I say a quick few words before we tuck in, which we'd better do very soon before this beautiful feast is cold."

"Go! Go!" said Polly. Her King Prawns were beginning to wink at her. She'd better eat them quickly before they spoke to her or got up and walked away.

"I'd like to propose a toast to the one and only . . . Melanie's Way!" said Tess and the girls raised their glasses with extra vigour.

"*To Melanie's Way!*" they chorused.

"As my mother used to say, God bless his little cotton socks!" said Gina.

"And to the waspy-waisted wee bastard that rode him home!" said Ruth. "I hope he chokes on his dinner!"

And at that the ladies tucked into the most scrumptious feast they'd had in a very long time. They shared dishes between them and *ooh*ed and *aah*ed at the different flavours. Tess's curry was as hot as she had requested and she had to order extra water to wash it down and Gina was delighted to have chosen the same as Polly. The King Prawns were fat, juicy and dripping with flavour.

By just after nine o'clock, they were resting back on their chairs, bellies full and wondering what to do next.

"I could sleep," said Gina.

"Me too," said Polly and she gave out a little yawn.

Ruth and Tess looked at each other in disgust.

"A brisk walk around town will put that notion out of the two of you," said Tess. "We didn't come here to sleep. Now, let Melanie's Way pay the bill and then we will go explore more. But before we do, for goodness' sake

emma heatherington

let's swap mobile numbers so that none of us gets lost again!"

"That's the most sensible thing I've heard all flippin' day!" said Ruth. "Let's make use of modern technology in the way God intended! Muppets!"

142

15

"No, no, no!" said Gina, stopping dead in her tracks. "I mean it. No. That's my worst nightmare. I'm simply not going in there!"

With the Chinese meal walked out of their system, yet still feeling a high buzz from alcohol, the girls were delighted to come across a bar just on the edge of town which advertised on a chalkboard: *King Kong's Karaoke To-Nite*.

All of them, that is, except Gina.

"I mean it. I can't stand karaoke. I had a bad experience in my twenties singing and I swore I'd never do it again. Please don't make me."

"Let's have a vote," said Tess, beginning to shiver now in her little white number. She wished she had brought a coat but she didn't have any to match her slinky little dress that made her look like a cross between a virgin and a sexy vamp – she was sexy and she knew it, even with goose bumps and a clear trickle under her perfect nose.

"I love karaoke," said Polly. "Sorry, Gina. I do. I never

143

have the courage to get up and sing but I love watching others. And you have an amazing voice! Remember that night at the clubhouse when you sang 'Like a Virgin'? You took the house down!"

"Yeah, watching others making a fool out of themselves and making noises they should only be making behind closed doors of their own home and then doing it myself!" said Gina. "Believe me, for reasons other than I wish to discuss, I will never forget that night!"

"Look, it's hardly like we're going to have a microphone forced down our throats," said Ruth. "I'm pretty easy. I say we go in for a while and if it's not our cuppa, we leave again. Simples."

"At last, someone with a bit of sense," said Tess, already through the door. "It's not as if we'll be locked in forever. Come on for the *craic*! I already know what I'm going to sing!"

"I bet you do!" said Polly, following her sister inside.

There was a cover charge of ten euro each and Ruth paid for it automatically.

"God bless you again, little horsie," said Gina when she was told to put her purse away. She kept forgetting about their big win since she had been otherwise occupied at the time of the race, which meant she kept being pleasantly surprised every time she was reminded that the night out was now to be totally on the house. Result!

Walking into the karaoke bar was like stepping back in time. It was carpeted in the wackiest combination of swirly colours including pink, yellow and green and Polly's head began to spin. Even the barman looked retro with his pink shirt and skinny black tie and the stools were one-legged silver dials that also span when you sat on them. King

Kong was giving it loads on the microphone and it wasn't hard to see where he got his name from. He was at least sixty years old, bald as a coot, with a huge body and a face that was as hairy as the top of his head should have been. Polly hated the place even more when she saw him.

"There's no one here," she said. "I'm sure there are other places that are less vomit-inducing!"

She had to shout over the dulcet tones of the karaoke master who was singing to a tiny empty wooden dance floor that was watched over by a ghastly UV light.

Gina saw an opportunity. She would put that horrible night with Trevor behind her and start enjoying life as it was. She would be the new Karaoke Queen and she would sing and dance her heart out if she wanted to!

"Watch this!" she said and she walked to the rhythm of the music onto the dance floor, dropped her handbag and danced around it. She glowed in places she had never glowed before and the girls laughed their heads off as she brushed off little dots of fluff from her glamorous dress.

"Ha! That reminds me of our clubland days!" said Polly. "Remember how embarrassed you'd be when your white bra showed through everything or worse, your knickers and all!"

Ruth danced her way to meet Gina and soon all four of them were circling their bags, unable to dance at times for laughing as they sang along to 'When Will I Be Famous?' and 'Robert de Niro's Waiting'.

Two cocktails later and Polly was feeling the urge to take the mike, but she would never admit it. Not yet anyhow.

"Three o'clock, three o'clock!" said Tess as they sipped their third Sex on the Beach in a little booth that had velvet green covers which totally clashed with the carpet.

145

The girls did a head-spin and their mouths dropped open when at least twenty men spilled into the bar, most of them looking a bit the worse for wear, with a very rugged, fit-as-hell ringleader who was wearing a T-shirt that said 'Stag Me Bitch' under a huge pair of antlers.

"Oh sweet divinity!" said Gina, and she lifted her straw to her mouth and took a long drink of the sweet liquid that she had fallen in love with. "A stag party! Woo hoo! Does his T-shirt say 'Shag Me Bitch'?"

"It says 'Stag Me Bitch'," said Polly. "But I think it means shag. How vulgar!"

"Dreams do come true," said Ruth, whose slanty eyes had become round and huge at the sight of so many virile young men. "It's like the Irish rugby team have entered the building! Oh God, I feel like playing Eenie Meenie Miney Mo! Where on earth would you begin to choose?"

"I told you we shouldn't have come here," said Polly, sinking further into the green-velvet seat. It smelled a little bit vinegary to her and she pictured the staff rubbing it with a dirty dishcloth which made her skin crawl. "This is going to be like a reverse version of that TV show Take Me Out! I'm afraid!"

Before they could say 'Karma Chameleon' (which was the song that was playing), Tess, Ruth and Gina had hit the wooden dance floor again with a vengeance as Polly watched in awe at how brazen they really were. This time there were no handbags in the centre or funky retro dance moves that brought them back in time. No, no, no. This was a show of all shows and they were shaking their money-makers as sexily as they could, even if King Kong was still stuck in an eighties time warp.

"You are being watched so badly!" said Gina to Tess

over the sounds of Boy George. "They can't take their eyes off you. The rest of us have no bloody hope when you're around!"

"Well, it's good for the ego!" said Tess. "But I only have eyes for my Rob. This is just a bit of fun. Believe me, I know my limits! They can look, but don't they dare touch!"

Ruth, on the other hand, hadn't noticed how Tess was centre of attention. She was in a world of her own, pouting and shaking her hips as if she was a Columbian babe like Shakira and not an overweight, divorced mother of two who was on the wrong side of thirty and who would look more at home at an underground Goth gathering than in an eighties karaoke bar!

Polly watched from afar from the vinegary seat with slight anger and slight envy. She wished she could be a bit more like Tess sometimes: assertive, gorgeous, self-confident and totally committed to her husband, yet not afraid to have a good time without feeling guilty. Tess was doing absolutely nothing wrong by dancing. What was wrong with dancing? Okay, so she knew she was making those men goggle-eyed, but it was back to the old saying *'If you've got it, flaunt it'* and that's all she was doing. She would never take it any further than that. Never. She loved her life with Rob too much to jeopardise it by doing anything so silly. But Polly would be ridden with guilt if she as much as walked past the stag party. She would definitely feel the need to go to confession if one of them even spoke to her or, worse, paid her a compliment!

She watched Ruth and Gina giggle and move around the floor like they were on *Top of The Pops*, like an oversized Pepsi and an undersized Shirley from the eighties. They too knew how to let their hair down, even

147

after all they had been through. Look at Gina – the victim of a monster who beat her to a pulp and openly flaunted his floozy on the side . . . and Ruth, whose ex gave her the good life with one hand and took it all away with the other while he got up to no good with his skinny little boyfriend.

So why did Polly find it so hard to go with the flow? Why did she have to be so stuffy and pious all the time? Why did she always feel so goddamn guilty about relaxing, even for one minute? Why did she always have to be so highly strung, as James told her on a daily basis? Why, why, why?

"Can I buy you a drink?"

Polly's guilt trip was interrupted when she heard a very deep, very raspy voice with a Belfast accent. She looked up to see the guy with the *Stag Me Bitch* T-shirt standing over her. She noticed how he looked drunk and a bit unsteady on his feet. She didn't notice his huge muscly arms or his gorgeous blue eyes but then why would she? She was a married woman. It was not her place to notice such things. He was a young man who had obviously had far too much to drink and he had no idea that he was talking to a thirty-something mother of three! He should be ashamed of himself! It's his stag do, Polly told herself. Stop being so bloody judgmental.

"A drink? *Me*? Aren't you getting married soon?" she said rather tartly, realising that her mouth acted a lot quicker than her brain. There she was again. Telling people off. Nagging someone she didn't even know!

"In two weeks," said the Stag Boy and he swayed slightly to the music. "I only asked you if you wanted a drink. I didn't ask you to run away with me to Outer Mongolia and never come back, and I certainly didn't expect to be met with an answer my mother would give me! Sorry for disturbing you! You just looked a bit lonely, that's all!"

He left to turn away and Polly stood up.

"Wait!" she called. "Please wait! Mr Stag Boy! Wait!"

Stag turned around very, very slowly so as not to spill his glass of vodka that slapped and slurped around in his glass. His T-shirt was stained at the back, Polly noticed. Red wine perhaps? Or a big dollop of ketchup? Or worse, could it be blood? She wondered if it would come out in the wash. Stop! she told herself again. Stop with the domestic shit for once!

"I'd love to have a drink," she said, raising her chin and pulling her shoulders back. "I was miles away when you asked. I'm sorry. I'm so sorry for being rude."

See? This was normal. And it was just a drink. It was just a drink!

"Cool," he said. "I'm going to the loo first. Meet me at the bar in two."

Polly slumped back down on the seat and let out a sigh as she watched Stag disappear into the tiny toilet cubicle at the far end of the bar. Ruth was still grooving and grinding to the beat on the dance floor, Tess was still swinging her hips and licking her lips much to the stag party's delight and Gina was trying her best to keep to the rhythm in between asking King Kong to play some Wham! at every given opportunity.

So this is what the single life would be like, eh? Getting drunk, dancing your legs off, meeting strange men and getting to know them for one night only. It was like the old days when she and her sisters would hit the town with the aim of getting pissed on cheap cider and having enough money left to buy a burger on the way home with change in your pocket for a taxi and a handsome guy left behind with your number.

This was exactly the same, only she was much older now. She wasn't *old* and she didn't *feel* old, but the *idea* was old. It was out of date. It was in her past. Tonight was the same format as back then only now she had a bit more money, a bit more sense and the knowledge in the back of her mind that something just didn't sit right about this scene. Something about it all felt way out of place. Something in her head told her that this was never going to be the life for her. Drinking in bars with young men wasn't really her idea of letting her hair down but, for now, well, Stag was approaching and she would try, just try, to ease off the punishment-beating that she constantly gave herself in a bid to be perfect for everyone else.

So she followed Stag to the bar and tried to ignore how much she was shaking inside and out when he asked for her name.

"I'm Polly," she said. "Polly Knox."

When she said her surname, the guilt rose in her throat and she felt it choking her. Relax, relax, she repeated in her head. It's just a drink. It's just a bit of fun on a girly night out.

"You are a very sexy lady, Polly," said Stag and he leaned in towards her. Either he leaned, or he stumbled, she wasn't sure. "What would you like to drink? Let me treat you to a cock . . . a cocktail of my choice."

Polly's stomach gave a huge leap when he said 'cock'. She was astounded and hoped the expression on her face before he said 'cocktail' hadn't told him so.

"Oh . . . okay," she muttered and waited until the

barman served up two concoctions that looked way too bright in colour for human consumption.

"I'll race you to the bottom," he whispered into her ear. "One – two – three!"

"Go!" she said and to her surprise she was laughing at the challenge. This was fun.

"Wow, that was fast!" said Stag. "Best out of three?"

"You're on," said Polly, leaning up against the bar. A group of younger girls were assembling nearby but this hot young stud had eyes and ears only for her and it made her feel so good inside.

After the third cocktail, she thought she was going to choke with laughter as she pondered what drink they could experiment with next. He was a very funny guy and his hand was resting on her waist now. She should ask him to move it but they were practically best friends by this stage. Surely putting his hand on her waist wasn't a crime!

"Polly!" Tess hissed from behind her sister's shoulder moments later. "Polly, can you come with me for a second?"

Polly ignored Tess. Following the cocktails, she was on her first vodka shot with Stag (she still didn't know his real name but she loved how he smiled when she called him Stag). He had an amazing smile. Just – just perfect – and he smiled a lot. Next shot down the hatch? Don't mind if I do! They were having a great laugh! A great laugh altogether! Stag had just told her a hilarious story about . . . about . . . well, she had no idea what they were talking about but it was very funny. Something about a goat and a sheep and . . . no, she had no idea. Hilarious though.

"Polly!"

Tess dragged her sister away from Stag by the arm and whispered in her ear. "Come back and sit with us! Come on. Right now! You're making a show of yourself with that boy."

"A show of myself? How dare you! I'm just having fun!" said Polly, making faces back at Stag who couldn't take his eyes off her.

"Enough is enough," said Tess. "Now walk."

"No, Tess! No!" said Polly in sheer defiance. "I'm letting my hair down! I'm having fun! Isn't that what I'm always told to do these days? Be more fun, Polly! Stop always nagging, Polly! Stop telling everyone what to do as if they are your children, Polly! Well, now I'm doing it and you are treating *me* like a child. Now, let go of my arm!"

Tess let go. She looked over at Stag and back at Polly.

"Just be careful, okay?" she said. "We've all had a lot to drink. It's perfectly okay for Ruth and Gina to flirt their asses off and talk about sex with strangers and do whatever it is they want to do. They have made their decisions within their marriage. But you haven't. Please don't let a drunken night out make your decision for you."

"You'd think I was snogging the face off him!" said Polly. She winked across at him. He really was cute even if he needed a good wash.

"Two minutes later and I fear that's exactly what you would have been doing," said Tess. "You were so close, Polly! So close!"

Tess walked back to her seat and Polly watched her until she reached the other two who were now joined by another member of the infamous stag party. He was sitting in between Ruth and Gina and was obviously enjoying the attention he was getting from two, very horny, very drunk women who were at least ten years older than he was and therefore lots more experienced in life.

Polly took a step in their direction. She really should follow Tess. Then she looked across at Stag again and took a step towards him. Then back to Tess. Then back to Stag, but by now he was talking to his mates and then two girls who were barely out of their teens in very short skirts joined their company and his eyes locked onto their legs, then ran up their tiny perfect figures and landed on their chests.

"Hey!" she called but he couldn't hear her over the King Kong Karaoke Fest. Or if he did, he didn't answer.

All of a sudden, Polly felt a bit silly. But then, what had she been expecting from him in the first place? A man on her arm for the rest of the night? A man who was about to enter the jungle of marriage himself to flatter her so she could feel good about herself and feel that she was still capable of having fun? A man who hadn't a clue of the ups and downs and highs and lows of the commitment he was about to enter, but who was out for one last night of fun for the hell of it?

She felt herself sway a little. The booze was really going to her head. How could she have been so stupid? She wondered how close she really had been to making a very silly, very drunken mistake! Far too close for comfort!

"Slide on, Stag Boy," she mumbled and made her way back to her own territory. She had to thank her sister! She had to get away from Stag now and thank Tess who had just rescued her from potentially ruining her life for one drunken moment of flattery from a stranger who would either boast about her or totally deny her within seconds of their parting.

"Tess, you are an angel and I love you!" she said and Tess eyeballed her in the 'I told you so' way that only Tess could do. "Let's sing a song! It can be your choice. You know me. You may *be* an angel, but I have the *voice* of an angel. I can sing anything! Name that tune!"

Tess looked down the list in front of her that had King Kong's ugly mug (clearly Photo-shopped to death) at the top of it.

"'Sisters are Doin' It For Themselves'," she said within seconds.

"It's a no-brainer!" said Polly. "You really are the best!"

"I know I am. Now, let's have a sing-off and leave these two to drool over their latest conquest. And then you and I are going to have a good boogie and remember that you don't need a strange man to tell you how beautiful you are. We both have one of those at home and, despite their faults, life just wouldn't be the same without them."

"So, what do you do for a living, Ruth?"

Ruth had stepped outside for a breath of fresh air and had somehow attracted the attention of the only sober person in the whole nightclub. She, however, was pissed. She was feeling really nauseous now as the cocktails were taking their toll and the chicken fried rice from earlier was threatening to make its second appearance of the evening.

"What do I do for a living? You're very polite for someone who is out on the razz on a stag!" said Ruth. She was focusing now. Really focusing.

Polly and Tess were still having some sort of sibling-bonding session on the dance floor after their karaoke debut which actually wasn't too bad all things considered.

They were dancing their hearts out, hugging each other lots and giving the karaoke guy strict instructions as to what to play in between the stag boys and others taking their turn on the mike.

Ruth had slipped a kitty behind the bar so that each of the girls could order their own drinks as they liked and she had tipped the barman a healthy fifty quid to look after it honestly. She didn't really give a shit if he did or not. They were all so pissed now that she didn't really care and they hardly needed any more alcohol.

"I don't drink," said the guy who was insisting on striking up conversation. "Not any more."

He had joined her only minutes ago at a very dodgy time when she thought the pavement was moving right up to meet her.

"Really?" said Ruth. "At this present moment in time, I can't say I blame you. If you had asked me half an hour ago I would have called you a freak, but right now I can only be very, very jealous because I really wish I was more sober. Oh God, oh God, oh God!" Her stomach heaved into a very near miss.

"I used to drink a lot," said Mr Chatterbox. He was sucking now on a menthol cigarette.

Ruth was going to ask him not to smoke but then it was a public street and it wasn't his fault she was pissed as a fart and about to vomit rings round her.

"Really?" she said again. It was all she could muster. She *was* listening, she really was, but she couldn't really offer a lot to the conversation. Besides, she was doing him a favour by concentrating on not puking her very curried rice all over him.

"I had some bad times," he said. "Really, really low. Can't

155

believe it now. It's funny how when you look back . . . you know, my ma kicked me out of the house and everything. I had nowhere to go. I sofa-surfed for a while with some mates but soon they got pissed off and if it wasn't for Bert saving me, I don't know where I'd be right now."

"Good ole Bert!" said Ruth. She really was struggling now. "Whoever he is. May he be rewarded by the angels in heaven."

"He's my bestie," said the boy.

She realised he was just a boy when he used the word 'bestie'. Surely a man would never come out with that? She didn't have the strength or the energy to lift her head to see his face.

"What's your name again?" she asked. She was curious now, even in her drunken daze. Here was a young guy who was out with a crowd of drunken eejits and he'd managed to refuse a drink all night. Fair play to the lad. She didn't think she would ever be so disciplined. Ever.

"Christian," he said.

"Of course it is!" said Ruth. What else would he be called with high morals like that? Hardly Lucifer or Damien, that's for sure!

"I just threw myself into horse-racing after that," said the holy one. "Turned my whole life around, so it did. Only for Bert and horse-racing and the love of God I'd be a screwed-up mess by now. Might even have called it quits. I was suicidal, you know."

"Hic . . . horse-racing?" asked Ruth, looking at the boy with one eye closed and one open. Oh no, the vomit! The vomit!

"Aye. My da said it was the making of me. Someday I hope to ride in the Grand National. I want to be just like my hero, Spencer Baker. He won today. A horse called Melanie's Way. He's a beauty, that horse – and Spencer Baker, well, he's simply the best jockey in the world."

"Spencer? Spencer . . . *beurrrrrghh*!" And Ruth emptied the contents of her stomach all over the pavement at the sound of Spencer Baker's name. The recycled chicken fried rice and spring rolls splashed over her shoes and over young Christian the wannabe jockey, so badly that she thought she heard him whimper. She tried again to apologise but again the vomit lashed out and again and again until all she had left was a dry mouth, soggy feet and the vilest smell she could ever imagine all around her.

Cocktails, white wine, shots, Chinese . . . not a nice combination at all when you meet it at the other side.

"Fuck," she said to the boy. "Can you be an extra-good Christian and call me a taxi? Pretty please?"

"Er, yeah," said Christian. "You had a lot of stuff in your stomach. That's the most vomit I've ever seen in my whole life!"

"No shit, Sherlock," said Ruth. "Just a taxi. Please."

16

Gina was beginning to feel a bit weepy as the evening grew to a close. The young guy from the stag party who was still trying to chat her up was beginning to get on her nerves now. She wasn't interested and she had made that very clear without being rude but if he pushed it much further she would have to tell him, very politely of course, to piss away off.

She'd already had her man-fix for the day and she didn't really care if this young cub whose name was Tiernan thought she looked like a young Audrey Hepburn or if he couldn't believe she was over thirty or if he thought she would make a great kisser. His name said it all – she really liked the name Tiernan and some of her friends had children called Tiernan. But she didn't know anyone over the age of twenty-one with that name. He was just a baby – just a boy. He was almost young enough to be her son. She tried to do the maths in her head which was quite difficult at that moment in time, Tiernan was breathing down her neck and she pushed him away, wondering what her own little man was doing back at his gran's.

She really missed her son. Her precious Danny Boy. She blanked out King Kong Karaoke's droning in the background and started to hum the famous song to herself. She used to sing it to Danny to get him to sleep. She still did sometimes. He would be fast asleep by now, she hoped, all tucked up in his gran's spare room. He was a good boy. Nothing really ever annoyed Danny. He never complained about the way his dad flitted in and out of his life. He never complained about finding his mum with another bruise or about the noise when things got hot and heavy when it was past his bedtime. He didn't even complain when he had to learn how to inject himself twice a day with insulin to control his diabetes.

Danny never complained at all. Gina just wanted to be with him right now. She wanted to hug him and tell him he was a brave boy who was going to go on to do wonderful things for others when he was older. She pictured him as a passionate, tireless charity worker . . . someone who would make a real difference to humanity. Her son was unique like that. He was a special boy. But he would be asleep by now and he wouldn't know she was thinking of him. She would see him in the morning. She would never leave him again. He would be fast asleep.

But what if he wasn't? What if he was playing his Xbox that he'd insisted on taking with him for his big overnight stay and worrying about stuff but using the video game as a mask? Or maybe he was . . . maybe he was sad and lonely and was wondering what on earth was going on and was lying in bed staring at the ceiling and afraid to tell his gran in case he upset her? Maybe he was wondering why Daddy had disappeared and why Mummy had gone away with Polly and her sister for the night and was wondering if they would ever come back? Oh, she wanted to be with him now so badly! She wanted to hold him close and tell him everything was going to be okay. Everything *was* going to be okay, she had no doubt about that, but right now she wanted to be back at home and starting to make it so. She didn't want to be in some back-in-time nightclub in County Donegal with its dizzy carpet, surrounded by strangers who didn't give a shit about her life and who only wanted into her knickers for the night because in their drunken eyes she looked like Audrey Hepburn and might make a good kisser!

She looked at her phone to check the time. It was still only eleven forty-five and yet she felt like it was three in the morning. It had been a long, long day. Enjoyable in every way. Crazy too. And then there was Marco!

Marco had been different, she tried to convince herself. She would not beat herself up about her crazy early-evening fling with a stranger. She had known what she was doing. He had known exactly what she needed and he didn't mind giving her her way. He was her then, this was her now.

Gina stood up and Tiernan slumped down onto the booth. He had obviously been leaning on her to keep himself upright. When she staggered, she realised that she too had been leaning on him for support. She really was drunk.

"Silly boy," she said to him. "I bet your mother is worried sick about you. If that was my Danny . . ."

She wrapped her arms around her own waist and grabbed at the sides of her dress. What was she doing here? Why was she all dressed up in a town she didn't know when her whole life was falling to pieces? She should be at home sorting everything out, not running away from it all and sleeping with strangers to help her pretend that this wasn't happening! She felt totally out of place. She shouldn't be here. She was a mother. She had responsibilities.

The music seemed extra loud and the bar had become quite crowded now with hordes of scantily clad young girls pumping and grinding on the dance floor. King Kong was on a break and the new DJ had jumped the pace with his heavy beats and throbbing bass in songs that Gina had never heard before. They seemed to have the word 'mutha-fucka' on repeat, making her feel even more out of place.

She wanted to go back to the hotel immediately. She wanted to take off her make-up and her dress which now felt grubby and worn. She wanted a hot shower and to slip into her cosy jammies and cuddle up under fresh bedclothes until she woke up in the morning knowing that getting back to her son was a step closer.

"Shots at the bar!" said Polly who had taken on a whole new lease of life during her time on the dance floor. "Shots at the bar! Come on, Melanie's Way! Giddy up, giddy up, for vodka shots at the bar!"

"Not on your life, Polly," said Gina. "You go ahead but I swear I'm ready for the road. I couldn't look at another drink if you paid me millions to. Speaking of paying for stuff, where the hell is Ruth?"

She was nowhere to be seen. Polly, Tess and Gina all searched in their handbags for their phones to check if she had sent any messages and, if not, to try and get in touch with her.

Tess found hers first.

"Boked everywhere. Not good. See you back at hotel.

Party on, dudes!" read Tess. "Oh dear. I wonder should one of us go back and see that she's okay?"

"Maybe we all should?" said Gina. "We've had such a lovely day and such a fun night. It might be the right time to try and make our way back and that music is getting on my nerves, plus I can hardly see past my own nose. I'm hammered."

Polly, who was just a little bit more wobbly on her feet than earlier, squinted at her watch.

"It's only twelve o'clock!" she said. "No way, José! I'm only starting to loosen up now. You two go back if you want. I'm ready to *parrrr-tayyyy*!"

"I'll go back to the hotel," said Gina. "You stay with your sister. I really don't mind. In fact I was going to suggest that anyhow."

"Are you sure?" asked Tess. "No, that's not very fair. I don't think you should go back by yourself and we *could* call it a night . . ."

"Yeah, I'm happy to do that," said Gina, lifting her handbag.

"But, having said that," said Tess, "Karaoke King Kong is just about to come back on and he has promised me he would play a bit of Wham! just for you. It would be a terrible shame to miss it after the amount of convincing it took him to even find it on his collection!"

Gina looked over at Karaoke King Kong who was giving her the 'okay' sign with one hand and holding his headphones on with the other as he took his place back on the decks. He thought he was shit cool. He wasn't.

"You are having me on!" said Gina, feeling a shot of adrenaline pump through her tired veins at the very thought of hearing her George singing in a nightclub. "He is actually going to play it? Oh my God . . . George? For me? I can't leave yet then!"

Gina's sense of responsibility wavered as she thought of her teenage idol. No one understood Gina's love for George Michael. Not even her own mother, God rest her, who had to endure constant tape recordings and video recordings every time he came on the telly for years and years, and constant playing of his LPs and cassettes on Gina's little pink HiFi system in her bedroom. Gina had a George Michael schoolbag, a George Michael duvet and pillow set (which she kissed every night, sometimes a little bit too passionately for her own liking) and her bedroom was plastered from floor to ceiling with posters of her icon. George Michael was her number one guy and no man would ever live up to him, ever.

"He's gay," her brother Tim would say.

"You're gay!" she would say back. Turned out she was right with that one. Tim now was well and truly 'out' and had a different man every turn around.

When George Michael did eventually 'come out', she had cried for weeks but then she forgave him and decided that she would just have to settle with being his best friend forever. Her love for George was too strong to just dump him because he didn't like women, and to be honest, she was glad because she would have been terribly jealous if he had ever married some skinny supermodel. Men were fine. She could cope with that.

It had been more than twenty-five years since she had danced to his music at the school disco. By the time she was hitting real nightclubs, George had turned a different corner so to speak and when he made his comeback she had been stuck at home changing nappies and watching him on MTV.

"I can't believe he's going to play it! But we go after George?" she said. "Deal?"

"Deal!" said Tess. "He is playing a double set, just for you! I told him I'd snog him if he did."

"*What?*" said Polly, disgusted. "I may be drunk, but don't think I didn't hear that!"

"I'm joking!" said Tess. "Jesus, you need to learn to lighten up!"

Gina fanned her face with her clutch bag. The excitement was too much to bear.

Just then, the opening lines of 'Wake Me Up Before You Go Go' filled the air and Gina closed her eyes, absorbing every beat.

"Will we dance or sing?" asked Tess. "King Kong with the big dong said he would give us the microphone, or he would sing it for us."

"I think it's time I learned to sing again!" said Gina. She would do it! She would sing her heart out as a big two fingers up to the life she had suffered through since the last time she sang. This was the beginning of something new and she would mark it by singing one of her favourite songs in the whole world!

"Okay, you sing and we'll dance!" said Polly, still stung by Tess's 'lighten up' comment. She would prove her wrong should she have to snog King Kong herself.

"You girls are the best!" said Gina and within a jitterbug heartbeat they had shoved Karaoke King Kong out of the way and had taken the place by storm.

"I'm pissed as a fart," said Tess when they finally stumbled off the dance floor and back over to the vinegar booth where Baby Tiernan was fast asleep. They squeezed in around him and sat swaying to the music, not wanting to admit that they really couldn't take any more.

"I'm pissed as forty farts," said Polly. Her eyes were glazed now and she had to squint to see. She was a mess. A terrible mess altogether. Imagine if James saw her now! He would be so ashamed of her.

"There's only one thing worse than a drunken man, Polly," he would say to her if she ever got more than slightly tipsy.

"And what's that?" she would ask.

"A drunken woman."

Oh fuck it, she thought! James wasn't here, he wasn't going to see her, this was a one-off and she would probably never, ever do it again and, besides, it's not as if she had been in any trouble or offended anyone, was it? She was 'lightened up'. She was drunk, she was merry and apart from feeling dizzy and have to squint to avoid seeing double, she was fine. Just fine.

Gina couldn't really speak at all. Every time she tried to, it sounded like gibberish and she felt like her mouth was full of suds. All that dancing and the last shot that Polly had insisted on in between George tracks had made the alcohol swirl around her bloodstream all the more and she was afraid to stand up. Putting one foot in front of the other was going to be a huge challenge. She clumsily took off her shoes and slumped her head down on the table in front of her. Surely a snooze would help? Just five minutes of shut-eye to stop the room from spinning. Then she would be fine. She would be just fine.

"We need to get out of here," said Polly and then she started to giggle.

"What?" asked Tess. Her eyes felt so heavy and were fighting against her attempts to keep them open.

"You look so funny!" said Polly. "You look really dopey and I can see two of you, *ha ha*! Two Tesses! As if one Tess isn't bad enough! There are two – no wait, there's another one! Three!"

Tess gave a lazy smirk. She was too drunk to laugh. She needed her bed.

"Well, you look like the Bride of Frankenstein," she said. "Your mascara is like a river down the sides of your face and you look . . . oh I can't even be bothered. Come on. Taxi."

Polly stood up and breathed deeply through her nose and out through her mouth, in through her nose and out through her mouth. *Concrentate, concentrate, concentrate.* She remembered James teaching her that exercise when they would go out and get terribly drunk in the early pre-children days and she would always be the first to fade and to complain that she felt sick.

He had stood with her on many occasions, holding back her hair as she threatened to puke up her breakfast, lunch and dinner in front of him. How attractive! No wonder he hated her having any more than two glasses of wine these days. She couldn't handle it any more.

She nudged Gina who was almost comatose on the table. Polly really couldn't take any more of this. She wanted out of there and she wanted out now and she never wanted to see another shot or glass of wine in her life again. She felt wobbly and woozy and totally out of control.

"Gina? Gina, love, come on! We need to get a taxi! Gina!"

Tess was flopping about like an impatient schoolgirl. She was becoming irritable. Alcohol did that to her. She was what Rob called a 'twister' when she drank. She was opinionated enough in sobriety but, with a few drinks in her, she could have a tongue like a viper and had often been forced to apologise to others the morning after the night before by having too much to say. She was careful not to drink around the village of Cranmore! Imagine how her reputation would suffer if she called the parish priest who adored her a dirty rotten pervert or if she told her principal that she'd flash her boobs at him if he gave her a promotion!

"Oh, we should have gone earlier when she suggested," she said. "And I think I've broke my wee toe. Ruth stood on it earlier on the dance floor and it's throbbing."

Tess picked up Gina's shoes from the floor and, realising that doing the same might solve her toe problem, she slipped off her stilettos and carried them too.

"Gina! *Gina*!" called Polly. It was like trying to wake the dead.

"What, what, what?" said Gina eventually, wiping dribble from her mouth. "God, where am I? Where's Danny? I want Danny!"

She slumped back on to the back of the booth and her little pixie-like head swung from side to side.

"*Ohhhhh* . . . I want to go home!" she moaned and then she started to cry. "I'm sorry, Trevor. I want to go home now. Ten years! Ten years we were married. Trevor!"

Tess and Polly looked at each other with concern. Ruth had got the vomits, Gina had got the tears and Tess had got the injury to her toe. Three inevitable parts of a big night out. Poor Gina. She had so much ahead of her, she

167

had no idea. This was probably only the beginning of a long road to recovery from her marriage breakdown.

There was nothing else for it. Gina was not going to move from that seat unless she was escorted. Without discussing it, Tess took one arm and Polly took the other and they hauled Gina up from the booth then pulled her arms around their shoulders so that they could bear her weight. She slumped between them and her legs folded underneath her like an accordion. This was going to be difficult. Very difficult indeed.

They managed to force her to get her legs under her again, by dint of shouting at her and shaking her awake, and then they staggered towards the door, Gina hardly helping them support her weight at all.

Polly felt very stupid when they had to pass Stag and his mates at the bar. She could hear them snigger and then they began to chant like hooligans on a football terrace.

"*Cheerio, cheerio, cheerio!*"

"*You're drunk, you're drunk, you silly wee skunk!*" sang another.

"Don't worry about it, ladies," shouted Stag. "You're only young once!"

And the rest of the lads laughed their heads off, big belly laughs that came from the pit of their beer-filled tummies.

Tess stopped and glared at them. Man, but she wanted to give them the middle finger so badly but, hanging on to Gina's arm with one hand and carrying her shoes in the other, instead she had to settle for a very childish tongue-stick-out which made her feel even more frustrated. God love the next person to pass comment on them tonight! Didn't they know she was a teacher? Didn't they realise she was a respected member of the community and that her gorgeous husband was too? He was a fireman! He was a life-saving public servant! How dare they belittle Tess and her friends on a night out! Immature little bastards!

"Oh dear!" said a burly bouncer who seemed to appear from nowhere with a short-ass side-kick when they stepped outside. "Too much to drink at your age? Not a pretty sight."

Tess stopped as if she had pulled on the brakes, much to Polly's despair. They had finally developed a rhythm to their weaving walk and now they would have to start all over again!

"You cheeky fucker!" said Tess. Oh, he was in trouble. He had no idea what trouble he was in. "Why don't you just focus on doing your job and leave the smart comments behind? I could report you for coming out with that."

"Report me?" said the bouncer.

He was chewing gum like it was going out of fashion, stank of cigarette smoke and cheap aftershave and he wore a snarky grin that made Tess want to knock his lights out. And as for his stumpy colleague? He would get it too if he didn't shut his mouth – he laughed way too high-pitched for her liking!

"Yes! *Report* you!" she spat, realising she was sounding like one of her pupils involved in a schoolyard rant. "Are you deaf?"

"Report me for what? And to who?" he asked. He looked at the three of them up and down, up and down, as if they were scum.

To *who*? Good question . . . Tess scrambled for an answer. She hadn't really thought of who she would report him to.

"To your management," she said. "Or to the Society of Bouncers!"

"'The Society of Bouncers!'" He let out a huge guffaw. "Oi, Mickey! Are you a member of the Society of Bouncers 'cause this one says she will report us?"

"You mean the *Official* Society of Bouncers?" shouted Mickey, wiping tears from his eyes as he laughed. "Sure, I'm the President. Report us for what, Missy?"

"For being ageist!" said Tess, fearing she was losing her case the more she tried to speak. "Just because we can't walk doesn't mean we're drunk, you know! I am injured if you must know! My toe is on fire! It might even be broken!"

She could have kicked herself for coming out with such nonsense. They were all rat-arsed, pissed, wrote off, whatever you wanted to call it. They were a mess. They were a disgrace. But she didn't need some jumped-up asshole in a dickey-bow to remind her of the fact! She hated doormen at nightclubs almost as much as she hated traffic wardens. It was like the authority had gone to their big fat heads and they just thrived on any excuse to pull you up on something. She wouldn't let him away with it.

"Off you go home to the babies, Mummies," he said, lighting up a cigarette and blowing the smoke into the cool night air without making any further eye contact. "I'm sure Daddy is fed up baby-sitting by now!"

Mummies? *Mummies*? Tess was livid! She was not a mummy! She was an independent glamorous career woman who would not be categorised by this dickhead in his jazzy shirt and tie!

"*What* did you just say?" she asked, trying her best to stand up straight which was proving very difficult with half of Gina's weight depending on her. Gina was a tiny little thing but, boy, she was heavy after a while, especially when being led by Dumb and Dumber!

"What's wrong with being a mummy?" snapped Polly. "Only for your mother you wouldn't even be here, you prick!"

"Prick!" mumbled Gina, who was slowly coming back to life. Slowly.

"Never mind," said the bouncer. "Taxi shouldn't be long."

"You said to go home to our babies, didn't you, you smarmy git?" said Tess. "God love the woman who ever has your babies! You'd be lucky if you even got a ride in the first place!"

She was seething. She could feel her insides burn and the rage pumped through her more and more when she looked at his pompous acne-scarred face. He looked her up and down and then licked his thin lips before taking another draw from his cigarette.

"Well, I have no problem in that department," he said, patting between his legs. "I could have a different woman every night, especially when they get into the state you girls are in. I could have anyone!"

"Well, whoever you'd get, she'd need to be more than drunk! She'd need to be blind or deaf or both to put up with your bad manners if that's how you speak to women!" said Tess. She knew she should just walk away but he had a face that was in dire need of a good slap. A face only his mother could love.

"Look, lady, move along and get into your bed," said the bouncer. "Just as well you're already wearing your nightie! You're only asking for trouble if you go out like that!"

Tess looked over at stumpy Mickey who was enjoying this little show to the full.

"And as for you, short-ass," said Tess. "You couldn't get a turn at a roundabout!"

Mickey spat on the pavement and then stubbed out his cigarette.

"Hey, Joe," he said. "All this coming from mutton dressed as lamb! Maybe that term MILF is dead and gone! Chase them back to *Cougar Town*!"

That was it. Tess let go of Gina who fell into a drunken slump and Polly caught her just in time. She took her stiletto in her right hand and swung it at the bouncers who ducked and the shoe bashed up against one of the small panes of the window of the bar.

"Tess! Stop!" squealed Polly. "Don't rise to him. He's not worth it!"

"He said I was lamb dressed as mutton," she slurred. "He is not getting away with that! I have a gorgeous husband who thinks I'm sex on legs!"

The bouncer ducked again and laughed as her second shoe missed him and bounced off the window again.

Tess grabbed Gina's shoes from Polly's hands and flung them, quick as lightning and this time she hit the first guy, Joe, full whack in the chest.

"Charming," he said, still wearing the same grin and his colleague sniggered beside him. He casually lifted the shoes and handed them back to Tess. "Want another go? I should charge for this sort of entertainment."

Tess felt like doing a war dance or throwing a childish tantrum right there on the pavement. He was enticing her! He was laughing at her! No one ever laughed at her! No one since Ruth Monaghan back at school! She hated bullies! She would not let him away with it.

She flung a shoe with double force this time and the

172

bouncer coolly stepped out of the firing line and let it hit the window. The sound of breaking glass was one that Tess would not forget for a long, long time but the sound of the police siren that followed soon after, as they stood there gaping, was even more memorable.

"Oh fuck!" said Polly.

"Oh *fuck*!" said Tess, covering her mouth with her hands. "*Shit!*"

"Looks like *you* have been reported," said the bouncer and he put his hands in his pockets and began to whistle. Then, as if he saw it all the time, he turned to his colleague. "Have this cleaned up, Mickey, before someone is injured. Stupid drunken women."

He kicked bits of glass across the pavement and shook his head, still smirking and knowing that, once again, he had won when affronted by people who'd had one too many.

Tess could feel her heart thump in her chest. She wanted to kill him. She couldn't believe he had riled her so much but there was no way she would let anyone speak to her or belittle her friends like that. She breathed in and out, in and out, as the squad car braked to a halt. She could hear them radio through to the station and she wanted to cry. But she wouldn't. Not a pup's chance.

"Tess, are you okay?" said Polly. "You broke the window!"

"Oh, tell me something I don't know!" hissed Tess. Talk about declaring the obvious! Sometimes Polly was so bloody thick!

"Ladies," said one of the police who was putting on his cap as he spoke, "would anyone like to tell me what is going on here?"

"Is she in trouble?" asked Polly. Tess might be all bravado, but she was about to cry.

"Why don't we have a little chat and find out?"

He took out his notebook and Polly felt like she might faint.

17

"I need you to talk to me," said the policeman.

Tess was being very quiet but every time Polly tried to explain, she was told by her sister to shut up.

"Don't you dare touch me!" said Tess when the policeman stepped closer. He was a young man, possibly around her age and he looked mightily pissed off.

"He's gorgeous!" said Gina, and Polly covered Gina's mouth to prevent them getting into any more trouble. "Cop-alicious!"

"That bastard started it!" said Tess, pointing her shoe at Joe the bouncer. "He said we were lamb dressed as mutton."

"Mutton dressed as lamb, you mean!" said Polly. She hated when people got sayings the wrong way round.

"Oh, shut up, you! I am not discussing this any further, officer!" shouted Tess in defiance. "I am getting into a taxi and I am leaving this place and never coming back, ever in my whole legged life!"

"Make sure your legs can work if you ever do come

back," said Joe and he winked at the cop who seemed to know him.

"See! See!" said Tess. "He started this!"

"Come along now!" said the policeman.

"I am not going anywhere apart from to my hotel!"

"I think you'll find that it's not as simple as that," said the policeman. "I need to take a statement from you. You broke a window and assaulted a doorman. You can't just walk away, I'm afraid."

He was calm and he spoke quietly in comparison to Tess's high-pitched, hysterical tone. She could feel tears prick her eyes but she wouldn't cry. She wouldn't cry!

"I don't believe this!" she said. "Do you know who I am? I cannot just give you a *statement*! Who knows what that will lead to? I have never been in trouble in my whole life!"

The policeman rolled his eyes like he had heard it all before.

"No, I don't know who you are," he said, "but I will need you to tell me who you are – in fact, when we get to the station you will have to give me a lot more information than that."

He flashed a badge at her. His first name was Simon. She normally liked people called Simon. She didn't like him at all.

"What? *What*! When I get to *what* station?" Tess really was going to cry now. "I am *not* getting into a police car! My husband is a fireman, you know! He serves the community just as much as you do and he will go mental when he hears this nonsense! He is six foot three! He is stronger than you! And that asshole enticed me! He started it."

"Just step into the car, ma'am."

"Get out of my face!" said Tess.

"Tess, just do what the man says. Don't cause any more trouble," said Polly. Her mouth was filling up with salty saliva. She was so going to puke and she was trying her best to hold it back. Plus her legs were like jelly. She really did feel faint. Gina was like a dead weight hanging off her.

"I will not do what *anyone* says!" said Tess.

"Maybe that's your bloody problem!" said Polly. She was really tiring of Tess's stubbornness. It was a good trait most of the time, but sometimes she took it too far. Like she was doing now. "If you had just kept your mouth shut we wouldn't be in this situation!"

"*We*? I don't see you being asked to get into a squad car! As always, Perfect Polly comes out smelling of roses and good old Tess with too much to say gets into trouble! Some things never change!"

"Oh, here we go!" said Polly. She shrugged Gina off her. Sod it. She would have to learn how to stand up unless she wanted her dress covered in vomit which was coming very, very soon. Polly needed to focus on her own fragile wellbeing.

"I have to go through all this and I may have broken a toe! It's a hospital I need to go to, not a bloody police station! I am *not* getting into that car!"

"Ma'am, unless you give me a full statement here and now, you would be advised to get into the –"

"No! You can't make me! No one can make me! I have rights, you know! Don't you dare touch me! Don't touch me!"

The policeman put his hand on her shoulder once again and she shrugged him off in bad temper.

"You have the right to remain silent –"

"*Piss off! No way!*" she screamed. "I've watched the movies! I know what that means! Are you for fucking real?"

"You have the right to remain silent. You do not have to say anything, but –"

What the hell was he on about? He couldn't arrest her! His voice was a fuzzy blur and Tess's head was spinning round and round and round. She thought that she might faint now too. She thought she might be sick. Polly was just standing there swaying and Gina was sitting like a rag doll on the pavement as a member of staff from the bar brushed broken glass around her.

The policeman was still talking but Tess couldn't hear a thing. He might as well have been singing the National Anthem for all she knew. What was she going to do? Rob would kill her for this! He would be so embarrassed – and what about her parents and her sisters? Or Rob's stuffy parents! Oh God! And her job? She might never work again! She had never heard of a teacher being arrested and then staying in their job! This was enough to ruin her! All because of some jumped-up security guy who thought he could talk to women whatever way he wanted just because he wore an ear-piece and a stupid cheap suit!

She had to get away. She had to get away now. She simply could not let this happen. She looked over the policeman's shoulder. She would run. Yes, she would run and he would never catch her up! She was a cross-country champion, you know! She would run and run like Forrest Gump and the cop would give up and go find a real criminal who really deserved to be arrested.

She dropped her shoes. Her toe was so sore. She

couldn't let it stop her. She had to at least try. Her eyes darted around her. She would go after three. Yes – it was her only option. She didn't have any other options. She had to run. One . . . two . . . three! And she was off!

"*Oi!*" called the policeman. "Come back! *Oi!*"

Tess ran and ran, the pain in her right baby toe making her feel like she was being stabbed with every step she took but she couldn't stop, not if her toe fell off was she stopping! No way!

"*Tess!*" called Polly. "Tess, don't be so bloody stupid! Come back here now!"

But Tess couldn't hear her. She was staying focused. She was back in the Cross Country Championship final where the one thing that drove her on was the sheer blind determination that no one would ever get the better of her. She would never be beaten. Not then and not now.

"*Arrrgh! Fuck!*"

The pain! The pain was just too much. She slowed down to a hobbling jog, telling herself to keep going, to rise above the pain. She could do this. She could. She could.

"*Ow!*" No, no, she couldn't. She stubbed her sore toe across the pavement and the pain – the really excruciating, searing pain that went right to her heart and caught her breath meant she just had to stop. She had to. She couldn't breathe. She could barely see.

She stood on the pavement, tears streaming down her face now, and fearing she might choke with the agony she was in.

"Come on!" said the policeman who had obviously been only inches from her the whole time. "Let's get you some medical attention for that and then we'll do what we have to do. You don't like to make things easy on yourself, do you?"

Tess looked at him through her watery eyes. He had a kind face and his dimples were actually kind of cute. If she wasn't married and wasn't in such agony and if he wasn't arresting her, she just might fancy him. She always loved a man in uniform.

"I am begging you," she sobbed, afraid to look at her toe. "I am begging you so, so much. Please do not arrest me. Please don't. I will lose my job. I teach young people. They don't let criminals teach young people. Please."

The policeman took a step back and his face crumpled when he saw the blood oozing from Tess's toe.

"Ouch, that looks sore! You're a fast runner, I'll give you that! Broken toe or no broken toe!"

"Cross Country Schools Champion 1996," she said. "Record breaker too."

"You seem to like breaking things, then?"

"What?"

"You broke your toe *and* you broke a window, Miss. You assaulted a doorman and then you resisted arrest by running away. I don't have a choice."

The squad car crawled alongside the pavement and stopped beside them.

"Let's go. And for goodness sake, don't pull a stunt like that again or I will have to handcuff you, and that, contrary to popular belief, is not a pleasant experience."

He opened the car door and Tess looked back into the distance where Polly and Gina stood watching from afar in disbelief.

"Can my sister come with me?" she asked with a sniffle. She felt so alone and afraid and she didn't want to go to the police station. She wanted to go back to the hotel and put on her fluffy slippers and wake up in the morning to a Full Irish and a sauna and swim and put on the pretty blue dress she had packed for the journey home, where Rob would meet her and tell her how much he had missed her and cook her Sunday lunch as she read the papers in the sun, just as he always did.

"I'm afraid not," he said, shaking his head.

He had sticky-out ears, she noticed. Maybe she wouldn't fancy him ever.

"Okay," she whimpered and she hobbled across to the squad car and got into the back seat. She had no shoes on. Her toe was throbbing. Her face was a mess and her hair was sticky from sweat and tears. What a night this had turned out to be. She looked out through the back window of the car. Traffic whizzed by, their bright lights forming a blur so bright it stung her eyes. She could see Polly stare ahead while Gina clambered into a taxi. Tess lifted her hand and waved at her sister.

"I'll be alright," she mouthed.

She put on her seatbelt and closed her eyes, shivering from pain and the cold interior of the cop car. She would love a blanket. One of those really soft, furry blankets that her mum always had for them when they were little and feeling poorly. She wanted her mum. She wanted Rob. She wanted anyone.

"Car two . . . minor accident on Letterkenny Road . . ."

The crackly sounds of the radio messages coming through and the traffic whirring past as they drove towards the town centre made her feel like she was having an out-of-the-body experience. This had to be some sick joke. She would open her eyes and she would be in a taxi with the others, heading back to the Cove Country Club where they would laugh about the antics they had got up to that day . . . the massive win on the horses, the revelations of Ruth and her jockey-loving husband, the disappearance of Gina and the hot sex she had in a Jacuzzi with Marco, the delicious Chinese meal and the poor embarrassed waiter, the sounds of the eighties with Karaoke King Kong, the stag party and their flirting and Polly's near-miss with its ringleader . . . things to talk about, laugh about and recall when they got old and grey. One night away to forget their troubles . . . one night away to make everyone at home appreciate them more . . . one night away to reflect on life as it was and to realise what it really was that was important to each of them.

This had been her idea. She had been excited about the spontaneity of it all. Eager to prove that Polly could let her hair down and relax, just like she could . . . keen to show Ruth Monaghan that she was a confident, successful woman despite all the bullying of days gone by . . . determined to show poor wee Gina that there was life after living with an abusive man.

It had all been her idea.

So why had it all gone so horribly wrong?

18

"Don't cry, Polly," said Gina. "Please don't cry."

They pulled up outside the Cove Country Club and the taxi-man awaited his payment.

"That's forty-five euro, ladies," he said. "Forty-five euro."

"Forty-five euro, *please*!" said Gina. "And you don't have to repeat yourself. We heard you the first time, you robbing thief! We know you taxi drivers talk!"

The fright of what had happened to Tess had sobered her up a lot and she had found a second wind on the journey home and was now surprising herself at how she could take charge of things when it really came to it. She'd never felt enough confidence to be a leader type, but Polly needed her and she had to buck herself up and stop always playing the 'poor Gina' role and she was feeling very comfortable being boss.

She handed the taxi-man his money and they climbed out of the car.

"Congratulations on your big win!" said the man and Gina slammed the door.

Polly looked a mess and she smelled even worse. Her lovely red jumpsuit was stained with beer and the crotch seam was coming apart, so Gina made sure that Polly positioned her handbag over the offending hole to avoid any stares when they went into the very posh foyer of this very posh establishment.

"Should I phone Rob?" asked Polly as they walked through the revolving doors. It was well after one now and she was terrified of what was going to happen to her sister.

"No, not yet," said Gina. "Let's just get changed and freshened up a bit and then we'll try and get our heads round what we can do for Tess. We need to check on Sleeping Beauty too. I hope she got back here okay."

Polly's head was doing burleys and she couldn't even think about Ruth, who was no doubt snoring in a deep slumber up in her room, blissfully unaware of how the night had ended.

The hotel foyer was peacefully quiet. Soft music played very, very subtly and the fresh flowers that were arranged in long tall vases across the Reception desk filled the air with a beautiful fragrance that made the girls feel even more disgustingly filthy as they walked past them towards the lift.

"I just wish Tess would learn to shut her mouth," Polly said, trying to push the button on the lift. She kept missing it.

Gina tried but she kept missing it too. They were both still obviously a lot drunker than they were pretending.

"*Ahaaaa!*" said a familiar but highly unwelcome voice from behind them. "Can I help you, ladies?"

Gina looked around to see Pee-ta the Porter standing with one hand on his hip. He looked down his snooty nose in distaste at the sight that stood before him.

"Tell him to go away," said Polly under her breath, refusing to look at him. "I really can't cope with him right now."

"We are perfectly in control," said Gina. "We would just like to use the elevator to get to our rooms."

She made sure to say 'elevator' and not 'lift'. She knew he thought they were common as muck and, even though he did have a point judging by the way they looked right then, she wouldn't stoop to accepting his assistance.

He leaned his scrawny body in between the two of them and pressed the 'Up' button with sober ease.

"*Voila!*" he said as the elevator doors opened. "Easy when you know how, eh?"

He sniggered and Gina threw him the middle finger when he turned his back.

"I hate men," she said. "All of them."

Polly could feel the bile in her stomach burn. Her mouth was dry and her lips kept sticking together as if she had used a Pritt Stick instead of the very expensive lipstick she had in her handbag. She caught a sight of their reflection in the mirror inside the elevator and it frightened her. What a difference a few hours made! That evening they had been freshly made-up, turning heads everywhere they went with their glamour and sophistication and beauty until the poisonous sins of too much alcohol seeped under their skin and ruined everything.

"Why aren't we moving, Gina?" said Polly. "Please get me to a bed quickly. I need to lie down."

She slid down the wall of the elevator. She wanted to crawl into a little ball and close her eyes and wake up when this whole sorry mess was fixed.

"*Oops!*" said Gina, and she let out a giggle. "Silly me!

185

I forgot to push the button! There we go. Floor three. Here we go. There we go."

She squinted as the elevator began to move upwards.

Polly had never experienced exhaustion like this before. Not even when the twins were tiny babies and she had to do double night feeds for the first nine weeks of their lives. No, no, this was a very different type of tiredness. She felt dirty inside and out. She had a cut on her elbow that was just beginning to sting and she had no idea where it had come from. Her mouth felt like the Sahara desert and she could smell booze from her clothes. She was a dirty rotten stop-out. Her little sister had just been arrested. She was so ashamed of herself for letting it all happen.

"Right, that's us! Let's go!" said Gina, taking Polly by the arm and hauling her out of the lift before the doors closed and she was sent back down to the wrath of Pee-ta the Porter.

"Where on earth are you finding the energy to be so chirpy?" asked Polly. "Please stop. You're making me jealous. I have the energy of a mouse."

"Remember, I had a power nap in the nightclub!" said Gina and they both giggled hysterically at the thought.

"Clever girl! I wish I had thought of that instead of thinking I was a bloody teenager and giving it all on that slippery dance floor!"

They staggered down the corridor and came to Gina and Ruth's room first.

"You coming in?" asked Gina.

Polly shook her head and stared at the floor. More swirly carpet. Her head spun. What was it with this part of the world and swirly carpet?

"Why don't you go get your jammies and toothbrush

186

in your room and come and stay with us for the night?" said Gina. "I don't want you to be on your own."

"But what if . . . what if Tess comes back? Oh God, Gina! What is going to happen to her?"

"Get your stuff and we'll talk about it later. This is no time for you to be fretting in your room by yourself. You need to be with your friends."

"Thanks for being such a good friend, Gina," said Polly. "I really don't want to be on my own."

"Of course you don't," said Gina. "No woman is alone when she has her friends."

Polly sniffled and choked back more tears as Gina linked her arm and they went to Tess and Polly's room. Polly found the key card in her handbag which Gina swiftly took from her hand and swiped, then opened the door.

The room was exactly as they had left it. It was like visiting a crime scene, kind of like going back in time. It was almost ghostly, with Tess's belongings strewn across the bed, just as she'd left them. The room smelled of perfume and make-up and freshness and hope and various dresses and other outfit options lay everywhere.

Polly could hear Tess's voice from earlier.

"It's about time you dressed for your age and not like our mother. You have a figure to die for, now show it off!"

She really was so bossy and to the point but Polly loved her sister with all her heart. She was loyal and kind and would go to the ends of the earth for her family and she loved Rob so, so much. She was an excellent teacher – everyone's favourite. She had won the annual school extra-curricular award for Best Sports and Best Arts teacher, which was outside her main job as French teacher, for three years in a row. She didn't deserve to be taken away in a police car even if she did throw stilettos at a bouncer. It was just a pity she didn't hit him harder!

Polly looked in the mirror and remembered earlier in the evening when she and her sister had both done so with such pride. How did it get like this? They had set out with such good intentions.

"Come on," said Gina. "There's no point stewing over everything now. What's done is done and it's not like any of us murdered anyone, is it?"

"Mutton dressed as lamb," said Polly quietly to her reflection. "Maybe he was right. Maybe we're all just mutton dressed as lamb."

"Or lamb dressed as mutton, as Tess would say!" said Gina. "As if we are! Now, come on. Let's go and see if Ruth is alive. That's all we would need. A bloody heart attack or something to have wiped her out."

"Don't even joke about it," said Polly, taking her pyjamas and toothbrush and following Gina out of the room.

Ruth was out for the count when the girls got to the room seconds later. They didn't know whether or not they should wake her and fill her in, or to let sleeping dogs lie and allow Ruth to be the only one of them to get a full night's sleep.

"I say leave her be," said Polly, slumping down on the bed.

"But what if she gets angry tomorrow that we didn't wake her? She may think she has missed out on something. She may even be able to come up with some sort of help? Ruth seems to be clever –"

"And I'm not?" said Polly. Her eyes were closed and

her arms were folded as she lay on the bed, still in her jumpsuit. She didn't have the energy to change. Not yet.

"That's not what I meant!" said Gina from the bathroom.

"It's okay, you're right. I'm not academically clever like Ruth or Tess," said Polly, her voice trembling with self-pity. "I never was the sharpest tool in the box. Pretty Polly, that's all I ever bloody was. Good enough for having babies and cooking and cleaning and maybe the odd shag on a Saturday night, but certainly not clever. *Nuh-uh!* Maybe that's why my husband is so bored with me."

Gina walked back into the room. Her mouth was full of toothpaste and she waved her toothbrush as she spoke.

"Never ever say that," she said.

"And I never am listened to," said Polly, knowing the tears that were streaming down the sides of her eyes and into her ears were heaped with pure self-indulgence but she was too drunk to care. "Even my children turn a deaf ear when I try to tell them off. I'm weak and pathetic and I can see why James is so fed up. I'm bored to tears with him being bored to tears and –"

"Polly Knox, you listen to me!" said Gina, sitting on the edge of the bed. "You are one of the kindest, smartest, caring people I know, Miss Madam! If it weren't for you over the past few days, I'd be in the clinic by now. You may not have a big fancy job but you have qualities that will last well beyond anyone's retirement. You have soul!"

"Who has soul?" came a voice.

"Well, look who it is!" said Gina. "The dead has arisen!"

Ruth slowly revived from her slumber and the very sight of her lightened the mood. Polly broke into a smile. She was glad that Ruth was awake. She never, ever

189

thought she would see the day when she was glad to hear Ruth Monaghan's voice.

"What? What are you two talking about? And where's the gorgeous one? *Ow!* My head!" she squealed. "I shouldn't have got up so quickly."

Ruth really was a sight. Her bright red hair was sticking out in clumps and she had a deathly white face with black panda eyes. Polly marvelled that even in bed Ruth wore all black. Not sexy black. Just black.

"We have had a terrible ending," said Polly. "And now we're all weepy and sentimental and shitting ourselves. If I were you I'd go back to sleep."

"I'll sleep when I'm dead," said Ruth. "I'd love a glass of wine. Did you bring any back?"

"*Eurgh!*" said Gina. "The very thought of it!"

"Joke! Now, seriously? Are you the last two to survive the party? Please tell me I wasn't the only one to give up the ghost early! Is Tess asleep?"

Polly and Gina looked at each other and both began to speak at the same time.

"It's a long story," said Polly.

"I fell asleep," said Gina.

"On the table in the bar," said Polly.

"We had to carry her out," continued Polly. "The stag party gave us awful abuse, but it was when we got outside –"

Ruth was wide awake now. This was good! Suddenly her vomiting outside over the wee wannabe jockey wasn't so bad after all!

"Tess threw her shoes at the doorman and broke a window. She thinks she has broken her toe too 'cause you stood on it."

"Did I? Shit! So is she at the hospital?"

"I don't know. I suppose they're going to take her to hospital on her way to the Cop Shop," said Polly.

"*What?* Has she been arrested?"

"Yip," said Polly and the fear overcame her once again. Her poor baby sister!

Ruth's mouth dropped open. Gina looked at the floor. Polly stared at them both. None of them knew whether to laugh or cry.

"Arrested? Tess Woodhead? I can't believe it!" said Ruth.

And a deathly silence filled the air as all three pictured Tess in prison wear, all alone with her sore toe.

In the end, they cried. All of them.

19

It was dark in the holding cell.

Tess never had been so frightened in her whole life. Not even when she broke Stacey Edwards' nose with a hockey stick during a friendly with the rival school in first year.

Not even when she told her mum that her teacher broke all her new pencils in bad temper when it was really Ryan Arthurs who did it because Tess had broken his heart in fifth year.

Not even when Rob's great-grandmother's antique vase smashed into smithereens all over her kitchen floor when she was dusting it, seeing the family out of a few grand and a sentimental heirloom that was at least a hundred years old and worth enough to feed a small family for a year.

Not even when she thought she was pregnant when she was nineteen and swallowed a full bottle of gin to try and make the baby go away.

"Oh God, please help me!" she said, clasping her

hands in prayer. She never really was one for prayer and had to pretend to be interested at school Masses or when Rob would make her go to Mass every Sunday because his parents would somehow find out if he didn't go.

She had tried to break that tradition once she got a ring on her finger, but Rob was having none of it.

Maybe the policeman was right. Maybe she *did* have a habit of breaking things. She had certainly broken plenty of hearts in her day, that was for sure . . .

At fifteen years old, Ryan Arthurs was the first – she told him she was in love with Robbie Williams and could never ever love another man in her life. He was gutted and hadn't spoken to her since, even though his daughter was now a pupil at her school. He still couldn't look her in the eye.

Then there was Brian Marshall who she'd gone steady with for two years. The pregnancy scare put her right off him and he cried for days when she dumped him once she found out that she wasn't really pregnant after all. She cried tears of relief while he sent her letters and songs every day for a fortnight. Then he got over it and got married to his next-door neighbour who was a single mother of two. Maybe he just wanted a family.

The last break-up before she met Rob was the worst of all. She had been engaged to be married to Todd Evans – a rugby player from Galway who was destined for big things. Her father had been in his glory, telling all his mates that his future son-in-law was a professional sportsman and that he was picked for Ireland but missed out due to a hamstring injury. Tess was madly in love with him, but a drunken snog in the back of a bus after her sister's hen party put a stop to all that. She panicked, questioned her love for Todd and broke off the engagement. He had never loved again. She knew that for a fact and he still hadn't forgiven her for the emotional turmoil he went through afterwards.

Yes, she knew how to break things alright. And now, here she was stuck in a cold, sterile holding cell as she waited to be called to make her statement. They wanted her to sober up first, they said. They asked her did she want to make a phone call. A relative? A lawyer perhaps? She didn't want anyone to know about this. Not even Rob unless he really had to.

They had taken her phone, her jewellery and her purse from her. Even her precious fine gold necklace that she had worn every day since her grandmother had left it to her. It was antique and it was her signature look. What did they think she was going to do? Hang herself with it? Apparently, according to Simon the Cop, or Copalicious as Gina had called him, that was exactly what they were afraid she would do.

He wasn't such a bad old skin, once she calmed down and stopped calling him Big Ears. Not to his face of course. She wasn't that bad. But he did have sticky-out ears.

He *was* cute though. And he had a wicked sense of humour that, as the alcohol and shock wore off, Tess brought to the forefront with her one-liners bouncing off his.

"Do you come here often?" she asked him as he led her to the cell.

"Only to deal with bad teachers," he said. "You need to work on your aim, you know. You'll never make a sniper with that shot. It was pathetic."

"I must practise more next time I throw whiteboard pens at one of my pupils when they refuse to *parler Français*."

His name was Simon McGuinness and he was from Letterkenny. She liked Simon now, even if he had arrested her. She felt safe with him, familiar almost, and now that he had gone and left her in the cell all by herself while he followed up on paperwork, she wished he would come back and talk to her. It was sort of like a patient clinging on to their doctor even though he had just told them they had a terminal illness. Or a grieving mother who turns to God for answers as to why he took her son. She needed someone to talk to. She couldn't just sit here all on her own like – like a criminal! Maybe she would be allowed to make that phone call now? But to whom? Polly! Yes, she wanted to call Polly.

She walked towards the heavy cell door and looked through the letterbox-style peephole. Her toe ached when she walked, even though it had by now been well bandaged up. It was broken alright and she knew all about it with every step she took.

"Hello!" she called out. "Hello? Simon? Constable Simon or whatever your name is? I mean Garda Simon? Officer? Anyone?"

She heard footsteps along the corridor and her heart skipped a beat. She felt like she was trapped on a desert island and that her smoke signals had been answered by a ship in the distance. Yes! They hadn't totally abandoned her! Someone was coming to her rescue at last!

"Simon?"

"Garda McGuinness is busy," said a strange, older face. "What's up?"

He glared at her through the peephole and she could

smell his breath. He looked like a teddy bear with a blonde moustache and his breath smelled like coffee and mints.

"I'd like to make my phone call now," she said, her lip trembling with fear and anxiety. "I need to talk to my sister. I need to tell her to bring me shoes when I'm allowed out of here. I need to tell her I'm okay even though I'm not okay. I'm so scared, officer. And my toe is so sore."

The man glanced downwards, looking at his watch.

"You're statement is scheduled for 3 a.m.," he said. "You can make your call after that. Not long to go now."

He dropped the shutter on the peephole and she listened as he walked away, *clip, clop, clip, clop* echoing along the corridor. Then he began to whistle, just like Joe the Bouncer did when he had beaten her in their argument. She hated whistlers! It was such a smug, arrogant, irritating sound!

She thumped the steel door but it didn't make as much as an echo. Then she stood against it, the coldness of it almost burning her bare back and she slid down into a huddle on the floor. This was a living nightmare and she had a terrible feeling that it wasn't going to be over as quickly as she had hoped it would. She was in big, big trouble.

She was broken.

The walk to the interview room was long and cold and lonely. Moustache Cop wasn't as friendly as Copalicious and there certainly was no banter or making her feel at ease. He kept looking at his watch – she wondered was it a habit he was aware of, or if it was because he really hated doing nightshifts and couldn't wait to get home, but no matter what the reason, it was very noticeable and very irritating. It was like one step, two steps, three steps, look at watch. One step, two steps, three steps, look at watch, and repeat. Well, not just quite that bad, but almost.

"In here, Miss," said Moustache Cop.

"Thanks," said Tess and she tiptoed inside. She still had no shoes but they had given her a pair of plastic socks to wear which were extremely uncomfortable and they really didn't match her tiny white dress which was no longer white anyhow.

Garda Simon McGuinness, as she felt she should call him now since she was entering a formality zone, was there, seated at the far end of a large wooden desk. He had a tape-recorder and was looking very efficient. She smiled at him but he didn't smile back and she felt rejected. What the hell had happened to him? God but she was tired!

Moustache Cop introduced himself as Sergeant Bill McCloskey and he stated the time and date and began the interview. It was all so formal and Tess was beginning to feel like a real convict. Had she really committed a crime? Was it really such a big issue? Didn't they have drunk drivers to arrest or murderers or rapists to chase after? Not tonight, obviously. This was as exciting as it got in this little town.

"So, he called us names," said Tess, as she told her story.

"What were the names?" asked Garda McGuinness.

"He called us . . . he called us '*mammies*'," said Tess.

Garda McGuinness raised an eyebrow. Sergeant McCloskey cleared his throat.

197

"*Mammies*?" asked Garda McGuinness.

"Yes, *mammies*. He told us to go back to our babies. Oh, and he also – he also said that we were drunk."

Again, more astounded expressions across the table.

"I'm not saying he was wrong!" protested Tess. "But he didn't have to *tell* us that we were drunk! We may have been pissed but we weren't stupid! I can tell when I am drunk, thank you very much. I didn't need him to remind us!"

"Just keep going. What happened next? Was this when you lifted your weapon?"

"My weapon?" said Tess, exasperated now. "That was a Louboutin shoe, I will have you know! It was not a weapon!"

"But you used it as a weapon," said Garda McGuinness. "You know, it would be much quicker if you just told us what happened from your point of view instead of getting precious about brand-names of shoes. You threw your shoes, and then . . .?"

"I missed."

"Okay, you missed. And then what?"

"Then I used Gina's shoes."

"Okay . . . so you used your friend's shoes as a secondary weapon."

"Were they Louboutin too?" asked Sergeant McCloskey with a chuckle.

"No, they were the High Street's best!" said Tess. "Gina doesn't wear Louboutin. And anyhow, I can't believe you are calling our shoes 'weapons' no matter where they're from! They're just shoes! And very nice shoes at that!"

"So at what stage did you hit the gentleman on the chest?" Garda McGuinness yawned silently.

Sergeant McCloskey looked at his watch. Again.

"I was aiming for his fat *head*!" said Tess. "Oh God, I didn't mean that! Please rewind the tape! I really didn't mean that!"

"But you missed on that occasion, didn't you?"

Tess's eyes darted from McGuinness to McCloskey to McGuinness to McCloskey. She was panicking now and her breathing was becoming very unsteady. She couldn't think straight.

"Please, just let me start again. I didn't mean to hit him."

"So you meant to hit the window, then?" said Garda McGuinness. "Just tell us, in chronological order of events, what exactly happened so that we can record your statement, Mrs Matthews. I'm finding you very hard to follow."

"I just want to go back to my hotel," said Tess. "Please let me go now."

"Nearly there," he said, making more notes. "Just keep going. So you threw your friend's shoe, which wasn't a Louboutin . . . and you missed the doorman."

Tess was becoming pissed off now. They were taking the mick and she didn't like it one bit.

"I threw Gina's shoe, yes," she said. She was angry now. "And it smashed the window. *Boo hoo!* I'm sorry about that, I really am. I'm not normally a destructive person. It's just . . . he was so smug and rude and pass-remarkable. He should have just let us leave the place with whatever dignity we had left. Yes, we were drunk but we were by no means disorderly up until that point when we were antagonised! I bet he wouldn't have said those smart comments if we were three drunk men, would he?"

McCloskey and McGuinness looked at each other.

"Well, would he?" repeated Tess. "Would he have said 'Oi, Daddies, go home to your babies'? No, he wouldn't have because he would have had much more than a shoe thrown at him! He was picking on us because he is a sexist pig and doesn't like to see women out having a good time!"

"We cannot comment on the doorman's intentions," said Sergeant McCloskey.

"Oh, you two probably agree with him! It's alright for men to get rat-arsed on the weekends, to run to the pub, to leave the wife and children behind while he 'watches the football' or 'meets his mates' or 'needs a pint'! That's mighty fine and if they come rolling home, I mean if they decide to come rolling home, well, no harm done, is there? But a woman – a woman! How dare she! How bloody dare she?"

Sergeant McCloskey stood up and adjusted his fat belly around his belt. "Mrs Matthews, I would ask you to remain calm. Try not to get upset."

"Upset? I'm absolutely fuming! I'm the one treated as a criminal all because that bastard thinks he can treat women like second-class citizens!"

"And he too will be invited in to the station to make a statement," said Sergeant McCloskey, "and the bar management will obviously be deciding now whether or not they want to press charges in relation to the damage done to their property. As will Mr McAleer."

"Who?"

"The doorman you assaulted. Mr McAleer? The man who offended you by calling you a 'mammy'? He may wish to press charges for assault. We will be deciding on just how disorderly your behaviour has been."

Tess put her head in her hands. The whole event was a muffled mess. She was sure he must have said more than that but she couldn't remember exactly. The stag party had made her mad with their horrible chants and Gina was proving difficult as she slumped about like a drunken scarecrow. At least if she had been able to actually walk it might have allowed them to exit with a tiny bit of grace.

"Can I go now?" she asked, tears filling her eyes. She dreaded looking in the mirror. She had bruises on her knees and her make-up was long gone. She felt like she had been dragged through a hedge backwards so God knows what she actually looked like.

"Just read the statement over and sign the bottom if you are happy that this is a true record of the events in your opinion."

Tess read through what Garda McGuinness had recorded in print. It was all on tape anyhow but she imagined that was only a back-up in case she retracted that she had said anything that he now had on paper. It made her seem like a ridiculous drama queen, there was no doubt about that, but she would stick to her guns in her case against Joe McAleer. He was a prize asshole and he had no respect for women. He deserved to be whacked with a stiletto, but he wasn't really worth all this hassle, was he? Ah well, she had no choice now. She had made her bed, she would have to lie on it.

"I really want to go to bed," she said, signing the bottom of the white lined paper.

"You can make that phone-call now," said Sergeant Bill. "You're free to go. We will be in touch in the next day or two."

"And then what happens?" asked Tess, her eyes

saucer-like with fear. She pictured a courtroom, with Rob standing beside her in shame and her name all over the newspapers with headlines such as *'Drunken Teacher Attacks Doorman'*, or *'Teacher Tess's Drunken Tantrum'* or *'The REAL Bad Teacher'*. Oh she was so afraid of what was going to happen, she could barely even think about it.

"We can't foresee what the next stage will be," said Garda McGuinness.

She had the distinct impression he was a bit of a kiss-ass when it came to old Sergeant McCloskey. He definitely had lost that cheeky twinkle in his eye and was very business-like. Perhaps he was in line for a promotion. She had to kiss ass in her job too. She and Simon had so much in common.

Sergeant McCloskey ended the interview formally and then left the room, leaving Tess and McGuinness alone.

"Is he your boss?" she asked him. She was angry with him and she didn't know why.

"Sort of. Well, for tonight he is. We have two sergeants. Bill is one of them. He has been here a long time. Why?"

"Nothing," said Tess. She would keep her mouth shut for once.

"Look, between you and me," said Garda McGuinness (he was no longer Copalicious), "there is a long, long queue of people who would love to throw more than a stiletto at Joe McAleer, so don't beat yourself up about it."

"There are?" asked Tess. "Why?"

"He has a fine reputation around here," said Copalicious (he was now Copalicious again). "Bit of a bad boy. It should be him sitting across from me, not you, and someday soon it will be if I get my way. I had to do my job tonight, but secretly I was raging you didn't get him full whack in the face with that shoe. It would have made my night."

Tess couldn't believe her ears. Copalicious was rubbing his hands and sucking his teeth, just like he was imagining finally nailing McAleer for all he was worth.

"So why the hell did you arrest me?" she asked. "You could have just let me go!"

"I had to arrest you, believe me," he said. "But there was one thing for sure and you said it tonight. If you and your mates had been three drunken men leaving that bar, Joe McAleer wouldn't have opened his gob. He's a coward when he's outnumbered by men, but when he puts on that security uniform and there are women to take the piss out of, he thinks he's God. You did the right thing. He's a . . . what was it you called him again?"

"A prize asshole?"

"Yes. That's it. He's a prize asshole."

"Now, young lady. Here you go," said Sergeant McCloskey, entering the interview room. He was carrying a deep plastic tray, the kind you would see in an airport security check, which contained all her belongings.

"Thank you," said Tess, still digesting Copalicious's openness with her in such formal surroundings. Maybe he didn't know . . .

"I have lots to catch up on," Copalicious said, standing up and gathering up his paperwork. "Good luck, Miss. Keep up the good work at school and remember to practise your aim. *Au revoir.*"

"I will, Garda," said Tess, totally bewildered. "*Au revoir.*"

When he left the room, she put on her necklace again

as Old Bill shuffled about, making himself seem busy and constantly looking at his watch.

"Oh, the tape," he said. "Is that still running?"

He muttered to himself, something about Simple Simon, and he switched it off, rewound it and put it in his breast pocket.

"Everything okay, Miss?" he asked her. "You can make that phone call now. Get yourself out of here at last. No place for a lady in here."

Tess smiled to herself and picked up her phone to call Polly. Simple Simon was a good name for Garda McGuinness. Way better than Copalicious. Maybe he was a bit slow off the mark even though he tried to act the tough guy. Whatever he was, she didn't really care. Because, by recording his opinion on Joe McAleer, Copalicious might have just saved her bacon.

"Bless me, Father, for I have sinned!" Tess stood at the police station door with open arms as the girls ran towards her from their taxi.

It was past 4 a.m. and Ruth was still in her black pyjamas. Polly and Gina had showered and changed into day wear but Ruth, despite her sleep, still didn't have the energy.

"My God, Tess, get into the car quick. Here are some slippers. I hope no one sees us!" said Polly, leaning down to help put the slippers on. One wouldn't fit her thanks to her broken toe, so she had to make do with just the other which made her hobbling very difficult indeed.

"I think I'm starting to feel hung-over," said Gina. "I must be one of the very few who hasn't puked yet."

"I haven't puked yet," said Tess and the other three glared at her.

"No, you don't really qualify for a puking pass," said Ruth. "You're in enough trouble as it is!"

They got back into the car, ducking and diving like real-life criminals (which one of them now potentially was) and then each breathed a huge, exaggerated sigh.

"That was a sigh of relief, by the way," said Ruth. "I am so glad this night is over at last."

"Me too," said Polly. "I never want to go through that again. Ever. Give me boredom and school runs and spaghetti-stained clothes any day."

"Oh, what did you have to mention spaghetti for? Now, I really want food," said Tess, luxuriating in the heat of the car as she stretched her long legs.

"Ooh, me too," said Gina. "I'd love a big greasy kebab. And a cheesy chip. I've never had a cheesy chip before but I've always wanted to try one. Whoever thought of putting cheese on chips? *Mmmm* . . ."

Polly leaned back in the front seat of the cab and closed her eyes. She was peckish now too. Any tiredness had left her and the shower had sobered her up somewhat but there was no doubt about it, the munchies were setting in.

"There's no chance getting a takeaway at this time round here, ladies," said the taxi-man, deflating their hopes and making their bellies seem even emptier.

"Unless . . ." said Polly. "Unless we order room service when we get back. I'm nearly sure there are a few hot food items on the menu in the room. Imagine how irritated that poncey Pee-ta will be when we order as much as we can!"

"Yes, let's!" said Gina. "It will cost a fortune, though!"

"I think you're forgetting about Melanie's Way," said Ruth, patting her handbag. "You can order whatever you want!"

The taxi-man raised an eyebrow and looked in the rear-view mirror at Ruth who was squashed between Tess and Gina.

"Are you the one they were all talking about in the Top O'The Road?" he asked. "The one who's a psychic with the horses?"

The girls played dumb and shook their heads, remembering how the other taxis had ripped them off once they got a sense they had won money on the horses.

"Nah," said Gina.

"Who?" asked Tess.

"I did a couple of runs from there tonight," said the taxi driver. "They were all talking about this big – I mean, this lady who had been there in the afternoon with some very glamorous friends and they say she was a pure genius. Picked every winner for the full two hours she was there."

"My, my," said Ruth. "Definitely wasn't me. I'm more of a psycho than a psychic. I have no idea what you're talking about."

"Ah, I must be mixing you up with another four young women who won a fortune in the pub earlier," he chuckled. "That'll be twenty-five euro, please, each way, so fifty in total."

The girls looked at each other.

"Only twenty-five?" said Gina. "Maybe we should give him a wee tip for being honest. The rest just took the piss all night and not one of them said please, not even Larry the Leprechaun. Will we throw him an extra tenner?"

"I'll do one better than that," said Ruth and she leaned across, paid the man and whispered into his ear. "Two thirty, tomorrow, Doncaster, a horse called Ivor Rocket.

206

It's a sure thing. And believe me, that's more than any tenner tip I could give you!"

The taxi-man let out a strange noise. It was a mixture between a squeal of delight and a groan but whatever it was, it showed he was really, really excited. He quickly wrote the name of the horse down on the back of his firm's business card, gave Ruth a big slobbery kiss on the cheek and then wore a huge grin as he drove away. He even tooted the horn which was totally un-PC for that time of the morning.

Daylight was already breaking through as the four women stood outside the Cove Country Club and watched his lights disappear into the night.

"Right, ladies," said Polly. She could feel her eyes get heavy again but her stomach needed immediate attention. "Let's give Pee-ta one more run for his money and then we need to get some sleep. It's way, way past our bedtime."

"I couldn't have put it better myself, sister," said Tess and they walked for the last time in through the revolving doors of the Cove Country Club Hotel.

20

"Oh sweet God in heaven, please tell me it was all a nightmare."

Tess tried to open her eyes. She couldn't. They were stuck.

"What time is it?" asked Polly. "Please don't say it's time to get up."

"Ask Sergeant Bill McCloskey," said Tess. She had buried her head under her pillow by now. "He always knows what time it is."

"I hope you never have to see Sergeant Bill again," said Polly.

They had sat talking and eating till almost five thirty with Tess giving them the full account of her 'night' in a cell down at the Cop Shop. It was both fascinating and frightening as she recounted that lengthy hour in captivity, all alone and cold and scared out of her wits. She tried to remember the name of the famous guy who had been famously rescued from captivity but it was too late and she was too tired for her brain to function on that level. She would Google it when she got home. She had a new found empathy with his suffering. In fact, she might even see if she could do voluntary French classes at the nearest prison. They couldn't all be criminals in there.

"I never, ever want to see Sergeant Bill again. Never. I want to see Rob and I want to go home."

A few doors down, Ruth was lying wide awake while Gina snored loudly across from her.

She hadn't really slept much since Polly and Tess had called it a night, full of toasted sandwiches and tea. Pee-ta the Porter was a pain in the ass as they had expected and refused to bring them anything more exotic than a sandwich, but it had filled a gap in their empty tummies and they couldn't exactly look a gift horse in the mouth.

All in all, Ruth had thoroughly enjoyed her break away. She loved the adult company, the sense of freedom, the chance to prove to people from her past that she was not the ogre they remembered her as. She had feelings and problems and history. She had humour and talent and personality. She had come so far since that day she packed up her belongings in London and boarded a plane with her head held high and her heart lying as low as it could be.

And now what? Now what was she supposed to do? She would go back home to her son and daughter who had outgrown her. She would try and concentrate on a business that never really was hers to call her own. It was Jeffrey who had set it all up. It was to serve all his cronies who would much rather have given their business elsewhere but who were too afraid to say no to him. She had to start from scratch, really. Yes, she had one or two jobs outstanding to email across the water, but once that was done, it was Bye Bye London. She had to cut the cord. She didn't want to be known by any of those fakes again.

She needed a new direction, a new focus. Designing brochures and websites was a passion she enjoyed but it reminded her of the dirty betrayal her husband dumped on her. She remembered Michael, the guy in the bar, and his offer of a sports column on horse-racing. Not even Jeffrey could steer her away from her love of horses and anything to do with them still got her excited. She would probably never hear from him again though. Yes, she had his details and, yes, he had said to contact him but did he really mean it? He was drinking at the time. Hell, he might even have been a bit the worse for wear when he made the suggestion. And how did he know she could do it? He didn't. She could do it with her eyes closed, but she was too afraid. No, she would push that to the side for now. If it was meant to be, it would happen but she had been let down in the past too much to get her hopes up again.

She remembered a saying her mother once told her: *Trust no one but yourself and you will never be disappointed.* Oh, she knew what she was saying when she told a very young Ruth that advice! Her mother would never, ever trust her again. Ten years had passed since that awful, horrible day when their relationship, friendship and mother/daughter bond was burned down forever.

She wondered what her mother looked like now. She wondered if she even knew that Ruth was back in the place she grew up in. She wondered if she would even care.

Ruth rested her head farther back and stared up at the ceiling. She breathed in and out in a bid to control her emotions. She wanted her mother so badly. She wanted someone to tell her everything was going to be okay, she wanted to say she was sorry, but it was too late for all that now. She had done so much damage. She had hurt too many people. Polly and Tess might have forgiven her and she was so grateful for that. But her mother? No. Her mother *never* would.

"You awake? Gina?" she whispered a little louder than she should have, but she couldn't lie there all alone for much longer. It had to be at least nine o'clock. They would need to be having breakfast soon. Well, they had planned to have breakfast, rain, hail or shine but of course that was hangover-dependent and Ruth was a few hours ahead of them in the sleep department.

Gina mumbled something. It sounded like "Marco" but Ruth couldn't be sure. She picked up her phone from the bedside locker and texted Polly. She really couldn't lie there all alone for any longer. She was wide awake and she had to do something.

"U UP?" she wrote. She would always text in capital letters which drove her children mental. Remembering that brought a smile to her face. They were great kids. They had their moments, but who didn't?

Her phone bleeped back almost straight away. Polly was obviously a champion 'texter backer'. Ruth loved people who texted back straight away.

"Almost. Breakfast in 20? Need shower. Honking."

"SEE U THEN!!!" wrote Ruth, feeling better already. She used exclamation marks a lot when texting too which Melanie said was 'so uncool'. Knowing this made her use them even more.

She sat up on the bed and tried to muster up the strength to walk across the room and pull the curtains.

When she did, the morning sunlight threw a hazy beam across the room and Gina stirred.

"Sorry!" whispered Ruth. "We're going for breakfast in twenty. You coming?"

Gina let out a groan and then she kicked the covers off and lay still, so still that Ruth was sure something strange had happened to her mid-groan.

The deep breath that followed and the sudden spring up in the bed assured her that Gina was just fine.

"I am so hung-over," she said. "What time is it? Get me something to drink quickly."

"Vodka shot? Cocktails? Wine? We have everything," said Ruth.

"Shhh!" said Gina. "Not funny. Quick. Fluid. Liquid. Mouth like sandpaper."

"It's just gone nine," said Ruth, handing her a glass of water. "How are you feeling, apart from hung-over? I don't know about you, but I am dreading going home. I have a major case of the heebie-jeebies and it's not pleasant at all."

Gina threw herself back onto the pillow. "*Ouch!* Oh no! Oh God, what did I do yesterday? Ruth! This is a nightmare!"

Ruth gathered some clean underwear and her outfit for the day – a long black jersey dress and flat silver pumps.

"Don't," she said. "Don't think about it now. Don't think about any of it. No post mortems, remember? What happens in . . . what happens in . . . where are we again?"

"I have absolutely no idea," said Gina. "Somewhere in Donegal. That's about as much as I ever want to know."

"Fair enough," said Ruth, heading for the shower. "What

happens in Somewhere in Donegal, stays in Somewhere in Donegal. I won't be long. Now, pull yourself together."

"You nervous?" Polly asked. She was applying her make-up and was surprised that she looked almost normal. Almost.

"Bricking it," said Tess. She was finding it a little harder to recover some of her usual get-up and go. She had managed a shower but the task of choosing something to wear was making her dizzy.

"Wear the blue dress," said Polly, now applying lipstick. She was miles ahead.

"You think so?"

"I know so," said Polly. "You need something to brighten you up and the yellow one will make you look like you're about to be sick. You're yellow enough, believe me."

"I *am* about to be sick. Honestly. Breakfast? Do I have to?"

Polly giggled at how the roles had reversed. It was only the evening before that Tess was telling her what to wear and what to do and how to do it.

"You should try and eat something," she said, "even if it's only some tea and toast. We need to get on the road soon, I suppose. So much for spa treatments! I couldn't be bothered. Could you?"

Tess swallowed hard. "No . . . no, I couldn't. The very thought of sitting in a steam room in silence is enough to drive me over the edge. I'm doing battles in my brain as it is. I'm in hate-myself mode."

"Don't say that," said Polly. "You don't hate yourself. You may be a criminal, but hate is a very strong word."

Tess stepped into the blue dress and turned her back to her sister who zipped it up without having to be asked.

213

"Joking aside, I may have fucked up my whole career, Poll," she said, glancing in the mirror. She was looking more like her old self now that she had her hair washed, dried and straightened and had put on her clothes. A lick of make-up and she would be good as new. On the outside, anyhow. On the inside she was a shivering bag of nerves.

"We'll just have to say a prayer that you haven't," said Polly. "I'll pray to St Jude all the way home."

"St Jude? But isn't he for hopeless cases?" asked Tess.

"Exactly," said Polly.

"Gee, thanks, sister."

"You're welcome. Now, I'm going to check on the other two eejits to make sure they're almost ready. I think we'd all agree that the quicker we get out of here, the better."

After nibbling over breakfast, the girls brought their bags to reception and Polly took the lead on checking out.

"Let me," said Ruth, producing her credit card. "It all goes on Melanie's Way, remember?"

"You're a star, Ruth Monaghan," said Polly, letting Ruth do the honours. "At least that's one good thing to come out of this weekend! That really was a great win!"

Ruth handed the receptionist her card and entered her PIN.

"There are lots of good things to have come out of this weekend, believe me," she said. "Tess will be fine, Poll. Don't worry about it. It was hardly a first degree crime! A good solicitor and she will walk away scot free. That's if that asshole even decides to press charges. He might just let it go."

"You don't know what he was like, Ruth," said Polly, glancing back at her sister who was now in the foyer on the phone to Rob. Gina was on the phone too. It really was like Confessions of the Night Before.

"Well, if he has any conscience at all he will let it go. It's not like he was even injured, the stupid gobby prat! But we will have to go and pay for the damage you did at the karaoke club before we leave."

They packed their bags into the boot of the Jeep and climbed in, taking up exactly the same seating positions as they had on the way there the morning before.

"So, how's Rob," asked Polly. "Did you tell him?"

"No," said Tess, staring at her fingernails in the front seat. "I couldn't . . . I just couldn't. Can we just go to that place so I can pay for a new window? And then . . . well, then I will decide how and when I am going to tell Rob."

"Oh," said Polly. "You're going to have to just tell him. And today!" She hated stating the obvious, but felt that Tess was going to need more than a gentle nudge to break the inevitable to her husband.

"I just . . . He was telling me about his evening. He had gone to the cinema with a friend, had a beer and then was in bed by twelve. This morning, he has already done a three-mile run, been to early Mass and read the morning papers. Where in all that was I going to tell him I had been arrested for drunken disorderly behaviour and spent half the night in a police cell?"

"Sweet God," said Polly, gripping the steering wheel. "I forgot how perfect Rob is. God, I don't envy your task."

"He isn't perfect," mumbled Tess. "None of us are. He just likes to do things properly. He is thoughtful and kind and I'm a drunken slapper who doesn't deserve him."

"Oh shush," said Polly. "He's not that perfect. And you're not a drunken slapper *all* the time."

215

They stopped by the bar and Tess did the walk of shame to settle the one hundred and fifty euro bill for the broken window pane. Then they drove in silence for a good while, each wrapped up in thoughts of what they had ahead of them.

Gina couldn't wait to see her son. He had told her on the phone that he had missed her as much as she missed him and she pictured holding him tight, telling him that they had so many good times ahead, reassuring him that life would be better even though it was going to be very different. He didn't ask any questions. He didn't mention his father and he didn't even ask if she'd had a good time. All he wanted to know was when she would be home. He needed her and that made Gina warm up inside.

She thought about Trevor who was probably slating her name to his family, blaming her for all his wrongdoings and searching for sympathy from anyone who would give it to him. She didn't have the strength to argue with him. She would keep her dignity, find a good solicitor (if there was such a thing) and try and pick up the pieces of her life as it was. Then she would quietly move on, just as Ruth had when she was faced with a similar conundrum, and make sure that Danny wasn't affected by the mess his father had created.

Ruth was thinking of her mother and how or when she could even begin to build bridges. But where would she start? She couldn't just land on her mother's doorstep unannounced, could she? That would be enough to put the woman into an early grave and she had already been responsible for her ill health down the years, or so she was led to believe. No, she would have to think of another, more subtle approach. A way of making amends would be her focus from now on. Polly and Tess had proven to her that it was never too late to forgive and forget. Yes, she had made many mistakes but hopefully, just hopefully, she could fix this very last part of her life that had been broken for way too long.

Polly's mind was a flurry of dread and anticipation of what the future held for her marriage and her young family. She had been so close to losing it all last night. She would never forget how Tess had stepped in, just moments before she let herself down so badly. If she had as much as kissed that young guy in the bar, it would have been enough to make her doubt her feelings for James forever. But she really had been close. What did that tell her? That she didn't love him? That she didn't respect him? Or was it just a drunken encounter that she was over-analysing and that she would learn to forget and forgive herself for?

She knew there was something wrong and she was terrified as to how she was going to get her life back on track again.

And then there was Tess. Rob had been his usual chirpy self on the phone. Sometimes he really was too good to be true. His structure in his life and his positive outlook had always complemented Tess's potential wild streak. He was the only one who could straighten out her mind, who could reassure her that she was a good person and who would go to the ends of the earth for her. So what on earth would he say when he found out she was potentially in a lot of trouble? She would have to go to court and defend her name. Her name would be in the local papers. She would be such a let-down to Rob, to her family, to her school . . .

"Stop the car!" she said and Polly pulled into the side of the road, yanking on the brake so hard that it made everyone jolt out of their daydreams and back into the here and now.

"What? What's wrong?"

Tess opened the door and leaned outside, undoing her seatbelt with a shaking hand.

"I'm going to be –"

Sick. She was so sick. She crawled out onto the grass verge and held her hair back with one hand but nothing would come, only tears which streamed down her face which were sodden with guilt and shame and remorse.

"I'm so scared, Polly," she said. "What am I going to do?"

Polly was standing by her side now. The smell of potential sick wouldn't do much for her own hangover but she couldn't leave her sister to puke on her own. It was an unwritten rule from their teenage days. If someone was even thinking of being sick, you stayed with them, helped them clean up and went on about your business. But this wasn't a teenage night out. This was a real-life adult 'stand up and be counted for' mess that Tess had found herself in. Polly was scared too but she couldn't admit to that.

"I can go with you, if you like?" she suggested. "Maybe if I was there to back you up, Rob might even see a funny side to it. And you did break your toe, don't forget? Surely you deserve a little bit of slack for being injured?"

"Oh God, yeah!" said Ruth out through the window. "I don't think I said sorry about that. Sorry! But are you sure it was my fault?"

"Yes!" spluttered Tess. She had acknowledged that she

couldn't be sick and wiped her mouth with a fresh tissue which came straight from Polly's ever-available pack of Handy Andies. Polly always had Handy Andies.

"I honestly don't remember," said Ruth. "I can't apologise enough. But it may be your get-out-of-jail card with your husband. Every cloud and all that . . ."

Gina was sniggering as she pictured the scene. Tess had looked so glamorous the night before and she really had been giving it all on the dance floor.

"When exactly did it happen?" she asked.

Tess climbed back into the car, feeling a little bit better. Polly handed her a bottle of water from the glove compartment. She had a box of stuff stored there that she called her 'Just In Case' box – some water, baby wipes, a hairbrush, hair bobbles, tissues and a sewing kit. Polly would never be caught out in a crisis, that was for sure.

"It was around the time that Karaoke King Kong was gyrating to that 'Tarzan Boy' song from the eighties."

"Oh God, yeah!" said Ruth. "I think I may have been giving him the eye at that stage! After each drink he was beginning to look more and more like George Clooney!"

"Holy shit, what were you drinking?" asked Polly. "You would have needed to be on some sort of drugs to make that comparison!"

"Exactly!" said Ruth. "But it's the best I can do in my defence. I was in a little world of my own and was thinking I was a Size Zero supermodel. Never in a month of Sundays!"

Polly cranked on some tunes and they relaxed back in their seats for the duration of their journey, interrupting the silence only now and then to give out some random flashbacks of the night before.

"Remember the guy who was wearing two left shoes!" said Gina. "He was so drunk he didn't even notice!"

"Remember the poor waiter in the Chinese. God, we will go to hell for that!" said Tess. "Polly was so cross with us!"

"Oh shush!" said Polly. "No post mortems. I am cringing enough as it is."

"And we won't mention Gina's Jacuzzi!" said Tess. "I think you could write a juicy bestseller about that. *Making Love with Marco*! You wee slut!"

Gina laughed at the idea but deep down she was beginning to feel ever so slightly bad about her antics with Marco. She was still a married woman, after all. But then she imagined Trevor and his fist and his silences and his disappearing acts and his liaisons with She Who Must Not Be Named.

"I don't regret it for a second," she said.

Perhaps if she said those words enough, she might just believe it.

21

"Ruth, is it okay if I drop you off home first?" asked Polly.

They were approaching their home village now and the mood was a mixture of anticipation, relief, sorrow and fear.

"Yes, of course," said Ruth. "No doubt my son and daughter will have the red carpet lined out onto the street for me. They're always doing that. I told them no fanfares this time. That would be just embarrassing."

Polly pulled up outside Ruth's smart townhouse. There didn't seem to be any sign of life inside, never mind red carpet or fanfares.

"Looks like I'm going home to a silent slumber," she said, disappointment dripping from her voice.

"That's teenagers, I suppose," said Polly. "Enjoy the peace while you have it. I will probably go home to a monstrous mess. At least you can suffer your hangover at your own pace."

Ruth opened the car door and stepped outside.

"Thanks, girls," she said, feeling teary and emotional.

"It really was a blast and I can't tell you how much it helped me."

"Me too," said Gina. "We should arrange another one soon."

"Not in this lifetime," said Tess from the front seat. "I'd rather have boiled cabbage for breakfast every day of my life than see another police station!"

"Well, minus the police station, the arrest and the excessive puking," said Gina. "All in all, it *was* a great night out. It was just what the –"

"Don't say it!" said Tess.

"I'll be in touch," said Ruth. "Catch you lunatics later."

She closed the car door and Polly got out and helped her with her luggage, then walked her up the short path that led to the house.

"You'll be fine, Ruth," said Polly. She rubbed the other woman's arm as she spoke. "Soon, this place will be so much like home, London will seem worlds away and you'll never look back. You deserve happiness and I really think you will find it here."

"I hope so," said Ruth. "Please don't be a stranger. I may look like a tough cookie but I'm a big softie underneath."

"You're a wonderful person," said Polly. "And please don't be lonely. You know you can call on me any time."

"Thanks," said Ruth. "Thanks so much."

Polly turned to go back to the car and Ruth watched her walk away. She was such a gentle soul, was Polly Knox. Ruth had so much to thank her for. But for now, she would go inside, have a coffee and wonder what her next move would be to getting her life sorted once and for all.

"Do you think Gina will be okay?" asked Tess when they

parked the Jeep outside Polly's house. Gina had been left off right at her own front door, despite it just being a few yards away. Polly had insisted so that she didn't have far to carry her bag. Despite her being the littlest of the bunch, Gina's bag weighed the heaviest and Polly wondered if she had kidnapped Marco and taken him home with her.

"It's going to be so tough," said Polly. "I do hope she stays around here, though. I'd hate to see her go. A few months will make a great difference to her and I can already see a streak of confidence coming through, but she has a long, rocky road ahead."

"As do we all," said Tess. "Look, I can just head on home if you want. Maybe it's better if I tell Rob myself? I mean, it's not the end of the world. I was only arrested for shoe-throwing. Surely that's not as bad as stealing or mass murder?"

Polly couldn't help but laugh. "No, nobody died and let's keep it that way. But it's up to you. I can come with you if you think it would make things easier but tell me quickly so I can let James know if you want me to go and help you explain . . ."

Before Tess could make up her mind, young Frankie had opened the front door of the house and was on his way to greet them.

"Hello, baby boy!" said Polly, stepping out of the vehicle to meet him. "Have you lot been good for Daddy?"

"Sort of," said Frankie. "I didn't go to bed when I was told so I'm supposed to be grounded, and the twins wouldn't eat their breakfast but Daddy didn't make it properly. It was soggy."

"Oh dear," said Polly, ruffling his hair. "Maybe we can negotiate that grounding, now that I'm home."

223

Tess got out of the car and grabbed her bag from the boot. Her own vehicle was parked along the kerb from the morning before.

"Looks like you have your own stuff to contend with, so I'll just run along and face the music," she said to her sister. "Being grounded is tough, Frankster! But I bet your mum can pull out some tricks to get you off the hook."

"And I'm sure we can do the same for you, Tess," said Polly. "Just be honest with him, sis. Try and see the funny side. It will be a big fat nothing, wait and see. I bet that Joe McAleer or whatever his name is antagonises someone different every night. Let me know how it goes, won't you?"

"Okay," said Tess. She walked towards her car. "Apart from that, I think our wee night out was a success?"

"I think it was too. Are you sure you can drive with your sore toe?"

"I'll manage," said Tess. "Believe me, this toe is the least of my worries! Please don't tell James what happened to me or I will never hear the end of it."

James was at the doorway now, a toddler in each arm. He looked exhausted which made Polly glow a little. Now he would know what she had to go through every day and every night.

"Hey, James!" said Tess, making an effort to sound much more chirpy than she felt inside.

"Hey, Tess," he replied. "I'd love to say you look well, but – nice limp!"

"Oh shut your face!" said Tess and when she was sure none of the children were looking, she gave him the finger.

"Charming, Mrs Matthews," he said. "Hope you don't teach that to your pupils at school."

224

He chuckled and stepped aside to let his wife through the door of their family home, leaning forward to kiss her on the cheek as she passed. She stopped and wrapped her arms around him and the twins. She never wanted to leave them again. Well, not for a long, long time.

Ruth drummed her fingers on the coffee table and stared at her phone. Her mother's number was emblazoned across the screen, waiting for her to be brave enough to press the dial button. Her house was eerily silent and it would be the perfect opportunity to just bite the bullet. She pictured her mother, scurrying around her house in the city, watering plants, running after the dog, reading the newspaper cover to cover twice over, visiting her late husband's grave twice a day . . .

She wondered if she had changed any over the past ten years. Would she be greyer? Would she be frailer? Angrier? Or would she have become more subdued in her later years? She always had been sharp of the tongue and was never afraid to change her mind.

"Oh, you're home. I didn't hear you come in."

Melanie walked past Ruth without making eye contact and slumped onto the sofa, flicking the TV on and automatically finding the music channel of her choice.

"Yes, I'm just in," said Ruth, waiting for her daughter to ask about her night away. She didn't.

They sat there, like two strangers with no conversation between them. There was just the hum of the television to break the deafening silence. Ruth went to speak and then stopped. She tried again, but the words wouldn't come out. Who was this young girl anyhow? Why were things always so strained between them? Surely they wouldn't go in the same direction that she had with her own mother? She couldn't let it happen.

"So, what are your plans for today then, Mel?" she asked. "You doing anything nice?"

She always called her Mel when she was trying to be on her wavelength. Mel used to love it as a young child. Now it got right up her nose.

"Don't call me that, Mum. My name is Melanie."

"Sorry, Melanie," said Ruth. She crossed her legs and then uncrossed them. Why did her own daughter make her feel so uneasy? "So, what have you been up to then?"

"Nothing much," said Mel, still staring at the TV. "Is there anything to eat? You left here yesterday and there was nothing for dinner. I was starving. I had to go get a Chinese."

Oh boo hoo, thought Ruth. *I had to go get a Chinese.* Normally, Melanie would break her arm for a Chinese.

"Which is why I left you money," said Ruth. "Had I left food as an alternative, I doubt if you would have cooked it, would you? I didn't imagine you would turn into Nigella Lawson overnight."

"Nigella who? At least I would have had the option," said Melanie. "I didn't have a choice."

Ruth sat back in the armchair and put her feet up on the coffee table. She wasn't normally so slobby, but sod it. It was Sunday and her daughter was being a little bitch and it was her house so she would put her feet up on the coffee table if she bloody well wanted to.

She closed her eyes for a few minutes, and then opened them when she heard footsteps upstairs.

"Is that Ben?"

Melanie let out a noise. It was a mixture of a grunt and

226

a snort so Ruth was unsure if it meant yes or no. In saying that, who else would it be? Tom fucking Cruise? Hardly!

"Ben!" she called. "Is that you?"

Maybe she would get a more pleasant and productive welcome home from her son. He was always such a pleasant boy, just like his father had been. Perhaps Melanie was a chip off the old block when it came to the Landsburys, but she wouldn't allow herself to think that way.

"Hey, Mum," said Ben, bouncing into the living room. "Have you seen my rugby shorts anywhere? I'm supposed to be at the pitch for one and I can't find them anywhere?"

Ruth dragged herself off the sofa and walked out to the laundry room where Anneka, her housekeeper, had all the laundry piled into neat stacks. Sitting on top of one of them were, funnily enough, Ben's 'missing' shorts.

"Here you go," she said, throwing them at him playfully. "I wonder how they got in there? Imagine! All folded and clean in the laundry room!"

Ben gave his mother a quick peck on the cheek and stuffed the shorts into a raggedy sports bag. He was a solid big fellow and hadn't wasted any time in seeking out the nearest rugby club on his arrival back to Ireland. His Sunday friendly kick-a-bouts down at the school grounds had made sure he made lots of new friends in addition to those he had met at the more formal mid-week training at the clubhouse.

"So how was, em . . . where were you again?" he asked.

He scrunched up his face which showed his dimples and she noticed that he needed a shave. Sometimes she looked at him and he was just like his father. Well, what his father was like at seventeen. She hadn't seen him since so had no idea what he might look like now. Maybe she

227

would look him up one day and let him know they were back home. There never had been any hard feelings between them. Ben's dad was only a child and was in no way in a position to raise a young son. With her mother whipping her into shape, she had enough to contend with at the time other than fighting with Charlie Robinson to stand by her. He knew about Ben, but the last she had heard he had emigrated to the States a long, long time ago.

"Where were we? That is the question. Somewhere in Donegal," she said and she tittered at the idea that she really didn't know where they had been. "It was great fun. Just what I needed."

"So, did you – did you score, Mother?" he asked playfully and she rolled her eyes in response.

"I think my days of scoring are long gone," said Ruth. "But thanks for the vote of confidence, son. And what did you lot get up to in my absence? I was sure I would come home to a party house and bodies lying everywhere."

Ben raised an eyebrow. "Now, dear Mother, would I do such a thing in your absence?"

God, but he really did look like his father!

"I am just trying to think of what I might have got up to as a teenager. But then, by the time I was your age . . ."

He zipped his bag up on the kitchen table. "Oh here we go again," he said. "You were a single parent living in London without a penny to your name and not a friend to call your own. Now where have I heard that before?"

"Oh hush, you," said Ruth with a smile. "You need to eat something before you go. Have some tea and toast. Or can I make you a quick sandwich?"

"Sorry, Mum, I really gotta go!" he said, giving her

another kiss on the cheek. "I'll be home in time for tea. Catch you laters."

He sped out the front door where a fancy car was awaiting him. Ruth followed to the door and watched and waved as he drove off. At least one of them was happy and content in their new lives, she thought. Melanie was finding it harder to fit in, there was no doubt about that and she spent most of her time on the phone (or BBM, or Facebook, or Skype) to her friends in London.

She walked past the living room and took a peek inside to where her daughter lay curled up in a ball in her pyjamas, flicking through music station after music station on the television. Ruth thought of joining her, of trying to drum up some conversation about how it would take time but that she would settle in soon. There was a great life for them in this village. It would be different to London but it would be better in many ways. But Melanie seemed miles away so Ruth made her way to the kitchen with only her thoughts and a cold cup of coffee for company.

'It was just so funny. I mean, even the policeman said I shouldn't have been arrested. You would have laughed with disbelief. It just all got out of hand and he even apologised afterwards. It was a big fat mistake.'

No, that wouldn't do. Tess was practising what she would say to her husband and was getting nowhere fast.

To her despair/delight (she couldn't decide which), he had popped out to the shops and had left her a note to say he would be back in five and she had already been home for ten minutes. So that meant an extra ten minutes to sweat and panic and dread what exactly she was going to tell him about the events of the night before.

'You see, the bouncer . . . well, he was really nasty and he grabbed my arm and then he stood on my toe and it broke, it actually broke! Look! Evidence!'

Oh God no! Definitely not! Rob would be after Joe McAleer like a shot if she told him that and then they would all end up in jail! No, there was no point in trying to flower it up or skirt around the issue. She would have to bite the bullet and tell it how it was.

She heard the key turn in the door and her heart skipped a beat.

"Where is my precious girl?" she heard Rob say from down the hallway.

She walked (well, hobbled) to meet him and the smile on his face turned sour when he saw that she had been injured. He dropped the bags of shopping onto the hall floor, including a huge bouquet of flowers, and walked towards her, concern etched over his gorgeous face.

"What happened?" he asked. "Are you okay?"

This was good, thought Tess. He was full of sympathy. She would have to play on this whole toe issue, big-time!

"Oh Rob, it is so, so sore! It's broken! It was an accident." She actually thought he was going to pick her up and carry her through to the living room but that would be just ludicrous so she kissed him slowly and then eased away, leading him inside.

"But what *happened*?"

"Well . . . we went to a karaoke club and Ruth stood on my foot by accident on the dance floor . . . I didn't realise it was so badly hurt at the time . . ."

"What? That's incredible!"

She lay on the sofa and he put a cushion under her foot, staring at the broken toe as if it was a life or death injury. Sometimes his love for her was so over-the-top that it got on her nerves, but not now! Now, she needed every ounce of attention she could get from him.

"Did you have it seen to?"

"I . . . well . . . yeah, I spent most of the night in hospital. Those A and E departments are so busy, Rob! Honestly, the wait was atrocious!"

She couldn't tell him! She just couldn't tell him!

"Tell me about it!" he said. "I was talking to that Sheila lady who works down at the Spar. She spent last night in hospital with her grandson and they had to wait for four hours to be seen. He had pulled a muscle when trying to kick his sister when they fell out over a game of Super Mario Brothers. Bloody ridiculous if you ask me!"

"I know, imagine fighting over Super Mario! That is ridiculous!" said Tess, hoping to raise a smile. It worked.

"Ha ha," said Rob. "I mean the waiting time. Oh come here, you! I have missed you so much! Do you realise how hard it is to fall asleep without you?"

He leaned forward to kiss her and his leg brushed against her toe.

"*Ow!*" she yelped and he pulled away.

"Oh, I'm sorry!" he said. He kissed her gently, reached for the remote control and gave it to her, then pulled a furry throw from off the back of the sofa and put it round her.

"What did I ever do to deserve you?" she asked.

"I ask myself that question every day," said Rob and Tess threw a cushion at him. "Now, do you fancy a cuppa? Or something stronger to ease the pain?"

Tess didn't. The very thought of any food or liquid was enough to make her nauseous. Rob hadn't had a hangover since his teens and even then they were mild from what he had told her.

"I might just wait a while," she whispered. "It was a long journey and I feel like I need to rest up, what with this sore toe and everything."

Rob stood at the doorway. For a moment she thought he could see right through her.

"Well, I'll be in the kitchen if you need anything," he said. "Just call."

He really was too good to be true. She couldn't tell him now. It would burst his bubble. It would ruin his day off.

"Okay babe," she said and when he left the room she closed her eyes tight. What was the name of that Patron Saint of Hopeless Cases again, she thought? Oh yeah, St Jude. She would use this time to have a good old word with her buddy, St Jude. He would be able to help, wouldn't he?

22

"So what happened to Tess?"

Polly felt her cheeks burn so she turned away from her husband, pretending to be busy unpacking her bag. There was no way she was telling James the full story. It would be right up his street to hear that Tess got into trouble. Tess never got into trouble. Not since she met Rob, anyhow. If James knew that she had been arrested, he would break into a *Riverdance* right there on the kitchen floor with delight.

It wasn't that he disliked Tess as such – in fact they were very similar characters in many ways. They each had too much to say and they were not afraid of saying it and sometimes that was funny, but sometimes it crossed the line and they would enter a full-blown argument over subjects that ranged from the political state of Northern Ireland to the benefits of cottage cheese when watching your weight. Anything, yes anything, could spark a row between Tess and James and this would be enough to give him ammunition against her for the rest of their days.

Tess was determined to keep it to herself for as long as possible.

"What do you mean?" she asked, sorting out the clothes she had worn from those she hadn't. She picked up the red jumpsuit and shuddered. If clothes could talk . . .

"She looks a deathly shade of white and her toe is all bandaged up," said James. "Put it like this, I haven't seen her looking as rough as that since the morning after her hen party and we all know what happened then!"

"Oh, here we go again!" said Polly. She brought her clothes to the adjoining laundry room and tipped them into the basket by the machine. She'd put the jumpsuit in a delicate wash cycle, she told herself, shuddering at the memories it brought back. The Stag. Oh, the Stag! She came back into the kitchen and made herself busy at the sink.

"What?" asked James, a huge smirk growing on his face. "You're hiding something, I can tell."

Oh fuck.

"I'm not."

"Yes, you are. Tess made a fool of herself and I want to know how. You don't know how long I've been waiting on some fuel to light up Miss Goody Two Shoes Teacher's fire."

"It was nothing like the hen party," said Polly. She could feel resentment at the look on his face and she was too tired and too hung-over to talk to him.

He really did love any given opportunity to bring up Tess's hen party, just as she loved to remind him of the antics of his own stag trip. It was like a never ending ping-pong game that no one would ever win.

"Ruth stood on her toe on the dance floor, if you must

know," said Polly. "It's no big deal. She'll live. But never mind all that, did you manage okay without me then? No dramas? No meltdowns?"

James wasn't letting it go so easily. In fact, he was finding it so amusing he had to sit down. He was buckled over with laughter.

"It was wee buns," he said between spurts. "No problems whatsoever . . . but back to the broken toe? *Who* stood on it?"

"Ruth," said Polly.

"*Ruth*?"

"Yes, Ruth! What's the big deal?" asked Polly. She really wanted to throw the dishcloth at him right now.

"Big is the very word!" he said. "Isn't that the big one who used to bully her at school?"

"Yes, why?"

"Oh sweet Jesus, this is hilarious! Where is my phone? I have to call her!"

"No!" said Polly. She dropped the dishcloth into the sink. "No, don't call her yet. She isn't ready to see the funny side. Not yet."

Polly tried to keep a serious face but then she kept picturing Ruth bouncing around the dance floor and her clumsy heel scrunching on top of Tess's dainty porkies. She could see why James would find it funny, but she was too stubborn to let him see her laugh along with him so she lifted the dishcloth again and began to wipe up breakfast cereal from the worktops.

"Okay, okay, you've had your laugh," she said. "I'm sure Tess isn't finding it quite so funny but, yes, I can see why you would find some humour in her injury."

"Honestly," said James, wiping his eyes. "That is the

235

funniest thing I have heard. I can just imagine Tess giving it all, posing for all she was worth, lapping up all the attention of every man in the bar and then *crunch!* I wouldn't like Ruth Monaghan standing on my toe! From what you have told me, she's no lightweight!"

"Enough, James!" said Polly. He really was starting to get on her nerves now. He was yet to ask if they'd had a good time. All he was interested in was taking the piss as usual. "I was thinking of taking the kids around to see Mum after lunch," she said, hoping to change the subject. "You fancy coming? We could go for a walk in the park afterwards. Get some fresh air into their lungs."

James was putting on his socks and shoes as she spoke to him. He had found it all such a doddle, he hadn't even had time to get dressed and it was lunchtime. *Pah!*

"Eh, let me think about that one," he said. "No. Thanks for the invitation but I'll give it a miss."

Polly threw the dishcloth into the sink again in bad temper.

"Why not?" she asked.

"Because I can think of other ways of spending my Sunday afternoon, thank you very much, but you go ahead. I just can't be bothered hearing of all the antics you got up to last night, which no doubt will be centre of conversation with you and your sisters once you get together around your mother's table."

Polly could feel her blood really boil now. Antics? That's all he could think of it as? Antics? He didn't give a shit if they'd had the time of their lives or the worst night out in history. He was so caught up in his own wee world that he just didn't want to know!

"You really are one ignorant pig these days, you know

that!" she said to him. "Why does everything have to be riddled with sarcasm or else silence with you lately? I am this close . . . *this* close . . ."

James stared at her and then shook his head, making her feel as pathetic as he always did.

"You're only home and you're at it again," he said.

"At what again? I only asked you if you'd like to come to my mum's to visit and you threw it back in my face."

James stood up. "Do you know what?" he said in defiance. "We had such a lovely time last night, just me and the kids. It was peaceful round here for a change!"

"Peaceful? What the hell are you saying?"

"I just don't know why you always get so stressed about everything," he spat. "The simplest things are turned into this great big deal every minute of every day. I don't know what goes on in your head but it isn't healthy! There's always a fucking issue, isn't there?"

Polly could feel herself well up. She wanted to run out through the door, just like she had felt the night before she left. Why did he make her feel this way? Why couldn't he be a bit like Rob sometimes? Tess was treated like a queen no matter what she did. No doubt she had told him about the incidents of last night and had his full support from the outset – but James? All he could do is belittle her and make her feel so worthless! And now he had told her that they had a lovely time without her! She had to get away from him before she said something she would regret.

"I'm taking the twins next door to see if Gina is okay," she said. "Maybe you could knock yourself out by serving lunch since you're so good at this domestic shit? No wonder it was all such a walk in the park. I had it all laid out for you. I'll be back in half an hour."

She left him fixing his belt onto his trousers and took the twins from the garden, trying to stay focused so that her tears wouldn't flow. He had made her cry far too much lately. Every time it happened, it was like he was hammering her slowly into the ground. Down, down, down she was going and every time it happened, she vowed she would never let him do it to her again.

Gina had left her husband because of his violence and fondness for other women. Ruth had left hers because he had an affair with another man. Polly knew she shouldn't think that way, but she wished sometimes that James would give her an excuse to get out. She didn't wish for violence or infidelity of any sort – that would be just sick, but something, just something so she could pinpoint exactly why she had to get away from him because she wasn't so sure she could cope with his attitude any more.

Gina was on the phone when Polly arrived at her door.

"Oh! Sorry!" whispered Polly. "I'll call back. I was just –"

Gina shook her head and stepped back from the front door, ushering Polly and the children inside as she cradled the phone on her shoulder.

"I don't care if it suits you or if it doesn't, Trevor!" she said, guiding them into the sitting room. "I'm having the locks changed this afternoon, so either you come by and get your belongings before then, or they end up in the dump!"

Gina stomped around as she spoke and Polly sat down on the huge cream-leather sofa, trying to distract the twins by flicking through a magazine that sat on Gina's coffee table. It was one of those psychology-filled glossies with lots of tips on how to change your life, be more creative and focus on positivity. The twins were having none of it and found a basket of potpourri much more fascinating.

"*Oh, is that so?*" asked Gina, her voice quivering with temper now.

She was doing laps of the ground floor and Polly assumed she was somewhere near the kitchen now.

"Is that *so*? *Over my dead body!*" she squealed. "And you can tell that bitch that if she as much as drives past my house she will have her tyres slashed and I mean it! I mean it, Trevor! *Ew!*"

She came into the living room where Polly was and threw the phone on the armchair.

"He hung up!" she said. "He fucking hung up! Oh, I'm sorry!"

She covered her mouth, realising that Polly's three-year-old twins were within earshot.

"Gina said fuck," said Thomas and his brother let out a giggle.

"Fuck!" repeated Max with great delight.

"Boys!" said Polly. "Honestly, it's like their ears are specially tuned in to pick up that word – like they have secret radar that lets them hear it from a certain distance. But anyhow, how are you? I'm sorry for landing in on you but I just had to get out of the house."

Gina put her head in her hands. She was less than a shadow of the bouncy, bubbly girl who had discovered herself in Donegal only the day before. She was back to looking small and thin and frail and, Polly didn't like to say it, but Gina looked weak.

"Can you park those two in front of the telly and we'll have a coffee, or is that asking for trouble?" asked Gina.

Polly thought about it. "We could chance it," she said. "I can't guarantee they won't pull the place apart or kill each other, but I'm up for it if you are. I can check on them at five-minute intervals."

"Great!" said Gina. "I'll go put the kettle on while you find something on CBeebies that might mildly amuse them."

Polly looked around Gina's living room. To an outsider, it was the scene of a picture-perfect family life. The huge deep cream-leather sofa with its inviting fluffy cushions, a shiny polished wooden floor centred with a tasteful rug that looked like it cost a fortune, exotic potted plants that certainly didn't come from Asda on either side of the antique fireplace and framed photos of smiley happy family life on a bureau in the corner. Gina had put a lot of effort into making her house a beautiful home, but its fine décor was merely a mask that hid the heartbreak and hurt that it held within its walls.

"Boys, would you like to watch something on telly?" Polly asked her twins.

Asking Thomas and Max what they would like to watch on TV was like inviting an unnecessary political debate your way. They had similar tastes, as most three-year-old boys do, but they loved a good argument and sometimes Polly felt that they knew their disagreements were enough to set her over the edge and, better again, bribe them with chocolate to shut their little faces.

"Postman Pat," said Max. He was a tad obsessed with Jess the cat these days. He was a retro kind of kid.

"No!" said Thomas. "I don't like Pat. *Yuk*."

Thomas had more modern taste. He was a big fan of Iggle Piggle.

Polly flicked through the children's channels until she

found an old episode of that annoying Australian sing-along show where the five adults were a bit too happy for her liking.

"*Yeah!*" the twins said in chorus.

Great stuff!

"*Yeah!*" said Polly in return. Maybe she did like those happy people after all. "Now you two sing along and Mummy is going to be in the kitchen with Gina, okay?"

They didn't answer her. They were too engrossed in the happy people. Polly couldn't blame them. She knew her own face looked like a miserable Monday.

"Oh Gina, it really is horrible, isn't it? I can only imagine what you're going through!" she said when she joined her friend who was impatiently waiting on the kettle. She could keep an eye on the twins through the glass doors between Gina's living room and kitchen, which settled her nerves ever so slightly.

"I just don't get him," said Gina.

Her wee face was pale and she looked like she had been crying a lot.

"I mean, why can't he walk away with a bit of grace, you know? He has no need to fight with me and make it even harder."

She served up the coffee, visibly fighting back tears, and joined Polly at the kitchen table.

"Why, what's he saying to you?" asked Polly. "I can't believe he has the cheek to put you through more torture after all the time you put up with his stinking behaviour!"

She would love to get Trevor Humphries by the throat. She really would.

Gina sniffled and shook her head. "It's like he is the victim, I swear! It's like I plucked this idea to leave him

241

out of the blue and for no reason at all. He thinks I have no right to end our marriage, that I have no right to assume that Danny and I can stay here in our family home. He says he will put up a fight even though I've been fighting it out for years and years."

She broke down again and Polly rubbed her shoulder. Poor Gina. She didn't deserve any of this.

"Where's wee Danny now?" asked Polly. She didn't think it was a good idea for Danny to see his mum in such a state. "I could take him for a while if it gives you time to get your head around things."

"No, no, it's fine. Thanks, Polly, but I kind of need him, you know?" said Gina, trying to talk without sobbing. "He's down the road playing with that wee fella with the funny voice, but I need to make him something to eat soon – and it might sound stupid but something as simple as that gives me strength to carry on. Just knowing he needs me."

Polly nodded in silence. She could totally understand where Gina was coming from. Danny was the only thing keeping her together at the minute. He was the only reason why she was still functioning. Without him, she would go to pieces altogether.

"Well, is there anything I can do to help?" asked Polly, knowing it was one of those stupid questions that people were asked over and over again at the time of a crisis such as a break-up or a death in the family, but that there was no 'yes' answer to. (Unless you could mend a broken heart, bring someone back from the dead or change a violent, cheating bastard's ways – and most humans were incapable of those things. Funnily enough.)

"Just be there for me, Polly," said Gina, grasping her friend's hand. Her knuckles were white against her pink skin and her hand shook despite her tight grip. "I just need to know you're there for me."

"Always," said Polly, feeling emotional now. If this was what a marriage break-up was like, she dreaded the day it might ever happen to her. "You know that I'm only a phone call or a text away, or just call over to me any time day or night. You don't have to go through this on your own. I'm here for you and so are Tess and Ruth. Tess might be in prison, mind you, but she'll have you in her thoughts and prayers."

To Polly's relief, Gina saw the funny side.

"You know, I totally forgot about all that. Any word from her? Has she told Rob?"

Polly shrugged. "I haven't heard from her since she left here earlier. No doubt he's too busy fussing over her broken toe to even have noticed the word 'arrested'. Honestly, he is so good to her it would make you sick."

Gina stared at the table. "It's funny that, isn't it?" she said, twisting a tissue in her hands.

"What's funny?" asked Polly. "Tess in prison for battering a doorman?"

"No," said Gina. "I mean, when a man is really, really good to someone, we say it would make you sick. And then, as in my case, when a man is really, really bad to you, it makes you sick too. So how the hell do we find the right one then, if they all are going to make us sick?"

Polly thought for a moment. Gina had a good point. It was the butt of all jokes in their family that Rob treated Tess like a princess. Her thirtieth birthday was just around the corner and the sisters had a sweepstake on how sickeningly romantic he might be to mark the occasion. Tess would say they were all just jealous, and sometimes Polly was, but most of the time she wondered if all that attention and adoration would be too much to bear?

But then there were the Trevor Humphries of the world. Pig-ignorant bullies who would make your skin crawl. Much more sickening than Rob being a 'pussy', as James often called him.

"I don't want to be so clichéd as to say 'a happy medium'," she said to Gina. "But too much one way or another cannot be healthy. Trevor is an extreme that no woman should have to put up with, but you wouldn't want them grovelling to you twenty-four-seven, would you? Otherwise, there is no passion, no spark. It's hard to beat a healthy row where each party gives it their all and then have great make-up sex afterwards."

Polly peeped in at Thomas and Max as they spoke. Those Aussie dudes were playing a blinder and the twins were still dancing merrily to their tune. Little angels! For now . . .

"Oh good God, don't mention that word!" said Gina, burying her head in her hands again. "I swear, Polly. I won't sleep for days with the guilt and shame of that carry-on yesterday. I'm mortified. On top of everything else, that's really not helping me at all!"

Polly let out a hoot of laughter at poor Gina's face. She really was in the horrors over Marco.

"Don't be so silly!" she said. "You were letting off some steam, letting off some anger! You didn't do anything wrong! Marco was a hot stud! Be proud of it!"

"But I *did* do something wrong!" hissed Gina. "I slept with a young man I had only met minutes before. Not hours. *Minutes*! I'm a slut! And I'm still a married woman! It was reckless and inappropriate and irresponsible and I'll go to hell for it!"

Polly was in stitches now. "It *was* reckless and irresponsible and whatever that other word you used –"

"Inappropriate," said Gina very seriously.

"Yes, that too and it's not behaviour that you would recommend on a day-to-day basis, but look at it this way – you have been treated like a dirty dishrag by that Trevor monster for years and you finally took a very brave step on Friday. You left him. You were free. Marco made you feel young and new again and, if I recall, you were walking on air yesterday!"

"I was pissed out of my mind! I could barely walk on the pavement at all at the end of the night, never mind on air and look at how much trouble *that* caused, but that's another bloody story!"

"*Ha ha*, okay," said Polly. "Well, to be honest with you, I don't think you should annoy your wee head any more about Marco. You have enough to deal with right here, right now."

"But I can't stop thinking about it!" said Gina. "I was even contemplating going to Confession. I haven't been to Confession since I was twelve!"

Polly looked her in the eye. She really was putting herself through terrible mental torture. And Confession was a bit extreme. As pious as Polly could be at times, she didn't agree with telling a priest your deepest darkest secrets. They were between her and the Man Above. She didn't need a middleman knowing her business. No way.

"Stop that immediately," she said to Gina. "You have done nothing wrong. In fact, you did what a lot of us would only dream of doing. You followed your instincts, it made you feel on top of the world and now you should close the door on it. Focus on today. Focus on Danny and

245

focus on getting that asshole his clothes back so he can get out of your life and let you get on with it."

Gina's face froze at the sound of a car arriving outside. Trevor. She looked terrified and she grabbed Polly's hand again.

"It's him," she said, her bottom lip trembling. "He'll know, Polly! He'll know I was with another man! The second he looks at me he will know!"

Polly felt panic rise into her throat. She had only spoken to Trevor Humphries over the fence on occasion, when he was putting out the bins or when he was getting into his car and it was only ever a polite hello. Sometimes he didn't answer at all. She should go. She should leave now, shouldn't she?

"Please don't leave me, Polly!" said Gina as the key turned in the door.

Polly's heart was thumping and she knew Gina's was too.

"Deep breaths," said Polly. "I'm not going anywhere. You will be fine. I'll stay to make sure."

Trevor entered the kitchen, whistling casually and wearing a two-day stubble. He stank of alcohol and stale smoke and his shirt was stained with beer down the front.

He placed what looked like a boxed toy on the counter, then glanced at Polly but didn't acknowledge her. She couldn't speak. She could see the twins dancing in the sitting room and it looked like two totally different worlds were about to collide. She couldn't let her children witness this. She had to go.

"Don't go, Polly," whimpered Gina. "Please."

Trevor Humphries raised his chin and pointed at Polly, but kept his eyes on Gina.

"I want to talk to my wife alone," he said. His voice was gravelly and matched his appearance no end.

Polly wanted to scream for help. She wanted James to burst in right there and then. She didn't know what to do. She wanted to go, but she needed to stay. She had no idea! What should she do!

"Polly . . . Polly is just finishing her coffee," said Gina. "Your clothes are packed at the top of the stairs. In your suitcase. You can get them and then go. *Now.*"

"I want to talk to my wife alone," he repeated. His eyes were wild and he breathed in and out of his nostrils. "I'm sure Sally can give us some space, can't you, Sally?"

"It's Polly," said Polly. "Not Sally, Polly."

He turned his head slowly towards her and Polly felt a shiver go straight to her bones. He was a slightly built man, about five foot eight but his tone was fierce and, up against Gina, he was like a world champion heavyweight. She wouldn't stand a chance.

"Okay, I'll go . . . but I'll be back in five minutes," she said, slowly standing up from the table. She saw the look of pleading fear in Gina's eyes.

"Five minutes," said Gina, with a gulp. Polly nodded.

Trevor was staring at his wife again.

"I'm just next door if you need me before then," Polly said and she walked slowly towards the sitting room where the twins were caught up in innocence and laughter.

She took the boys by the hand and, ignoring their resistance to leave, she left Gina alone with her husband and walked next door with a fear in her heart that she had never experienced before.

247

23

"Don't touch me, Trevor. Please don't touch me," whispered Gina. Her voice was breathy and her mouth was so dry. She kept glancing towards the back door, waiting on Danny to burst in from his play.

Trevor's silence was petrifying. He stood over her, shaking his head and clenching his clammy fists. It was only seconds since Polly had left, but it seemed like an eternity. Gina glanced at the clock, willing it to move forward. It was coming up to two in the afternoon. Danny would need a snack soon. He had barely touched his lunch. Maybe he would have a sandwich? Tuna perhaps? Or banana. Yes, he loved banana sandwiches. As soon as Trevor left she would –

"*Arghh!*" His fist landed across her cheek and it throbbed! Oh God, it throbbed so badly!

"*You dirty, filthy whore!*" he said, shaking his right hand and shuffling his feet like a frustrated animal.

"Where were you last night? Where did you go, you slut? I'll kill him! I'll fucking kill him!"

Gina cowered into the kitchen chair, almost into the foetal position. He knew. She could tell he knew. He knew everything about her. She knew barely anything about him these days but he always knew what she got up to. If she visited a different grocery store than usual, he would hear it before she got home. If she took a different route to school with Danny, he would quiz her as to why. So why the hell did she believe that she would ever get away with what she did yesterday? Why did she think she would ever have the ability to leave him? He wouldn't let her. He had full control.

"I . . . I don't know what you are talking about," she said. "I was with Polly. I needed a break. *Arrgh!*"

The second was always the worst. It was like childbirth. The first time it's unexpected and you take the blow, but next time around, you know what's ahead and it's even more terrifying than before.

"You left our son with my mother so you could go whoring around town with that posh bitch from next door, didn't you? Look at me! *Didn't you?*"

Gina was trembling from the very inside. Five minutes must be up by now, she thought. Please, Polly. Please come back. Please. She couldn't take any more. She was on the brink of telling him about Marco. She felt so dirty and he was so convincing. She was a whore. She slept with a stranger. She deserved what he was saying.

"I . . . I didn't mean to . . . I didn't . . ."

"You did!" he said. "You fucking –"

A flurry of footsteps from outside slowed down the

mood and they both waited to see who their visitor was. Trevor had a river of perspiration above his lip and his forehead was dotted with glassy beads. Gina could feel a trickle of cold sweat travel right down her spine.

"If she is back," whispered Trevor, his fists clenching again. "If that nosey tart doesn't know when to stay away from my house, I'll chase her. I'll fucking chase her!"

His chest heaved in and out as he waited and then the back door burst open.

"Daddy!"

Oh God! Oh God, thank you! thought Gina.

It was Danny and, like a deflated balloon, Gina almost collapsed against the table. Danny was home. He had saved her much more than Polly could. Trevor would never touch her in front of their son. Yes, he had battered her black and blue when the boy was asleep, but never in cold daylight in front of his eyes.

"Hello, my boy!" said Trevor and, like someone had flicked a switch, his whole personality changed into that of a doting father who had returned from a legitimate trip away. Even the beads of perspiration that had sat above his lips and on his forehead had disappeared.

"You smell like bad beer," said Danny, pulling away when Trevor leaned in to embrace him. "*Yuk!*"

Gina discreetly wiped her mouth with the back of her hand and looked at it. Yes, just as she thought, she was bleeding. She couldn't let Danny see her like this. She had to slip away before he noticed her tear-stained, blood-stained face.

"Look what I have for you!" said Trevor and the young boy's eyes danced in his head with anticipation as his father picked up the box he had placed on the counter earlier.

As Danny tore the box open and pulled out a toy plane, Gina saw her opportunity and left the kitchen to find the solace of the downstairs bathroom.

She closed the door behind her and leaned against it. She felt dizzy and drained and she could barely breathe. Her jaw hurt and the blood was coming heavier now. She leaned over the sink and spat bright red pools over the stark cold white porcelain, then rinsed her mouth and tried to ignore the sting where her tooth had pierced the inside of her cheek. It wasn't the worst she'd had to suffer, not by a long shot, but the timing of it all, after Marco, made it all the more fierce. She didn't deserve it. No one deserved to suffer like that. But she had betrayed him and, deep inside, she knew he could tell.

Ruth was in her car. She was driving it. She was driving it towards the city. After that, she had no idea what she was going to do, but she was hung over and feeling brave. Her Alfa Romeo zoomed down the motorway towards Belfast and she felt a fire in her belly that she hadn't felt in a very long time. It was a 'carpe diem' feeling. A now or never. A 'sod it, I'll take the chance' notion that had come on her moments after her son left for his rugby game.

She had been sitting alone at her kitchen table, nursing a cold cup of coffee when the idea came into her head. Melanie was still vegetating on the sofa inside and the trill of pop music was booming on Ruth's fragile head. She didn't realise it until afterwards, but she had been staring at the same spot on the kitchen table for at least six minutes, her mind emptying as she focused on the here and now.

Jeff was gone. There was no more life with Jeff. Her business was a sham. She had no more desire to design brochures or websites than she had to go back to her bogus life in London, full of pretentious assholes who truly believed that money made the world go round. She had two healthy, if sometimes ungrateful, teenagers. She had a beautiful roof over her head, a nice car, she had been reunited with people that used to hate her and who now called her a friend. She had to stay in tune with the present and look towards the future. But every time she thought of that word, she saw her mother's face.

"I'll be back . . ." She didn't know what to tell her daughter. "I'll be back by six. I've left money in the kitchen if you want to go get a snack."

"Chinese again?" snarled Mel.

As if she didn't love an excuse to stuff her face with noodles and chicken and curry sauce!

"You could buy something and . . . what's that word?" asked Ruth. "Oh yeah, cook it? You could buy something and cook it?"

Melanie mumbled and went back to flicking the channels on the television and Ruth left her to it.

She didn't fear for her relationship with her fourteen-year-old daughter. Girls were strange creatures at that age. Full of hormones and change and frustration so it was best to just ride the storm, even if it did threaten to send her into an early menopause sometimes.

She checked her make-up in the hallway mirror, fixed her lipstick, sprayed her favourite perfume and brushed her red hair. She really, really did need to get her roots done. With her long black dress and pale skin, she looked like someone from *The Addams Family* but that was her style and she sort of liked it.

Now, she was hurtling towards the city with Radio 2 blaring as she drove, singing along in denial as she made her way to her destination. But with only twelve miles to go, she released her foot from the throttle and slowed down to give herself a little bit of time for it all to sink in.

She couldn't just turn up unannounced, she knew that. It would be like World War III on the spot. Instant carnage. Murder. Well, maybe not murder, but it wouldn't be pretty.

It had been ten years. Almost to the day. Ten years was a long time not to have any contact with the woman who brought you into the world and the idea of it made Ruth sick to the pit of her stomach. She remembered the day so clearly, as if it was yesterday. She remembered it scene by scene, word by word, as if it was a detailed diary entry she had scripted and learned off by heart. She remembered her mother's face, etched with hurt and disappointment that she could be arguing so deeply with her only daughter on such a dark day of their lives. They were both to blame, there was no doubt in Ruth's mind. There were things said that should never have been said. Things that could never be forgotten. Things that could never be taken back. But she could try. She could only try.

Belfast was now in the near distance and she could see the new art piece called RISE, a huge transparent web in the shape of a ball, which guided her to the short tunnel that took her onto the city's Westlink. Ruth thought that the ball looked more like a huge testicle than a piece of art, but who was she to comment?

Belfast was a changed place since she left home as a teenager and she felt proud to be linked to such a beautiful city, enwrapped in history and culture and hope. Her mother had always been a city girl and had detested and resented the country life forced on her when she married Ruth's father. She was more than delighted to escape back to her roots when she left to live with Raymond. And that's when her relationship with Ruth went terribly downhill. After the divorce went through, she married Raymond in the City Hall and Ruth, under pressure from her mother, attended.

Ruth drove off the Westlink and onto the Crumlin Road. She could feel sweat trickle under her arms and down her back and she turned the radio off in order to concentrate. It was a bright, breezy Sunday afternoon and the traffic was light which allowed her time to get her breath back and to get her bearings. She hadn't been here in such a long time and the sights and sounds were taking her right back to that fateful day in 2002.

"Raymond is dead."

Her mother's voice had been so cold and stoic and overflowing with grief and shock. She had spat the words down the phone to Ruth, as if it was somehow her fault that her mother's husband had kicked the bucket. As if she was telling Ruth exactly what she had been longing to hear for years.

"I'll be right there," Ruth had replied, equally clinical, and she had set about making arrangements with their nanny to look after Ben and Melanie while she made the trip across the water for the funeral.

She remembered the plane. She could remember the

very seat she was in as she flew into Belfast City airport.
It was cold for the time of year. There was a certain nip in
the air and Ruth had been sure it was Raymond pinching
her from the skies, blowing a cold wind round her neck as
she made her way across town to her mother's home.

He hated her. He really did and she had made no bones
about how she felt about him too.

Her brother had greeted her at the door with a light
hug. Brian was always the peacemaker. A gentle soul who
had wasted far too much of his life playing referee to the
women in his life. When he married Fiona, a country girl
who was as easygoing as he was, he thought his days of
arguments were over, but there would never be an
argument like there was the day of Raymond's funeral.

"Mum's inside," he had told her in his soft, gentle tone
that reminded Ruth so much of her dad. She missed her
dad. She was always a daddy's girl.

Ruth would never forget the look of scorn on her
mother's face when she greeted her. The house had been
packed with visitors – a traditional Irish wake with
neighbours, friends and relatives rallying round to look
after the grieving widow and her nearest and dearest.

"You must be Ruth," said a voice which was laced
with acid and venom.

The room went silent. Ruth looked to where a girl not
far from her own age stood, her eyes bloodshot and her
face puffy from crying.

"Yes," said Ruth. "Samantha?"

Ruth extended a hand but the girl, a chubby blonde
who gripped a set of rosary beads tightly in her hands,
didn't return the gesture. Instead, she glared at Ruth with
glassy green eyes and then she spoke.

"Why are you here?" she asked.

Ruth was stunned and she looked to her mother for help. She could feel all eyes on her as she stood adjacent to the coffin of a man she detested with all her might. She shouldn't have come. It was no secret that she blamed Raymond Dillon for the break-up of her happy home. But her mother was her mother, wasn't she? She wasn't here for Raymond. She was here for her mother.

"I – I wanted to pay my respects to the dead," she lied and Samantha gave a fake laugh.

"Respect?" she said. "You wouldn't know the meaning of the word! You had no respect for my father when he was alive so why would you claim to respect him when he's dead? You're too late, Ruth. He told me all about you! Why don't you go back and crawl into whatever sewer you came out of?"

Ruth felt the room spin around her. It was hot and clammy and it smelled like death and she needed to take her coat off before she fainted. She was so hot. She was humiliated and the people around her – far too many to be in such a small space – whispered under their breath and paranoia rose up to Ruth's throat and began to choke her.

It was her brother, as always, who came to her aid. He guided her, by the shoulders, out of the room, away from the corpse and her mother and the stepsister that she had met only very briefly at the shoddy civil service of their parents' wedding. Ruth had left before the reception, too upset to stay, knowing her father was at home in Cranmore breaking his heart. Brian led her outside into the cool air and they sat down on the back step of her mother's house.

"Why didn't she say something?" Ruth asked. "Why

didn't she tell her to be quiet? They're all talking about me now. I can feel it!"

Brian lit up a cigarette and passed it to his sister who took a long draw. They used to share cigarettes as teenagers and, even though she no longer smoked, doing so then with Brian made her feel at ease, as if she still belonged . . . as if the family bond was still there.

"She is heartbroken," said Brian. "She has barely spoken in days. She really loved him, you know. Despite how angry we have been about it, she really did love him and she is in deep shock. Samantha was out of line, but I suppose we have to allow for grief there too. You did the right thing by coming today. Mum might not realise it now, but she will appreciate it once the dust settles."

Ruth rested her head on her brother's shoulder and felt her body temperature simmer back to normal. She had been nervous about the trip and she did feel hypocritical. She had never acknowledged her mother's second marriage, not after she witnessed her father drink himself into an early grave with heartache at losing his family to another man. Raymond Dillon had blood on his hands as far as Ruth could see, and she had never been afraid to say it.

"Why won't she ever forgive me?" she whispered. "Can't she understand why I felt the way I did about him? He hated me too. He hated me more."

Brian patted her leg, and then stubbed out his cigarette under his shoe.

"You're her daughter," he said, his voice steady and gentle. "You're her flesh and blood and once this is all over it may be the perfect time to start all over again."

"Oh, would you listen to them playing happy families!" a spiteful voice interrupted them.

Samantha had been standing behind them the whole time and had saved announcing her presence until she had heard what she wanted to.

"Not now, Samantha. I think you've said enough."

Brian was calm but Ruth's heart was thumping with fear of what the other woman would say to her next.

"I'm only starting," said Samantha. "You may be her *flesh and blood*, but I have been more of a daughter to your mother than you have ever been!" She lit up a long white menthol cigarette and exhaled like a rebellious teenager.

"Don't say that!"

"You make me sick," continued Samantha. "How dare you cast judgement on my father when you didn't even give him a chance? You don't belong around here any more. You're not part of this family! I think it would be best for us all if you just go home to your rich man and your big fat fancy lifestyle in London with your two-point-four children! We were never good enough for you so just leave us alone!"

"That's enough, Samantha," said Brian. "This isn't the time nor is it the place to dish the dirt on my sister. She has come here because she has a right to be here. And there are people watching!"

"Oh stop sticking up for her – you said the same," said Samantha, looking at Brian now. "She has no place here any more. You said it!"

Ruth froze. Had Brian really said the same? Her own brother? Her heart was being crushed now, so badly she could almost hear it, crumpling up into a tiny ball inside her chest.

"I didn't say it quite like that," said Brian.

Ruth stood up, away from him. She was an outcast. They had all been talking about her. They hated her. All of them. She wasn't part of the family. Samantha had said it. And Brian too?

"What *exactly* did you say then, Brian?" asked Ruth. Her lip quivered. Hearing this was worse than anything Samantha could have thrown at her.

But Samantha was on a roll now. And it was two against one.

"Your mother says that since you moved to London –"

"Shut up, Samantha!" said Brian. He had lost his cool and his voice was raised so that everyone inside would surely hear. "I think you have said enough. This is between Ruth and me now. Go back inside immediately!"

Ruth's hands were trembling. She put them in her coat pockets, then she took them out and folded her arms, but no matter what way she stood, she couldn't feel in any way in control. She wanted to get out of there and never come back. The hurt she felt burned right into her soul.

Samantha stood her ground.

"Mum has been feeling very lonely since Raymond took ill," said Brian to his sister. "She has relied a lot on Samantha and me, but that's because you don't live nearby. If you did –"

"If she did it wouldn't make any difference," said Samantha. "Ruth couldn't bear the sight of my father so she would have stayed away regardless. Everyone knows that."

Brian's eyes darted between the two women and once again he was playing peacemaker, trying to explain as best he could how his mother felt without hurting his sister so badly that she would never want to come back again.

"She needed you, Ruth," he said. "She needed you and you didn't call. Her husband was dying –"

"He was nothing to me!" said Ruth, feeling the dam burst as the tears streamed from her eyes. "He wasn't my father! I nursed my own father on his deathbed because that man stole his wife! If it weren't for him, we wouldn't have already buried the man who gave his life to us! Raymond Dillon gave us nothing only a broken home!"

Samantha squealed. "You hateful bitch!" she shouted and then she lashed out at Ruth physically, her chubby hands gripping Ruth's hair as Brian tried to part them. She was out of control, scrabbling and scraping Ruth's face and pulling at her clothes like a raging tiger. Brian eventually jolted her away, out of breath, and Ruth fell onto the grass in a wave of shock and exhaustion.

She looked up to the back door of the house where faces peered out through the net curtains. Tea-makers had stopped making tea, grieving relatives had stopped being consoled. Amongst them was her mother who walked to the back door and stared at Ruth.

"Why do you always cause such trouble, Ruth Monaghan?"

"I . . . I only wanted to see you."

"I have had enough of you," her mother had said, her voice weary and sad. "I think it might be best if you leave us to grieve for Raymond in peace. He is gone now. Let him go . . . in peace."

"Mum?"

Ruth felt like she was carrying a lead ball inside her as she watched her mother turn away, being comforted by Samantha as they moved inside. She walked back into the house, staring at the floor, in through the tiny kitchen, past the grieving relatives and tea-makers, past the room where the corpse of Raymond Dillon lay and she lifted her overnight bag and walked out through the front door. She would never hear from her mother again.

24

Polly heard Trevor Humphries' car pull out of the driveway next door and she let out a huge sigh of relief. She walked towards her bedroom window which looked out of the side of her house and onto Gina's driveway. Yes, he was gone.

She raced downstairs and out through the door, down her drive and across to Gina's. She didn't knock on the front door and, when she burst inside, she was frightened to death of what she might find.

"Hello?"

Gina walked from the kitchen, wiping her hands on a tea-towel. She was shaking and her lip was beginning to swell. Polly ran towards her and held her tight.

"I'm okay now, Polly. That's it all over now. I'm okay."

Polly felt hot tears trickle down her cheeks and onto Gina's wispy hair.

"I am so sorry!" she gasped. "It was five minutes. I said I'd be back in five minutes but I was too late!"

Gina shook her head and released herself from Polly's grasp. She smiled at her neighbour but the inside of her mouth stung when she did and she let out a hiss of pain.

"Onwards and upwards," said Gina, closing the living room door where Danny was playing with his new toy plane. "I'm just getting Danny a banana sandwich. He loves banana sandwiches."

She turned away from Polly, went back to the worktop where she had laid out two rounds of bread and some butter and continued slicing up the banana.

"So, what happens now?" asked Polly. "Are you just going to forget he did this to you, or are you going to call the police and screw the bastard? You need to get a restraining order on him so that he doesn't come back and do this to you again!" She felt more distraught about it than Gina seemed to be. She had never witnessed domestic violence so closely and she could feel anger and frustration boil up inside her.

"I am having the locks changed at four," said Gina, ever so matter of factly. "He has taken all his belongings. I assume he has gone to live with her but I didn't ask him. His mother refuses to give him the time of day and he doesn't exactly have any friends apart from his employees and I'm sure none of them will want to home him."

"I didn't mean what would happen to him," said Polly. She leaned against the worktop and watched as Gina made the sandwich for her son with such precision. It was almost like a work of art as far as banana sandwiches go and, if it weren't for the horrible circumstances, Polly would have made a joke about the symmetrical row of little circles that lay so perfectly on their bed of bread.

263

"Oh, me?" said Gina. She reached into a cupboard for a plate for the sandwich, then poured a glass of milk and brought the lot in to Danny.

"Yes, you," said Polly when she returned. It was like talking to a robot.

"I'm just going to get on with things," said Gina. She wiped her hands on the tea towel and then ran her fingers through her hair. Her mouth was starting to bleed again and she dabbed it with her finger. "Coffee?"

Polly stared at her vacantly. "Coffee? Yeah, okay. Listen, Gina. I'm not sure if you are aware but –"

"I deserved it, Polly, okay?" said Gina. "Just drop it. He knows me inside out. He could tell just by looking at me that I had been with another man. He's not stupid!"

"He *is* stupid!" snapped Polly, a little louder than she had intended. "He is stupid and ignorant and a violent bully and there is no way that he could have known! Stop making excuses! No woman deserves to be beat around like that!"

Gina slammed two cups down on the worktop, fetched the milk from the fridge and slopped it into the cups, ignoring the fact that she had spilled most of it over herself and the worktop in the process.

"A cheating woman does!" said Gina. "What sort of a wife and mother am I, anyhow? Who the hell did I think I was, jumping into bed with another man the very day after I had ended my marriage! Would you do that to James? Why did I do it?"

"I almost did it too!" said Polly. "I was seconds away from cheating on my husband the other night! Seconds! Only that Tess stopped me, I would be in a very different position today but that's not something I'm proud of!"

264

"But you didn't! So why did I do it? Why does anyone feel the need to cheat?"

Polly held her hands out. "I don't know why anyone does!" she said. "It scares the shit out of me, even admitting it to you now. Saying it out loud makes it real and my skin is crawling at what could have happened, but you? Your case is different. Your marriage was over long, long ago. Trevor has been with his mistress for ages now and he made no effort to hide it – not from you, not from your friends or family, not even from his own mother! And then he gives you the odd slap in the mouth to remind you who is boss? Don't you dare feel guilty, Gina! I don't care if you slept with the entire *army* yesterday! Don't you dare feel guilty!"

Gina poured the coffee and they stood in silence. The radio was playing a George Michael song and Gina didn't even notice.

"I should probably get on with things now, Polly," she whispered. "Thanks for calling. I just need some time to think, on my own, you know? I need to go to the shop. I promised Danny we would have a movie night. It's important I spend some time with my son. Alone."

Polly poured her coffee down the sink and sat the cup to the side. She couldn't drink it. She knew when she wasn't wanted.

"Okay," she said. "But you know where I am. You don't have to do this on your own, unless you really want to."

"I have Danny to think of," said Gina. "I have Danny and I have locks to change and I have to focus on the future. I never want to look back. I never want to be treated like this again."

Trevor had left in an awful rage earlier, vowing to be back, but Gina couldn't even think of that now. She'd tidied herself up and hung out some washing and was on autopilot, convincing herself that she had seen the last of him. She knew deep down that she hadn't.

"That's good," said Polly. "Stay strong, Gina. I will be cheering you on from the sidelines or the front row or wherever you want me to be."

"Thanks," said Gina, and Polly left her standing in the kitchen, clasping her coffee cup as if it held the secret path to a pain-free future.

"You didn't eat much."

Tess was staring at her plate, unaware that she hadn't touched her food in at least ten minutes. Rob had prepared her a dish to die for but she couldn't taste it. Her mouth felt numb, as if her tongue was riddled with lies and the guilt of what she was keeping from her husband.

"I'm in trouble, Rob," she said, afraid of looking into his eyes.

She felt him stir in his seat and when she did look up at him, she could tell his mind had gone into overdrive.

"You didn't –"

He couldn't finish his sentence and Tess knew exactly what he was thinking. She clasped his hand and squeezed it tight.

"Oh baby, no! Nothing like that!" she said.

She could almost feel the adrenaline run into his hand and his breathing was obvious and unsteady.

"What . . . what sort of trouble then?"

Tess took her time. No matter how many times she had

266

rehearsed it in her head, there was no way round it. She would just have to spit it out.

"I was arrested last night," she said.

Rob laughed. It was more a nervous giggle and he pulled away from her in disbelief.

"You what? Arrested? What on earth?"

He was still giggling and it irritated Tess. She could feel her temper rise. This was not the reaction she had expected but it was making her angry.

"It's no laughing matter, Rob! I could lose my job over this!"

Rob stood up from the table and paced the kitchen floor.

"I'm not laughing! I mean – arrested for what? You? Arrested? Are you serious?"

"Yes, I am very serious!" she said. "I spent the night in a cell. It was so scary, Rob. If they press charges I am screwed. I have been worried sick about telling you and all I get is a smarmy giggle. You have no idea what I've been through!"

Tears sprang to Tess's eyes and she sniffled back her emotion. She had been expecting a lecture, a shameful telling-off, a 'what will the neighbours say' type of sermon but he wasn't saying anything like that. Instead he was pacing the kitchen floor like an expectant father in a labour ward.

"But for *what*? What the hell were you arrested for? You weren't drinking and driving, were you?"

"No!" she said defiantly. "I'm not that reckless! It was so stupid. It was a drunken argument with a doorman that got out of hand and I . . . well, I got angry and they

arrested me for assault and . . . and damage to property . . .
a window. I was taken away in a car and everything. It
was the worst experience of my life. I mean, I know I
shouldn't have reacted the way I did but . . . oh God, Rob,
what have I done?"

Rob sat back down at the kitchen table and took his
wife's hand. He leaned across and kissed away her tears.

"Oh baby," he said, a sympathetic smile on his face,
"don't get upset. We will deal with this. It's not going to
come to anything."

"How do you know?" sobbed Tess. "I've paid for the
damage but the police may press charges and so might the
bouncer. Plus I am so humiliated. Imagine if the school
finds out. Or my mother, or worse, your mother! I will be
ruined, Rob. My whole reputation . . . my career . . . oh
God, I wish I could turn back the clock. He was just so
rude. So demeaning. I should have hit him harder. No,
that's not true. I shouldn't have hit him at all!"

Rob couldn't help but laugh again, no matter how he
tried to hold it back. "I think you are getting upset over
very little," he whispered. "I thought you were going to
tell me you did something really serious."

"Like what? Like I was arrested for breaking and
entering? Would that be serious enough for you? It wasn't
funny, Rob!"

"Okay, okay!" he said. "Look, why don't you go have a
nice long bath and let me call a few people. Find out what
we can do to nip this in the bud before it gets out of hand."

Tess sniffled more. A hot bath sounded so appealing
right now. She was tired and emotional and she felt sick
to the core. The smell of the police cell was still on her

skin, the sounds of the doors banging behind her were still ringing in her ears. She wanted to scrub it all away. She felt like she had something crawling inside her and she needed to make it stop.

"How can I go to work tomorrow feeling like this?" she said. "I'm worried sick. The guy is a well-known asshole – even the cop said so – but he is also known to be a troublemaker. I'm so scared, Rob. I never want to see another police station in my life!"

"Leave it with me," said Rob. "Go have your bath, wash away that hangover and we'll have an early night. I don't care who or what this guy is. He is not going to ruin you, I can assure you. We will get the best advice on this, I promise. "

"Thanks, babe," said Tess. "And dinner was lovely. I just don't have an appetite right now. Go figure."

Tess stood up and tried to muster up the energy to go and run a bath. She had so much running through her head. She was worried about Gina, she was worried about Ruth, she was worried about Polly and James and what would become of them. She was worried about herself.

She walked into the hallway and hobbled up the stairs to try and get her head around how everything had become such a mess.

Polly saw the police arrive at Gina's door and her heart jumped into her mouth. Had Trevor come back? Ordering Frankie to stay and watch the little ones, she ran outside, leaving all three of them pinned to the living-room window with open mouths, staring at the police and squad car.

"Hello?" she called to the officer who was knocking on

269

the front door of Gina's house. Another was peering in through the front door. "What's happened? Is Gina okay? I only left her an hour ago!"

"Your neighbour has been in an accident," he said. "We are trying to contact her husband. Do you know where we can find him?"

"What sort of accident?" asked Polly. She was physically shaken now. Gina had been in such a bad way earlier. What on earth had happened to her now?

"We need to talk to her husband," said the man again.

"They . . . he . . . look, I've been with Gina all weekend. Her husband has left her. They are no longer together. They are . . . well, they had an argument. A serious one. He left. I need to know what is going on. Is she okay? Where's Danny?"

"Mrs Humphries was involved in a crash. She appears to have lost control on a bend and hit a stone wall. She has been seriously injured."

Polly gasped and felt her legs weaken beneath her. "Oh my God! Danny! Is he okay?"

"He's being treated at the hospital – he had some injuries. We need to inform her husband who is her next of kin, estranged or not. Can you help us trace him?"

Polly's mind was a muddle. She didn't want to find Trevor. She wanted to get to Gina and Danny right away. But the police did have a right to know, she supposed.

"I think . . . he . . ."

She thought of him tucked up in his lover's home, stinking of alcohol, with the pain of Gina's face where he hit her still probably throbbing on his fist.

"I don't know where he went when he left . . . but his

mother lives in the next town. I don't know her name or where exactly. Gina's family are all in Dublin. Their name is Kelly."

The policeman pulled a notebook from his pocket and made a few notes, then asked Polly for her own name and phone number and jotted them down also.

As the policeman nodded and turned away, Polly raced back inside her own front door and called for James. As the children burst out of the living room, she grabbed her jacket and handbag, and scooped her keys up from where she had left them on the hall table earlier.

"Mum, what's happened?" said Frankie, all agog.

James was on his way down the stairs now. He had been in the shower and had missed the arrival of the police next door.

"Call Tess quickly!" she said. "Tell her Gina has been in a serious accident. I'll meet her at the hospital."

"Oh God! Is it really bad?"

"Mum, is Danny okay?" asked Frankie.

"I hope so," said Polly, leaning down to kiss her son goodbye. "He and his mum have been in a car accident. I'm going to see them both now. It will be fine, baby."

Frankie looked terrified now. She sometimes forgot that he was old enough to understand much of what went on around him these days.

"Tell him he can have my Nintendo DS if he wants. He always wants to play with it."

"You are so kind, baby. I'll call you soon," said Polly and she left her family, got into the car and reversed out of the driveway, barely able to steer her hands were shaking so badly. If Gina was as bad as what her gut was telling her, this was going to be a nightmare end to what was supposed to be a wonderful weekend.

"Can you get it?" Tess called to Rob when she heard the phone ring. "It's probably *Crimewatch* or the Official Society of Bouncers after my blood!"

She could hear Rob giggle as he walked to the phone, but when he answered his tone took a U-turn.

"Okay . . . Christ. We'll be right there. Tess!"

"Rob?"

Tess turned and hobbled down the stairs as fast as her sore toe would allow her to. She could tell the news was bad.

"Rob, what is it?"

Rob grabbed his coat from the bottom of the stairs and lifted the car keys from the hall table.

"We have to go quickly! Your friend Gina has had an accident. It's bad. Come on! I'll drive you there now!"

Polly was in the foyer of the hospital when Tess arrived.

"Oh God!" Polly said, her hand clasped over her mouth. "Thank God you're here!"

"What the hell happened? Is it really as serious as James said?"

Polly nodded and hugged her sister tight. "Oh Tess, I've just seen her being taken into the ICU. It's bad. It's worse than bad. She looks so fragile and tiny and weak. They wouldn't tell me much, only that she has no broken bones but has a severe head injury and I could see that she's hooked up to all sorts of machinery and she is unconscious and –"

"Slow down, Polly," said Tess, leading her sister to a seated area in the foyer. "Can I get you a coffee? Water?"

Polly shook her head. "The police said it was a serious crash and the doctor is waiting on Trevor to arrive before we can hear any updates on how Gina is. He was at his mother's and they want to speak to him first, naturally. Oh Tess, she was a in a terrible state of mind when I left her earlier. I should have stayed. I didn't –"

"Shh!" said Tess. "This is not your fault. Where was she going, though? When the accident happened? Did she mention going out?"

"She mentioned going to the shops," said Polly. "She just said she had things to do but she was almost zombie-like. She was in some sort of trance and all she could talk about was looking after Danny. She's in intensive care and she looks so frail . . . oh God, Tess, if she doesn't pull through . . ." Polly dabbed her eyes with a tissue as memories of Gina lying on the hospital bed upstairs filled her mind.

She had wanted to see Danny but he was asleep. The staff had told Polly that he was responsive and bright when asked questions on arrival to hospital, but since then had found it difficult to remember what exactly had happened. He had a broken leg, but nothing more serious.

"Are you sure you don't want a drink?" asked Tess. "I could be doing with a coffee."

Polly looked up at her sister and shrugged. "I can't even decide," she said. "Oh no, Tess. There he is. It's Trevor."

Trevor arrived through the huge revolving doors of the hospital. It was evident that after his moody departure from Gina earlier, he had drowned his sorrows in more alcohol. He glared at the two women but they could see flickers of shame cross his face. His mother was with him, a strong-looking, striking woman.

"I suppose you think this is my fault," he said.

"I'm not here to judge you," said Polly. "I am here to support my friend. This is not about you."

He was trembling and rightly so. Polly could almost smell the guilt seeping from his ugly pores and she looked away when she noticed tears bulge in his eyes.

"You must be Polly?" said Trevor's mother. "Gina talks a lot about you. You've been a great support. This is just so hard to take in."

She was shaking too but Polly had a feeling that, unlike her son, Mrs Humphries was shaking with fear for her daughter-in-law and grandson.

"Have you seen her or Danny?" she asked.

"No, I didn't see Danny – he was asleep – they said he's okay but for the broken leg, though he doesn't seem to remember much. But I saw Gina . . . Gina is . . ." Polly's voice broke when she said Gina's name.

"Take your time, love," said Mrs Humphries. "This is a terrible shock to all of us."

"She's still unconscious," said Polly. "They wouldn't go into any detail with me – they want to talk to Trevor."

Trevor let out a monstrous sigh and his mother supported him as his shoulders heaved in sorrow.

"Take me to see her, please," he said. "I want to see my wife and son."

25

Ruth felt like a proper stalker. She was in her car on Scotstown Park in Belfast, the radio turned down low, sunglasses on, visor down, and was watching the comings and goings of a neighbourhood that was unfamiliar and full of bad memories.

Her mother's house was still exactly the same – a little bungalow in the north-west of Belfast where retired couples lived in neighbourly bliss. The red door with the huge green pots at either side was as shiny and perfect as it had always been. The white net curtains were still gleaming and the summer seat that used to be at their old house where they lived with their dad sat underneath the front window.

Ruth thought of her dad and how he had made that summer seat with his own hands. He was a fine tradesman and he had always made sure that their young lives were full of adventures and memories. Ruth smiled as she thought of him building a tree-house in the garden, making a seesaw from old bits of wood, lighting little bonfires at Hallowe'en and then bobbing for apples at the kitchen table while her mother hovered round them impatiently with a tea towel in case any of the water would spill.

But the summer seat had always been so special to her. She would sit by his side and listen to stories of days gone by when he was a young boy growing up in the village of Cranmore. He let her carve her name on the seat and he carved his name on the other side. It was like their secret chatting place at the bottom of the garden. It was a tranquil place Ruth would escape to when she was feeling sad or lonely. It was the only place where she would feel like she belonged sometimes. She loved that summer seat and the memories it held and now it sat outside a house where she was not welcome. She stared at it and heard her father's gentle, sorrowful voice in her head.

"Don't let anyone ever bring you down, Ruthie," he used to tell her on repeat. "When the whole world seems against you, rise above it and take a big step back. Never, ever hold a grudge against anyone. Life is too short to hold a grudge. Always be the better person and never be afraid to say sorry."

She had always been a daddy's girl – she could never deny that. It was as plain as the nose on her face. It used to cause rows between her parents, how he favoured her over anyone who came his way. It was like he was mesmerised by her and she by him too, so when her mother decided to end the marriage to be with Raymond Dillon, it was no surprise that Ruth was going to despise the man.

But both men were gone now and she needed closure. She wanted to know that she had done absolutely everything she possibly could to show her mother that she had room in her heart for both her parents, even if she resented the choices her mother had made in the past. Perhaps without Raymond Dillon in their lives they could rebuild a relationship, get to know each other again, be as close as they could be considering their past.

Ruth slid down in her seat when she saw movement inside the house. She wasn't close enough to be noticed but her heart was racing at the thought of laying eyes on her mother. Then the door opened and she leaned forward again, taking off her sunglasses to get a closer look. It was Samantha.

She hadn't changed a bit. She was still peroxide-blonde, still a bit overweight and still as rough as a badger's backside. She had a toddler by the hand and another older child followed her out through the door. Ruth felt like she was being stabbed all over. Samantha's children were in and out as if they owned the place while Ben and Melanie were treated like they were invisible. No matter what Ruth had done to upset the applecart with Raymond Dillon, it pained her to think that her own family had chosen his daughter and her children over their own flesh and blood.

She wanted to get out of the car and approach Samantha Dillon and let her know just how much her actions really did hurt her. She longed to scream out all the anger that had festered in her since she was a teenager when her mother dismissed her pregnancy with Ben and told her to 'get rid of it'.

But she couldn't. Not yet. She didn't have the energy,

or the strength to argue against people who really just didn't care. Her children had grown up, her husband had left her and she had moved back to Ireland to try and rebuild her life, and her family didn't give one shit about her. They weren't worth her time, or her tears. She would drive away, back to her little corner and she would never go near Scotstown Park in Belfast ever again.

"We should go," whispered Tess into her sister's ear. They had been sitting in the corridor outside Intensive Care for over an hour now and the silence was crushing. It was a daunting place and Tess felt like they were beginning to get in the way.

"I can't leave her," said Polly. "I shouldn't have left her earlier and I am not leaving her now."

Tess was really worried about her sister. She had taken Gina's accident so badly and was adamant that, had she been a more attentive friend and neighbour, she could have prevented it.

"But Trevor and his mum will be here all night, and her brother and her mum might turn up," said Tess. "You can come back in the morning. I'll ask our Helen to look after the twins and I can take Frankie to school on my way. There is nothing more you can do for Gina, or Danny, tonight."

The police had managed to contact Gina's brother in Dublin and her mother, who was holidaying in Spain, was flying home later that night.

Polly shook her head, still reluctant to go. She thought of Marco, the hot young Englishman who had put a huge smile on Gina's face only a day before. She thought of

George Michael and she smiled – Gina would always remind her of George Michael! She remembered how beautiful and confident Gina had looked when they had all dressed up for their big night out. That's the Gina that she wanted to see back again. She didn't want Gina to live a life of misery ever again. When she pulled through, Polly was going to make sure that Gina Humphries was the radiant, fun-loving, beautiful creature that she had grown to know and love. Trevor Humphries was a dirty rotten pig and his crocodile tears of guilt did nothing for Polly at all.

"He seems so sad," Tess had said earlier after Trevor and his mother had returned to Gina's ward after spending time by young Danny's bedside.

"Sad my arse," said Polly. "He's drunk and emotional and full to the brim of stinking guilt. I will never forget the way he made her feel, or the way he lifted his fist at every turnaround. He hurt her more than any car accident ever could. I can't bear the sight of him."

Tess had been shocked at how 'to the point' Polly was when it came to Trevor Humphries, but then she had more or less witnessed his antics first-hand for years. She had wiped up Gina's tears on many an occasion, had taken Gina and her son for daytrips on sunny days when she was so low that she couldn't drive, she had even sent over home-cooked meals for Gina and Danny when Trevor did a disappearing act and when Polly sensed that Gina was in no fit state of mind to realise it was dinnertime. No wonder she hated the bastard. She had every right to.

"You need sleep," said Tess. "Come on. I'm sure if

there is any change in Gina or Danny, Trevor will let you know. He knows how good a friend you have been to her. Surely he will have the decency to do that."

"I'm not leaving until he does," said Polly. "I will sit him out. Gina wouldn't want to be here with him on her own."

"Polly, would you listen to yourself!" said Tess. "You have a husband and three children at home. You need to switch off and get to bed. Gina is being looked after here by the very best of medical staff. He can't harm her now. And you can't help her any more by sitting here!"

Polly wiped a tear from under her eye. She had cried so much all evening that she was surprised she had any more tears left.

"I remember the first day she moved in next door," she said with a smile. "She was ordering those removal men around no end. I'll never forget how bossy she seemed."

"Yeah, I remember," said Tess, picturing the sight as if it was yesterday. "She was a stubborn wee thing back then. And she was so, so pretty. I remember wondering where she got all her gorgeous clothes. I was so jealous of her."

"She soon had that beaten out of her," said Polly. "That dickhead stripped her right down to an unrecognisable shadow of the girl from Dublin with the nice clothes and feisty personality. And you know what the saddest thing of all is, Tess?"

"What?"

"Yesterday – yesterday in Donegal, I thought we had got her back again."

Tess put her head on her sister's shoulder and closed

her eyes, listening again to the eerie hospital sounds and the gentle whispers of medical staff as they cared for the select few patients in rooms off the corridor and behind the doors of the ICU.

"Just one more hour," said Polly, clasping Tess's hand. "Just let me stay for one more hour and then I will go home. I don't want to leave her just yet."

"Mum, your phone has been going mental all evening! Where the hell have you been?"

It was almost ten when Ruth got home from Belfast and she was so tired she'd had to have the window down on the car the whole way down the motorway to keep herself awake. Now, all she wanted was her pyjamas and a good book in bed to distract her from the flurry of emotions that were racing through her.

"Where's Ben?" asked Ruth, checking her phone. Gosh, it had been busy! She felt popular for a split second.

"He's gone for a drink with some girl – I don't know who she is. Some bimbo, no doubt, knowing Ben!"

The first message was from Polly and Ruth gasped as she read it through.

"Oh my God! Oh no!"

"He always goes out with bimbos . . . Mum, what's wrong?"

"It's Gina!" said Ruth. "Oh God, she's been in a bad accident with her son. I need to call Polly."

Melanie looked at her mother in bewilderment and then the penny dropped. "Oh, the girls you were out with last night? Is it serious?"

Ruth nodded in reply, scrolling through the numbers

281

on her phone. She dialled Polly's number but it went straight to voicemail. Then she tried Tess and got the same response, so she left a message.

"Tess, I'm just home. I was in Belfast and didn't have my phone and . . . oh, please get in touch as soon as you get this and let me know what to do. Are you at the hospital? Call me quick!"

Ruth hung up, redialled Polly's number and left a similar message.

"What were you doing in Belfast?" asked Melanie.

"Huh?" Ruth was still checking her missed calls and text messages. They were mostly from Polly and Tess. This was terrible!

"You just said you were in Belfast? What on earth for? That's miles away?"

"I wasn't in Belfast," said Ruth. She didn't want Melanie to know anything about her stalking her own family.

"Mum, you just said!" said Melanie. "What's going on? Did you go to see your mother? I hope not!"

Ruth felt like a schoolgirl who had been caught playing truant. It was like role reversal again, just the way it was so often these days. Melanie would chastise her as often as it would happen the other way round.

Ruth pretended she didn't hear her and continued to look at her messages. Her stomach was churning at the thought of Gina lying in hospital in such a bad state. Should she go to the hospital or would that be intrusive? Surely there was something she could do.

"Oh, and I answered one of your calls earlier," said Melanie. "I was going to turn it off because it just kept ringing but, when I lifted it, it rang so I answered. It was some guy, Michael . . . from the pub last night. He said for you to call him. *Twit-twooo!*"

Ruth stopped what she was doing and looked up at her daughter. "Michael? What did he say exactly?"

"Is he your new boyfriend?" asked Melanie.

"No, he is not indeed!" said Ruth. "It's business. What did he say?"

"He said . . ." Melanie cleared her throat for effect. "He said '*Hey, Hotstuff, remember me?*' I said no and then laughed my head off! He was mortified!"

"Melanie!" Ruth's eyes were wide as saucers.

"I'm joking," said Melanie. "He just said you would know why he was calling and could you call him back. He said you have his number."

Relief flooded through Ruth and then it hit her again about Gina. Why was she getting excited about a phone call from a stranger when her friend was in such a critical state?

"Look, I have to go," she said. "I need to see what's happening with Gina. This is really serious, Melanie. I'll keep in touch. It's too late for me to go to the hospital so I will call at Polly's house and see if she's there."

"Okay," said Melanie. "But take your phone with you this time! I'm not playing secretary again!"

Melanie handed Ruth the phone and walked her to the door.

"I'm sorry to have to race out again," said Ruth. She gave her daughter a peck on the cheek but Melanie wiped it away. "I really won't be long. I'm just so worried about Gina. Sorry, love."

Melanie didn't look too perturbed to have the house to herself once again.

"I need to get an early night," she said. "And who wants to hang out with their mother, anyhow?"

Ruth walked away from the front door, took a few steps and then stopped.

"Someday you might regret saying that," she said, but Melanie had already gone inside.

26

Ruth yanked the handbrake, jumped out of the car and walked as fast as she could up Polly's driveway. She pressed the doorbell and then checked her watch. It really was late to be calling, but she didn't know what else to do. There was a light on in the living-room window but apart from that the house was in darkness.

At last she heard footsteps and James opened the door. He looked like he had been asleep.

"James, I'm so, so sorry to call at this hour. I can't get through to Polly and I'm worried sick about Gina."

"It's Ruth, yeah?" said James. He opened the door and beckoned her to come inside.

"Yes, that's me. Is Polly here?"

"No, she's at the hospital. But come on in. I'm sure you're shocked like all of us."

The house was silent apart from the low hum of the television in the sitting room and the air smelled like freshly baked cookies. It was warm and cosy and Ruth felt her heart tug at the thought of anything going wrong with Polly's seemingly perfect existence with James and her children.

"I was away this evening and stupidly forgot my phone. Have you heard any news from Polly? Is it really that bad?"

"The last I heard was that Gina is in ICU. No broken bones but she hasn't responded yet and her head injuries seem pretty fierce."

James led her to the kitchen and invited her to have a seat at the table where she had broken down in tears only days ago. She took a deep breath. Things had really changed tenfold in all their lives since then. She had made new friends she now depended on wholly, and the confidence it gave her to have people who cared made her realise that she didn't need her own family as much as she thought she did.

A bottle of whiskey sat by the draining board and an empty glass was beside it. Ruth looked at it and then at James.

James poured a large whiskey, then offered her a drink. Ruth shook her head. "And Danny?"

"He isn't so bad – a broken leg – some loss of memory," said James, downing half his whiskey.

He looked really tired. Tortured almost. Perhaps she should leave. It was late and he didn't need strangers in his kitchen on a Sunday night when he looked like he would much rather be in bed. Or alone with his whiskey and his thoughts.

"Well, I have left messages with both Polly and Tess so I'm sure they'll be in touch," she said, getting up to leave. "Sorry to have bothered you. I just didn't know what else to do. I'm so worried about Gina."

James was staring at her and she was feeling rather uncomfortable in his company. She had only met him once before, on the day they were leaving for Donegal, and she had envied Polly so much when she saw him at first. He was a very handsome man who had looked gorgeous in blue jeans and a black T-shirt that emphasised his dark hair and eyes, but now he looked weary and worn and she wasn't sure what he was thinking.

"I'm just really tired," he said. "Sorry if I seem rude or a bit spaced out. I've had a few whiskeys to try and keep the demons from in here . . ." He pointed at his head.

"It's fine," said Ruth. "Thanks for inviting me in. I'll let you get some sleep, then."

She wanted to get out straight away, but he was almost delaying her departure with his stare. She walked towards the door, feeling his eyes on her back.

"I'm afraid, Ruth," he said. "I'm so afraid."

Ruth stopped dead in her tracks on the kitchen floor. She turned towards him.

"Afraid? What are you afraid of?"

She didn't know what to say. She didn't even know this man who was looking at her like he wanted to confide in her at this hour of the night while his wife was holding vigil by her best friend's bedside. He was drunker than he was letting on. Why else would he come out with such a statement to a virtual stranger? She had never met the man before and he only knew her from what Polly might have said about the weekend past, or those terrible years at school.

"I'm afraid that Polly is going to leave me," he said. "That's what your big night away was for, wasn't it? So she could consider her options. So she could see what life was like on the other side."

Ruth shook her head. Oh God. She wasn't sure how to respond. His statement had knocked her for six and she didn't know what to say.

"Em . . ."

"I know she isn't happy. Neither of us are right now. But that's what happens in marriage, isn't it? It goes off the boil, you charge on, you fix it. Did she say anything? I need to know."

"No, not at all," she said, and then she remembered Polly's confession in the Chinese restaurant where she said she didn't know if she wanted to be married at all and Ruth's advice with the metaphor that matched his exactly – things simmer, go off the boil, but when they boil over there is the danger of there being nothing left. "Well, I'm not really the one to ask. I have a failed marriage behind me and I don't know an awful lot about others. I really think you should talk to Polly about this."

James sat down at the kitchen table and rubbed his forehead. As if she was on autopilot, Ruth fetched the bottle and topped up his whiskey. He gulped it back like it was his lifeline.

"I don't normally drink much," he said. "It's just . . . well, I don't say much either these days and that's part of the problem. I just can't find the words, you know. Did you ever just get to the stage in life when finding the right words is the hardest thing of all?"

He swirled the whiskey in his glass as he spoke and Ruth sat down at the table again.

"Have you . . . have you ever thought that you might

be . . . maybe you're clinically depressed, James? Perhaps you should see a doctor? I've been there. I know that horrible feeling of hopelessness when everything, even holding down a conversation with the people you love, feels like climbing a mountain."

James looked up at her. He shook his head in denial.

"Me? Depressed?" he said emphatically. "Sure, what on earth would I have to be depressed about? I have it all, don't I? A gorgeous wife, a good job, three beautiful boys who think the world of me? Other men would kill to walk a day in my shoes and all I can do is moan about it."

"On paper, yes, it does sound ideal. It isn't always as straightforward as that, though, James. Depression can hit any of us at any time. If you tell your doctor how you've been feeling, he'll be able to decide if you are or if you are not. It's nothing to be frightened or ashamed of."

James drank the dregs of the whiskey from his glass and wiped his mouth. He looked at Ruth and gave a nervous laugh.

"You probably think I'm some sort of nut-job sitting here spilling my guts out to you. I've had a few too many whiskies. Just ignore me. I'm sure you need to get home. I'll probably have forgotten all about it by the time the morning comes and, with Gina in hospital, I'm sure Polly will have a lot on her mind over the next few weeks."

Ruth thought for a moment. She had suffered at the hands of the Big Black Dog, as it was known, on many occasions as she battled with life after Jeffrey. She knew the signs. She knew the dangers if it got out of hand. She couldn't just get up and go after he had given her only a tiny part of his feelings.

"I'm in no hurry," she said. "I can listen if you want to talk. You know, being depressed is more common than you might think. A lot of men with lives just like yours go through exactly how you're feeling right now. It's better to talk it out. I don't know you but I've a good ear and I'm willing to listen. Sometimes it's easier to talk to a stranger than it is to your own nearest and dearest."

James nodded and let out a long sigh. "I don't want to let Polly down. I don't want her to think I'm weak and that I can't cope with our life. We have a great life, you know. Maybe I'm just ungrateful."

"No! You are not ungrateful at all. If you were, you wouldn't be talking to me with such concern right now. How long have you been feeling like this?"

"Months." He stared at the table and bit his lip, then shook himself out of it again. "A few months at least."

"A few months is a long time when you're feeling desperate."

"It's nothing. Honestly, ignore me. It's the whiskey and –"

"It's not the whiskey," said Ruth. "It's too easy to say it's the whiskey. Maybe Gina's accident has made you realise just how bad you've been. Maybe this has triggered you to talk about it at last. But don't blame the whiskey and, if I were you, after tonight I'd lay off it for a while. Drinking helps numb the pain but, believe me, it doesn't provide the answers."

James walked to the sideboard and poured another glass. He stared at it and then he threw it down the sink.

"I can't hide it any more, Ruth!" he said. "I need to get out of this terrible rut in my head. I need to talk to Polly and tell her how I feel but I can't!"

"Then please, please talk to your doctor." She feared for James but she also feared for Polly. How would she cope, knowing that James was going through this on top of Gina's accident? This was going to have to be treated very carefully.

"I'll think about it," said James. "I'm going to go to bed now. Polly has a key. You can wait for her here if you want but I've no idea when she'll be back. She might even stay at the hospital."

"No, no, I'll go," said Ruth. "But please promise me one thing, James."

James ran his hands under the cold tap and splashed his face. She waited for him to respond.

"I can't," he said. "I can't promise anything. I'm sorry."

"Okay," said Ruth. She wouldn't push him. He had taken a huge leap of faith by telling her what he already had. Maybe he had spoken enough for one night.

"But thanks," he said. "Thanks for not telling me I'm a wimp or a basket-case or a selfish loser. I didn't mean to burden you with all that. I don't know what came over me."

Ruth wanted to hug him. He looked so forlorn and in need of a hug, but not from her. He needed to talk to his wife and have her hold him and reassure him that it would all be okay.

"It was no burden at all," she said softly. "I'm glad you were brave enough to tell me. I'm always available to lend a non-judgemental ear if you feel the need. Just don't bottle it up, James. It's better out than in."

James nodded his head and his eyes drooped heavily as they blinked beneath the tiredness and drunkenness that had overcome him.

He walked her to the front door. "Good night, Ruth," he said.

"Yeah, get some sleep," she replied. "I'll be thinking of you. Don't ever feel you are alone."

She walked down the driveway and got into the car, glancing back to where James stood watching her. She waved him goodbye, turned the ignition and started the car, looking across at Gina's house in sorrow.

What a difference a day made, she thought. What a huge difference one night away could make on four very ordinary lives.

Polly awoke before the alarm to the sound of birdsong and for one blissful moment didn't remember what had happened the night before. The sun streamed in through her window and she could feel the weight of James's arm around her waist.

"Are you awake?" she whispered but he didn't answer so she snuggled further into him and closed her eyes to try and savour the moment. She remembered the good days when this was all in life that mattered . . . a time when she felt so secure in his arms, when everything would be okay if he was by her side. Now, even though he was physically right beside her, and no matter how much she tried to relax and feel secure, she felt like she was a world away from her life as she once knew it.

She turned in the bed to look at him and their faces were so close they were almost touching. She could feel his breath on her face and, when she watched him sleep, she could almost see the pain and worry in his face. What was he dreaming of? What on earth was going on in his mind that made him seem so far away?

"You awake?" she asked again, wanting him to stir even though she knew he was miles away in a land of unsettled dreams. He had tossed and turned all night and the empty bottle of whiskey that greeted her when she came home told her that he was hiding something from her that she couldn't convince him to tell her.

He groaned and turned on the bed to face the opposite direction, so she crept out from beneath the covers and walked to the en-suite bathroom, hoping that a warm shower would ease some of her worries away. She stood beneath the pulsating water, inhaling the fresh smell of the tea-tree shower gel and leaned her head back so that the warmth ran right down her back, tingling her skin and washing her whole body out of the cocoon-like feeling of sleep.

It had been almost one o'clock when she'd finally left the hospital. She had bought a toy aeroplane to replace the one that had been destroyed in the accident and placed it in beside Danny, kissed his forehead and whispered that his mummy would be able to see him soon.

"You are a very brave boy," she told him after reading him a bed-time story. The story was possibly a bit too babyish for a six-year-old but she wanted to try and drift his mind out of the clinical feel of the hospital ward with its strange sounds and faces and names he didn't know.

Trevor had left the hospital long before her. His mother was so apologetic and thankful for the grace that Polly and Tess managed to show her wayward son. Mrs Humphries had been good to Gina down the years and the fear she felt for her little grandson was tangible. Polly tried to remind herself that no matter how much she was afraid for Gina's recovery, Mrs Humphries's fears were probably tenfold as she dreaded a future for Danny without his mother.

Tears mixed through the sudsy water on her face and Polly wondered how she would get through the day ahead. She had her own family to think of as well as Gina and Danny and she had to make sure they were taken care of before she could go back to the hospital. It was Monday morning and Tess would have to go to work so she would have to make it across there by herself. Her sister Helen had promised to keep the twins while James went to work and Frankie would be in school until three so she had a fair stretch of the day covered before she would have to rethink any childcare plans for whatever the evening held in store.

She rinsed off and turned off the shower, knowing that when she stepped outside and got dressed she would have to find the strength to face what new challenges the day would bring. Would Gina have progressed overnight? Would she be facing another day of silence and bleeping monitors and the horrible lingering sense of death in the air? She shuddered at the very thought.

"You're up early."

James was awake when she came back into the bedroom. He looked hung-over and groggy but it didn't bother her as much as it might have a few days before.

"I couldn't sleep much," she said. "I need to get organised and get back to the hospital."

James climbed out from under the duvet and sat on the edge of the bed. He sighed and stood up with a stretch then made his way to the shower without saying anything more. Polly got dressed, making the most of the early morning peace before the children awoke. It looked glorious outside so she chose a long, pale-blue summer dress and flip-flops and slid a hairband onto her long blonde hair, then touched up her clear complexion with a light layer of foundation and a brush of mascara.

"I can take the day off if you want?" said James. He was behind her now, looking and smelling a lot fresher than a few minutes before, a towel wrapped around his waist.

"It's okay, thanks," said Polly. "I have the kids organised till three and then I can see to them until you come home."

He walked towards where she sat at her dressing table and put his hands on her shoulders, squeezing them lightly. His touch felt so good. She had missed him so much. She wondered what had changed in him. He hadn't reached out and touched her like that in so long and she needed him so badly right now. She had a feeling that he needed her too.

"We will get through this," he said and when she looked at him through the mirror, she saw tears in his eyes as he spoke.

"You think so?" asked Polly. She held his stare. He was finally facing up to their problems.

"Of course we will," he said. "Look, Poll . . . I know I haven't been myself lately, but . . . but I think I can learn to deal with things if I get some help."

Polly turned around to face him. She stood up and put her arms around him and held him tight.

"Help?" she asked. "Do you mean marriage counselling?"

James nodded. "And help for . . . well, for whatever it is that is making me so damn miserable lately. It's not your fault, Polly. It's just . . . it's just a sense of hopelessness that I can't explain. I need to talk it through . . . face it, deal with it. I need to finally admit that my head isn't in a very good place right now and that it hasn't been for a long time."

Polly was shocked. Was James depressed? Is that what he was trying to say? She felt a knot in her throat, choking her with dread at the thought of her husband battling this horrible nightmare for so long.

"I think you've taken a huge step already by telling me, James. I am your wife and I will always be your best friend so please don't hide your feelings from me. How long have you been like this? Weeks? Months?"

"Months," he whispered, kissing her forehead. "I think Gina's accident has put a lot of things into perspective for me. My head has been a mess lately and I think I need to dig deep and find out why. It's like I don't have energy to do anything any more. But I know that I can get it sorted. You and the children are the most important things in my whole life. I need to get it fixed for all of us."

Polly rested her head on her husband's bare chest and inhaled his manly scent, feeling invigorated as she felt his heart beat beneath her face. She was so proud of him. It took a lot of guts to admit to needing help and, although it had taken a long time, she felt a great sense of relief now that he had identified the problem.

"I will be there for you every step of the way," she said. "I have missed you so, so much. I was so afraid we might have drifted apart so far we would never find our way back."

"I would never let that happen," he said.

"Please don't," she whispered.

He kissed her long and hard and led her over to the bed. She felt her whole body rise with desire as they lay down. He kissed her neck, running his hand up underneath her dress and squeezing her thigh.

She wrapped her legs around him as he let the damp towel drop onto the floor.

"Nothing or no one will ever come between us, Polly," he said. "Never."

27

Gina's eyes flickered. She felt drunk, or hung-over. She couldn't decide which. Her mouth was dry. She turned her head and squinted at her bedside locker. She was back in the hotel with Ruth. She definitely wasn't in her own bed. Perhaps she was dreaming.

She opened her eyes fully now, but they blinked back heavily in defeat as if a huge weight was resting on her eyelids. She tried again. No joy. Everywhere was silent. Danny must be still asleep. And Trevor? Yes, Trevor was gone. The knowledge of that gave her great relief. She stretched her eyes open again, but they didn't have the strength to stay open. She didn't have the strength to do anything.

Her eyes opened again slowly and she managed to keep them that way at last. She couldn't see much . . . there was a strong white light at first, followed by a glowing beam of yellow that stung her so badly she closed her eyes tight and stayed like that before trying once more. If this wasn't a bad dream, then she was living a real-time nightmare.

She tried to speak but her mouth felt numb. It wouldn't move and she could only hear the words she wanted to say in her brain. She needed Danny. She needed to see him so she could tell if this was all real. Or was she dead? Could she possibly be dead?

"Da –" she mumbled and then a noise came from beside her. It was a voice. It seemed so loud. Wherever she was, they spoke very, very loudly and it was hurting her head. She could hear the beeping sounds, the tip-tapping of heels on a floor and voices! There were voices everywhere!

The yellow light was slowly fading and the outline of a familiar face came into view. Her vision was blurred but it was an outline that she knew like the back of her hand.

"Trev –"

"Gina! I'm here. You're okay! Oh, thank you God!"

Why was he shouting? He didn't need to shout!

"St-stop . . ." At last! She could speak but she didn't recognise her own voice. It was hoarse and deep and her throat hurt when she spoke. She could see him now. He looked awful. He looked as if he hadn't slept for weeks.

"Gina! Oh thank God! Nurse! Nurse!"

He was pressing a bell frantically and he was crying like a baby. Trevor never cried. He made other people cry, but he never shed a tear himself. What the hell was going on?

"Where am I?" she mumbled. "Danny? Wh–where's Da . . ."

A nurse came rushing over and bent over her, peering

anxiously at her face, then glancing away towards some monitors.

Gina's head was throbbing. Everywhere was white and she was cold and with every word she spoke it felt like a hammer was hitting her with each and every syllable. She was freezing cold. She wanted to get up but it hurt so much to move. And her head! Oh God, her head hurt so, so badly.

"Gina? How are you feeling?" asked the nurse urgently.

Gina shook her head, unable to speak.

"Do you remember what happened to you, Gina?" asked the nurse.

Trevor was gripping her hand now. She didn't want him to hold her hand. She wanted him to let go. He was hurting her. Trevor always hurt her. She wanted him to go away and never come back.

"We thought we had lost you," he said. "Please don't leave us, Gina!"

"Water," she said and the nurse poured a glass from a jug on the bedside table. She held it to her mouth but only allowed her to take a few sips. The water wet her throat but it felt like she was swallowing nails.

"Gina? Can you remember what happened to you?" asked the nurse insistently.

Why did the nurse keep asking her that?

Then she remembered.

"The accident. Where's Danny? Where's my Danny?"

"Your son is fine, Gina," said the nurse. "He's here in the hospital but he's fine." Then she hurried off, saying "I'll go to get the Staff Nurse now."

Like a slowly starting engine Gina's brain unfolded,

reliving the moments of the accident. She remembered Danny in the backseat, making zooming noises and whizzing his toy aeroplane through the air as they drove to the shops. She was thinking about how her life had changed so much in just a few days. She was thinking of Marco and trying to decide if he had been a mistake or a revelation. She was thinking of the week ahead and dreading how on earth she was going to get through it as a single parent. She wasn't thinking of the road ahead though. She should have been thinking of the road.

"Danny . . .?" she whispered again.

"Ssh," said Trevor. "He's okay. Our boy is okay."

Gina could feel her heart race and the bleeping of the monitors was piercing on her brain. She wanted to get out of here. She needed to go to the shop. Danny wanted a movie night. She'd promised him a movie night!

Another nurse leaned over into her vision space and gave her a huge smile.

"Welcome back, Gina," she said softly. "My name is Anne and I'm the Senior Staff Nurse here at the Royal Victoria Hospital. We are taking great care of you, but your body has been through a severe trauma so we need you to take things nice and slowly. Do you understand?"

"Yes," said Gina. Her lip was trembling now. She could feel tears slide down the sides of her face, past her ears and onto the pillow. "I just want to see my boy."

"Of course," said the nurse. "Danny leg was broken in the accident, Gina, but he's doing fine. We'll bring him to you as soon as the team on Children's allow him to come over. This morning's report says he has had a good night and he sat up this morning and had breakfast."

"Weetabix," said Gina. "Make sure . . . they give him Weetabix."

She needed to see him. She needed to touch his soft, pale skin and his spiky brown hair and hear him talk about his comic-books and the programmes he watched on television. She wanted to hear his voice sparkle with enthusiasm when he talked about football and how he scored a goal at school and how he said 'it's not fair' when he didn't get his own way. She needed to see for herself that he was okay. She was his mother. Only she could tell if Danny was really okay.

"You need to take things really easy," said Nurse Anne, scribbling down notes as she spoke. "Dr Brady will be delighted. He is on his way here now and he will explain everything to you."

Trevor was sitting down on the armchair by her bed again. She could see him rock back and forth in the chair, staring at her almost in disbelief. She really must have scared the shit out of him, lying there hooked up to the gadgets that were making sure she was still alive. He was probably riddled with guilt at the way he had treated her and dreading that she might slip away. She was almost tempted to play dead just to give him one final scare!

"I don't want you here," she said and Nurse Anne did a double take.

"Pardon?"

"Not you . . . him," said Gina. "I don't want him here. Get him away."

Trevor stopped rocking and his look of disbelief turned to utter fear. He was white as a sheet and his cheeks were sunken and gaunt.

"Mrs Humphries, please don't be upset," said the nurse. "Just try and relax. I know you must feel very confused but –"

"Then get him out of here now, the wife-beating, bullying *bastard*!"

It exhausted her, but she made sure to say the word *bastard* as loud as her weakened voice-box would allow and Nurse Anne jumped at the shock of how such a frail, small person could make such a giant noise.

Trevor stood up, shuffling his hands in and out of his pockets and jingling his keys. Gina hated when men jingled their keys. He was an all-round asshole and it had taken a severe knock on the head to make sure she realised it once and for all.

"I'm going," he said. "I'll go and check in on our Danny. Make sure he has eaten his Weetabix."

Gina felt her stomach churn. He was playing the ideal husband and father! He was anything but, with his floozy and his fists, and she would be letting him know it!

"Yes," she said, more softly now. She closed her eyes. "Go anywhere you want, but don't ever come back in here because you make me sick."

She opened her eyes to see Nurse Anne whose expression was pleading for Gina to stop and for Trevor to go. The nurse waited as Trevor stood at the bottom of his wife's bed.

"Your wife has suffered a severe brain injury, Mr Humphries," said the nurse quietly. "Behavioural changes are common at this stage of recovery, so perhaps it's best you leave for now."

"Yeah," he whispered.

303

"Try not to be too upset," the nurse continued. "She's very heavily medicated and may not mean what she is saying."

Gina was not going to let him away so easily.

"He knocked me around more than the car accident did," she said. Her throat was aching now, but she forced the words through. No matter how sore she was, she wanted to say her piece before he left. "He is a cheating wife-beater and it didn't take a brain injury for me to know it. Get him away."

Despite the excruciating pain she was in when she spoke, she managed a wry smirk as Trevor walked out of the tiny room with his tail between his legs. The nurse watched him leave and then walked to Gina's bedside.

"Please try and rest, Mrs Humphries," she said. "Let's just settle down and compose ourselves, shall we?"

"But –"

"No buts," she said firmly. "The doctor will be here any second. I will inform my staff that you don't wish your husband to have access to your bedside again. I promise you that, for the good of your health."

Tess wasn't feeling so good. She stood in her classroom, teaching her first-year students the French alphabet but she couldn't make it through the full twenty-six letters without feeling so nauseous that she had to stop.

Rob had made an appointment for after school with his solicitor friend who had assured him that he would do all he could to avoid any charges being brought against Tess. That was easing her mind, but the fact that she would have to tell everything about her night out to a solicitor in the first place was incredibly embarrassing. She just didn't do things like that! She was a teacher. She had responsibilities. She had a career to think of. And she had Gina on her mind. Life was spiralling out of control.

"Are you okay, Miss?" asked one of her pupils. "Maybe you should sit down. You look weird."

Weird? Yes, that was exactly how she felt. It was a swirly, dizzy feeling that drained her energy and made her just want to lie down and switch off. It wasn't even break-time yet and it was only her second period of the morning so she couldn't just give up already. She had to fight it off, to ride the storm and see this day through. She was tired and emotional after the rollercoaster weekend and she couldn't concentrate on her job with the fear of her future. She felt unsettled and in limbo and she wanted to come back down to earth and find her way again.

"Can I go to the toilet?"

She came back to her senses with the request of a young girl who was desperate to be excused.

"Sorry . . . I'm sorry I was miles away there. Where were we?"

"You got as far as 'G' in the alphabet?" said the girl. "But I need to 'P'. I've asked you three times."

The class erupted with laughter as the young lady was permitted to leave the room at last. Tess sat down at her desk and took a drink of water. She had mints in her drawer somewhere. Maybe that would settle the nausea and at break-time she would have a nice strong cup of tea. She had a lot on her mind with the police and the solicitor, not to mention worrying about Gina and her son lying in a Belfast hospital.

"Okay, let's get this nailed," she said to the twenty-five faces in front of her. "I think we'd better start at the beginning again – *Ah, Bay, Say, Day* . . ."

She popped a mint into her mouth and sucked it desperately but the nausea was growing worse. She couldn't breathe properly and the room began to spin.

"Miss, you don't look so good."

"Excuse me," said Tess. "Bronagh, you're in charge. I'll be right back."

She rushed through the doorway of the classroom, out into the corridor and across a foyer to the staff bathroom where she made it to the toilet bowl just in time. She had never felt so ill in her life. She was violently sick and the French alphabet was ringing in her ears. She was dizzy and confused and so, so ill and she just wanted to go home.

Polly picked Ruth up at eleven and they set off on the short motorway trip that took them to the hospital in Belfast.

"It's just a nightmare," said Ruth when she got into the car. "I've hardly slept a wink with worry and I'm sure you're exhausted too."

"I'm so tired I can barely think straight," said Polly, stifling a yawn. "I intended to be on my way much earlier than this but Helen called to say she was running late and then I was on the phone to the hospital. I can't tell you how relieved I was to hear that Gina had a good night and was comfortable. She's a little fighter, isn't she?"

Ruth smiled when she remembered some of the fun she had with Gina over the weekend. She really did show her true colours and was a far cry from the meek, vulnerable young woman who had walked into Polly's kitchen only a couple of days ago.

"Does it mean she'll make a full recovery?" asked Ruth.

"I don't think she's out of the woods yet," said Polly. "She suffered a huge blow to her head so they'll want to keep a close eye on her for quite a while, but at least she is out of Intensive Care and wee Danny is able to go and visit her around now. It was so frightening seeing her like that last night. It's an image I never want to see again."

Ruth was wondering if James had told Polly about their late-night chat the night before. She had thought about him, as well as Gina, all night long and her heart went out to him for how he was feeling. Mental exhaustion was something she could closely identify with and she totally understood how it could come about without rhyme or reason.

"Was it late when you got home?" she asked, hoping to break the ice on the subject matter. She wasn't being nosey. She was concerned. "I called at the house because I couldn't get you on the phone and I couldn't settle."

"Did you? James didn't say."

Shit.

"Maybe he forgot," said Ruth. "He seemed to have a lot on his mind."

"He does," said Polly. "You know, I have learned so much over the past few days, Ruth. I really have."

Ruth knew exactly where she was coming from. "Me too."

"I've learned that you can live with someone and not

really know them at all. James talked to me, Ruth. At last he talked to me. Told me he's been suffering from severe depression. I had no idea what he was going through and it took a night away, a near-miss with a stranger and the tragedy that could have come from Gina's accident to make me realise what really is important in my life. It's been a frightening experience but I think I've come out the other side."

Ruth was delighted for Polly. "And you also learned never to throw stilettos at a stranger," she said with a chuckle. They had had enough doom and gloom and she felt like they should lighten the mood.

"Or chat up a hot young Stag when you're full to the throat with shots and vodka!"

"It was a great night. Thanks again for inviting me." Ruth checked her make-up in the mirror on the sun visor. "I don't know how I would have coped over the past few days if you hadn't taken me under your wing. I really appreciate it, Polly."

Polly reached across and gave Ruth's arm a squeeze. "You don't have to thank me," she said. "You have taught me how strong a person can be in the face of adversity, Ruth Monaghan. It took guts and courage to leave your home in London and start again here."

"Well, I might as well be in London because my family are only down the road in Belfast yet they might as well be in Outer Mongolia."

"How do you mean?"

Ruth realised that she still had so much to fill her new friend in on.

"Let's just say, you are so lucky to have your family,

Polly," she said. She didn't feel this was the right time to stress Polly out with more drama. "I envy your relationship with Tess so much. To cut a long story short, my brother hasn't spoken to me for years and don't even start me on my mother. She really hates me and I feel so alone. It's a horrible feeling to be isolated from the people who are supposed to love you unconditionally."

Polly gulped at the thought of being estranged from her family. She had no idea that Ruth had such a battle going on.

"Well, I don't know the details of the story but I do know one thing, Ruth Monaghan: your mother and your brother really don't know what they're missing out on. It's their loss, but hopefully they will realise that sooner rather than later."

Ruth leaned further back in the front seat of the car. Every time she closed her eyes the night before she saw her father's summer seat outside Raymond Dillon's house. When she finally got to sleep, she dreamed of Samantha and her mother sitting on it, chatting and drinking tea while Samantha's children played in the garden. She hated the bitterness and jealousy she felt when she thought of their cosy relationship.

"I drove to Belfast last night," she said. She fixed the buttons on her top. They didn't need fixing. "To see my mother."

"Oh my God, Ruth! What happened?"

"Nothing happened," said Ruth with a shrug. "I drove to the street where they live, watched for a while like a lunatic stalker, saw Samantha, my stepsister who caused most of the trouble between us, coming out through the front door, then chickened out and came home. That's why you couldn't get in touch with me. I was playing desperate detective games with my own mind. It didn't do me any good at all."

Polly concentrated on the road as she digested the torment that Ruth had put herself through. She just couldn't understand how a mother could turn her back on her own flesh and blood and treat her like such an unwelcome outcast. Whatever had happened to cause such a rift? Whatever it was, Ruth wasn't ready to tell her yet.

"You should have driven over the silly bitch," she said. "I need a drink. We are getting a bottle of wine tonight on the way home. I just can't imagine what you're going through. I couldn't cope without my family. You deserve a medal."

They arrived at the hospital just around noon and, as they walked towards the hospital entrance, Polly pointed out Trevor pacing the paving outside, sucking on a cigarette and staring at the ground.

"He turns my liver sour," said Ruth. "I'd love to kick the shit out of him right now. A good dig in the kidneys is what that boyo needs!"

"Don't even think about it," said Polly. "One of us with an assault charge is enough, thank you very much. Wait until a time we can get him when no one else is looking. They probably have CCTV here."

They marched towards Trevor and Polly painted on a smile.

"Great news, isn't it, Trevor? I can't believe she had such a good night! It takes more than a bash or two to the head to beat our wee Gina, doesn't it?"

Trevor stopped. He dropped his cigarette, stood on it, exhaled the last mist of smoke and looked Polly directly in the eye.

"Enough of the smart-ass comments," he said. "That's my wife and son in there. Don't you dare even think you can speak to me like that!"

"You don't scare me, Trevor Humphries," she hissed. "I hope you are proud of yourself. I hope you are crawling inside with guilt for all the years of agony you put my best friend through. I hope you rot in hell."

Trevor opened his mouth to defend himself but he was flummoxed as the two ladies marched past him and in through the hospital doors.

28

Tess sat in the car outside the school building and twiddled her phone in her hands. She wanted to call Rob and tell him how ill she felt. She needed comfort and a hug and a cosy blanket in front of an open fire. She was blessed to live so close to work but the thought of driving felt like climbing a mountain and she just couldn't muster up the energy. She thought of Gina lying in hospital, critically ill, and tried to pull herself together but the deep sickness she felt inside just would not go away.

She would have to rise above it. She would drive home and she would have a lie-down, perhaps a bit of a snooze and she would be right as rain in no time.

"Are you sure you're not pregnant?" her colleague had asked her before she left. "Morning sickness can strike at any time of day, you know?"

It was a running joke with a jag that Tess had faced since the moment she came back from honeymoon.

"Do I hear the pitter-patter of tiny feet?" they would ask her.

"Your clock must be ticking now?" was another favourite. Or "Aren't you feeling all clucky now you're married?"

Every time she was faced with the question she would dismiss it with a jokey answer but she longed to tell everyone to mind their own bloody business. It was bad enough in her home life with her sisters and her mother nagging at her constantly to get a move on, not to mention Rob with his puppy-dog eyes every time he saw a baby in a pram.

She couldn't be pregnant, could she? She took her pill religiously at the same time every day.

But accidents did happen. No contraceptive was one-hundred-per-cent guaranteed and everyone she spoke to about it knew someone who'd got pregnant despite taking precautions.

It was stress, it had to be! It was stress, plus recovery after a heavy, heavy weekend of booze and late nights. Her body was telling her to give her head a break. She had too much going on and now it was affecting her work life. She hated giving in to illness of any sort, especially when it meant taking time out of her precious job. She hadn't taken a day off since she started at St John's and was determined to maintain her record of excellence as she aimed for promotion.

But she would have to be totally sure. Yes. She would eradicate pregnancy immediately by buying a pregnancy test on her way home. And if she was pregnant . . . well, she would have to deal with that later.

The very thought of it made her heave again.

"Look who it is!" said Polly when they entered Gina's new side ward. It was much more pleasant than Intensive

Care with its pink walls and bright (though glaringly fake) flowers on the windowsill. It even had a television which was showing a re-run of *Friends* which had young Danny super-glued to it from a wheelchair at the side of Gina's bed.

"Hi, Polly," said Danny. "Look!"

He pointed to the cast on his broken leg and then held up his wrist to show the light bandage he had on it.

"Wow!" said Polly. "Your friends at school will have a field day signing those bandages!"

"And look," he said, pointing at the gash above his eye. "I don't need the bandage any more. It's stopped bleeding but I really wanted to keep the bandage to show everyone. It was cool!"

Ruth had barely noticed the boy because her eyes were locked on Gina who stared back at her visitors with heavy, dopey eyes.

"How are you feeling, love?" she asked her. "Or is that the stupidest question in the world?"

It was one of those moments where Ruth was sure she would say the wrong thing – a mixture of nerves and emotion had her tongue-tied and she just couldn't find the words.

"I've been in much better places," said Gina. "Food's not bad though, even if I do have to be spoon-fed like a baby."

She looked a lot worse than Ruth had imagined she would.

"You look . . ." Polly was finding it tough as well. She was glad that Danny was there to provide an easy distraction.

"Like a car-crash victim?" said Gina. She tried to laugh

but gave up, closing her eyes for a few seconds. When she opened them again, her friends were crying silent tears.

"We thought we'd lost you," said Polly. "What on earth happened, love? How did it happen? Can you remember?"

Gina slowly nodded her head. She licked her lips and Polly handed her a cup of water to sip.

"If you're tired, you can tell us later," said Ruth. "She looks tired, Polly. Maybe we should come back later."

"I'm still here, you know," said Gina with a cheeky smile. "I may be battered but my ears still work."

Her lips were dry and crusty and her eyes had dark circles that blended in with the blue-and-yellow bruises that dotted her forehead.

"Sorry," said Ruth. "Do you want to sleep?"

Gina shook her head but her drooping eyes told a different story.

"We'll come back in an hour," said Polly. "You rest up and then you can tell us all about your rally-driving debut and how it all went terribly wrong."

"I'll never be a Schumacher," said Gina. "You okay if I get some sleep, Danny boy?"

Danny gave his mum the thumbs-up and they called the nurse to arrange to have him taken back to his ward.

Gina had drifted off into a deep sleep before any of her visitors had even made it out through the door.

Neither woman spoke as they walked down the corridor, out of the Neurological Ward and into the lift that led to the ground floor. They were heading for the canteen. The hospital was buzzing as always with teams of doctors marching past in teams of three and four, some in white coats, some in surgical greens and all chatting ten to the dozen. The entire place smelled of chlorine and sanitising fluid and they were glad to be met with the warmer yet still frantically busy atmosphere of the canteen.

"I'm dying for a coffee," said Polly.

They lifted a tray and queued along the wooden counter, sliding the brown trays along past pre-packed crackers, cheeses and yoghurts, then buns and cakes and biscuits, two self-service pots of soup and a hot food counter that was serving up everything from chicken curry to sausage rolls and a sweet-and-sour pork dish that looked quite appetising.

"Do you fancy something more substantial before your coffee?" asked Ruth. Her tummy was rumbling as she had missed breakfast in the usual Monday morning rush to get Melanie out to school. She was worse now as a teenager than she had been when she was at primary school.

"I don't really have an appetite for much more than a coffee," said Polly. "But you go ahead. It all looks good. I just couldn't stomach it."

Ruth let out an exaggerated sigh. "Don't tell me you're one of those lucky people who cannot eat when they're stressed or worried? I would eat the leg of a buttered donkey no matter what I was going through. In fact, in times of stress, I'd eat the four legs of a buttered donkey! You lot sicken me!"

Polly laughed and made her way to the coffee machine. A little girl stood a bit too close to it for her liking and she looked around to see who she was with. She was reaching up to fill a cup with hot water from the machine and, at no more than four years old, Polly was afraid she would scald herself.

"Sapphire! Come here immediately!" said a peroxide-blonde dressed in track-suit bottoms and a yellow T-shirt.

"I want coffee," said the child.

Polly winced. A child drinking coffee?

"You can have coffee when you get home!"

Bemused, Polly helped herself to coffee and made her way to the till to pay. She was just opening her purse when Ruth sidled up behind her with a full tray.

"Ah-ah, madam!" she said. "Put that purse away. Don't forget, we have a big hospitality budget still on this card. That horse can keep us all in comfort for a while yet and I will make sure we spend every penny of our winnings unwisely."

She pulled out her bank card and handed it to the check-out girl.

They took a seat by the window and Ruth attacked her food with gusto.

"How's your chicken?" Polly asked.

"It's pork," said Ruth, munching away. "I can't believe you're not eating. Honestly, it would take a nuclear bomb to go off in my belly before I would go off my food. And, before you say it, I know it shows."

She rubbed her stomach and shovelled another spoonful of rice and pork and sweet-and-sour sauce into her mouth. Hospital canteen food sure had come a long way since the last time she had sampled it. Those doctors and nurses were spoilt rotten. Ruth wondered if she could come here more often for a spot of lunch without the traumatic circumstances. She giggled to herself at the thought of bringing a date to a hospital canteen for dinner! Then she stopped chewing and the taste of the food left

317

her mouth. She swallowed hard, took a drink of water and felt her blood run cold.

"Ruth? Ruth, are you choking? Ruth?"

Ruth couldn't speak. Her eyes were fixed on a woman and child who were arguing loudly at a table at the far end of the canteen.

"It's . . . it's Samantha," she said, the food now cartwheeling inside her. "That's Samantha Dillon. Over there."

Polly's eyes darted across to where Ruth was staring. It was the coffee kid and her mother.

"Sapphire's mum?"

"What?" said Ruth. "Who?"

"I was at the coffee machine and the little girl, Sapphire, was trying to reach for a cup of hot water because she wanted coffee and it drew my attention. I just found it all a bit strange. So that's the infamous Samantha? Why are they here, I wonder?"

Ruth was concentrating on her breathing. She thought she might pass out as she watched her nemesis across the room and all sorts of thoughts were going through her mind. Was her mother in hospital? Was she really ill and no one had told her? She had to find out.

She stood up and Polly followed her in between tables, excusing herself as they bumped into chairs on the way past in Ruth's haste to find out what the hell was going on.

"I know what you're thinking," said Polly to Ruth's back, even though she knew her friend wasn't listening. "Ruth, just keep calm. Don't assume it's anything to do with your family. It might just be a friend of hers. Maybe someone has had a baby? Don't panic, please Ruth. And for God's sake don't hit her!"

But Ruth was charging on, her mind full of possibilities. Her mother had cancer and was dying on a ward just above them. Or maybe she'd had a bad fall and a broken hip, or a serious car accident like Gina. Why didn't they tell her? Surely she deserved to be given such life-changing information?

"Samantha!" she said and the other woman looked up at her, mid-argument with her daughter over spilling a yoghurt.

"Ruth!" said Samantha. "How did you find out?"

Ruth swallowed hard. "Found out? I'm here visiting a friend. What is there to find out? Tell me! Is it my mother?"

Samantha pushed back her seat and grabbed her daughter's hand, ignoring the child's request to finish her lunch. She dragged the child across the canteen as young Sapphire craned her neck behind her to watch the strange lady who was following them in despair.

"You were told to stay away," said Samantha when Ruth caught up with her and matched her stride. "Why can't you get the hint? You're not wanted in our family!"

"Your family! *Your* family!" said Ruth.

Polly was pacing behind them. Samantha could move quickly, that was for sure.

"You heard me," said Samantha. She stopped and faced Ruth, head to head. She didn't seem to care that passers-by were noticing the commotion, or that Sapphire had started to cry.

"You and your father hijacked my family," said Ruth. "Now tell me what the hell is going on! I have a right to know!"

Samantha looked Ruth up and down in disgust. "We

319

thought we had got rid of you, once and for all," she said. "But you are worse than any cancer. You just won't go away, will you?"

Ruth clenched her fists as Polly looked on in horror. Cancer? Shit! Please don't hit her, she thought, even though the girl deserved more than a good slap across the jaw.

"I will not let you poison my mother any longer," said Ruth. "*You* are the cancer. *You* are the one who took my place in her life and convinced her I was some sort of evil offspring who was out to ruin her marriage!"

"Which is exactly what you are!" said Samantha. "You gave up your place in the family when you made my father feel like a criminal! There could have been room for both of us, but you couldn't handle the fact that your mother loved him more than she loved you!"

That was it. That was the final blow for Ruth. She couldn't listen to this venom any longer. She would find her mother, in whatever ward she lay on in this hospital and she would talk to her, get the closure she needed and then she would move on. She didn't need permission from the stranger who stood before her. She wasn't afraid of Samantha Dillon. Not any more.

"Let's go, Polly," she said, still staring into Samantha's face. "I don't need to look or listen to this any more. I'm going to find my mother."

"Your mother has cancer, Ruth," said Samantha. "She has had it for months."

Ruth froze to the spot and her eyes blurred and her ears heard nothing more that Samantha had to say. Her mother was dying.

"Ruth?" said Polly. "Ruth?"

Polly's heart was thumping and she could feel her whole insides shake.

"Thanks for letting me know, Samantha," said Ruth and she slowly walked away, leaving Polly to follow her. "I at least deserved to know!"

Tess tied her hair back in a low pony-tail then twisted it into a bun and pinned it at the nape of her neck. She had dark rings around her eyes which were bloodshot and sore from lack of sleep, over-indulgence and vomiting, and her skin was pasty and dry. She glanced at the white paper bag that sat on top of the toilet cistern. It was challenging her to take the plunge and find out one way or another if her illness was connected to impending unplanned motherhood or if it was simply the strains of a very heavy weekend.

She opened the bag and slid out the long blue-and-white box, her fingers trembling as she opened it and removed the plastic stick that was to determine her future. She had always been so careful with contraception and had not had to perform this task since that horrible scare at nineteen when she was young and stupid.

But what was the worst that could happen? If she was pregnant, would she learn to live with it, learn to love the prospect of being a mother? Or would she resent the lack of choice she had when she was so determined to do things her way and wait until she felt the time was right?

"None of mine were planned," her sister Helen would say. "And I wouldn't change them for the world."

"I got the shock of my life when I found out I was having twins," Polly had told her. "I had only ever planned to have two children, but now I can't imagine life without my two little rascals."

There were worse things that could happen, that was for sure. But being a mother just wasn't in her plans yet. She wanted to go on at least two more foreign holidays with Rob and enjoy being free to do whatever they wanted to do without the responsibility of a tiny mouth to feed.

"Let's get a puppy," she'd once suggested in jest. "And every night we'll get up at 2am to feed it, and then we'll see if we are ready to have a baby."

Rob wasn't impressed and objected solemnly that she was comparing their child to a dog, which made her laugh even more.

She peeled the plastic wrapping off the white stick and removed the lid, then did what she had to do and waited. She watched as the moisture filled one window, then two, and the first blue line appeared. Beads of sweat formed on her brow and she dabbed them away with some toilet tissue, every second seeming like minutes.

And then it came. The second blue line.

"Oh *fiddlers*!"

She didn't know where 'fiddlers' came from and she started to laugh. She'd never said 'fiddlers' before in her life.

But she was pregnant! She was pregnant and to her surprise, a huge smile crept across her face. Maybe it was nerves. She hadn't planned on smiling, but against her better judgement she actually felt a rush of excitement.

She stood up, fixed herself and washed her hands. What was going on? She was supposed to be panicky, confused and distraught. She was supposed to be angry at the contraception for not doing as it was supposed to. She was supposed to be worried about how it would slow down her ability to make it to Head of Department at school. But instead, she had this soul-filling feeling of euphoria and she wanted to shout it from the rooftops.

She was going to have a baby! She and Rob were going to be parents! Despite all her protesting, Mother Nature had other plans in store for her and she just couldn't wait to tell her husband.

29

"I'll go back to see Gina," said Polly after Ruth had found out from the Enquiry desk the whereabouts of her sick mother. "I hope you know what you're doing, Ruth. I don't want to see you hurting any more over your so-called family. Just don't expect too much."

Ruth tilted her chin back, straightened her top and fixed her bright red hair. "I just want to say my piece, make my peace if you like, and leave. I don't want her to die without my having had the chance to do that. Samantha can say what she wants. I need to deal with this before it eats at me any more."

Polly nodded and gave her friend a tight hug. "I'll say a wee prayer," she whispered. "Stay strong and don't let that scumbag beat you down. You are better than that. You are Ruth Monaghan, woman of steel and power and don't you ever forget it!"

"Thanks, Polly," she said. "I feel a bit more like a big blob of putty than a woman of steel, but I'm doing this for all the right reasons, believe me. Once I have it dealt with I can move on with my life and focus on people who care about me, rather than worrying about those who don't."

They parted company and Ruth stopped by the hospital gift store which stood adjacent to the Enquiries desk. It was full of the usual hospital-type gifts – teddy bears in blue and pink for new arrivals, balloons, flowers and huge chunks of chocolate and honeycomb, rows of magazines and books and fizzy drinks. She stopped at the stand that held greeting cards which were dominated, naturally, with a variety of *Get Well Soon* designs.

She fingered one that said '*Get Well Soon Mother*' and lifted it from the rack. She opened it and read the verse aloud, feeling a lump in her throat as the words stung her empty heart.

"You gave me life, you wiped my tears.
You cared for me through all the years.
You nurtured me, you watched me grow.
I love you more than you'll ever know."

If only! With a deep breath she put the card back in its place, fixed her handbag on her shoulder and made her way to the lift. One was waiting already, so she stepped inside and pressed the button that would take her to the Oncology Ward. She still couldn't believe that she had bumped into Samantha. It was strange how things worked out. Maybe this was a sign that all was not lost.

The lift pinged open and she stepped out onto the corridor of the Oncology Ward.

She made her way to the nurses' station. The atmosphere was much less tense, less urgent and desperate than on Gina's ward but the same air of the unknown lingered around it. She gripped her handbag and felt her confidence lessen with every step she took.

"I'm here to see Hilary Monaghan, I mean Hilary Dillon," she said to a nurse who was ignoring a phone ringing to handle her query.

"Hilary Dillon . . . Bay two, second bed on the left," said the nurse and Ruth nodded but didn't move.

She couldn't get cold feet now. She was so close. She had to face up to this and close that sorry chapter of her life once and for all.

"It's tough, I know," said the nurse, who obviously thought she was delaying for other reasons. "I've been through the same with a close relative so I know exactly what you're going through. You are family, yes? It's close family only I'm afraid at such a crucial stage in Hilary's illness."

Crucial stage? Ruth looked down the lengthy green corridor and then back at the nurse.

"I'm her daughter," she said. "I'm her youngest child."

"Oh," said the nurse. "But I thought Mrs Dillon said she had only two children . . . Samantha and . . . oh, the name of her son has left me."

"Brian," said Ruth. "His name is Brian. And she does have only two children. I am one of them."

With a new-found fire in her belly she left the bemused nurse and made her way to Bay Two. She stopped, got her bearings and looked over to the left. The bed was surrounded by a floral curtain and she approached it with adrenaline pumping through her veins. She must be calm. She was not there to cause trouble. She was there to make her final peace.

A younger nurse stepped out from the curtain and swept it around the railings, acknowledging Ruth's presence with a smile. As she had expected, Samantha guarded the bedside while her daughter Sapphire stuffed her little face with chocolate. Samantha didn't meet Ruth's eye, instead she stroked Hilary's hand as the woman lay asleep. Hilary's body was barely skin and bone and she looked like a translucent doll as she lay against the stark white bed linen.

"How . . . how long has this been . . .?"

To her surprise the anger subsided at the sight of her mother, so weak and tiny and oblivious to her presence and pain. She didn't look like herself. How could she with such a violent, decaying illness eating her insides? She looked like she was already dead.

"She doesn't have long," said Samantha. "It was a short battle, but that battle is almost over now, isn't it, Mum?"

Mum! Ruth nodded slowly in acceptance of the news. This was not a time to show bitterness or resentment. There was no point looking back. What was done, was done. She was here now. She knew now.

"And Brian?" she asked. "Where is he?"

Samantha looked up at her at last. "He's at work. He does the evening shift, I do the daytime. It's been a rough time for all of us."

All of *us*. All of *them*. Such simple words that reminded Ruth that she was no longer part of this tight family unit. She wanted to stamp her feet and kick and scream at Samantha for not telling her that her mother was dying. She wanted to find Brian and call him the walkover wimp that he was. But most of all she wanted to talk to her mother. She wanted to rewind time so that she could find out just why her mother resented her so much.

"I want her to know I was here," she said. Her throat was dry and she really wanted to cry. "I want her to know that . . ."

"There is no point," said Samantha. "She won't know. She's so heavily medicated these days that she doesn't know day from night. We'll be taking her home within the week so that she can leave us with grace in the place she called home."

Samantha spoke like a bloody priest! Whoever said such drivel! 'Leave us with grace in the place she called home?' She wouldn't even know how to spell the word 'grace' never mind use it in her everyday language! Ruth recalled the nurse's words: she thought Hilary had only two children – Samantha and Brian. Hilary obviously didn't even regard her as her own blood, even in her last days. Ruth tried to let the reality of that sink in and, as she stood, staring at the woman who used to wipe her nose and soothe her when she was sick, she felt nothing but sorrow. Not for herself, but for the woman that her mother had become.

"I will pray for her then," said Ruth, feeling a rush of the warmth of acceptance run through her veins. "I hope she finds peace and doesn't suffer for too long. My suffering too is over now. Goodbye, Samantha."

She blessed herself and turned away from the two women who had made her life a living hell for as long as she could remember.

"Oh and by the way," she said, turning back again. "I

never want to lay eyes on you again, or my brother. You can tell him from me that he is nothing but a cowardly sissy who has let women dominate him his whole sorry life. I didn't expect much from you but by God I expected a lot more from him. You two suit each other. I'm glad I don't have to look at your ugly faces ever again!"

She left Samantha and walked tall, allowing her last tears for her mother to fall down her cheeks as she left the ward, past the nurses' station.

"Too upsetting?" said the same nurse who had greeted her on arrival. "My heart goes out to you. It really does. I remember when my –"

"No," said Ruth. "I'm glad I came. You don't know how glad I am. Yes, it was upsetting but perhaps not for the reasons you mean. And now – now I'm going home to my real family. I have two children too, you know. And I will never, ever deny them to anyone, no matter what they do."

The nurse looked more puzzled than ever but Ruth didn't explain any more. She left the Oncology Ward with her lips pursed together and her head held high, then entered the elevator to go back to see Gina. For the first time in a long, long time, Ruth Monaghan felt like she was going home.

The afternoon was going so slow and Tess wanted to make the evening so special, but first she had the appointment with her solicitor to contend with. She hated solicitors. Not the people themselves, but what they represented. Having to visit a solicitor was a sure sign that things in your life were stressful – be it buying a house, marriage disruptions or throwing stilettos at a bouncer. Solicitors were never a good thing.

She sat in the silence of the brown waiting room as a secretary tip-tapped on a keyboard a letter that was being dictated through an ear-piece. There were files everywhere, bound with various types of fasteners and Tess's head spun at the very thought of having to wade through them for information.

"I can't believe I have to do this," she said when she was called into Jim Smith's office. "Honestly, I am so humiliated, so can we make it as pain-free as possible?"

Jim was an old school friend of Rob's and Tess had met him on a few occasions down the years – mainly in posh wine bars and classy restaurants. To have to recount a drunken night out which ended in arrest to someone with whom she once socialised on a more sophisticated scale was worse than torture.

"I'm glad you've trusted me to handle this," said Jim. He was a baby-faced thirty-two-year-old who looked like he should be wearing a school blazer rather than the expensive shirt and tie he sported in his dull brown office. "Believe me, this will all be treated with strictest confidence and I promise not to take the piss on your aim when throwing stilettos."

Tess was still feeling nauseous and wasn't in the mood for jokes. She wanted to get this over and done with so that she could focus on the evening ahead when she would tell Rob what the future held for them.

"Just tell me what you need from me," she said. "I really do just want to be told what I have to do and then get out of here. No offense. Please."

"I've listened to your interview, but just to make sure

we've left no stone unturned, just tell me again what happened and we'll make this as smooth and pain-free as we can."

Jim took notes as Tess quickly recounted her version of the night in question once more. She told him about the stag party, about Gina being legless and how the demeaning comments from the burly fat bouncer were the last straw. She told him about her toe (which was still throbbing but had taken a back seat to her new vomiting sickness) and how she had run away when Copalicious tried to reason with her. It all sounded so childish and silly and she was so glad when she finally got to the moment when she was released from the police station further to enquiries. By now, her face was burning with deep humiliation.

"I think it's unlikely that this McAleer guy will press charges," said Jim, once he had received as much information as he needed. "I've done my homework on him and from what I have heard he would do well to stay away from the courts for a while. He is a well-known thug who has enough on his back catalogue of run-ins with the law. Plus, I have listened to the tapes of your interview with that young Garda –"

"Copalicious?"

"Who?"

"I mean Garda McGuinness."

"Yes, that's the one. His remarks at the end of the tape were obviously accidental but it weakens the police case against you for any misbehaviour."

"I hope you are right," said Tess. "But what happens now?"

Jim Smith chewed his pen which made Tess's teeth go

all funny. She couldn't stand pen-chewing. He slid the pen behind his ear, and then took it back for another chew which made the vomit rise from her belly again. She could see slobbers on the tip of it. *Boke.*

"We wait," he said, eventually. "I have contacted the Gardaí in Donegal and asked for all correspondence to be dealt with through this office, but I'd be highly surprised if there is another word about it."

"Really? Gosh, you don't know how good it feels to hear that," said Tess. "I just want to put it behind me and look to the future. One thing's for sure, I won't be going out on the town again for a long, long time." She felt like a weight had been lifted off her shoulders. "Thank you for your time, Jim."

She stood and shook the solicitor's hand. He had such a firm shake that she was surprised her arm stayed in her socket but his hands were damp and cold. *Yuk.*

"I'll be in touch if need be," said Jim. "Tell Rob we'll have to have a pint together soon. Is he still fire-fighting and making women swoon with his big hose?"

"Ha ha," said Tess with a smile. "He's still making me swoon which is all that matters."

She said her farewells and left the brown office via the brown stairs and out through the brown waiting room with its silence and mountains of files and tip-tapping of keys. She couldn't wait to see Rob. She couldn't wait to tell him that his big hose had made a baby!

Tess fixed her make-up and loosened the bun in her hair, letting it fall around her shoulders. She changed out of her work clothes into a long, multi-coloured maxi dress and flip-flops and sprayed some perfume on her wrists. Rob would be home any minute and she had his favourite dinner waiting for him in the oven and the table was set to perfection. To her great relief, her morning sickness had lifted since her appointment with Jim and she truly believed that a lot of it was to do with the stresses of the weekend past. Now, she had a totally new focus on her life and she couldn't believe just how excited she felt about it.

She heard the key turn in the door so she made her way downstairs. Rob met her with his usual cheery smile and a welcoming kiss, pulling her by the waist into him as he nuzzled into her neck.

"You smell good enough to eat," he said, nibbling her ear.

"Let's go through to the kitchen," said Tess. "You can eat your dinner instead."

Rob washed his hands and sat at the kitchen table, watching Tess almost float around as she served up a steaming hot Shepherd's Pie and fresh steamed vegetables.

"Have I done something to deserve this?" he asked. "Did Jim promise you that he would save you from a life sentence in prison for stiletto-throwing and is this a sign of your gratitude for my making use of contacts?"

"Better than that," said Tess. She was bubbling inside. She wanted to hold off and savour the moment but the words 'I'm pregnant' were fizzing on her tongue. She wanted to just spit it out, but she also wanted to build up some sweet anticipation.

She lay Rob's dinner down in front of him, and then sat her plate across the table from his. A candle flickered between them and she was smiling so much her cheeks were almost caving in.

"What on earth is going on, Tess? Did someone kidnap my grumpy, hung-over wife with the broken toe from earlier and replace her with the beautiful, cheery but very bossy model I know and love?"

He was mixing the Shepherd's Pie around on his plate and she could tell he was dying to get stuck in. Normally his child-like mixing irritated her but nothing in the world could wipe the smile off her face right now.

"I can hear something," she said.

"What? Probably my belly rumbling," said Rob. "I hadn't even had time for lunch today. Two accidents the other side of town and a young couple who had set their chimney on fire was enough to keep me out of McDonald's. I was craving a Big Mac all day."

"Craving?" said Tess. "Funny you should say that. I'd imagine I'll be doing some of that too very soon. Craving . . ."

Rob slowly laid down his knife and fork. He looked across at her beaming face via the flickering candle.

"What . . .?"

She stood up, looking radiant with her flowing dress and long blonde hair that turned him on so much, and made her way over to him.

He pushed his chair back so she could sit on his knee, and she draped her arms around his neck. Then she leaned back to be sure she could see the expression on his face.

"You see," she said. "The thing I hear, my darling husband . . ."

Rob gulped. She could tell he knew what was coming

but was too afraid to say in case he had read her signs all wrong.

"The thing I hear right now, is the pitter-patter of tiny feet."

"No way!" said Rob. "I thought you didn't –"

"So did I," said Tess. "I thought it was the last thing in the world that I wanted, but I did a test today and the minute that blue line appeared, I realised that being with you and having your baby is the one thing I want most in the whole world and I simply cannot wait. You're going to be a daddy!"

Tears ran from Tess's eyes as she watched her gorgeous husband swallow the news he had been longing to hear for over a year now.

"I . . . I . . . when? Oh my God, this is amazing!" His eyes widened and filled up and his voice was broken in shock.

"I reckon it will be May," she said. "So we have a while to wait. I must only be a few weeks. It's definitely very early stages but I'll find out more when I go to the antenatal clinic. I've made my first appointment for Friday!"

Rob nestled his face into Tess's shoulder and held her as close as he could. They stayed like that for minutes until they remembered their dinner was getting cold.

"I'm almost too excited to eat," he said when she took her place again at the opposite side of the table. "Are you sure you're okay with it all? Only a few days ago you chucked a wobbly with me for even suggesting it."

Tess pushed her food around her plate. Her appetite was waning too and deep in the pit of her stomach she still felt a tiny bit queasy.

"I feel like I'm on top of the world," she said. "I really do. I was so against it because I wanted to be in control and make sure it was me who decided when my body would be ready. But nature had other plans. It just seems so meant to be! I'm over the moon!"

Rob squeezed her hand and was smiling more than Tess had ever seen him smiling before – more than when she accepted his marriage proposal on a hot sandy beach in Tuscany three years ago, more than when he declared his love for her on their wedding day in a country church in front of two hundred guests. It really was the happiest moment in his life and she was so glad to have been such a huge part of it. Well, all of it really.

"So, what are the odds it might be twins then?" he asked with a grin. "I hope you know this is the start of that football team I've been planning and your sister has twins, so who knows?"

Tess lifted a pea off her plate and flicked it across the table.

"Don't push your luck, matey!" she said. "Let's just see how we manage with one little mouth to feed and take it from there!"

"You're quiet," said Polly to Ruth on their way to the car. "I won't force you to talk, but you know I'm here for you every step of the way. It can't have been easy for you to see your mother like that."

Ruth sniffled and focused on keeping her dignity. She would not break down in a hospital car park. She would not break down at all if she could help it.

"I need you to do me a favour," she said.

"Of course. Anything," said Polly. "I'll do anything I can."

They found Polly's Jeep and she bleeped the immobiliser to release the lock, then they climbed up inside.

"I need you to stop by my mother's house," said Ruth.

"Okay . . ." said Polly. "But who will be there? You're not planning on doing anything silly, are you, Ruth?"

"Oh, stop talking to me like that!" said Ruth. "You'd think to hear you I was going to rob the place or torch it or something. I may have been a bit of a rebel in my day, but I'm not a total gangster!"

Polly laughed at the way Ruth spoke in such a fluster. "I thought you might be after Raymond Dillon's ashes or something. You probably want to steal them and scatter them down a sewer!"

"Do you know, I couldn't even be arsed," she said, folding her arms like a defiant child. "I'm afraid you'll have to make some room in this Jeep because what I am taking is a hell of a lot bigger than Raymond Dillon's stinking ashes."

Polly put the Jeep into reverse, afraid of what she was going to hear next.

"Bigger?" she asked. "How much bigger?"

"You'll see," said Ruth. "Now just get me to Scotstown Park and all will be revealed."

Polly did what she was told and followed Ruth's directions to the south-west of the city where they travelled down a terraced side street that led to a rather pleasant cul-de-sac of tiny Lego-like bungalows – the retired couple's paradise. She was asked to stop outside a neat little whitewashed house which had window-boxes full of colour and a bright red door. It was a cosy spot and was much too nice for a wicked old witch like Hilary Dillon to reside in.

"I'll be a second," said Ruth. "It's times like these that I'm glad I'm not a skinny little runt like you!"

She stepped out of the car and Polly watched her open the red iron gate and make her way up the short pathway that led to the red door. A man opened the door and peered out, and then his face turned white with shock.

Polly wound down her window. She was not missing out on this!

"Ruth? What on earth? What the hell are you doing here?" he asked. His voice squeaked like a teenager's.

"Oh put a sock in it, Brian!" said Ruth "I won't be long. I'm here for one thing and one thing only."

Brian was a miserable-looking creature and Polly wanted to scream all sorts of obscenities his way, but she reckoned that Ruth had it all under control.

"You can't! No, you can't!" said Brian. He was in his sock soles and his beige slacks flapped in the wind when he stepped outside. His red-and-white stripy jumpy was like an embarrassing gift from an ageing aunt and his thick-rimmed glasses were lopsided.

"Oh, yes, I can and if you as much as come near me right now, I will knock your lights out and you know it," said Ruth. "You're nothing but a pussy-whipped wimp, Brian Monaghan, and I am ashamed to say you are my brother!"

She lifted a beautiful green summer seat as if she was lifting a small child and carried it with ease down the garden path as Brian looked on with his mouth open in shock. Polly had no idea what her friend was up to, but it certainly was having an effect on the 'Where's Wally' lookalike that stood so haplessly in fear of her. Ruth was still muttering as she manoeuvred the summer seat through the narrow gate.

Polly stepped out of the Jeep to help her.

"This should never, ever have been taken from my father's home and placed in front of Raymond Dillon's house! He would turn in his grave if he ever thought his own humble work was displayed so blatantly and so vulgarly! Turns my stomach! Well, I have it back now, Daddy, and no ass of no Dillon will ever sit on it again, you can rest assured. Don't come near me, Brian! I mean it, don't come near me!"

Brian was at the gate now but there was no fear that he would go any further. Without Samantha and his mother around, he was weaker than ever.

"I tried to talk them round," he said. "I told them you had a right to know but they made me swear that I wouldn't. You don't know how many times I almost called you! I had no idea you were back. How long have you been back? Maybe, you know, when all this is over, we can catch up?"

Ruth gave the summer seat one last heave into the back of the Jeep. It was easy as Polly had put the back seats down to fit it in and the door closed without any problems.

"Catch up? When it's all over?" said Ruth. She had her hands on her hips now and Polly noticed that her eyes were full of tears, despite her bravado. "You chicken! You absolute piece of stinking chicken-shit! If I wasn't good enough to 'catch up' with when our mother was here, then don't you even dare think of catching up with me when she is gone! I have been through hell and back over the past few years and not one of you gave a shit about me then and you don't give a shit about me now!"

"Ruth, you're upset," said Polly. "Let's just go home." She put her hand on Ruth's elbow but she shrugged it away.

"I haven't finished yet," she said. She was crying now. She was letting it all out.

"I'm sorry!" said Brian. He was gripping the top of the gate and he looked like a little boy. He really did look like he was sorry but for Ruth it was too late for apologies. She had waited for so, so long.

"All I wanted . . ." she sniffled, "all I wanted was just one sign. Just a sign to show me that there would be a glimmer of hope that I would be accepted by you all again. But that sign never came. I had to go looking for it at the hospital and I found out that there never was a sign. That's why it never came. There never was one in the first place. I wish you well, Brian. I hope you are proud of the decisions you've made but I get the feeling that it's your loss, not mine. Goodbye."

She walked around to the passenger side, wiping her face, and when she got comfortable in her seat, she pulled on her seat bell, fixed her make-up and let out a long sigh of relief.

"Now," she said to Polly. "I feel much better now. Let's get home to our families who love us. I just want to see my children and hold them very close, even if they do think I'm a nerd for doing so."

"Yes," said Polly. She was longing to snuggle her boys

too and have a cosy night in front of the telly with James. It had been a hectic weekend and she had a lot of catching up to do. "I think I need a glass of wine after all that!"

"Bring it on!" said Ruth. "Let's get the flock out of here! You have no idea how good I feel right now! I feel free at last! *Woo hoo*!"

30

Three Months Later

Gina sat in her armchair by the front window and watched the snow fall onto her front garden as Danny played outside, wrapped up in as many layers as he could carry. He was back on his feet again and although not completely mobile, he was certainly making up for lost time as he hobbled around outside with Polly's kids and some of the other children in Ardglass Villas. The sky was heavy and full of snow and although she was tired and was due her daily nap, she couldn't close her eyes in case she missed the magical flurry outside.

Polly was in the kitchen tidying after lunch – she had made lunch for Gina and Danny every day since Gina was sent home from hospital and would not hear of things being any different, no matter how much Gina protested.

"Right, missy," said Polly when she entered the room. "That's enough staring out of windows for one day. How about we put on our wellies and take a walk in this beautiful winter wonderland?"

342

Gina craned her neck to the side. She was so cosy in her fleecy pyjamas and the fire was roaring in the grate.

"I'm a bit too tired," she said. "But thanks anyhow. I'm happy enough to just admire the view, but you go ahead. I'm sure the kids would be delighted to go for a walk in the snow with their super-cool mum and leave old Misery Guts Gina behind. Danny needs to wrap up extra warm though. His leg could get very sore if he stays out too long."

Polly sat down on the armchair opposite.

"Danny is making a great recovery But you . . . well, you really are going to have to get out and about more, Gina. It's not good for your physical or mental health to be stuck in here all the time. The doctor says –"

"I know what the doctor says!" said Gina. "I'm bloody sick listening to what the doctor says. I'm sick of being told what I can and can't do! I am tired so I will sleep. I do not want to go out into the freezing cold and get soaked through, thank you very much!"

Polly clasped her hands, sat back in her chair and stared out the window, mirroring Gina's every move. Gina's temper tantrums were a regular sign of her ongoing frustration and anger for what she had been through and Polly had never risen to them. She understood her best friend's plight more than anyone as she had seen her suffer and slowly progress every single day.

"Fine," she said. "Let's just sit here then. No harm in that and the fire is lovely."

The silence between them was childish and they both knew it.

"Don't you have things to do?" asked Gina. "It's

Saturday afternoon. Most people with young families like yours are running around like headless chickens on Saturdays, not sitting with a grumpy neighbour who doesn't have the energy or the interest to go out for a walk in the snow."

Polly didn't answer at first. She squinted her eyes, watching a robin pick a worm from the snowy ground outside.

"You know, I can't imagine what goes through your head every day as you sit here, Gina," she said. "I'm not being smart or funny, I'm really curious. You spend a lot of time at this window and I do wonder what you think about to make the time pass by."

"I do spend a lot of time here," said Gina. "I find it very peaceful. I don't notice the time slipping by at all. I like it."

Polly wasn't letting it go. She had spoken to Gina's doctor on a regular basis and the main emphasis these days was to try and ease Gina back into a normal routine. Having worked with James through his recent bout of depression, Polly did not want to see the same thing happening to her dear friend.

"So, do you think about Trevor when you sit here? Or mull over your health? Or about Danny?"

Gina took a deep breath and shrugged. "Stuff," she said. "I have plenty of stuff to think about."

"Stuff like what?" asked Polly.

Gina felt a smile creep over her mouth. Before she knew it, she was grinning like a basket of chips. Polly smiled too. She knew exactly what Gina was thinking of.

"You dirty wee bitch," said Polly. "Three months on

and you are still thinking of your Jacuzzi session with Marco! It must have been bloody good! I don't think I've ever had such a memorable sexy moment that could make me smile or even recall three months later!"

"Believe me, it was so good," said Gina. She sat up in her chair and drew her legs underneath her. "And you have no idea how much that memory has helped me get through the past twelve weeks, Polly. When I was lying in the hospital, once I knew that Danny was okay and that I had my injuries well beaten, I would drift off to Marco's little room and imagine his brown, muscular glistening body rub against my skin as he sipped champagne beside me in those bubbles." She closed her eyes and took a deep breath, then let out a deep "*Aaaaah!*"

Polly was delighted. She had thought Gina was sulking and feeling sorry for herself as she sat at her window but instead she was savouring sweet memories of her sexual liaison with a handsome stranger!

"Do you ever wonder what he thought when he woke up after your marathon and you were gone?" asked Polly. Being a bit of a softie, she often worried if Marco felt used by Gina's *Wash and Go* style sex session. If it had been the other way round, they would all have been disgusted.

"Of course I do," said Gina. "I picture it in my head all the time. I hope he didn't think I was some fly-by-night slut who bed-hops with every man she bums a cigarette off. But . . . I think he knew that I needed to find some sort of release and feel good about myself again. With those good looks, I have no doubt but that he had another girl on his arm before we even left the village."

Polly shook her head with a smile. "You do make me

laugh! I wonder what he's doing now. Do you think he would remember you if your paths ever crossed again?"

Gina's eyes were sparkling now. It really was so romantic to think that she might come across Marco again and that they would have another chance to relive that wonderful evening.

"Oh believe me, I know he would remember me!" said Gina with a cheeky wink. "I left him with some lasting memories, that's for sure. I have years of experience ahead of him and I used those to my advantage. In fact, think I may have taught him a trick or two! He will probably never book that Jacuzzi room again for fear of having life-long flashbacks!"

Polly tried to picture the room in question. The tiny hotel . . . the ornate bedroom with the Jacuzzi bath . . . She couldn't really imagine Gina giving it her all but then what did she know about what would happen once the fires were stoked in Gina's loins? She must have been a proper little minx in her day!

"Do you think he ever comes back here to Ireland or did you scar him for life?" she asked. Gina was really bright right now and Polly didn't want her to let that feeling go.

"He comes back on the third weekend of every month, without fail," she said. "If I really wanted to, I would know exactly where to find him and when. He has business to attend to over here and, when he has it all wrapped up, he stays in *The Wayward Inn* . . . where he once met a wayward stranger . . . and he lets time slip by without even checking his watch. It's heaven!"

"Oh my word, I would nearly drive you there right

now!" said Polly. "I want to find a friend like Marco! He sounds simply divine!"

Their lusting after Marco was interrupted by Tess who came swanning in, looking as radiant as ever.

"*Knock knock!*" she called. "Oh my word it sure is Baltic out there! Frankie and the twins are making a snowman outside and Danny is director of operations. Don't kids feel the cold at all? *Brrr!*"

"No, they certainly do not," said Gina. "And to think that this time next year, your little one will be all snuggled up and looking out at his big cousins playing in the garden and then, before you know it, he will be in the thick of it all and you'll have wet socks and wet shoes and soaked-through coats and a little pink face coming in and out to get warmed up by his mummy."

Tess looked at Polly and her eyes widened with delight. Gina hadn't been so chatty since . . . well, since she came home from hospital. It was almost like she had visited the wrong house!

"I never thought I'd say it, but I can't wait," said Tess. "I like your fleecy jammies, Gina. Lookin' cosy over there!"

Tess sat on Gina's sofa and lifted a magazine from the coffee table. She flicked through it, feeling very much at ease. They had developed a rota between the three of them to make sure that Gina wasn't left alone for more than a few hours every day. Evenings were left free to spend with Danny but the girls were afraid that if the house wasn't busy during the day, she might not make as much progress as she should.

"So, you don't want to go for a walk then, before I leave you in the hands of Tess the Terrible," said Polly. "Going once, going twice . . ."

Gina looked outside. It had stopped snowing and the boys were having a ball in the garden. Could she really muster up the energy to get dressed and go out into the cold air? She knew it would make her feel better, but she had perked up already by talking about Marco and she was quite content with that.

"I have another idea," she said to her two friends who were all ears.

Gina never had ideas these days. She never made suggestions or showed enthusiasm for anything. This was truly a first.

"Go for it!" said Polly.

"Why don't we stick some pizzas in the oven for the boys, send your other halves to the pub and get Ruth around for a glass of wine and a good old proper catch-up together? It's been twelve weeks since the four of us really got stuck into a good old nitty-gritty gossip and I am finally ready to get back into the real world. I might even get dressed!"

"Get dressed! Now there's a first!"

"And put on make-up!"

Gina hadn't even finished her suggestion when Polly and Tess had taken out their mobile phones and were texting their husbands to offer them a few hours down the pub. They would be delighted with the chance to sip a pint and from what Polly could remember, there was a big game on that evening which James would kill for the chance to watch with the local lads. He was making slow progress and his counselling sessions were making him realise that depression wasn't as isolating as many thought it had to be. There were thousands of others in his position and there was so much help out there for men who were going through something very similar.

Family day trips, quality time with Polly and the odd evening out with the boys were the things he seemed to enjoy most now and Polly was delighted with his progress. Their sex life had improved too as James became more contented with his work and home life. His business was picking up and Polly found that when he felt good, it made her feel good too. She didn't feel so frumpy and old anymore. Gone was the *Bisto Mum* apron and the nagging subsided in order to give James the space he needed to get better. And he was getting better. And now, so was Gina.

"Ruth is on her way over," said Tess with a giggle. "She has been shopping with Melanie and says she has some hot news about Michael the journalist!"

"What!" squealed Polly. "Did she meet him at last? My God, you have to give the man kudos for being persistent! He has been texting and calling her for weeks and she wouldn't even talk to him! That's fantastic news. It shows she's willing to finally move on from that excuse of a family she has in Belfast!"

An hour later, the foursome were huddled around the fire in Gina's living room, eating Chinese takeaway from the cartons and sipping red wine while the children played in Danny's bedroom.

"What will I do if I have a baby girl?" asked Tess. "It's all boys, boys, boys around here! She would either be bored to tears or would be a little tomboy and join in with them all for the *craic*. Oh, it's so exciting. Is that wine nice? Let me just smell it . . ."

"You can have one glass," said Polly. "I'm nearly sure

you can, but then they change the rules so bloody often. One minute it's good to do one thing, then the next it's a total disgrace. I could never keep up."

Tess, as the others had predicted, was determined to do everything by the book. She had given up smoking, wouldn't touch a drop of alcohol, avoided soft cheeses and took her folic acid religiously. She even kept up some light exercise and her only craving so far was for mint Choc Pop lollies and she couldn't find them anywhere.

"So, tell us about Michael the journalist!" said Gina. She was in flying form now and the small glass of wine she was allowed on her medication was making her giddy.

Ruth pursed her lips and did a shimmy on her seat. She set down her empty carton of food and clasped her hands in front of her.

"Well," she said. "You know the way I have been avoiding him like the plague for as long as I can remember?"

"Yes!" said the chorus of eager listeners.

"Well, Melanie answered my mobile the other day. She is such a sweetheart these days. I don't know what has got into her but, anyway, it was before the snow came and the sun was shining so I decided to take a book outside and sit on my dad's summer seat as the world passed by. I couldn't concentrate on the book and so I laid it down and let the sun warm my face."

"I am going to bust you!" said Tess. "Would you cut out all the shite and just tell us what he said!"

"*Shh!*" said Polly. "Let her tell the story. I like a bit of anticipation."

"Me too," said Gina. "Go on, Ruthie. Sun on your face, book by your side . . ."

"Okay," said Ruth. "To cut a long story short –"

"No! Don't cut it short!" said Polly. "Tess, see what you've done now! You have ruined the whole flow. I was enjoying the sun on her face and book by her side bit!"

"Oh for God's sake, next thing there will be white turtle doves and an angel playing a harp. He rang, Melanie answered and then what?"

Pregnancy certainly hadn't changed Tess's ability to keep it real!

"Melanie told me it was Polly on the phone. I didn't look at the screen and said something smart –"

"Oh no, what did you say?"

"Look who's interrupting now!" said Tess. "Honestly, it's double standards with you lot!"

"I said something like 'Well, Fanta Pants, how's it going?'" said Ruth and the others laughed, covering their mouths in embarrassment.

"And he's ginger, right?" said Polly. "Oh, hell, slap it up you! That's sweet revenge if there ever was sweet revenge for calling me that horrible name for so many years!"

"Tell me about it!" said Ruth. "To my amazement, he laughed his head off. In fact, I thought he was never going to stop. But I still hadn't copped who it was. I looked at the mobile-phone screen, saw his name and hung up!"

"No!" said Tess. "Please tell me there's more! If I had to listen to all that sun on your face build-up for that, I'll murder you, Ruth Monaghan!"

"Of course there's more," said Ruth. "He rang back, didn't he?"

"I'm scarlet for ye!" said Gina in her best Dublin accent. "Jesus, the poor man must be keen!"

351

Ruth smoothed down her long black skirt and gave a sexy pout. Her hair was darker now and she had eased off on the pale make-up so she looked ever so slightly less Goth these days.

"Well, of course he is keen. I'd give Kate Moss a good run for her money, wouldn't I? Anyhow, he calls back and I answer with a very meek 'Sorry, I thought you were someone else who used to have ginger hair' and he is still laughing so I sort of calm my knickers a bit and wait for him to stop the giggles."

"I like Michael," said Gina. "He sounds like fun and he was so helpful to me when I was drunk and slutty. He called you to say I had made a magical return to the pub that day. I must buy him a box of Roses to say thank you very, very, very much."

"He did help," said Ruth. "That was very kind of him. So, anyway, small talk, small talk, how are you, *blah, blah, blah*, and then he asks if I'm still interested in writing for his online magazine. He tells me how impressed he was by my 'superior knowledge' and how he wasn't going to give up until he got a yes or no, hence the stalker-type phone calls he had been making since we first met."

Polly poured more wine for Ruth and then topped up her own glass. As the only two legitimate drinkers in the group, she felt she should make the most of the situation and it was the weekend so therefore it was a guilt-free exercise.

"So I said I would need to know more and he said he would like to get to know me more, and tomorrow night we are going out for dinner and he is picking me up at six! *The End!*"

352

The girls squealed and Gina even kicked her feet in delight.

"I'm so thrilled for you, Ruth!" she said. "It's almost like a blind date. Are you shittin' it?"

"Brickin' it!" said Ruth. "Now, I am going to need a lot of help to get ready because I haven't been out on a date since I was a teenager. I'm even thinking of adding a bit of colour to my trademark black!"

"Right, that's it!" said Tess. "I'm in charge of wardrobe! You have to admit, I'm the best at that!"

"You are," said Polly.

"No doubt," said Gina. "I think Polly should be conversation advisor. She is the wisest of us all."

"Agreed," said Tess. "Never a wiser word spoken, Gina."

"And what about you, Gina?" asked Ruth. "What are you bringing to the party?"

Gina looked out the window again. It was dark now but the blinds were still open and the navy night sky had cleared to let the stars shine through. She felt hopeful for the first time in ages. Trevor, through guilt and deep remorse, had made sure their separation was as smooth as it could possibly be, and she felt free from the days when she lived in fear. With a restriction order and a healthy deposit into the bank and his mother well and truly on her support team, Gina knew she would never look back and would never be alone when she had her friends.

"I'll be your cheerleader," said Gina. "It's about all I can offer at the moment, and I can't promise any backflips or cartwheels, but I will certainly be rooting for you and making sure you feel on top of the world, Ruth Monaghan!"

The girls whooped with delight and clinked their glasses in approval.

"And so what does the future hold for you, Miss Gina?" asked Polly. "Tess is destined for motherhood, I am a much happier wife and mum and Ruth has a whole new career and even a new man knocking on her door. What are your plans?"

Gina looked at the three women who had become her best friends in the whole world in such a short space of time. She had thought long and hard about her future as she sat at her front window, day in, day out. The itch to run her own business was now pumping through her veins and she had so many ideas she didn't know where to start.

"I'm thinking of finally getting off my arse and doing something with my brain," she said. "Pardon the pun, since I just bashed it in a car crash, but now that Trevor is out of my head I can finally concentrate on my ambitions once and for all. I've been smothering them for years and it's time to set this monster loose!"

"You can't just stop there!" said Tess, always eager to get the full story. "What type of business?"

"Well, I've always been fascinated by the tourism industry in this country and it's something I feel I can contribute to. I have a real passion for old hotels and their décor so I'm going to do a course on interior design and then when I'm feeling confident enough to get up and running, I will start scouting for business."

Polly looked around Gina's living room. She really did have impeccable taste and some of the paintings on her walls would sell easily to anyone with an artistic eye. The girl really did have talent.

"Wow," said Tess. "You go, girl! A woman of your ability should be out there flaunting herself to the outside world. Your eye for décor is just too good to be confined to one house only. You can use my nursery as a guinea-pig project if you want?"

"Oh how kind of you, Tess," said Ruth. "But Gina doesn't work for ex-convicts!"

"*Ow!*" said Tess, throwing a cushion. "I am free from all that! You bitches are never going to let me live that down, are you?"

"No," said Ruth. "But seriously, I was going to suggest that Gina takes on my whole house as her guinea-pig project. It's much more of a challenge than a nursery. Any old fool amongst us can design a nursery. You'd want a proper house Gina, wouldn't you? Not a poxy boxroom?"

"Ha ha," said Gina. "Thanks for your very kind offers, ladies, but I have a very specific place in mind where I would like to tout for business. In fact, in a few weeks' time, I plan to make a festive visit and see how I go from there. You could call it inspiration to guide me on my way into studying."

"Oh, go on," said Polly. She felt a little tipsy and warm inside and it felt amazing. Gina had colour in her cheeks for the first time in ages and her gaunt, tired face had broken into a wide eyes smile. A few more weeks and Gina would be as stunning as she was on her wedding day.

"Well, I'm not quite sure where exactly it is," said Gina. "All I know is that it is called the Wayward Hotel and that it can be found 'Somewhere in Donegal'."

"Somewhere in Donegal?" asked Ruth. "I do believe we have holidayed in that very location."

"I'd be very careful if I were you," said Polly. "There is a tendency to disappear when you go there for a few hours, like old Kitty O'Connor who was found by the river."

"And a tendency to get into lots of trouble?" said Tess. She rubbed her swollen belly, enjoying the banter with Gina. It really was a blessing to see her so content.

"And you can win lots of money there," said Ruth. "I know a guy who drinks in the bar. In fact, I'll be seeing him tomorrow night as you all know!"

"It's all falling into place," said Gina, with a naughty twinkle in her eye. "A place where you can win lots and lots of money and get into lots and lots of trouble? I think I'm almost ready for it. Now, who's for more wine?"

Ruth and Polly held out their glasses. They knew what was coming next from Gina.

"So . . ." she said with a smile. "Now that I've planted the seed . . . anyone fancy a road trip?"

"To Somewhere in Donegal!" said Ruth and she raised her glass. "I'll drink to that!"

If you enjoyed
One Night Only by Emma Heatherington
why not try
All Over Again also published
by Poolbeg?
Here's a sneak preview of Chapter One

All Over Again

Emma Heatherington

POOLBEG

1

Natalie locked her car and slung her handbag over her shoulder, slipping the car keys into the side pocket of the bag and reminding herself over and over again to remember where to find them later.

"Happy birthday to me," she muttered, closing the car door and going over her 'to do' list for the day, which so far didn't consist of anything celebratory at all. No cakes, no parties, no romantic meals – not even a birthday card as yet and it was already afternoon.

She had got a text from the delicious Dougie first thing this morning which had made her smile, just as his early-morning messages always did. Dougie, the love of her life and truly delicious in every way, was certainly a little forgetful at times. As much as she adored him and his habits both good and bad, sometimes, just sometimes, she would wish that on days like this he might be just a little bit more attentive. Like, a card would have been nice, or a bunch of flowers . . . or even a phone call in place of the usual text message to say hello.

But then again he *did* have more pressing things on his mind these days. Things like the survival of his laundry business in a recession, things like struggling with mortgage arrears as a single parent, things like where to buy everyday stuff for two very demanding, fast-growing preteens whose world revolved around designer clothes and Xbox games . . . yes, Dougie had a lot on his mind these days and Natalie knew that sometimes she just had to come a long way down on his list.

And besides, thirty-five wasn't really an age to celebrate anyhow, was it? There was nothing great about being thirty-five . . . nothing to really make a big song and dance over, so she shouldn't sweat that Dougie hadn't made a fuss. It wasn't 'sweet' like sixteen, it didn't scream 'get drunk legally' like eighteen, it didn't give you a key to the door like at twenty-one, it wasn't a depressing turning point like being thirty and you never ever heard of a thirty-fifth birthday bash. Well, Natalie hadn't anyhow.

Being thirty-five was . . . well, just ordinary really, and Natalie McKenna was slowly deciding that if anything, it was perhaps a time for her to reflect on where she was in life, and where she wanted to be when the next milestone came around (the one they say that life begins at). That age was only round the corner, but Natalie had been hoping that life would begin for her long before now. Her life hadn't exactly worked out as she had planned or hoped for, but it was life as she knew it for now and it was up to her to make things happen and that was exactly what she intended to do.

Yes, she had a lot to be thankful for, but things hadn't really changed too much in the past ten, maybe fifteen years. She still lived in the same coastal town where she had celebrated her very *first* birthday. She still worked for her parents at their busy but time-warped café where the same people with the same faces ate the same food year in, year out. She still had nothing to call her own apart from Penny the Peugeot 205 which had really seen better days and even Dougie, her boyfriend of two years, still wasn't really all her own.

He wasn't all her own and probably never *would* be with his family commitments and business tangles, but Natalie still believed that in all her thirty-five years, Dougie was the best thing that had happened to her, even if it was in a 'better late than never' kind of way.

He had his faults like any other man. He wasn't the romantic type at all, but he showed he loved her in many other ways – like the way she would catch him watching her with longing when she was doing the most mundane things such as fixing her hair or even washing the dishes, or the way he thanked her every day for coming into his life and making his everyday experiences seem worthwhile again. Or how when things were hectic with the twins and the demands of everyday life, he would do something that was so tender, like putting his fingers gently on the back of her neck and moving his thumbs in a light massage and she would feel tingles run right down her spine from his touch.

She didn't need big birthday presents or fuss to know he loved her today, no matter what her mother would say when she'd go through her daily rant of how Dougie "simply wasn't good enough". And just as she always did, Natalie would rise to the bait and it would end up in a row as it always did, with her mother using their debate to reach for another brandy, because she just couldn't cope with all the stress of life these days. As if her mother had any idea of the word *stress*! She spent most of her days with her chubby ankles up on a footstool in front of the television while Natalie and her father ran frantically around in the café downstairs. Stress was not part of Delia McKenna's life, nor would it ever be no matter how much she whinged about it!

Natalie walked in the late June sunshine across the cobbled street towards the café and as always Bert Parks, the newsagent from next door to Nellie's Café, came out to say his daily hello. It was the same conversation every day and, like all the characters on Scotch Street of Castle Bay, Natalie couldn't imagine life without him, no matter how much she sometimes bitched and moaned about living in a constantly repetitive existence.

But today the conversation was different.

"Happy birthday, Natalie," said Bert, his portly belly resting over the belt of his faded denim slacks that had been around since Natalie could fit on a tricycle. "Wednesday's Child is full of woe and you certainly don't look like a birthday girl today, pet. Why the long face?"

"Long face? Really?" said Natalie. "I'll try and turn my frown upside down then. I'm just lost in thought, Bert."

"Come on . . . penny for them?" asked Bert, handing her the usual bundle of afternoon newspapers for the punters in the café.

"Ah, nothing much," she replied with a smile. "Maybe just a case of one birthday too many and not a lot to show for it? Getting on, getting nowhere fast and feeling sorry for myself to be honest."

Bert let out a sigh and shook his head so that his fifties-style quiff threatened to actually move – but it didn't. Since she was a tiny girl, Natalie had only seen Bert's hair move once and that was on the day his wife died and he was just out of the shower and didn't have time to style it when he raised the alarm of her sudden illness.

"I remember the day you were born," he said, looking across to the sea like an old reminiscing sailor. "It was one of the busiest days of the year when the schools were breaking up for holidays and hordes of families descended here on Castle Bay to escape their city lives. Your poor father was up to his neck in that wee café when the call came from the hospital to say you had bounced into the world. Oh, you were a bouncy, bonnie wee lass! It was a day like today, and the smile on that man's face was one like I had never seen before. It was as if you were the only baby girl in the world."

Natalie smiled, picturing the scene in her head and was struck by the idea of her 'bouncing' into the world. She wondered how different Castle Bay would have been all those years ago and that made her feel even worse. It made her feel even older.

"He stood just right where you are now," said Bert, lost in the past, "and he bellowed into the shop, over the heads of maybe twenty, thirty customers who were in with me, searching for the last of my buckets and spades.

'I'm a daddy, Bert!' he told us all. 'Imagine, me a daddy at long, long last!' And off he went to visit you for the very first time and he has been smitten ever since. You're a special girl, Natalie McKenna, and don't ever forget it. You have a lot to show for your thirty-five years and you just have to look at the joy in your father's eyes to see it."

Bert's words brought a smile to Natalie's face and she felt herself beam from the inside out.

"Thanks, Bert," she said. "I'll remember that. You have a nice day and I hope the sun comes out and that you're run off your feet selling ice creams and ping-pong sets. Bye!"

"Oh, and bring the wee ones in after school and we can all have a birthday treat!" called Bert after her. "That'll keep you in their good books!"

Natalie gave out a chuckle. It was no secret in Castle Bay that Dougie's twins were hard work.

"I have no need to try to impress them today, Bert, but thanks anyway," she called. "It's the last day of term so they're being picked up by Auntie Ursula and anyhow, Wednesday is my day off the school run . . . and I love it!"

"Good girl yourself! At least they can't moan at you for being late. Have a nice day!"

"I'll try!"

Natalie felt a tiny weight off her shoulders at the thought of no school run today. Being late for Dougie's twelve-year-old twins was now part of her everyday life as much as losing her keys was, and an ordeal she dreaded more than a twelve-hour shift in her parents' café. The twins would be standing at the school gate each day, their eyes squinted and their lips pouted when they saw Natalie's car speed towards them, her face full of panic and fear. Yes, fear of what they would come out with when they clambered into the car, all long limbs and schoolbags and folders and the smell of stale deodorant and school canteens lingering on their navy uniforms.

They were always 'freezing with the cold' or 'mortified, just morto' or 'scared she had forgotten'. Which, in fairness, she sometimes had . . .

"I'm sorry!" she would plead the whole way back to the house they shared with their widower father, thanking herself she had not yet taken the plunge and moved in with them permanently. Her little flat above the best Chinese takeaway in town was her haven away from their world of boy bands and Match Attax Cards and she vowed to hold on to it for as long as she could.

"No, you're not a bit sorry. If you were sorry then you wouldn't let it happen again," Amy would say, twisting her hair around her finger so tight that it would almost break.

"And you always let it happen again and again and again," her twin brother Jack would chirp up in support. "We should just walk home. Yes, next time this happens we'll just walk to Dad's work and see what he says then! Better that than being humiliated and travelling in this rust bucket anyhow!"

"Rise above it," Natalie would remind herself and sometimes their accusations and outbursts would actually make her laugh.

Some days though, they would make her cry. Really.

Yes, daily battles with Dougie's children were part of

Natalie's everyday existence and at times she wondered if it was all really worth it. Sometimes her life was so predictable, she really did feel like she was living in *Groundhog Day* as the same things continuously happened, day in, day out.

Like the arguments she had with her overweight, overbearing mother about when she was going to give up on Dougie and find a *real* man of her own with no baggage who would give her children that she would actually have to give birth to and therefore be *forced* to take their grief and tantrums – at least in that way they could blame her for 'being born' in the first place when things got really bad.

Or the constant worry she secretly had that Dougie didn't really love her and that he might only be using her as a surrogate mother or a stopgap solution or was training her up for a life full of duties like enforcing the school run and thinking up ingredients for packed lunches.

Her weight was another worry and the way she habitually stuffed her face with at least two chunky Kit Kats after her evening meal at the same time every day to try and make herself feel better.

Actually, that wasn't really a worry. The Kit Kats she enjoyed immensely, but the rest she couldn't say the same for at all.

It's not that she didn't *enjoy* Dougie's children. She just didn't enjoy them as much as she did, say, chocolate bars dunked into tea or walks on the beach in summer or – or trips to the dentist. She enjoyed them in a way that anyone would enjoy prepubertal, attention-seeking twins that weren't your own and who called you fat and reminded you that you are "not our mother anyway so don't dare tell us what to do". She enjoyed them the same way she enjoyed going for a smear test or running out of petrol in the snow when her mobile phone had gone flat.

She enjoyed them because they reminded her of his life before her, with his pretty red-haired wife who was always smiling, always happy, always on top of her game before she died and left Dougie heartbroken.

Yes, she enjoyed them. She really did.

Sometimes the things they said *did* make her laugh, but most of the time it made her want to scream and run for the hills on bad days when she burnt the dinner or bought the wrong chicken nuggets or failed to iron their school uniforms properly.

Sometimes it made her want to slap their little faces when she would think they were asleep and she and Dougie would be finally 'getting it on' under the covers only for one of them, normally Amy, to walk right into the bedroom and scream like she was being murdered because "Daddy has his hand on Natalie's boobies!"

"I was checking her heartbeat!" Dougie would say in a fluster, jumping off her so quickly that he would take the bed covers with him and give young Amy a full-frontal view of Natalie's naked body, which wasn't exactly in tiptop shape thanks to the Kit Kat overload and extra wine consumption she needed for medicinal purposes these days.

"I love you, I really do," he would say afterwards as they tried to take up where they left off. "They're just kids. They don't understand."

Oh but they did understand, or so Natalie believed.

Like last summer when they took the twins on a quick getaway to Spain for a week and to say it brought challenges to the 'bedroom' was an understatement. Amidst the sunburn, heat rashes and threats of sunstroke and after a long day by the poolside in the sweltering heat, she and Dougie managed to find time for a quick fumble on the balcony. It was well after midnight and she was feeling gloriously tipsy and even a bit sexy as he told her what he would like to do to her on that hot August night. But just as they were about to reach home base and his hands and other bodily parts were doing what she wanted them to do, she saw the gruesome twosome doing handstands in the sitting area of the apartment – their beady upside-down eyes placed firmly on the action outside and on the extra flab on her belly – and the heat of the moment disintegrated like a damp squib. Her balloon was well and truly deflated that night and despite their efforts to rekindle the moment when the brats were chased back to bed, it just wasn't the same and Natalie ended up taking the sofa bed for the rest of the holiday while Dougie made room for each twin on a nightly basis in the bedroom.

Yes, sex with two demanding twelve-year-old delinquents was always going to be a carefully choreographed, pre-planned operation. Quickies were common, marathons were almost out of the question and Natalie secretly loved when Super Granny would come to the rescue and whisk them away to the city for a whole weekend once a month. Then, once the guilt subsided as she watched their little backpacks disappear into the distance, she and Dougie would do it in almost every room in the house at every time of the day and she would promise herself that she would never have ill feeling towards his innocent children again because he was worth it.

Oh yes he was.

Every second of the pain they put her through was worth that one dirty weekend a month when she could serve him breakfast in bed in nothing but her undies, or without them on if the mood was right.

He was worth it until Amy and Jack came back home and told her how she stank of chips from the café and that her homemade soup looked and tasted like vomit. Endearing little beings, they were. So endearing . . .

But, somewhere in the far corner of her very generous heart, there was a *little* space that had Jack and Amy's names written on it and in time Natalie knew that that space would grow and grow and she would learn to love them unconditionally, as *if* they were the fruits of her own loins. Even if, in Amy's case, that meant listening to Justin Bieber on repeat and with Jack it meant cheering from the sidelines as he kicked a ball round a muddy field on cold winter Saturday mornings. The love would come, in time, she was sure.

Others weren't so sure, especially her mother.

"It won't come in time and it's about time you found a man of your own and thought about having your own children," she would rant, on a more than regular basis. "You're nothing but a slave to that man. A slave. He probably thought he had died and gone to heaven when he met a soft touch like you."

"I am not a slave, Mum. I just like to help him out

with his children," Natalie would say defensively. "And it was his *wife* who *died* and went to heaven, not him. Plus I see him *very* much as my own and those kids come as part of the package, so they do. They're not mine, no, but they are Dougie's and I love him more than anything so I have to accept them too. End of."

"Well, I've said it before and I'll say it again," Delia McKenna would chant, her chubby ankles stacked on top of her floral footstool in her favourite pew in front of the television, "you are denying your own womanly rights by not having children and I will never tire of telling you so. You will only realise it when it's too late and you won't be able to say that I didn't let you know."

Given the chance, Delia would have reminded Natalie on the hour every hour that at "almost thirty-five" her biological clock was beyond ticking and was now screaming at her to get a grip and stop taking the piss. Which, in fairness, it was. Oh good God it was.

Today, being 'almost thirty five' had become a saying of the past and the dreaded age had come around, much to her dismay. She would now, if the time ever came for her to give birth to her own child, be officially known as an 'older mother'. She hated that phrase. It sounded freakish, unnatural, ancient even. She had read the '*Over-35 Older Mothers*' websites and pamphlets in the doctor's surgery. She would be classed as a sad weirdo who got called 'granny' at the school gates instead of 'mummy' and her poor child would be teased and taunted about mummy's greying hair or frumpy clothes. The very thought itself was enough to send Natalie into a panic and head-spin.

But then she would reassure herself that lots of people have babies as they approach the big four-oh nowadays. Look at Dannii Minogue – radiant and glamorous at thirty-nine when she had her first-born, or Rod Stewart's wife who oozed beauty and sophistication and she was *well* over thirty-five. But then they weren't real people, were they? They had stylists and nannies and, most of all, they had an other half who *wanted* a child in the first place.

Dougie didn't. And worse than that, he couldn't.

There wasn't a day that passed that Natalie didn't picture herself with a baby bump, or shopping for nappies and baby food, or pushing a fancy pram through the park as onlookers oohed and aahed and commented on who the baby looked like.

"Oh, he has your eyes," they might say.

"Not at all, he is the spitting image of his daddy," another might argue as she gushed and admired the baby's little pink cherub face beneath a soft velvet blanket of dark hair.

Her mother was wrong. Her biological clock wasn't ticking right now. It was begging, screeching, pounding in her mind and on really bad days it threatened to chuck out its batteries and give up ticking for good as the reality of being with a man with a readymade family and absolutely no hope of starting over again began to sink in.

She loved Dougie. She really did. She loved everything about him, twins aside. His smile, his brown eyes, his laugh and how he found the same things funny as she did, the way he sang all the time even though he couldn't hold a note, the way he called her "honey", and the way that despite the incredible pain he had been through that he always, always looked on the bright side of life. She loved when they went for long walks on the beach, just the two of them, and when she would catch him staring at her with a look of love in his eyes, as if he was the luckiest man in the world. And then he would tell her just how much he loved her and they would cuddle and she would feel like the luckiest girl in the world too.

Her relationship with him was so special, but when the reality of everyday life kicked in, she knew it was certainly not what she had planned and that marriage, babies and perhaps an escape from the claustrophobia of the family business was just not to be.

All of her friends had moved on and were now in the early stages of marriage with at least one or two 'mini-me's' running around their feet. Some even had teenage children, like her old friend Michelle who she was reunited with recently through the powers of Facebook. Michelle was a carbon copy of how life should be at thirty-five. Two gorgeous kids who she gave birth to when she was young enough to enjoy them, a wealthy husband who adored her and enough leisure time on her hands to ensure that the only stress she felt was when choosing what to wear in the morning. If Natalie didn't love Michelle as much as she did, she would hate her. Fact.

Life hadn't turned out so straightforward for Natalie, alas. The love of her life was a gorgeous but grieving widower, the babies in her life were stroppy teenage twins with attitude and issues, and her career continued to be serving hungry holidaymakers in Nellie's Café on

Northern Ireland's picturesque, if blustery, north coast. Hardly the white-picket-fence lifestyle she had dreamed about since she was a teenager.

"Afternoon all!" she called, making her way through the blue-painted door of Nellie's to begin her Wednesday shift. Her arrival was met with the usual cheery welcome that made her realise that life wasn't really so bad sometimes. Nellie's was a happy place to work and there was always a bit of news or gossip to make the day go quicker.

Natalie loved Wednesdays for lots of reasons. It was the one day she had a lie-in and watched daytime telly from the comfort of her own bed in her own little flat down the road. It was the day she left Dougie to his own devices on the school run (or rather his sister-in-law who often stepped in when his work commitments dictated it), and the day when she and her dad would reminisce and dream over endless coffees and the odd doughnut or flapjack while her mum spent the afternoon upstairs in front of endless repeats of *The Jeremy Kyle Show*.

Her father was balancing on a chair in the far corner of the café, sticking up the '*Happy Birthday, Natalie*' banner that was at least twenty years old with its frayed edging and faded silver lettering. They had bought it on holiday in America when Natalie was about twelve or thirteen years old, having never seen anything like it before, and despite Natalie's later assurances that plenty of shops stocked personified banners and cups and key-rings, her father would have none of it. This banner was special. It was one of a kind. It was 'American' after all, so it couldn't be bought on just *any* stall or tacky birthday shop.

"Here she is, here she is!" said Molly, the busty, chirpy waitress whose sweet pleasant nature made up for her lack of brain substance when it came to matters of the world. "Happy birthday, Natalie! Twenty-one again!"

"Thanks, Moll," said Natalie, feeling the warmth of the ovens and the sweet smell of homemade cupcakes giving her a welcome hug and the echoes of last year's birthday wishes from Molly who had said exactly the same thing at, well, probably exactly the same time twelve months ago.

"Your mother will join us in time for the party," said Bill McKenna as he climbed down from the chair, his hands shaking as he put it back in its place. He was a frail, tiny seventy-something who had recently handed a part-time role of chef in the little café to his nephew Ross after over thirty years of building Nellie's into the endearing, traditional, cosy corner it had become with just himself in the kitchen.

"Party? Oh, come on, Dad," said Natalie with a giggly sigh. "You know I appreciate it but having these annual parties only reminds everyone that I am getting on and I really don't need reminding of that today, thank you. I'm thirty-five not thirteen!"

The look on her father's face told her that, despite her effort to make a joke of it, she had said the wrong thing.

"But you're our only girl," said Bill, rolling a piece of Blu-Tack between his fingers with fear that it might now be defunct if the party was cancelled. "We'd have a party every day for you if we could. And it's tradition now. Everyone expects it. Miss Ada is on her way and she has bought you a present. I'm beginning to think this is the highlight of her year."

376

Natalie knew that the term 'party' was used in the loosest terms possible, as loose as her elderly neighbour Miss Ada's idea of a present. The party normally consisted of a carrot cake (her favourite) baked by her dad, a few sausage rolls and similar party nibbles and a free coffee and slice of cake for whoever came through the doors at the right time. And Miss Ada's present would be a lavender soap set as it always was, and Natalie would have to act surprised and tell her sweet old neighbour that it was just what she neededwanted was just about to buy for herself. What was it with old people and lavender soap sets?

There were no official invitations to this 'party', but some of the regular holidaymakers from the neighbouring caravan parks had Natalie's birthday marked in their calendar as part of their holiday celebrations and, while it was lovely to see familiar faces wish her happy birthday every year, it had become ever so embarrassing.

"Still going out with that poor man who lost his wife in that dreadful accident?" the posh Mrs Gallagher from County Down would be bound to ask as she wolfed down a second slice of cake. She always waited until she was on her second slice to ask and Natalie found herself wishing she would choke on it.

"Yes, I am and we are very happy," she would say through gritted teeth as Mrs Gallagher looked at her with an 'Is that the best you can do, poor mite?' look on her face.

"Have you lost weight, love?" Mrs Gallagher's henpecked husband would ask, but before Natalie got a chance to answer his wife would chirp in.

"Has she?" Mrs G would say. "Can't say I noticed but then it's hard to notice when you're big-boned, isn't it, Natalie? I think you look as healthy as ever."

It was fair to say that the Gallaghers weren't her favourite tourists in the world and their birthday wishes weren't the only ones she could be doing without.

Toria Kelly's were another. Her smug look of pity when she would arrive into the café every year with her growing brood and either another newborn or another baby bump on tow made Natalie feel even older and more out of touch with life's natural plans.

"Number three!" (or four or five) "Can you believe it?" Toria would say as loud as she could, oblivious to the fact that her words were making Natalie's eyes prick as she felt the emptiness of her womb inside her.

"Congratulations," Natalie would reply with a smile, her heart yearning for the latest little bundle of pink or blue that lay snuggled in the baby carrier beside his or her yummy mummy and her expanding family.

Toria wore designer clothes and her parents had a huge holiday home on the outskirts of Portstewart. She had honey-blonde hair, glistening super-white teeth and wore an all-year-round Algarve tan from their 'real' holiday destination.

Just the type of girl you would love to throw darts at, really.

"I think we'll call it a day now," her gorgeous husband would pipe up every single year. He, on the other hand, was the type of man you would love to bottle up and keep. "It feels like our house is bursting at the seams already."

But sure as ever, when they'd return the following

year in their huge Audi Q7, Toria would come in with a newly rounded bump and talk of names and due dates, and customers admiring her natural motherly instincts and glowing skin would cut Natalie to the core.

Natalie wasn't greedy. She didn't want three or four children like Toria had. She didn't even want an Audi Q7. Just one or two children would be nice. Just one or two.

"Busy this morning, Dad?" she asked, automatically fixing tables ahead of the lunchtime rush. The pale blue-and-white-checked tablecloths were as faded and ancient as the menu in Nellie's but, according to her father, that was the secret to the success of the little weather-beaten café.

"The usual," he said and then leaned in to whisper, "Ross is pressing on with a new menu despite my efforts to keep things exactly how they are. He just doesn't seem to be listening, Natalie. You'll have to have a word with him. A good stern word as no matter what I say around here, it just goes in one ear and out the other. I don't know what they're teaching him up at that college, but he's speaking of foodstuff that I've never heard of!"

Natalie put her arm around her dad's shoulders, which she was sure were becoming more narrow by the day. "He means well, Daddy. He's an ambitious boy and we knew when we gave him the job that there are only so many Cowboy Suppers he can serve up before he gets bored. Think of it this way, it's better to keep him on the team than have him leave for pastures new. Hasn't Nellie's always been managed with family at the reins?"

Bill McKenna sighed. "I try not to think about that

too much these days. The whole family thing, that is. I mean, you have always felt suffocated and it's not as if we have family members beating down the doors wanting to take over from me when I'm no longer fit to look after the place. If you and Ross go, we might as well shut up shop. It just wouldn't be Nellie's any more without a McKenna calling the shots."

"Hmm," said Natalie, feeling sad at the tears in her father's eyes. She worried about him so much these days. "Well, then let's keep my one and only cousin right where we want him, eh? Let him have his say on the menu, even if it's just a little for now. The odd cappuccino or panini won't kill us off. It might even make the place stronger."

"I can hardly pronounce those silly words," said Bill, throwing his glistening eyes up to the heavens. "Whatever happened to a sandwich and a coffee? No point being fancy for the sake of it, but I suppose I can let him get on with it as long as he does it in baby steps. Baby steps will be the only way."

And there it was again . . . the word that just kept tripping her up everywhere she went these days. *Baby*. It seemed to follow her around every day now, seeping under her skin, when she switched on the television, when she opened a newspaper or magazine, even when she logged into Facebook there would be photos of babies or pregnancy announcements from friends.

And right then, as if God wanted to rub salt in the wounds of her barren state of mind, in walked Toria Kelly for her annual visit, struggling to manoeuvre a twin stroller through the door as her husband balanced two older children on his hips.

"Oh, just when I thought this day couldn't get any better," sighed Natalie, and then she lifted her notepad, painted on a smile and went to help her nemesis get through the door while resisting the urge to kidnap one of her ever-growing brood of ducklings.

If you enjoyed this chapter from
All Over Again by Emma Heatherington
why not order the full book online
@ www.poolbeg.com

POOLBEG WISHES TO

THANK YOU

for buying a Poolbeg book.

If you enjoyed this why not
visit our website:
www.poolbeg.com

and get another book delivered
straight to your home or to a
friend's home!

All books despatched within
24 hours.

POOLBEG

WHY NOT JOIN OUR MAILING LIST

@ www.poolbeg.com and get some
fantastic offers on Poolbeg books

Published by Poolbeg.com

Playing the Field

Emma Heatherington

Donegal lass Cara McCarthy has always been a tomboy type of girl, who wouldn't care how to spell Versace, let alone have any desire to wear it.

On a career break in London, she lands a job as a cleaner which is right up her street just then. But this is no ordinary cleaning job. Her new boss is Sophia Brannigan – the fashionista girlfriend of gorgeous Fulton FC Premiership star, Dylan Summers, and her new place of work is their luxurious home, Summer Manor.

Cara is determined to stay in the background, but life has other plans. Before she can say 'Manolo', she finds herself plunged in at the deep end of high fashion, posh parties and a front-seat ticket to the down-side of being a celebrity. With a friendly father figure in gardener Sam and a delightful new arrival called Lola, Cara's new life is set to be both fun and challenging.

But as Sophia's hunger for celebrity grows, so does Cara's bond with Dylan Summers and soon everything she does at Summer Manor seems destined to land her deeper and deeper into trouble . . .

ISBN 978-1-84223-372-6

Published by Poolbeg.com

Since You've Been Gone

Emma Heatherington

They call it Little Hollywood, and Millfield – a village nestled somewhere in the north of Ireland – is truly stage and screen obsessed.

Taylor Smith, TV actor and media darling, is Millfield's pride and joy – and then he lands a juicy part in the real Hollywood . . .

Erin O'Brien is the love of his life. She's a TV personality in her own right but, with Taylor away in the Hollywood Hills, she finds it difficult to cope. But that's what a glass or three of red wine is for, isn't it?

Erin's not the only one at a loss. The Millfield Players Theatre Group is under threat, much to director Darryl's dismay. Who will take over Taylor's role in the annual production?

Enter choreographer Olivier Lauren – an uber-talented, super-sexy French dancer who is set to shake Erin's heart with every shake of his hips. But she'll be true to her first love Taylor, won't she?

Whoever said it was quiet in the country?

ISBN 978-1-84223-409-9

Published by Poolbeg.com

Beyond Sin

Emma Louise Jordan

The picture-perfect O'Neill family is both admired and envied, near and far. But in the week leading up to Andrea O'Neill's high-profile society wedding, life-changing trouble is suddenly brewing and sinister cracks begin to show in the previously solid foundations of the O'Neill household.

When the bride's angelic sister Jessie disappears from the wedding reception and is still not found days later, the finger of blame switches from person to person as the hours before her vanishing are scrambled together in a jigsaw full of missing pieces.

Could Jessie have been living a double life, unknown to those who love her? And could anyone hate her so much that they would make her suffer the ultimate punishment for her dreadful secret sin?

ISBN 978-1-84223-399-3

Published by Poolbeg.com

The Truth Between

Emma Louise Jordan

When **Estelle Lynch** takes her own life, she leaves in her wake a mystery that will rock her daughter Holly's world forever.

A box of secrets which holds the key to Estelle's true past is found among her possessions and the identity of Holly's father seems within her grasp. As Holly battles with her grief, the obsession to find the perpetrators who made her young mother's life a misery threatens to ruin everything she has ever known.

Soon, Holly finds herself dicing with a torrid and dangerous back story that leads her into a cat-and-mouse chase taking her from Ireland's northern shoreline to the heartland of Belfast . . . then to the city of Dublin and into the path of celebrity chef, **Max Kelly**.

Holly's instincts go into overdrive as she becomes more and more convinced that the handsome father of two is linked to her mother's death. But somewhere between her instincts, her mother's diaries and what she learns about Max Kelly lies the truth between the life she knows and the life she only thought she knew . . .

ISBN 978-1-84223-387-0